SON

"Fascinating! *SONZ OF DARKNESS* takes you on an extraordinary quest while keeping you in total suspense."
—Cartel: Castillo, author of *Ghost Town Hustlers*

"Wonderfully written, filled with intense drama, action and mystique, Dru Noble's debut novel is mesmerizing."
—Blue, author of *Tattooed Tears*

"Gripping and exotic…guides you on a mental tour into the world of sci-fi from an urban perspective."
—Joi Moore, author of *Dirty Windows*

"*SONZ OF DARKNESS*—hypnotic, upturning and riveting, with a modern, nocturnal flair."
—Emlyn De Gannes, publisher of *Sucka 4 Love*

"*SONZ OF DARKNESS* is the best urban sci-fi thriller of all time! Dru Noble has crafted a remarkable masterpiece."
—Jaa'Mall, author of *Tough*

"An intriguing, emotion-felt adventure that leaves readers on the edge of their seats from beginning-to-end."
—A. C. Britt, author of *London Reign*

"Mind-blowing! Dru Noble's novel is incredibly inventive. Takes readers to another dimension while being captivated."
—Jay Bey, author of *Club Avenue*

"Magnificent! *SONZ OF DARKNESS* is great literature, challenging readers to explore Dru Noble's innovative world."
—God Math, author of *Ugly/Beautiful: Me*

"Absolutely ingenious! Marvelous, imaginative, spell-bounding!"
—Treasure Blue, author of *Harlem Girl Lost*

GHETTOHEAT® PRODUCTIONS

GHETTOHEAT®
CONVICT'S CANDY
HARDER
AND GOD CREATED WOMAN
LONDON REIGN
TANTRUM
GHOST TOWN HUSTLERS
GAMES WOMEN PLAY
DIRTY WINDOWS
TATTOOED TEARS
SKATE ON!
SOME SEXY, ORGASM 1

A GHETTOHEAT PRODUCTION

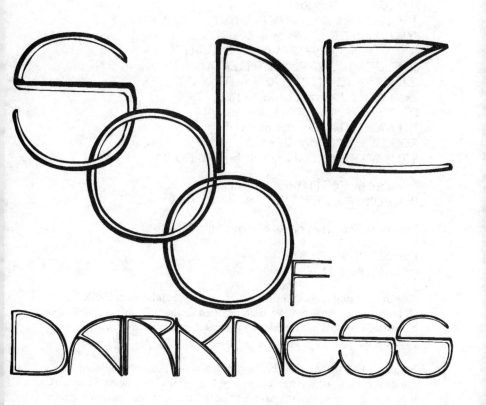

SONZ OF DARKNESS

MASTERPIECE CREATED BY
DRU NOBLE

Published by GHETTOHEAT®, LLC
P.O. BOX 2746, NEW YORK, NY 10027, USA

Library of Congress Control Number: 2008921077

ISBN: 978-0-9742982-1-4
Printed in the USA. First Edition, March 2008

PUBLISHER'S NOTE
This is a work of fiction. Any names to historical events, real people, living and dead, or to real locales are intended only to give the fiction a setting in historic reality. Other names, characters, places, businesses and incidents are either the product of the author's imagination or are used fictitiously, and their resemblance, if any, to real life counterparts is entirely coincidental.

ACKNOWLEDGMENTS

I first and foremost wish to acknowledge you, Doris. You always believed in me, and showed me the light I had within. Now, it can never stop burning bright. To my Grandma, your love for me never wavered. To my uncles, Donald and Sonny, thanks for supporting me, despite my failures. To my aunts, Sherrie and Ernell, for always reminding me to smile. Val, thank you for reading those first ten pages from that young boy so long ago, and challenging me to venture deeper.

To my sisters, Jackie and Altonese, now it's your turn to raise a nation. Stay strong no matter what. To my cousins, Tanya, Wanda, and Denise. So much beauty and compassion, I have no words to express how you've made me feel—thank you, always. To Dejon, since you were born, I've seen greatness in your eyes. Don't let anyone take that away from you, take care of your brother and sister and Jada—never lose that sparkling intelligence, baby girl.

I salute those who struggle and fight for a better day in this human void called prison, you all are more of my brothers than my own flesh. General a.k.a. "Who B. Mackin'", I would stand with you to face any and all battles. Fly Guy, we came a long way—it's almost over. A. G. (Show No Mercy), B.O.B., and you too, Wood, thank you for being my brothers, and showing me that my family is bigger than I believed. Don't think I forgot about you Kitab and Kernel.

HICKSON, you shared my vision, now it's time to share it with the world. Thank you for giving me the chance.

Lastly, to you who left me in the desert...I refused to die. In the end, karma has a way of delivering us all to our rightful fates.

Dedicated to my angel and her everlasting grace, my godmother, Doris. You saved my life and soul. Without you, I would be nothing. My little man, Justice Ziare, and to my nephews, Gabriel and Tykeem Noble. You three are the future—bring it glory.

ONCE A SLAVE, an essay by
DRU NOBLE
A GHETTOHEAT® PRODUCTION

This is not about my crimes. This is not about my redemption. It is about my life, and only that.

In the early summer morning of June 18th, 1979, there was a thunderstorm, and I was born. The falling rains would be a prelude to the struggles I would endure. Mere months later, my biological father would abandon me to an uncertain future; this was the first of many abandons. Like so many others of my generation, I faced the brute of an era of drugs, violence and pure apathy; lost souls and shattered dreams: cards placed on the table, a gun, placed on my head; my very sanity, daring me to play.

Years later, I would have two brothers and a sister who I'd have to watch over and take care, as if I were their father; in a single-parent home, with a mother on welfare. I learned in those early years that I possessed hidden talents while babysitting my siblings, as my mother gambled her nights away. Abilities like drawing, making up fantastic stories, and losing myself in my imagination to worlds that existed only in my head, but at that time, none of this would be harnessed. No, instead, it was buried. Only for a time.

Being a Gemini, there has always been two sides to me, each trying to conquer the other. One half, intelligent, forgiving and understanding, the other, violent and self-destructive—this internal war would play out in my soul, going into my teens. I ran the streets doing things most men twice my age had never done; a young man who'd aged before his years—taught things of wrong, learned in things of pain. Too many crimes, but this is not about that. Whatever I did, I knew that there was something out there better. I ignored that calling.... Mental chains shackled my mind, and I allowed it. I'd become a slave to the cycle of ignorance burdened to me. When I was seventeen, I participated in a robbery. Any dreams I had after that were destroyed, and my life as I knew it—would come to a tragic conclusion, only for a time.

Soon after, I was tried and found guilty of murder in the second degree. Sentenced to twenty years to life, more time than

8

both of my co-defendants put together, given three times the length than the actual murderer in my case. Less than two years later, I was abandoned by everyone I once loved, and would be treated with stark realization—as if I were dead. A living ghost, faced with the bitter truth that, people who I believed cared for me: family, friends, even my siblings, would turn their backs on me; no letters, no visits—nothing. My bid was done in the harshest of ways. It was done alone. And this would be for a time. Being in prison can bring out the worse in a person...I aged before my years, living with hatred, consumed with misery and animosity; I let it feed me, teach and mold me. This would be the darkest time in my life.

I learned that I wasn't abandoned completely. GOD sent the one person who would get through to me, my angel, my godmother; a woman with more strength and love in her heart than anyone I'd known. Even when I tried to push her away and show that my madness was stronger, my godmother's patience and understanding hand, did the impossible—she helped heal my demons, and eventually destroyed them. She told me, *"Son, you are not dead, the person you were is. GOD has other plans for you; I know this."* And she stood by me, unmoving—I love her for that; I always will. It was time for a man to be reborn.

Eventually, I let my past go, shed the brewing anger. The chains that held my mind since childhood, shattered in a million pieces, and ironically, in the pit of prison. For the first time in life, I was set free. Natural-born talents, along with the many I didn't know I had, returned to me. I began to re-awaken my imagination, and ventured back into worlds that had never left my dreams, which had never ABANDONED me.

I found out that some members of my family would stand firm beside me, and a door would be open where I would meet new ones. This would also be for a time. Then came a day where a brother I respected and known for years, would hand me a note that had the name and address of a new writer and publisher—one looking to publish works of other thought-provoking writers.

His company name is GHETTOHEAT®. His name is simply, HICKSON. The voice of my godmother played in my head: *"GOD has other plans for you."* I took that paper, and soon after, got a taste of those plans. My name is DRU NOBLE. I am an enigma of many things. But I am a slave *no* more. Now it's time...

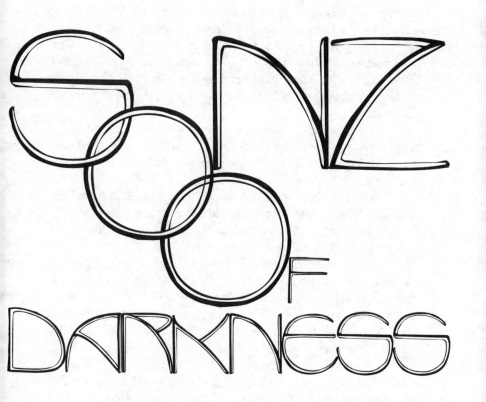

SONZ OF DARKNESS

PROLOGUE

Stars glittered warmly in the night sky above the rented car Wilfred Romulus had driven his family in, along the desolate *Haitian* countryside. Besides the vehicle's bright beaming headlights, the full moon and the stars were the only illumination.

Marylyn—his loving wife of two years, had sat in the passenger's seat beside Wilfred, clutching her newborn baby, Gary who smiled back and cooed at the attention of his young mother. Andrew—her three-year-old son, sat silently in the backseat.

Andrew gazed out the window, searching for any sign of people, but the dark night had revealed nothing, only darkness, which had given the toddler the impression that the car was floating in a black void.

He'd wished that his baby brother were in the backseat alongside him, so that Andrew could have someone to play with. Instead, he'd been left with his inanimate *G. I. Joe* action figure, which had stricken Andrew with boredom.

Marylyn could only see sandy road ahead in the glow of the headlights. She'd originally rejected her husband's request to visit his homeland two months prior—Marylyn was *American,* and had known nothing about this foreign country; only what she'd witnessed from *American* media, which truly appalled Marylyn from sanctioning the idea to visit *Haiti.*

Yet, Wilfred had continued to press her.
He'd told Marylyn that he wanted their children to be baptized in his native land by a Vowdun, who was famous in *Haiti.* Marylyn didn't even know what a Vowdun was until Wilfred had explained. He'd told her it was the same as a priest in the *United States.*

Marylyn eventually had become open-minded, thinking about the love she received from Wilfred. He'd come into her life when Marylyn was plagued by turmoil. She was on her own at the time with her one-year-old, first-born child, Andrew, who's biological father had deserted them when Andrew was still in Marylyn's womb; leaving the woman hurt and financially unstable.

Marylyn had no family or friends, only her son. Soon after, she'd met Wilfred—the loving, handsome man, Marylyn would come to marry. Wilfred saved her from loneliness, treating Marylyn like a queen.

Furthermore, he also loved Andrew, as though the young boy was a child of his own. When Gary was later born, their family had been complete. So, it was of no wonder that Marylyn would finally submit to Wilfred's wishes to visit his homeland. But, as they all rode in the car, Marylyn had begun to regret her decision. She then looked at her husband, wanting to tell Wilfred to turn back, but had resisted.

"How much further do we have to go, Wilfred? The kids must be starved—they haven't eaten since this morning," Marylyn said softly. Wilfred then smiled, taking one hand off the steering wheel as he'd pointed ahead.

"We'll be there soon. The old woman lives far out here so outsiders won't bother her. Very few people know of the Vowdun. Don't worry, Marylyn, it won't be long. We'll be back at our hotel before you know it, and tomorrow, we'll visit my mother," Wilfred promised.

Marylyn had become worried; nonetheless, she kept her watchful eyes locked on the road. Five minutes had passed before Wilfred seen the distant flickers of fire. He'd known that it was the torch the Vowdun kept outside her hut. Wilfred quickly drove to it, like a beacon to insects.

When the car pulled over and Wilfred stepped out, Marylyn had felt a knot forming in her stomach. Woman's intuition immediately then warned her to leave this strange place. Unwillingly, Marylyn opened up the car door and had stepped out, holding Gary tightly in her arms.

Andrew had become troubled when he saw the expression on his mother's face. His tiny fingers pulled the doors latch, and Andrew had quickly scampered to Marylyn's side.

The small, indigenous shack was a haunting image to the mother of two. Out in the middle of nowhere, so far away from society, it was as if whoever resided within its interior, hadn't wanted to be found. Wilfred on the other hand, had a hidden rejoice in his heart.

Wilfred then remembered when he was younger, how he'd broken his leg. When Wilfred's mother had brought him to see the Vowdun, the haggard old woman had healed Wilfred's ailment within one day. It was then when Wilfred's mother had explained to him the powers the Vowdun had possessed.

No one, not even Wilfred's mother had known the true origin or age of the Vowdun. Fascinated by what had happened to him, Wilfred promised himself to one day bring his firstborn to receive the blessings of the powerful elderly woman. Now, on this silent night, Wilfred had not only brought his first-born child, but his three-year-old stepson as well.

"Priestess, I have come to receive your blessing for my children," Wilfred had proudly called out in his native *Haitian* tongue. Shortly after, the raggedy sheets that covered the hut's entrance had opened. The Vowdun then exited her home and approached the family.

Her physical features were *frightening* to Marylyn!

The elderly woman had hunched over as if she couldn't bare standing. Long, disheveled garments covered the Vowdun's gaunt body. Her long gray hair was thin and stringy, revealing bold patches throughout her head. Watery, yellow-colored eyes had stared hauntingly back at Marylyn's own.

The young mother then held Gary even closer, protectively to her bosom. Andrew wrapped his arms around his Marylyn's leg, and squeezed with as much strength as he could muster—even Andrew was terribly fearful of the Vowdun's appearance. Marylyn instinctively reached down and gently placed her hand on Andrew's head, trying to comfort his fear.

The horrifying old woman had smiled obscenely, before her gaze met Wilfred. Marylyn had become appalled by the Vowdun's disgustingly, brown-colored, rotten teeth, when she'd spoken in a language that Marylyn didn't understand.

"So…you've come to receive my gifts, Wilfred Romulus. How noble of you. What sickness does your children possess?"

Wilfred was in awe when the Vowdun had said his name. He was a mere boy when Wilfred last seen the elderly woman, yet she'd remembered his name. Wilfred then silenced his thoughts.

"My children possess no illness. I want you to bless them; so no harm or sickness will ever come to my children in future days. I don't want my sons to *never* know of illness or suffering. *Please*, priestess, use your magic and *bless* them," Wilfred had pleaded.

Though Marylyn couldn't understand their speech, she'd still listened keenly. When the grotesque woman turned to look at

Marylyn, she'd gazed at her children with tentative eyes. Marylyn's heart immediately skipped a beat.

"I will do as you wish, Wilfred Romulus. But as you know, my services come with a price."

"I am aware of that."

The Vowdun then reached out to Marylyn with withered, thorny fingers, causing her to cautiously step back.

"It's okay, Marylyn, give her the baby. Nothing will happen to our child. I swear."

"But this is wrong, Wilfred," Marylyn had retorted.

"It will be over soon. This is my tradition, you understand that, don't you?"

Marylyn couldn't bare the thought of something awful happening to her newborn. She'd yielded to Wilfred's request and slowly handed over Gary. The baby becomes abnormally silent while being held in the Vowdun's arms. Wilfred then hugged Marylyn, trying to comfort her, as the priestess reached out for Andrew. Frightened to the point of screaming, little Andrew mercifully squeezed Marylyn's leg tighter.

"No, Mommy, N-O-O-O-O-O!" Andrew had pleaded, begging for his mother's supreme protection from the wicked-looking old woman.

Wilfred then saw the terror in his stepson's eyes. He'd bent down and touched Andrew's shoulder: "Everything's alright, son; you're my big man, right?" Wilfred said, smiling at the child. "You don't have to be scared, I just want you to go with your little brother for a while. Me and mommy will be right here waiting for you."

Andrew then sniffed, wiping the newly formed tears in his eyes. The sight of the discomfort had also brought Marylyn to the brink of tears.

"Can you do that for me, Andrew?" Wilfred then asked.

"Y-Y-Yes. Yes, daddy," young Andrew had stammered. Wilfred then kissed Andrew on the forehead before leading him into the waiting arms of the Vowdun. Andrew kept his eyes glued to the ground—he'd refused to even steal a glance of the elderly woman, as Andrew and Gary were being lead away from their parents.

Marylyn was pained with heartache when the three vanished within the Vowdun's shack. The filthy sheets at the hut's entrance had blocked her vision from what transpired in the interior of the makeshift home. Marylyn didn't want to be in *Haiti*—she didn't want to go through with Wilfred's will. At that moment, Marylyn only wanted her children.

Wilfred then wrapped his arms around Marylyn's waist, pulling her to him. He wasn't at all fearful of the priestess, nor what the old woman was doing to his sons. The Vowdun throughout *Haiti* had been highly respected—a spiritual asset to the land.

"I know you don't like this, Marylyn, but the gifts she will bless upon our children will be worth all this."

Marylyn had hated knowing that her sons were alone with the horrid witch—she'd hated herself even more for allowing it to happen. Marylyn then pulled away from Wilfred while having her nose wrinkled, glaring hard at her husband.

"I don't *care* about your customs, Wilfred! I can't *believe* I let you bring us out here with that *woman!* She has our kids, doing God knows *what* to them—I want to get Andrew and Gary *out* of there and go back home!" Marylyn had spat angrily, regretting her decision to allow the boys to be taken away from her.

As Marylyn had stared at Wilfred scornfully, her enraged state was shattered when the quiet night was filled with agonizing screams of her two children. Horrified, Marylyn quickly darted for the shack's entrance, fearing the worst for Andrew and Gary.

Wilfred instinctively grabbed her arm and wrestled Marylyn, keeping her from the Vowdun's shack.

"Let go of me, *bastard,* she's hurting my kids!" Marylyn then screamed, struggling to be free from Wilfred's tight grasp.

"No. It will be over soon," Wilfred had grunted. Marylyn then flailed wildly in his arms. Revolting images had run through Marylyn's mind. If the priestess had caused harm to her children, Marylyn would've not only murdered the witch, but she would've also found a gun and blew Wilfred's brains out. Marylyn couldn't fathom why her husband was stopping her from answering the terrified cries of her children.

She'd clawed at Wilfred, kicking and punching him with no abandon to obtain freedom. When Andrew and Gary's cries had fallen silent, the couple immediately froze. Marylyn, racked with despair, had freed herself from Wilfred's hold, and just when she stood, the hut's sheets were pushed aside.

The Vowdun stepped out of the shack. Gary and Andrew were nestled in her frail arms—both being in a deep slumber. Marylyn then frantically took her boys from the elderly woman with a scornful expression on her face.

"WHAT DID YOU DO TO MY KIDS, WITCH?" Marylyn had screamed. The Vowdun then grinned grotesquely. Enraged, Marylyn kicked the old woman in the belly, causing her to fall to the dusty ground. The Vowdun then gasped for air, as Marylyn had spat on her, before racing for the car with her children.

Wilfred then bent down and helped the elderly woman to her feet. He'd pulled a small knot of *American* money out of his pocket, and handed it to the priestess.

"I'm *sorry* for my wife's actions. I hope this will be enough for your services," Wilfred had offered respectfully.

The Vowdun then took the roll from his hand, and studied the money as if it were a foreign object. She'd snickered in distaste, then, in rejection, tossed it back at Wilfred. He was dumfounded, Wilfred couldn't understand why the old woman would refuse his payment. Three thousand *American* dollars had gone a long way in *Haiti*.

Cautiously, Wilfred bent down to retrieve the money from the ground. Once again, he'd held the cash out, trying to give it to the witch.

"What is wrong? Is it not enough?" Wilfred questioned.

"I do not *want* your tree bark. No, I will *take* an even greater payment for the gifts I have granted your seed," The Vowdun whispered in a hissing tone. For the first time that night, fear had begun to awaken inside Wilfred, because of the old woman's threat.

"*Please,* do not use your magic for evil against me, Vowdun. I will pay whatever you ask," Wilfred then pleaded. The elderly woman's mouth had opened, and Wilfred smelled her acrid breath. Her mysterious eyes had seemed to pierce his very soul.

"Yes, you *will* pay Wilfred Romulus," The Vowdun said, as she'd turned and had begun walking home. "Yes, you will."

The words haunted Wilfred, as the Vowdun mysterious vanished into her shanty.

Wilfred quickly made his way to the rental car where Marylyn was checking the children—she'd searched for wounds the Vowdun might have given them. None were visible.

Marylyn then strapped Gary down in his baby chair in the backseat, and laid Andrew beside him. The two boys were wide-awake before they'd entered the Vowdun's hut. Yet, Marylyn now had grown frantic—because she couldn't wake Andrew or Gary up. When Wilfred had approached the car, she'd looked at him angrily.

"They won't wake up! What did you let that *woman* do to our children, Wilfred?"

"GET IN THE CAR!" Wilfred had shouted. The expression on his face had told Marylyn that he was somewhat scared. She'd hurriedly got in the front passenger's seat, halting her frustration momentarily. Wilfred hadn't even glanced at Marylyn, as he'd started the ignition, and drove off at rapid speed.

Marylyn then stared silently at the right side of Wilfred's face for two minutes. She'd wanted to strike him so badly, for putting not only her but, their two children through eerie circumstances.

"I know your upset, Marylyn, but to my people, this is sacred—it's normal," Wilfred then explained, eyes being locked on the little bit of road the headlights revealed. Marylyn frowned at his remark.

"Andrew and Gary were *screaming* inside that hut, and now they're sound asleep! This is not normal! I don't care *what* you say, this was wrong, Wilfred! That *bitch* did something to our kids—it's like they're drugged. Why the *hell* did you bring us out here? WHAT DID SHE DO TO THEM?" Marylyn had screamed; budding tears had begun to run down the young, ebony mother's face.

Wilfred then took a deep breath, as he tried his best to maintain his composure.

"Take us to the hospital!" Marylyn had insisted.

"They don't need a hospital, they're perfectly healthy."

"How can you say that? Just look at them!"

"Marylyn, listen to me."

"I don't *want* to. I—"

"LISTEN TO ME!" Wilfred then said over Marylyn's voice. She'd immediately paused, glaring fiercely toward Wilfred as he spoke.

"The Vowdun *has* done something to our children—she's given them gifts we don't yet know. Marylyn, the Vowdun has helped *many* people with her magic—she once healed my broken leg in a matter of seconds! The Vowdun has brought men and women fame, wealth, even cured those stricken with deadly diseases. It once was even told that she made a man immortal, one who now lives in the shadows."

"I'm a *Christian,* and what you're talking about is satanic. You *tricked* me into coming out here to get Andrew and Gary blessed—you're a *liar!*" Marylyn had interjected.

"That is why we came to Haiti, and it has been done! The worst is over now."

As his parents argued, Gary Romulus' eyes had opened. He remained silent and unknown to his parents. The infant had been in a trance-like state, detached from his surroundings. Wilfred wasn't even looking at the road ahead; his vision had been glued to his wife as they feuded. Gary had been however.

The newborn had seen what his mother and father hadn't seen, way ahead in the black night. Two glowing crimson eyes had stared back at the baby. They were serpentine, eyes Gary would never forget. They were the same eyes he and Andrew had seen in the hut.

The Vowdun's eyes.

Gary then reached down and gently touched Andrew's shoulder. Strangely, the toddler had awakened in the same catatonic state as his sibling.

"Everything is going to be okay, Marylyn. I tried to pay the Vowdun her price, but she refused," Wilfred had stated. Marylyn then gasped.

"A PRICE?" Marylyn had blurted. She then refused to hear Wilfred explain anything.

Andrew and Gary had glared at those red eyes, which were accompanied by an ever-growing shadow that seemed to make the oncoming road even darker.

Lashing shadows awaited the vehicle.

"WHAT PRICE?" Marylyn had been consumed with anger; she'd easily detected the blankness of Wilfred's mind. Wilfred had been at a loss of words. Even he had no knowledge of what the Vowdun had expected from him; that was the very thought that had frightened Wilfred to the core.

The car then moved at seventy miles per hour!

The saddened mother of two had finally turned away from her husband's stare. At that moment, Marylyn couldn't bare Wilfred's presence. When her sight fell on the oncoming road, Marylyn screamed out loudly in terror. Wilfred then instinctively turned forward to see what frightened her. His mouth had fallen ajar at the sight of the nightmarish form ahead of him. Filled with panic, Wilfred tried to turn the steering wheel to avoid crashing.

It was too late.

The sudden impact of the collision had caused the car to explode into immense flames, flames that roared to the night sky. The evil creature that caused it had gone, leaving behind its chaotic destruction; and the reason for it.

Out of the flickering flames and screeching metal had come a small boy, who held his baby brother carefully in his fragile arms. An illuminating blue sphere then surrounded their forms, which kept Andrew and Gary, unscathed from the fires, and jagged metal of the wreckage. Incredibly, they were both physically unharmed.

Andrew then walked away from the crash in a sentinel manner. In the middle of his forehead was a large, newly formed third eye, which stared out bizarrely. Not until Andrew had been far enough away did he sit down, the blue orb then vanished.

Gary looked up at Andrew, speaking baby talk to get his attention. Andrew had ignored Gary. He was staring at the flaming vehicle as his parent's flesh had burned horridly, causing a foul stench that polluted the air. Through glassy eyes, Andrew's vision didn't waver; the child was beyond mourning.

Finally, Andrew had he gazed down at the precious baby he'd embraced. Gary then smiled, assured, unfazed by the tragic event. With his tiny arms, Gary tried to reach upwards, trying to touch the strange, silver eye on his brother's forehead, playfully. The new organ amused Gary, as any brand-new toy would've had.

"Mommy and daddy are gone now," Andrew then sobbed, as streams of tears rolled down his young face. He was trying his best to explain his sorrow. "I'll never leave you, Gary, I promise," Andrew had cried. Gary then giggled, still trying to reach Andrew's eye as best he could.

For the price of the Vowdun to bestow her gifts from her dark powers to the children, Wilfred Romulus had paid the ultimate price—the life of he and his wife. Their children were given gifts, far beyond their father's imagination, and for this, Andrew and Gary were also cursed with fates, not of their choosing.

The future held in store, untold suffering.

They were no longer innocent.

No longer the children of Wilfred and Marylyn Romulus.

They were now and forever, *Sonz of Darkness*.

As Andrew had cried underneath the midnight moon, a tear of blood welled in his third eye, running down his face. Fascinated, Gary then reached up earnestly, as the tear fell from his brother's chin, and into the palm of Gary's small hand.

* * * * *

The next morning, the *Haitian* authorities had found the children looking normal, without any trace of the eerie events that happened the night before on the roadside; not far from the wrecked remains of the car crash their dead parents had rested in. No one had bothered to ask or answer the mysterious questions as to what transpired.

It had been swept under the rug to avoid bad publicity.

Andrew and Gary were flown back to *North America* and placed in an adoption center in *New York,* because they had no known living relatives. While there, Andrew was extremely close to his Gary, never letting him leave his sight.

Two months later, a wealthy married couple had arrived at the adoption center. David and Valerie Taylor had not been informed that the child they wanted to adopt had a younger brother.

Andrew cried tears of agony when he'd been forcefully taken away from Gary. Powerless to stop what had happening, Andrew was mentally harmed in such a way that, it had buried itself in his mind for years to come.

The first three-and-a-half years of his Andrew's would be forgotten, but Gary on the other hand, had never forgotten the noble words of his bother: *"I'll never leave you."*

That, and the memories of the creature that had murdered his parents would forever haunt Gary.

ONE

Twenty years later…

Drenched in cold sweat that stains the hard mattress on which he sleeps on, Gary "Exodus" Romulus awakens, screaming out in terror. His horrid cries are heard throughout the cellblock that Gary is detained in at *Rikers Island Prison,* ending the peaceful slumber of other prisoners.

Breathing heavily, his brown eyes rapidly shoots back-and-forth in a disoriented, panicked state. Images of Gary's nightmare linger dreadfully, as he realizes he's safe in the cell, alone.

A neighboring cellmate begins banging on the cell wall angrily: "Hey Exodus, what the *fuck* is wrong with you?" Fly spits. Gary gets out of his cot wearily, wiping the abundance of perspiration from his brow.

"I'm alright, Fly; bad dreams. My fault for waking you," Gary answers.

"Listen, baby bro, you're going home in a few hours. You shouldn't even be *having* bad dreams. Go see your girl and hold your head—you can't lose it now," Fly offers his advice, now, just as awake as Gary.

The nightmares are returning again, now even more powerful than before: dreadful dreams of The Vowdun witch, and his parents' death. It's as if the tragedy has only happened moments ago, but this occurred when Gary was a baby. Strangely how he even remembers them at all.

As Gary now washes his face in the sink, he can still hauntingly feel the eerie embrace of his brother, Andrew's arms; the brother that was taken away from Gary so long ago.

Grabbing his toothbrush and toothpaste, Gary's thoughts returns to its normal cycle. It's been a year since his incarceration for the charge of grand theft auto, and Gary still feels no guilt about his crimes.

Gary's life leaves no time for remorse.

From foster care, to group homes, to prisons—it's just an expectation of the choices he'd made. Gary now has no family, the only recollections of one are the chilling nightmares and memories, which he knows in his heart are true.

After Gary rinses his mouth and spits in the toilet, the convict begins to get dressed. Gary smiles wholeheartedly as he thinks about who's waiting for him outside the prison walls.

Twelve months, with no sex, Melody is going to get it!

The vision of his long-time girlfriend washes Gary's mind of his previous nightmare.

"Exodus, are you *listening* to me? You done *woke* me up from my sleep, and now you got me over here talking to myself!"

"No, I hear you, Fly, I was just thinking about someone."

"You *better* be thinking about a job or something, so your *ass* won't come back here," Fly retaliates Gary sighs; a job is the *last* thing on his mind.

"You know I'm going to do my thing, Fly."

"Yeah, I know; just don't let me see you back here, baby bro."

A small chuckle escapes Gary's lips. He reaches for his *Walkman* and passes it through the bars to Fly.

"Take care of this for me, until I come back," Gary says in good spirits.

"Thank you, you stingy *bastard!*" Fly jokes back.

"Tell my people I said to take care."

"No doubt," Fly answers. The two then shake hands through the bars, as a correctional officer makes his count.

* * * * *

The sight of Melody's beauty brings a bright smile to Gary. She's leaning against her *Lexus* as he approaches. Melody immediately wraps her arms around Gary's shoulders, grasps him tightly. A rejoicing feeling now wells in Melody, as she passionately kisses her love.

Shortly, Gary removes his mouth from the Melody's lush lips, and gazes at the contours of her angelic face, as impulse causes Gary's hands to squeeze Melody's ample buttocks.

Melody has cut her long, black hair short since the last time he'd seen her—Gary loves the new bob style. Melody's wide brown eyes now look into his, as if she knows what Gary's thinking.

"Let's go home, Melody. I've missed you *so* much."

Melody lets out a small laugh as she gently grabs his hand: "I know you have, Gary. How was your stay at *Rikers?*"

"Unpleasant."

Melody then playfully traces her fingers against his cheeks before opening the car door on the driver's side.

"Let's get out of here," Melody whispers, as she gets in the car and starts the engine. Gary politely gestures for Melody to sit in the passenger's seat, which she instantly obliges. As Melody gets back into the vehicle, Gary becomes comfortable by pulling the seat position lever, having the seat fall back awkwardly.

Melody shakes her head in disbelief, *Five minutes out of prison, and his old ways still remain strong as ever*

Gary grabs several musical CD's and puts *Kid Capri's "The Tape"* in the CD player; music loudly blasts as he turns up the volume. Gary then firmly grips the steering wheel, and the Lexus speeds off recklessly towards *Harlem.*

Melody quickly frowns at his outlandish behavior, yet she holds her contempt in check—Melody's just happy that Gary is once again by her side.

* * * * *

The two young lovers spend the day and most of the night, reforming their long, denied passion for one another. Twelve long months has passed since the last time Gary and Melody has had sex. In all that time, Melody never strayed from her loyalty and companionship for Gary. She knows that he's a criminal-minded man, but that never stopped Melody from loving him.

Her own brother, Black is knee-deep in the crime underworld. He has his hands in everything from drugs, to running a car theft ring. The fast money Melody would make if she chose to inherit the lifestyle of her brother, hasn't tempted her.

Melody's only temptation is Gary Romulus.

As the two make passionate love, Melody wonders what path Gary will take this time around, because the sheer reality of losing Gary again will truly break her heart. Later, as their exhausted bodies lay entangled in each other's arms, sleep overcomes the couple.

The midnight moon glows in *New York City's* sky, as a terrifying dream returns to its tormented. Once again...*Gary is a child, a defenseless baby in his mother's arms, snuggled warmly to her bosom, with his older brother standing beside them. Gary then sees his father, so clearly Gary envisions him.*

The witch, haggard and old, takes Gary from his worried mother and his brother, Andrew. Yes, that's his name, Gary then remembers. It was Andrew, the one who used to amuse him by making funny faces, and calling him "Man-head". Andrew is taken with Gary into the Vowdun's home.

Now the dream becomes even more frightening.

Gary holds Melody tighter as he sleeps on.

The Vowdun places Gary's tiny body on a table and sits Andrew beside him. Andrew is shaking in convulsions, scared out of his mind, as the old woman retrieves a long, thin, sharp, silver knife and stares at the children maliciously. It's at that moment, both Gary and Andrew notices that the Vowdun's eyes have changed. They are no longer the eyes of a human. They are the eyes of a serpent.

Andrew screams out in horror when the Vowdun opens her mouth, revealing multiple rows of jagged fangs. He quickly tries to hop off the table and cry out for his mother and father. The demonic woman swiftly grabs Andrew by the throat, and lifts him up with one arm, choking the toddler savagely.

Worriedly, Andrew looks down, grabbing at the old woman's thorny fingers, struggling desperately for freedom, as the Vowdun hovers over his baby brother.

Gary sobs in his sleep, mumbling words in panic.

The Vowdun slowly lifts the knife and wickedly smiles. So defenseless is Gary, the newborn child, all he can do is cry, pleading for his parents, as the pointy blade rapidly comes down and stabs coldly into Gary's chest.

The agonizing pain inflames him. Gary's tiny lungs have filled with his own blood—his cry is silenced. The knife cuts straight through young Gary's fragile heart.

Andrew's eyes streams with tears, mortified, as he witnesses his brother's blood emerge from the fatal wound. The Vowdun witch then violently slams Andrew back on the table. The Vowdun takes a step back, laughing insanely at the mutilation it has caused. Then, the Vowdun's own skin begins to slowly tear and rip apart, revealing the true form within the witch's shell.

Both Gary and Andrew gaze at the hellish creature with fading vision. It's thin elongated, arachnid form, towers over the two. Big, glowing red eyes stares down at them, as yellow saliva falls from its mouth.

"You will not die my children. For now, you shall become one with me. In all the rest of your days I will haunt you, until you fulfill the destiny I have forge from my eternal essence. This I promise you," it hisses. The very flesh of the creature begins to illuminate in a blinding light, that bathes the hut's interior with an immense glowing radiation.

"LET ME G-O-O-O-O-O-O!" Gary bolts out of his sleep screaming, causing Melody to wake. Troubled by his state, she holds Gary tightly, as he tries to escape the evil creature from his nightmare.

"Gary, calm down. I'm right here, baby," Melody pleads; frightened because of his bizarre behavior. She felt Gary earlier when he was moving in his sleep, now, her lover is fully awake, crying hysterically—as if still trapped in the nightmare.

"N-O-O-O-O-O-O!" Gary howls in terror. A few feet away from the bed, Melody's full-view mirror suddenly shatters, startling her. She flinches beside Gary, and oddly, he freezes— ceasing his maddened display. Melody then views Gary cautiously; believing that his time spent in prison has affected him deeply than she's aware.

With his right hand, Gary inspects his chest just over his heart, still vaguely feeling a ghostly pain.

"Gary, are you okay?"

Gary turns to Melody.

Tears are running down his face.

She sees the distress in Gary's face. Lovingly, Melody hugs him comfortably, lightly placing a soft kiss on Gary's lips.

"Baby, whatever it is, we can talk about it," Melody states, wiping away his tears. Gary tries his best to regain his composure. This time, the nightmare was too real and extremely terrifying. Gary holds on to Melody, wanting to keep her against him, so that he knows that Melody is real.

She's the only hope Gary has of love and peace.

"Just hold me, Melody, that's all I want."

Gary places his head on her chest, as his girlfriend slowly caresses his low-cut hair calmly. Like a child afraid of the dark,

Melody comforts Gary's secret fear. Gary doesn't want to talk about his dream; worried that Melody would think he's crazy.

Melody wants to talk.

She needs to know.

But tonight...

Melody is satisfied with knowing that Gary's alright.

She's aware from past experience that he can be persuaded.

As Gary lay upon her bosom, Melody overlooks the broken fragments of the mirror on the floor. She decides to clean it up the morning; Melody doesn't know why or how it shattered.

That's very odd.

The shattering bothers her for a moment, but Melody pushes the thought aside and goes to sleep.

Gary doesn't.

Not this time.

If it's in his willpower, Gary will *never* close his eyes and return to those torturing nightmares again. The nightmares that seems too vivid and painful. Gary was so young, so innocent, and the Vowdun stole that from him—changing him beyond his understanding. Gary can't fathom how, but whatever it is, he feels it will never release him.

For the rest of the early morning hours, Gary clings to Melody desperately.

Fighting back tears of misery and loss.

* * * * *

That same morning, just as Gary Romulus is being released from prison, Andrew Taylor is growing aggravated from the sweltering northern *African* heat that bombards him. Andrew caked on insect repellent before leaving his campsite, but to no use, insects still swarm relentlessly above Andrew's head.

No one actually believed that the president of Lortech Industries wanted to visit the diamond mines his corporation owned, but the new secretive find within the mines has drawn Andrew's attention. Truth be told, no one wanted the twenty-three-year-old to be associated with the company, and he knows that.

His father, David Taylor had deemed it in his will that Andrew inherit the dynasty. An unexpected heart failure at age sixty-four has placed Andrew in the seat of power before predicted.

When his father passed seven months prior, Andrew had no idea of the responsibilities that would become his. Michael Masters, the chief of Lortech's security and information, has brought Andrew up to par with every detail of the current projects the company is developing. Protocol is practical to Lortech, in which its scientific achievements and weaponry for the NSA, and other *United States* organizations are the most prolific in the world.

It's of no wonder that no one wants to embrace such secrets to twenty-three-year-old Andrew. But he's no ordinary man of his age.

Andrew's education and intelligence are prodigious.

His parents were always astonished and bewildered by Andrew's superior mind power, and rapid ability to learn.

He'd risen through *Ivy League* schooling and achieved his Masters degrees in several sciences and professions, before the age of fifteen. This fact intimidated many, making enemies out of friends and foes alike. Andrew was the perfect prodigy child, for the great burden his father has left with him. His only problem is lack of experience, which Andrew is swiftly gaining.

As Andrew enters the mouth of the mine with a single guide, he contemplates on his mother, Valerie Taylor. His father's death has struck her deeply. She's a strong woman, the strongest woman in the world in her Andrew's eyes, justly so, for the wife of one of the most powerful Black men in *America.*

Andrew's mother will *never* get over the death of the man she so greatly loved, but she still has Andrew: the promise of a new dawn.

The stale air of the dark cavern Andrew and his guide travels through, makes Andrew's chest tighten. None of the other native mine workers would even attempt to return to the newly discovered sight they uncovered, but Andrew persuades one to show him. Andrew has to see it for himself, before allowing any archeologist on the grounds.

Lortech isn't in the business of rare jewels for sale; they need the diamonds for more valuable purposes, mainly for their light bending properties—to be used with other projects. It's a question of dynamics and resources.

Seventy feet down in the shadowy channels, Mefu, the dark-skinned *African* guide, glances at Andrew as if worried.

"What's wrong?" Andrew asks.

"Nothing, sir, I didn't believe you wanted to go any further."

"It's not your *job* to *think* for me. Now *carry* on," Andrew answers back snobbishly. Mefu sighs before walking on with the corporate mogul following.

A half hour later, Andrew and Mefu are so far into the mine, that it seems there isn't any air. Both men put on their air suppliers, as two beams of light from their flashlights shows them passage.

Clouds of dust float around Andrew and the guide, as if a ghost warning of danger. Andrew is fully aware of the many deaths that took the lives of miners in those depths, and the thought makes goose bumps form on his skin. Andrew advances a little further, until feeling a slight draft on his sandaled feet. As he points his flashlight to the ground, Andrew sees dust moving in the shallow air.

"There's a draft in here. That's strange, so far down here," Andrew states. Mefu looks even more uncomfortable.

"They say that this place is sacred, sir; that it is cursed. The other workers are afraid of this section of the mines, because of what they found."

"Cursed you say? Well I'm *not* a believer, bring me to the place now."

"But, sir—"

"NOW!"

Mefu does as he is told, and after several more minutes into their journey, Andrew finds what he came for. His sight falls on the opposite demolished, rocky wall, the miners had made when they discovered the sight.

Andrew's flashlight now beams into the unknown, and a humming wind fills the area. Mefu begins shaking uncontrollably, causing the industrialist to notice his fear.

"What are you afraid of? You are *not* a child. Don't let superstition control you," Andrew whispers through grinding teeth. Mefu's cowardly behavior angers him. "Pull yourself together!" Andrew orders.

"Yes, sir," Mefu answers, still letting his fear get the best of him. After he scolds the guide, Andrew begins to inspect the area. Before getting a good look at his surroundings, a voice comes screaming through the transmitting radio on his waist: *"TAYLOR, TAYLOR, COME IN, SIR!"*

Andrew quickly grabs the device and answers, "Yes?"

"We haven't heard from you in a while. I was just checking in on your safety. Is everything alright down there?"

Andrew recalls the voice over the radio; it's the head of his bodyguard team at a campsite, near the mouth of the mine.

"Everything is okay down here. We are just making renovations," Andrew jokes.

"Renovations?" the guard answers back, baffled at his employer's comment.

"Yes, I will clue you in when our business is done; copy?"

"Yes, I copy that," is the reply over the radio, the transmitter then goes silent.

Andrew raises the flashlight and looks over his surroundings once again. He's amazed at the sheer size of the area. It's ninety yards wide, and thirty feet high. The rocky walls are smooth, as if done by man. Andrew takes careful steps into the space, gawking as he went on.

Mefu stands frozen, refusing to move. Andrew turns to him and scowls his face.

"Mefu, *pull* yourself together this moment, or I promise you that you will be fired!"

Reluctantly, Mefu walks towards Andrew, and they continue their journey. As the two approach the back of the area, Andrew's jaw falls ajar at the sight of what's before him.

Two large stone statues stand on opposite ends of what looks to be a grave made of marble rock. The rays of flashlights illuminate the statues. Both statues appear to be lions. Their faces snarl in defiant expressions, frozen in time. Large wings sprouts from their backs.

They watch and protect the grave, Andrew gathers. "It's a tomb, Mefu!" he then comments while inspecting the top of the grave. Andrew notices what seems to be writing, with an abundance of dust covering its words.

Andrew then lifts the mask of his air device and blows down hard. The dusty layer is removed, revealing a form of writing Andrew doesn't understand, but he smiles nonetheless at the prospect of what is found.

Andrew quickly moves to the right side of the coffin and strongly grasp at its side.

"Well, come on, Mefu, let's get this lid off."

Mefu obeys, soon finding himself straining—the lid's heavy weight. Grunting vigorously, the two men finally raise the gravestone, and it falls to the side with a loud thump. Mefu shines his flashlight into the coffin's opening. What he sees makes Mefu tremble.

A decayed corpse lies peacefully in the embrace of death. Its hollowed eye sockets stare up into a world it has not seen for centuries. Andrew looks down further, and an array of sparkling lights shines back at him.

In the dead man's hands is a long wooden staff, having an abundance of multi-colored jewels encrusted into its frame. Mefu laughs happily at their find, no longer showing his fear.

"Mefu, I think we just stumbled upon the most rarest find this century."

"Yes, sir, *indeed* we have," Mefu states greedily. Without wasting another moment, Andrew reaches for the sparkling wood. The *African* guide forcefully grabs Andrew's wrist.

"Sir, what if it's booby-trapped?" Mefu questions. Andrew yanks his arm free from Mefu's grasp.

"I don't believe we would have gotten this far if this place was booby-trapped. Don't *ever* touch me again!" Andrew snaps. When he finally takes hold of the staff, Andrew feels the hard, encrusted jewels on his palms. He tries to pull it out of the coffin, but its deceased owner refuses to let it go.

Angrily, Andrew recklessly snatches the staff, breaking the bony, brittle fingers that held it. He then raises the artifact, adoring its splendid craftsmanship: "It's beautiful."

"Yes, it is, sir," Mefu interjects. As the two men gaze at the remarkable display of precious jewels, the ground underneath begins to vibrate, quickly becoming more powerful; almost taking their balance.

Andrew then hears rumbling. He turns and realizes that the foundations of the two statues are in fact cracking. Terrified, Mefu runs to the tomb's exit, knocking Andrew over, as he immediately flees.

"YOU'RE FIRED, *COWARD!*" Andrew shouts in fury, as the *African* guide vanishes from his sight. Andrew becomes startled when the head of one of the statues falls from its body and smashes into the ground, just a few feet away from him.

As Andrew stares at the foundation of where it fell, he notices that a strange, metallic liquid is oozing from both of the statues' crevices. Instinctively, Andrew stands up and tries to retreat from the tomb, just as Mefu has.

The fluid quickly blocks Andrew's way, moving as though alive. Andrew gasps at what he's witnessing. The liquid, which looks like molten gold, brings itself together, forming, as it lifts from the ground.

Andrew takes a step back, causing himself to slip on a silvery substance, coming from the other statue. As he hit the ground, Andrew is struck with the frightening thought that he's suffering from inhaling the mine earlier. Andrew thinks he's witnessing a mirage, something that his mind has conjured.

The liquids move distinctively, one apart from its shiny counterpart. Tremulous, Andrew watches in awe as the elements rise, forging two rippling images. Suddenly, the liquids become solid—one gold, the other silver; two humanoid figures stand in utter silence, facing Andrew.

The silver being approaches him and extends its hand, causing Andrew to coil back; he doesn't believe the sight in front of him. Then comes the voice, the voice Andrew doesn't hear physically, but rather in his mind. It's Andrew's own, but not he that brought it forth.

"We are AU and AG, we're cherubim that protect the staff of GOD, and the one who wields it. What is your will, Messiah?" the humanoids respond.

This is beyond Andrew's reason, afar from his imagination. He lives in a world of scientific fact: *How can the two beings above be real?* Andrew thinks. As he looks at the silver hand that reaches out for him, Andrew isn't afraid. In the struggle to make reason in what's transpiring, only one feeling emerges: power.

Carefully, Andrew takes the cherubim's hand, and the strange being pulls him to his feet. Andrew touches the beings' metallic bodies, reassuring to himself that he isn't hallucinating.

"I don't believe this. Who created you?" Andrew asks in wonder.

"HE who is, and will always be," his own eerie, calm voice answers back, as Andrew continues to inspect the cherubim. He then views the staff once again, wondering if he has stumbled upon some type of ancient technology.

"You wield the staff of GOD, what is it you will, Messiah?" The voice within Andrew's mind asks. He refuses to answer, instead, Andrew receives his transmitter radio and calls in: "Taylor to central, over."

"Yes, sir."

"I want a helicopter at the camp immediately; destination, airport. I have a package I want to get out of the mines, top security. And I want a team to secure this area, do you read me?"

"Yes, Taylor, what do you want us to do with your guide? He came running out of the mine, screaming something about ghosts."

Andrew hears the bodyguards' chuckle.

"Keep him detained until further notice. I believe he's inhaled too much of the air down here."

Andrew then places the radio back into its holder. From his experience and grooming at Lortech, Andrew knows that many things are to be kept secret. If knowledge is power, Andrew will reveal none of it. He wants nothing more than to get the two supernatural beings back to his hi-tech lab at Lortech for further analysis.

The staff is something Andrew will keep for himself.

The two humanoids wait for their master's request. Andrew watches his prize and speaks: "Gentlemen, follow me."

Without any notion of refusal, they follow their "Messiah".

TWO

The morning sun rises, spreading it's illuminating glory over the inhabitants of *New York City*. Melody opens her doe eyes to the golden shine, and reaches over for Gary's warm presence. There was no one at her bedside.

Startled, Melody raises her body out of bed, only to find her lover on bent knees, diligently picking up small fragments of broken glass, placing the contents into a small trash bin next to him. Melody now feels relaxed, realizing that Gary is in fact with her; she'll no longer be alone because of his incarceration. Gary looks over his shoulder at her naked form and grins.

"Why are you up so early, Gary?"

"So I can kiss you before you go to work."

Melody lazily stretches her arms outwards as she yawns. A quick glance at her clock tells Melody that she's late for work. Melody quickly scampers out of her queen-sized bed, careful not to step on any of the broken glass.

Gary playfully embraces Melody, lifting her off her feet. He carries Melody out of the bedroom, trying to kiss her evading face.

"Stop it. I have to brush my teeth and take a shower," Melody protests weakly, as Gary releases his affectionate bear hug.

"Let me take one with you. You *know* how I am in the morning."

Melody looks down towards Gary's crotch area and raises her eyebrow: "Well, you will have to wait until later. I'm already late for work."

Melody then enters the bathroom, swaying her hips seductively, and to Gary's dismay, she slams the door. Clearly let down, Gary places his head on the door.

"P-L-E-A-S-E?" Gary asks, as if a child, begging for a new toy. When he hears the bathroom door lock, Gary knows the reply.

"I said no, Gary, and *don't* try to pick the lock neither, 'cause you're not stealing any."

Gary shakes his head and retreats back to the bedroom to finish what he'd started. As Gary carefully puts more glass into the bin, he reflects on his nightmares. Melody thought that he'd woken up earlier, but the truth is that, Gary never went back to sleep. He stayed up all night with watery eyes, denying the tears to fall.

Lost in his thoughts, Gary's finger gets cut, because of the sharp glass he holds. The stinging pain arises, causing Gary to drop the fragment. He clutches his hand and grimaces. Blood immediately emits from the fresh wound.

Gary stares at it, intrigued, as though looking at an alien substance. The blood slowly runs into his palm, and Gary remains in a trance. Flashes of images burst forth in his mind, of blood within his palm, long ago, his brother Andrew's blood.

Unexpectedly the blood vanishes, causing Gary to stumble back in bewilderment. He gazes at his own hand, wide-eyed, as if it weren't Gary's own. The wound has miraculously healed, leaving no trace of the fresh cut, which seconds ago bled.

Gary begins breathing heavily…

Shuts his eyes tightly.

Re-opens them.

Fears that he's losing his sanity.

Gary then rubs his hand, attentively.

Studies it.

"What are you doing, Gary? I refuse to make love to you, and you're now getting your hand ready to play with yourself. You're not in prison anymore, baby," Melody states jokingly.

Before Gary turns to view her, he composes himself; Gary stands up, hides his distraught emotions.

"Stop playing," Gary interjects, as he turns to her. Melody has on nothing more than a pink plush cotton towel to cover her frame. As she puts on her teardrop diamond earrings, Melody overlooks her boyfriend.

"Well if you want it that bad," Melody says before seductively dropping the towel. She then places her body against a nearby dresser and squints her eyes. "I guess I can give you a little something," Melody offers.

Gary, now ignorant to anything else, slowly comes to her, but before he even touches Melody's soft, smooth skin, the phone rings.

"Too late. It's probably my boss wondering why I'm late," Melody indicates, as she moves to the phone, pushing Gary's thirsty hands aside.

"*Fuck* your boss!" Gary yells.

Melody quickly places her index finger on her lips, quieting Gary, before lifting the cordless phone. "Hello?"

"Yeah, what's the deal, sis? Put Exodus on the phone!"

Melody frowns while hearing the voice of her brother, Black.

"What do you want him for? Gary just got out yesterday, and your already trying to pull him back into trouble?"

"Melody, who the *hell* do you think you're talkin' to? Exodus is a grown-ass man, now put him on the *motherfuckin'* jack!"

Melody wants to hang up on her brother, but reluctantly, she drops the phone onto the bed and glares at Gary.

"It's Black," Melody sourly alerts Gary. He then retrieves the phone, looking concerned at his girlfriend's distaste.

"What's going on, Black?"

"What's up, my dude? How you been?"

"I've been fine."

"I know what you mean. Listen, Why don't you come down to my club 'round eleven, I have some things to discuss with you."

As Gary speaks with her brother, Melody dresses quietly, pondering on their conversation.

"Yeah, I'll be there, Black."

"Alright, you know I got love for you. It's goin' to be like old times." *Click.*

The receiver goes dead.

Gary hangs up the phone, feeling uneasy by the tone of Black's voice. Melody, now fully dressed, removes her bouncy hair from her face, and puts on her *Dior* glasses.

"What did he want, Gary?"

"Nothing major, Black just wants me to come see him."

"Come see him? Gary, I don't want you in that *nasty* booty club. Those chicks probably got all types of diseases. Don't get any ideas *either,*" Melody warns.

Gary approaches her with a sarcastic smirk upon his face, "Do you think I would try something with your brother right there? Hell, why would I go astray when I got the *best* woman in the world right here?" He then wraps his arms around Melody's thin waist, trying to ease her growing tension.

"You know what I mean. Black is poison. He only cares about himself, and I *don't* want you to get in trouble because of his rotten ass."

"Melody, he's your brother, so stop it," Gary replies, before giving his woman a quick peck on the cheek.

"Don't let him pull you into anything, Gary," Melody says seriously. She impatiently retrieves her pocketbook, releasing Gary's grasp.

"The clothes I bought you are in the closet, and there are many other things you can do today, instead of what you're planning. If you need money, there's some in the dresser. I'll be home late from work today, so *don't* do anything you'll regret."

"Yes, mom," Gary says jokingly.

"Mom, huh? Well instead of messing around with Black today, you *need* to go look for a job," Melody indicates sharply, making her way to the apartment door. Melody then turns again to look at Gary before she leaves: "Don't forget that I love you."

"I know that," Gary answers with a smile.

It isn't the answer Melody wants.

She leaves feeling slightly troubled, and it's then when Gary realizes that he said the wrong words.

Regretfully, Gary retreats to the bathroom.

* * * * *

Tonight, Gary finds himself on the "2" train, heading to the *South Bronx* to Black's club. He spent the day doing as Melody told him to: job hunting; discovering the process harder than expected. With no formal schooling or previous work experience, it is futile. Gary's only talent is armed robbery and car theft, teachings no school administered.

Gary felt awkward every time he stepped into an office, and when asked if he had a felony record, Gary felt as though he's being slammed into a concrete street.

"We'll be in touch," Gary's told over-and-over—a broken record of false promises.

With five hundred dollars of his girlfriend's money in his pocket, and a fuming attitude to match, Gary knows that there's a strong possibility of crime in his future. He doesn't consider himself a parasite, so it won't do Gary's ego any good to live off the funds of Melody.

The train now stops to a halt on *Prospect Avenue*. As he walks out the subway and onto the streets, Gary's tightly balled fists reflect the tension in his heart. With no sleep, and for so long, the effects are starting to show. Gary feels that it's cowardly of him to fear his nightmares, but Gary couldn't bring himself to face the terror again.

No matter how fatigued he'd gotten.

Five minutes later, Gary arrives to his destination. He sees several men, and surprisingly women, standing outside the establishment; waiting to be frisked by Brown, the intimidating doorman.

Gary steps right to the entrance of the club, grinning from ear-to-ear, and the doorman swiftly turns to him. Everyone believes a fight is about to break out, because of the way the doorman stares at Gary, but the notion quickly fades when the two men begin laughing heartily.

"Exodus, what the *hell?* I thought you were doing time," the doorman shouts.

"I got out yesterday, Brown, I came to see Black," Gary answers, as they shake hands; Brown's powerful grip is cutting off the circulation to Gary's hand.

"Go ahead, *shit* is off-the-*charts* in there tonight!"

Brown then pats Gary hard on the back, nearly knocking him off his feet. The doorman then turns back to his job, aggressively frisking a customer—Brown attentively searches for weapons.

Brown hasn't changed a bit, Gary thinks to himself.

The loud reggae music hurts Gary's eardrums when he enters the club—the raw scent of sex instantly fills his nostrils, as Gary ventures into the area. Naked and scantily clad women are all over the place, dancing seductively.

Gary looks to his right, and witnesses several men receiving lap dances. Some are also in dark corners, receiving sexual pleasures for a bargained price. When Gary views the stage, he sees other nude dancers gyrating their bodies to the vibrating beats.

Something quickly catches Gary's interest: the live-sex show two women are uninhibitedly displaying. The scene is extremely arousing to Gary, so stimulating, that he looks away.

Temptation is abound, and being that Gary was just released from prison makes it worse. Staying focused, he finds his way to the back of the club, where a narrow walkway awaits Gary.

He soon races up the passage where Mex, Black's personal security, greets him with a phony friendly handshake. Shortly thereafter, Gary enters the dimly lit office.

Black, standing with his back turned to Gary, views lustful scenes of his club through a two-way mirrored wall.

"Look at this freak show, Exodus. I swear, if all the crime in the world would cease to exist, you could *still* make money off of sex. Don't you know that prostitution is the oldest profession in the world?"

"Yeah, I heard that somewhere before."

Black laughs before he faces Gary. His bald head has reflected the dim light. Clean-shaven and well dressed, Black can easily be mistaken as an executive of a high-powered conglomerate, but the abundance of platinum he wears, won't allow Black to be mistaken for such a profession.

"I'm happy that you're out of prison, Exodus. Have a seat, we have some catchin' up to do," Black says, pointing his finger to where he himself sits; Black now interlaces his fingers.

Gary immediately feels uneasy.

He tries his best to mask his insecurities, but the wicked, dark-brown eyed man sitting across from Gary, seems to stare straight through him.

"Why didn't you come see me in the pen, Black? You could've sent me a letter or a postcard, something to acknowledge that I was alive. *Shit,* I could've *died* in there, you know how those pigs get down," Gary says spitefully.

Black's cool demeanor is taken aback. He clenches his jaw to refrain from outburst; instead, Black forces a smile.

"Write you? Come visit you? *Motherfucker,* I'm the one who got you that high-paid lawyer who got you that one-year deal. *I'm* the one who should be askin' you questions. Melody took care of you on the inside, didn't she?"

39

"I'm not *talking* about her, Black, I'm talking about you," Gary interjects. Black bites his bottom lip and stands up; his ill temper comes to surface.

"Shut the *fuck* up. I *took* you in when you came to me. Exodus, you were *nothin'* but a fourteen-year-old kid that ran away from a group home. I put *cash* in your pocket, showed you how to be a man. I *treated* you like my own flesh and blood by bringin' you into my family. Even when you started *fuckin'* my sister, I let you live. So don't you *ever* in your *fuckin'* life, come at me with that *bullshit* you talkin'. 'Cause if you do, I *swear* to my dead mother, Exodus, I will bury you."

Black's words run deeper than the blood in Gary's veins—truthful, hurtful words. Gary now believes that he let his anger cloud his better judgment, like so many times before. Even though Gary had gone to prison because of Black's crime influence, it was the life *he* had chosen; in a world where Gary felt that he had no other options.

Gary bows his head to the floor, in regret of how easily Black has made him feel lowly, as Black still breathes angrily.

"Black...I apologize, I should have never—"

"No, *nigga,* don't be sorry, it's time to get your *ass* back in gear, that's all!"

Gary lifts his head in surprise: "I'm going straight this time. I'm going to get a job or something, so I can take care of Melody."

"I don't want to hear that get a job *shit,* Exodus; be for real. Who's goin' to hire *your* ass?"

Black slowly moves in front of Gary, systematically he begins counting his fingers: "One, you *don't* have any schoolin'. Two, you *don't* have no trainin'. Three, you have no job experience whatsoever. Four, you're fresh out of jail. And five...wait this is the big one...with *all* that stacked against you, Exodus, your *ass* is Black!

"How you goin' to beat them odds, Exodus? ...Huh? Get a job at *McDonalds?* Sweat your *ass* off fryin' French fries? Don't be a *fuckin'* joke! You couldn't even buy Melody lunch with that chump change."

Black then bends down to Gary until they're face-to-face, looking at the veins in each other's eyes.

"Face it, *nigga,* we in this *shit* together until the end of time. We get rich, or we *die* tryin'."

Black quickly spins away from Gary and approaches a nearby closet, leaving his words to infect Gary's mind. Black speaks again: "I like you, Exodus, you've always been in my heart, even when you were comin' up. You get knocked and you *don't* snitch, you hold your composure. That's why I want you to do me a favor," Black states as he opens the closet door, revealing the contents inside.

Gary views several handguns that hang on the inside of the closet door; also seeing a large safe in the middle of it.

"What do you want me to do?" Gary asks inquisitively.

Black doesn't answer.

Instead, he takes a handgun from the door, along with three fully loaded clips. Black cocks the hammer back, briefly inspects the gun, making sure it's unloaded. Calmly, he walks back to his desk, sits down, and places the contents on the desk.

"It's your favorite gun, a snub-nosed .32 automatic. No serial number either. Go ahead, it's yours; a present from me," Black says while chuckling.

With a familiar uncanny speed, Gary retrieves the weapon. He loads it with one of the clips, making sure that a bullet is ready in the chamber. Afterwards, Gary places the gun into the back of his waist, and retrieves the rest of the clips for later use.

"Very thoughtful of you. Now, what do you want me to do?" Gary repeats.

"A-h-h-h, yes, *that's* the Exodus I know and love! Let's get down to business. That last car you stole, the one the police caught you in?"

"Please don't remind me."

"You left me with a very unsatisfied customer. Exodus, I need you to get a new one for me, the latest model. I'll give you two days."

"But I might need more time, first I have to find one."

Black puts up two fingers: "Two days, Exodus; no more, no less," Black orders before reaching into his pocket. He pulls out a roll of bills and tosses it to Gary. "That's ten thousand to get you on your feet; *don't* let me down!"

Honestly, Gary doesn't appreciate the fact that Black's giving him deadlines and dilemmas. Gary soon stands up, and begins to exit the office.

"Why don't you stick around for a while, Exodus? Go and get some of that action downstairs."

Gary doesn't turn to Black as he answers, "I'll pass; I've got work to do," Gary indicates as the door slams.

"You sure do, *nigga*," Black replies sarcastically, as he leans back in his chair and begins to sing off-key, as *Miles Jaye* plays in the background: *"Let's start love over, back to the way things were."*

Staring again through the two-way mirrored wall, Black's evil eyes are bombarded with extreme perverted images going on downstairs.

They're all his to control.

THREE

The Lortech tower in *New York City* is a colossal creature, amongst the many giant buildings there. From its genetic research lab, to its other numerous secretive projects, Lortech runs like an unrelenting beast.

Security is enforced to the extreme.

Cameras, bodily scanners, and a multitude of other surveillance devices are not only on every level of the building, but also outside of it—to the circumference of five city blocks in *Tribeca.*

Andrew sits on the top floor in his incredibly spacious office, like a king rightly so, for Andrew is the head of it all. He arrived back from *Africa* in a matter of hours in his private jet, along with his precious cargo: the twin sentient beings, AU and AG, who now stand silently in Andrew's office.

Yesterday, he had them analyzed at the company's futuristic lab, but to Andrew's surprise, the findings had all come back the same: atomic number 79, atomic weight, 196.967; and atomic number 47, atomic weight, 107.870.

The lab found nothing else out of the ordinary. It seems the two beings, or cherubims, as they refer to themselves, are nothing more than their namesake.

Science has not given Andrew the answers he seeks.

Andrew wants to know why he heard the voices, and how can inorganic matter move with so much likeness to life. Andrew can't deny any of it is possible, because they're staring at him from opposite sides of his office.

Andrew doesn't like the notion of what seems to be a supernatural puzzle, which lingers out of his grasp. The fact that he controls AU and AG's actions, calms Andrew in a definitive strange way.

He never allows the two beings to move in the presence of anyone. Instead, Andrew lets everyone believe in ignorance that he'd wasted funds, by having the living statues forged for his own amusement.

Soon after, Andrew places the jewel-encrusted staff into a case that's electronically activated in his office wall. It's highly secured, and can only be retrieved by using voice-activated protocols; to Andrew's understanding, the staff is better out-of-sight to anyone.

The two living statues still obeys his orders, because Andrew is the beholder of the strange, ornamented stick, which he concludes is the main source of AU and AG's abilities.

Andrew now continues waiting on the team he sent in to decipher the words written on the tomb—his patience is also growing thin. As the corporate mogul overlooks his mysterious prize, the phone to Andrew's secretary's line begins blinking. He presses a button then speaks: "Yes, what is it?"

"Mr. Taylor, your ten o' clock appointment with Ms. Sharon Puwa is ready," his secretary indicates through the telephone's intercom.

Andrew frowns.

In all his previous excitement, Andrew forgot about the planned meeting.

"Y-Yes, yes, send her in," Andrew stutters. After a few quiet moments, his office door opens, interrupting the deadened silence. The vivacious woman waltzes in like a lioness, beauty radiating from her every movement.

Andrew wants to smile, but he holds the expression, fearing that Sharon will know what lay in his heart. She soon glares at Andrew, her slanted eyes meticulously taking in what he'd become.

Sharon wears a short black skirt, with a white tailored blouse that exposes the top of her ample breasts. The crocodile high-heeled pumps Sharon sports, causes her strong calves to flex in stride while approaching Andrew's desk.

"So nice to see you, Ms. Puwa. Have a seat," Andrew says and instructs, admiring Sharon's presence. She places her palms on the desk and stares at Andrew distastefully.

"I don't need to sit, Andrew, I don't anticipate being here very long," Sharon says calmly, letting the words float from her soft lips before continuing, "Why haven't you made up your mind about the 'Shattered Dreams' donation? I've been waiting to hear your answer for months. Andrew, you could really make a difference for the foundation, you are more than able."

Andrew now follows Sharon's movements, as she now makes her way to AU and AG to examine the statues.

"Ah yes, now I remember, that foundation you started for underprivileged Black youth. When will you *wake* up Sharon, and stop living in a dream? Everyday they're *dying* out there, influenced by the media and self-serving desires, that ultimately have *no* meaning, nor purpose.

"Every time you watch television, look at what the world's views of black youth, they see *nothing* but a criminal culture; with no hope of becoming *anything* else but that. Sharon, why do you waste your time?"

"How can you say such *ignorant* things, Andrew? Those are *our* people, *our* future."

"Our people? Don't make me laugh."

Sharon scornfully stares at Andrew, wanting to strike him. He's changed so drastically from when they were young, Andrew now being a totally different person.

He and Sharon were once passionate lovers, but she parted ways from Andrew years ago, sensing the monster he was becoming. Now, lo and behold, Sharon's worst fears had come true.

"What *happened* to you, Andrew? You use to have so many dreams of how we could uplift our people; you were so brilliant. How could you have let yourself change so quickly?"

"Simple, Sharon, I grew up and saw the truth."

"That is *not* the truth!" Sharon screams in disgust. "There was a time when you figured out ways to stop the systematic genocide of the Black race, ways to kill the power of the oppressor. Now look at you. The man I once loved has become my worst enemy, you're the oppressor, Andrew!"

Sharon's statement bothers Andrew; it causes the blood in his veins to circulate faster. Here is the woman who watched Andrew become a man, the one whom he swore would someday be his wife, cracking down the wall of confidence that Andrew himself chiseled.

"You were always blessed, Andrew. You grew up in a loving environment with unimaginable privilege. Your intelligence is phenomenal, and now, you have the power to do the things you said you would once do. All I'm asking is for you to help me save these kids, by giving them a better chance at life," Sharon pleads.

Her face now reflects her inner pain.

Sharon is a successful fashion designer who gives back to the less fortunate communities handsomely. She wants more than Andrew Taylor's donation for her youth foundation, Sharon wants to pull him out of the depths of the solitude Andrew is drowning in, because of his responsibilities to Lortech.

Andrew simply shakes his head at her proposal: "Do you know what happens to a school of dolphins stuck in a net, Sharon?"

Sharon doesn't reply to the out-of-place question.

"Even if there's a small hole in the net, and a few of them see it, the dolphins will not escape, because they will not leave the sanctuary of the captive school. Eventually the dolphins will all die together, even though some might have lived if they chose to. I'm not going to *die* in that net, Sharon. Never!" Andrew spits coldly.

Sharon clenches her fist before calming the turbulent storm welling inside of her.

"Andrew, am I the reason you act so stubbornly? It's because I left you, isn't it?"

Sharon now walks past AU the frozen statue, unaware that it watches her every movement. She sits down on the desk in front of where Andrew is seated. Sharon slowly hikes her short skirt up, and exposes her voluptuous thighs. She places her stiletto heels on Andrew's armrests and grabs his tie, pulling Andrew towards her.

Andrew feels awkward.

Sharon's actions catches him off-guard.

Aggressively, she pulls his face to hers and kisses Andrew roughly. Afterwards, Sharon pushes him back into his seat, Andrew now being pinned between his chair and Sharon.

Seductively, Sharon arches her back, protruding her breasts, before spreading her bent legs even wider.

"Is *this* what you want, Andrew?" Sharon asks through curved lips. Her alluring eyes are not only inflamed in lust, but also in anger.

Andrew stares hard at Sharon's delicate, black lace panties. He clearly sees the imprint of her feminine slit. Almost beyond himself, Andrew reaches upward and caresses the underside of Sharon's thigh.

His touch is very familiar to Sharon, so knowing, that it causes the woman to bite her bottom lip in anticipation. Sharon seems so wanton, as though she knows Andrew's lust. His face begins to come towards Sharon's.

"You can have my body, Andrew, but you can *never* have my mind or soul."

Andrew immediately freezes, and as the two look into each other's eyes, passion begins to awaken him. Sharon now knows that she made her point strongly, feeling Andrew's hand tremble against her smooth skin.

Clenching his jaw, Andrew lifts Sharon's leg before closing her thighs tightly; finally, placing Sharon's feet towards the floor.

"Our meeting is over, Sharon. Get the *hell* out of my office!" Andrew roars, fighting back the feeling that threatens to overwhelm him. Angrily, Sharon smacks Andrew across the face, enraged because of his hostility.

Instinctively, AU takes a step, ready to mutilate the woman. Andrew dismisses the being with a glance without Sharon noticing. After fixing her skirt, Sharon walks away quickly, wanting to get away from the man's apathy. Before stepping out the door, she forces herself to take one last look at Andrew.

"Maybe you're not as intelligent as your IQ would lead people to believe. You're going to grow old, Andrew, stuck in your father's corporation—alone. I don't want that to happen to you. I love you, can't you see that!" Sharon yells across the office, as her sorrow-filled eyes begins to water.

"Get *out* of my building, *NOW!*" Andrew strongly demands. Sharon shakes her head, feeling distraught. "I *never* want to see you again," Andrew nearly cries out.

"You don't mean that, Andrew. Take your own advice, don't die alone."

"GET OUT!"

Noticing his miserable state, Sharon rushes out the door, letting it slam behind her. Andrew falls back into his seat; Sharon leaves him with re-opened wounds, her words echoes in Andrew's mind, over-and-over again.

As time goes by, he begins to regain composure. Andrew now believes that he's too strong for Sharon, too powerful for his *own* race. The flicker of self-pity abandons Andrew, as he promises himself to never lay eyes on Sharon again.

*   *   *   *   *

Staring at the kitchen table, tired eyes wavering from lack of sleep, Gary drinks his coffee, quietly. Melody was already fast asleep when he returned to her apartment at six in the morning.

Gary doesn't wake Melody; he refuses to disturb the young woman's peaceful slumber, something that Gary himself can't grasp. Sleep means returning to his tormented past, re-living those moments as if they're actually taking place in the present.

Gary's irregular heartbeat soon tells him his body is under much strain, but fear keeps Gary disciplined. He drinks more of the hot liquid in vain, attempting to boost his fatigue.

Melody soon stirs from her pleasant dream, lazily rising out of bed. Coming home from work at one o'clock in the morning, Melody was very unhappy to find an empty apartment. Yet, she knew that Gary went to see her brother, Black yesterday.

The thought of Gary being in the presence of the filth and corruption that thrives around Black, gave Melody a migraine headache. Before she turned in, Melody took two *Tylenol PM* aspirins. The pills did the job, giving an effect of drowsiness, perfect for Melody's temporary worry.

Melody yawns gracefully, grabbing her white bathrobe to conceal her nudity. When she leaves the bedroom, the first thing her eyes see is Gary, sitting at the kitchen table across from the living room.

To Melody, he seems very unsettling, which causes her to approach him. Gary raises his head and smiles when seeing her. Melody doesn't return the gesture.

The robust scent of freshly brewed coffee that she inhales causes Melody to walk to the coffee machine, pouring a cup while keeping her mood revealed.

"I stayed up late waiting for you. I was worried sick," Melody says, her eyebrow arched.

"I apologize, Melody, I got caught up."

Melody sits down in a chair beside Gary, crossing her legs. Immediately, she sees the newly formed bags underneath her boyfriend's eyes. Melody instinctively reaches out to feel Gary's forehead, suspecting an oncoming fever. Gary catches her hand, and gently brings it to the table.

"Are you okay, Gary? You look tired. You shouldn't have been out all night with Black."

"I was only at the club for five minutes," Gary lowly whispered, not wanting Melody to think he'd partaken in any extracurricular activities. "Things haven't changed around there. Nothing ever does."

Melody sighs, "But I hope *you* have," she states truthfully. Gary instantly reads the hurtful expression upon her face. He reaches into his pocket and pulls out the funds Black had given.

Melody frowns as Gary counts out eight thousand dollars from the bills—he then places it on the table in front of her.

"*What* is this for? *Where* did you get this money from?" Melody asks angrily, already knowing the answer to her questions.

"It can help pay some bills, Melody. I *don't* want to be living off you, it isn't right for me to let you carry my weight on your back. I can't live like that, so take it."

"I *don't* want it! *Wherever* it came from, my brother has blood on it. Someone suffered for this…. Why Gary? You don't even give yourself a chance, the first thing you did was *run* to Black. He doesn't give out money for free. Gary, you're falling right into his trap!"

"What trap? Why are you acting like this, Melody?"

"Because you don't need Black, and you *don't* need to do anymore crimes, Gary!"

Melody's rising voice is quickly bringing Gary more to the edge. Instead of hearing her loving advice, he hears only insult.

"WHAT THE *HELL* DO YOU WANT ME TO DO, HUH? GET A JOB? WELL NOBODY WILL *HIRE* ME!" Gary hollers, startling Melody. Tears begin to well in the corners of Melody's eyes; Gary never lashed out at her like that before.

"…All I'm saying is try, Gary. Baby, I know you can make it, you just have to give yourself a chance," Melody whispers.

"I've been trying all my life. This world is *fucked* up! Ever since I was a kid, I've been struggling my *ass* off, trying to make it. So what you're saying to me is *bullshit,* and I'm not trying to hear it! Just give me a reason, just *one* good reason why I shouldn't work for Black!"

Gary stares at Melody hostilely, with one fist balled on the tabletop. Melody bites her bottom lip and takes a deep breath. She's unbearably upset, but Melody withholds her emotions.

Glaring at Gary with watery eyes, Melody answers: "I'll give you more than one reason. I couldn't cope with seeing you locked up again because of Black. Lord knows how much time you could get, if you get caught doing whatever....

"I couldn't stand being alone, Gary, knowing that you're not with me again. You don't know how much it hurts. Black doesn't *care* about you, Gary; he doesn't even care about me. So don't fall into Black's web, 'cause in the end, he will desert you.

"And, the main reason is, because you don't need Black, Gary," Melody replies, as she reaches out and softly cups her lover's balled fist, gently trying to ease Gary's tension.

Staring desperately into his eyes, Melody continues to speak, "You don't need anyone else in this world, because you have me. *I* love you...you're not alone anymore, I'm with you. We can struggle together, Gary, you and I," Melody adds compassionately.

Gary's anger doesn't falter. His hand remains tightly balled under Melody's soft caress.

"That's not *good* enough," Gary hisses through clenched teeth. His cold words strikes Melody like a bolt of lightning. Her eyes widens in disbelief, causing Melody's restricted tears to fall freely down her face.

Letting go of Gary's hand, Melody covers her mouth as she gasps; utter despair erupts in Melody's heart. She soon rises from her chair and rush to the bathroom, crying aloud—wanting to be away from Gary's total apathy.

Gary soon hears the bathroom door slam hard, followed by the clicking of its lock. His lips quivers, as he stares at the chair Melody recently sat in.

Gary is frozen in the moment.

His hateful words are destroying Melody's feelings.

Regretting what he did, Gary shuts his eyes. Melody's unbridled cries come through the bathroom door. At this point, Gary knows he's losing control, gaining more stress because of insomnia.

He didn't mean what he said to Melody, it came out all wrong. But, the simple fact that Gary said those terrible things is beyond redemption. He eventually leaves the kitchen and approaches the locked door, Melody weeps behind.

Inside where Gary fears to tread, Melody sits on the bathroom floor with her knees pulled to her chest; Melody's head is lowered, hiding her grief. Gary's heart jumps every time he hears Melody's cries.

Her tears are his.

"Melody...Melody, I'm sorry. I didn't mean what—"

"GO AWAY!" Melody screams with burning lungs.

Gary takes a step back away from the door. Melody's reply tells him again how badly Gary has hurt her.

Nothing he'll say now can make things right.

All of Gary's efforts would be in vain.

"Melody, I...I love you," Gary says sympathetically.

"I said go away."

Gary can't stop her pain, the agony he caused Melody. Gary has to let her deal with it alone.

Maybe she'll forgive me later, he thinks, having no other choice but to believe that. Eventually, Gary walks away, and retreats to exit the apartment. If he chose to stay, Melody would never leave the bathroom.

Gary has a job to do, and after he got Black his merchandise, Gary plans to leave Melody's brother alone, for good. No matter *what* happens.

Melody is right. She's the only love I have, the only person that cares about me. Melody's the one who always stood by me, not Black. I definitely have to make things right for her.

Gary leaves the apartment soberly, with one mission in mind: to do one last job, before leaving his past behind.

Melody hears the apartment door close. She wishes that she hadn't awakened and confronted Gary. *How could he say that I wasn't good enough, after all the suffering I endured for him?* Melody thinks to herself.

All the times that Gary was incarcerated, leaving Melody alone without the presence of her man, she faithfully carried Gary. Melody always visited him when she had the chance, giving Gary all of his needs, as if she was his wife.

I'm not good enough for him?

Gary has only been home three days, and already he's chosen Black over Melody.

It's unforgivable.

As tears soaks Melody's bathrobe, she fights with the idea that Gary could do such a thing, but the more Melody sobs, the more the haunting thought that she will lose him sets in.

* * * * *

Andrew gazes through the dark tinted windows of his limousine, transfixed on the pedestrians he views. Andrew wonders what lives they lead, what professions they hold—a silent game he's played since his youth.

Three of Andrew's personal bodyguards are sitting beside him. All four men are silent, as they drive to their destination.

It's one o' clock in the afternoon, Andrew is already ten minutes late for his visit with Alberto McKoon, another entrepreneur, who is the president of Taterax Industries, a rival corporation to Andrew's own.

He knows that whatever McKoon wants to meet with him for, will surely bring on hostility to them both. In their profession, business is war, and generals have to know who their enemies are up-close and personal, in order to create strategic defenses. The main reason why Andrew didn't back down from his competitor's invitation.

If there's one thing his father, David Taylor had taught him, it was to: *"Never let anyone know of your weakness or strengths, always let them fall into a web of their own making."*

And that's exactly what Andrew intends to do.

As his limousine stops in front of the Taterax tower, Andrew's security quickly escorts him into the complex. Arriving at an elevator, Andrew notices the abundance of Taterax security forces standing everywhere. "Black suits", he always refers to name them.

Andrew also has a strong suspicion that he and his three companions are being scanned with hi-tech devices, as they step into the tower.

The elevator accelerates until it hits the top floor, where McKoon's headquarters is stationed. When the doors open, Andrew and his men are greeted by two more of Taterax's security; dark sunglasses they wear, hides the guards' cold stares.

Andrew steps past them and orders his men to wait outside, as he enters McKoon's office. When Andrew walks inside and approaches the throne of the head of Taterax, he carefully hides his contempt.

McKoon stands up from behind his large, oval glass table, pausing to simultaneously switch off twenty individual television screens, which are imbedded into his office wall.

He then smiles in an attempt to appear friendly, but Andrew knows better than that. McKoon gracefully approaches

Andrew, and holds out his hand to shake. Andrew refuses to amuse him.

"What do you want, McKoon?" Andrew questions.

"Don't be so stiff, Mr. Taylor. I only wish to speak with you," McKoon answers flatly.

Andrew sits in one of the twelve seats at the table and crosses his legs, placing his arms on the armrest.

"I can't ponder why. Please, *enlighten* me," Andrew retorts defensively.

"Well, first and foremost, I'm aware of your AI project for the mobile military units. We at Taterax have been developing a similar venture."

Before his opponent spoke another word, Andrew's jaw clenched, McKoon now studies him.

"Don't get upset. I have many friends in the NSA, after all, information is power, is it not?" McKoon adds before continuing. "Well, the problem is…wait, what I'm saying is totally confidential."

"I believe that point was made clear, just by us being in the same room together, McKoon," Andrew affirms. McKoon chuckles at Andrew's comment.

"That's why I think I'm going to like you, Mr. Taylor. As you know, when dealing with Artificial Intelligence, it is a very sensitive science. You can store an incredible amount of information on computer chips, all the data in the world if you would choose, but in all honesty, it is not liable for what our corporations want from the AI.

"After all, the mobile units are being made for military combat, they don't need to count the stars in the heavens. The NSA only wants the technology for one purpose, and you know what that is, Mr. Taylor."

McKoon waits for Andrew's answer.

Andrew only smiles faintly.

"I don't know, McKoon, why don't you tell me."

Andrew witnesses the adversary's left brow arch in aggravation.

"To kill, Mr. Taylor, to take out foreign and domestic enemies with proficient skill and stealth. But the key to this situation, the foundation of the AI project is something that the world would be horrified to know, if they ever found out.

"The human brain can store, analyze and calculate more information than any computer chip could imagine to store. This is why if the mobile units are to succeed, man and machine must be combined. Human experimentation. Which brings me to the fact of why I have asked for this meeting, Mr. Taylor."

Andrew becomes intrigued by what McKoon reveals to him. His rival tells Andrew more then he expected, and now, Andrew knows that Taterax is on the heels of Lortech's latest developments for highly secretive AI cybernetics.

The NSA didn't choose sides—they chose options. Lortech or Taterax, the fastest achiever won the game in an unyielding war of arms.

"My associates have revealed to me that the Governor of *New York* has suddenly become interested in our corporation's headquarters in this state. He wants to know about our experimental projects."

"Don't make me laugh, McKoon. You know as well as I that he *isn't* a threat," Andrew defends.

"Yes, I'm well aware of that, but Governor Peterson could possibly become a thorn in our sides. We develop technologies for the security and benefit of *America.* The NSA and other organizations I dare not mention, know who we are, and very well what we do; but the senate doesn't.

"It's a double-edged sword you might say. At one end, we are saviors, and at the other, we are committing crimes against humanity. You and I, Mr. Taylor, are above it all, but these ignorant, power-hungry politicians are *puppets,* with egos beyond their means. I don't *want* our corporations to be in jeopardy."

"What is Taterax planning to do?" Andrew asks peculiarly. McKoon's aqua-blue eyes widens before he grins.

"No, it's not what I plan to do, the question is, what do *you* plan to do, Mr. Taylor?" McKoon's tone of voice holds a sense of delivery that startles Andrew.

"Pardon me?"

"Mr. Taylor, I believe in growth. We are now entering an age where wars are fought silently, and to the victor goes the spoils. I'm ready to lay down our race against time, and call a truce."

"Get to the point, McKoon."

"The point is that, after careful deliberation, I've realized it's better for Taterax and Lortech to work together. It's dubious not to, after all, we are the same."

Andrew feels his temper rising but, he holds his tongue in check.

"We can benefit from each other, cutting the time our scientists and developers consume in half. Just think, Mr. Taylor, you are very young, you're put into a position which is strenuous, I can help you; by giving you the experience you need to run a corporation such as Lortech....

"I have people who can handle the governor, and if you would just be considerate, if Lortech and Taterax were to merge, you would have no future threats. We can be unstoppable," McKoon boasts.

Andrew now has had enough of his game. Just the audacity of McKoon's proposal was enough to enrage him. Andrew takes one sullen breath to relax, then stares at McKoon with piercing eyes; eyes that reflects the anger within Andrew's heart.

"I'm *insulted* by your weak offer, McKoon. You brought me here and tried your best to undermine me by offering me fear," Andrew states. A slight smile appears on his lips before he continues.

"I'm not the *least* worried about Governor Peterson, nor the senate. They are as much of a threat to me as a fly on the window of my limousine, and you're very well aware of this.

"You tried to coerce me into doing something that is beneath me, and yet, hoped that I would fall into your trap. You were mistaken to use such insidious tactics. Do you honestly believe that I'm some *ignorant,* young black man who inherited a corporation that he's too weak to run? Is that it, McKoon?"

McKoon's cheeks redden.

His upper lip begins to quiver.

McKoon motions to speak.

Andrew silences him by raising his hand.

"You are mistaken, unforgivably mistaken. Lortech will *never* merge with Taterax. I would be dead and buried before I *ever* allowed that. If my father was alive today, you wouldn't even have the balls to dream of such a gesture. You're pitiful," Andrew spits with a grace beyond his years.

"If your father was alive today, you wouldn't be in this office!" McKoon retaliates, his frustrations unhidden.

Andrew quickly stands up from where he's sitting, giving McKoon the impression that he's about to strike him.

"Yes, you're right about that fact, so I guess this is where we depart. Give me a call when you get your act together."

Giving McKoon one last pitiful glare, Andrew turns his back on the man and exits the office; the older man stares at the closing door angrily while grinding his teeth. McKoon's eyes burn, with failure that his scheme didn't work.

His plan was to combine both corporations, and eventually dispose of Andrew. It would've left McKoon with absolute power of both entities. Andrew saw through that.

Now, McKoon knows that he has to resort to a darker tactic. Soon, he hears a strange hissing sound coming from above where he sits, but McKoon refuses to look up. He's well aware of the presence above him, feeling its arrival in his blood.

A thick trail of hot, yellow saliva, falls from above, and begins to pool on top of McKoon's glass desk. It comes from the evil beast that clings to the ceiling—its large, glowing, red serpentine eyes, stares down at the man in disgust.

Alberto McKoon is *not* a normal man by any means, being part of a secret order that has existed for ages. In fact, he's the leader of the cabal, given his position of power by a creature that is old as time itself. Those of the Jinn Legion worship the eternal one.

For the price of power, McKoon has given his very soul to the wicked being, as men from all walks of life had done throughout the ages; for wealth and power the eternal one had granted.

Those of the Jinn Legion sought domination of the world, under the servitude of their divine god, the creature that changed them all, the eternal one, Lord Moon.

McKoon finally raises his head and views the horrid form above him. Its elongated jaw filled with rows of jagged fangs, grotesquely smiles back at McKoon.

"Why do you stop me from killing Andrew Taylor, my lord? He is nothing," McKoon says calmly to his master.

"In due time. Be patient, McKoon."

"But why? We don't *need* him in the Jinn Legion. He doesn't deserve Lortech, nor power he wields," McKoon argues.

The huge beast falls from the ceiling, causing its massive frame to slump hard onto the floor. The creature slowly rises beside its minion, standing nine-feet-tall. Several tendrils rip freely from the scaly skin that covers its flesh. The living vine flails wildly.

McKoon gasps, as many of the vines quickly wrap around his body, lifting the man from his chair. The tendrils begin to constrict, cutting off McKoon's blood and oxygen.

The evil being brings him closely to its large head, and begins to speak in its curdling, eerie voice.

"You *will* do as you are told, as will *all* of the Jinn Legion. My darkness shall fall very soon."

McKoon starts to choke. Desperately struggles for air.

"Do not *question* me or I shall rip you apart; bone-for-bone, mortal."

Suddenly, the beast's coils loosen, dropping McKoon violently onto the ground. He feels his heart beating erratically in his chest, as McKoon heaves for much needed oxygen.

"Yes, my lord, I will *never* question your wisdom again; never!" McKoon pleads.

Perspiring with tired, bloodshot eyes, McKoon raises his head, but the eternal one is no longer present. McKoon is relieved that the supernatural creature has spared him, as he rises to his feet.

McKoon is extremely loyal to Lord Moon, as are all those of the Jinn Legion. They know their master is beyond the rules of this being. Its power is greater than the gloomy universe it was born from; following the many paths it had set forth so long ago.

The time is coming to awaken its chosen.

Lord Moon's children.

Sonz of Darkness.

FOUR

In the twilight of the midnight hour, Gary finds his prize. Earlier, after his bitter feud with Melody, he shops for the tools of the trade. Gary first purchases a book bag before buying screwdrivers, and a fifteen-pound pulley at an Auto-mechanic dealership.

He is now ready.

Gary spent the whole day searching for the car he needed, but now that he found one, Gary sits silently across a nearby street and smokes a cigarette. Diligently, he views the area. Very few people walked up-and-down the street of the curb that the automobile is parked at.

"Two minutes, that's all I need," Gary whispers to himself. Casing is part of the game. The excitement of getting the car is only a thrill. But, something's holding Gary back.

He feels that it isn't wise for him to steal the car, too risky—because of his recent incarceration. Gary also believes that he shouldn't have shown Melody the money that her brother, Black had given him.

Why don't she understand this is what I have to do? Gary thinks. Fighting his own mind, Gary stands up from the curb where he sits. Tossing his cigarette aside, Gary makes his way across the street.

Almost unnoticed, he pulls a thin metal *Slim Jim* out of his sleeve, and sticks it in between the vehicle's door and window, fishing for the lock. Gary hears the click of the lock, immediately followed by a loud, shrieking alarm.

He isn't deterred; the security is to be expected. Gary then slips into the car, closing the driver's side door as he enters. Quickly, Gary unzips the backpack and reaches for the tools of his trade.

He is ready to tame the wild horse, as Gary always refers to his job.

* * * * *

Homicide Detective Lon Lee, "Lonely", to everyone who knows him, sits in his jeep, smiling at the crime that's taking place a few yards away. Off duty at the time, enjoying a fresh cup of coffee, he sees the young, black male move into action—it isn't hard noticing him.

The cop would've spotted anyone sitting on a curb at one o'clock in the morning with a black book bag.

What school is open at this time? ...The school of hard knocks, Lonely thinks to himself.

When Gary pulls the tool out from his sleeve, Lonely is assured that his suspicions are made. He thinks about calling for backup to take care of the situation, car theft isn't his criteria.

Lonely doubts that he could bring himself to drive away and act like he's blind to the crime that's taking place; Lonely will not leave it to that.

When he hears the purr of the vehicle's engine, and the car's alarm go silent, Lonely makes up his mind. He retrieves the receiver to his vehicle's speakers: "Turn off the car, and step out of the vehicle with your hands above your head!"

The warning from the loud speakers startles Gary. He feels flush, and a bit afraid, as Gary gathers his thoughts. With a growing frustration that he's been caught, Gary now sighs, exhaling the anger that slowly escapes his lungs.

"TURN OFF THE CAR, AND *STEP* OUT OF THE VEHICLE WITH YOUR HANDS ABOVE YOUR HEAD!"

Gary hears the detective's warning again, this time, Lonely with a sharp, threatening tone to his voice. Gary turns the rearview mirror, now clearly seeing Lonely's unmarked jeep.

"Only one pig," Gary lowly whispers, already, he's scheming on an escape. Refusing to stomach his bad luck, Gary loudly turns on the radio before loading his handgun. He simply won't turn himself in or listen to the cop's orders.

FUCK THAT! Gary thinks, *I'm not going back to jail.*

Melody will *definitely* leave him if he did. After all, she warned Gary countless times.

Gary then quickly grabs the wheel with his right hand, leaving the gun on his lap. Rapidly, Gary speeds out of the parking space with his heart racing, zooming as fast as the vehicle he's driving.

Lonely grimaces, as he witnesses the car drive off: "Stupid Ass kid," he says to himself, as Lonely starts his jeep's engine and begins to chase the car thief.

Swerving in-and-out of lanes, Gary swiftly dodges through numerous vehicles, picking up speed as he goes. Lonely is in hot pursuit following Gary, with the determined psychotic drive of his loose canon ways. He matches Gary move for move.

Gary becomes seriously troubled by the tenacity of the cop—the hunt is pushing him to the edge. Recklessly, Gary turns the steering wheel while braking hard, causing the vehicle to turn one-hundred-and-eighty degrees.

Pushing hard on the accelerator, making the car drive against traffic, Gary drives in the direction of Lonely's jeep.

The detective's keen eyes, widens at the wild stunt.

Lonely now sees the suspect's hand come out of the window and point in his direction, as both vehicle's accelerate at one another, speeding at a hundred miles per hour.

Momentarily, Lonely sets his eyes on the reflection of light shining from the object Gary's holding in his hand. Instantly, Lonely ducks, immediately pressing his foot on the brakes, as Gary fires at the jeep; bullets shatters the front window, fragments of glass falls on Lonely's crouched body.

Gary's fleeting car flies by the cop's jeep, as he continues reaching out his window, squeezing the trigger of the .32 automatic. As Gary passes by, he fires his gun until the clip is empty, now satisfied, believing that the detective is dead.

"YOU *FUCKED* WITH THE WRONG ONE!" Gary shouts, feeling victorious that he's free from the threat of capture.

Lonely raises himself up cautiously before peering through the back window, seeing Gary's car driving away in the wrong direction. At this point, Gary is placing others in danger with his plight.

Cocking his hammer back to his gun, Lonely begins putting bullets into the chamber of his nine-millimeter: "You want to play rough, do you?" Lonely says through grinding teeth. "I'll teach your Ass." He turns his jeep around, once again on pursuit; this time, Lonely has deadly intentions.

Laughter comes from Gary's mouth. His tension begins to fade, believing that he's safe for the moment. Gary then retrieves a cigarette, lights it, inhales, relaxing more as he exhales; until noticing the blinding high beam of Lonely's vehicle in his rearview mirror.

Gary immediately turns into a nearby street and speeds up. Lonely is persistent Gary gathers, as the cop gets closer. Lonely now points his gun through the shattered windshield, and aims at the left rear tire.

One shot rings out.

The rubber tire burst.

It quickly tears apart because of the excessive speed both drivers are in, leaving the rim bare, scraping against the concrete street. Hot sparks fly with the steel's friction.

Involuntarily, Gary swerves into a back alley street, knowing that he has to abandon the car. The steering wheel jerks in his hand, causing the car to spin uncontrollable. In panic, Gary abruptly force turns the steering wheel, trying his best to gain control. The car flips over violently several times, until it crashes horrendously into a red brick wall.

Lonely immediately stops his jeep, troubled by the sight of the disaster he caused. Concerned, Lonely hastily runs towards the crash. Gary stares at the detective through hazy, blurred vision, his broken form screams out in agony.

Gary's head lays limp on the steering wheel, dashboard now pushed into his chest. It smashed his ribs in on the moment of impact; broken bones tear into Gary's heart and lungs, causing massive internal bleeding.

Lonely gasps at Gary with regret, the young black man's shoulder bone is protruding through his skin. Blood is also tearing out of Gary's eyes and mouth. Lonely frowns at the sickening image.

"Damn, why you have to run, kid?" Lonely asks worriedly. Choking on the blood that constricts his throat, Gary stares pleadingly at the cop.

"Help me," Gary begs. His request can barely be understood through the crimson gurgling. Bitter guilt now rises in Lonely's thoughts. He knows that Gary is beyond saving.

This is the consequence of the young man's actions.

Even if Gary does live, he will probably spend the rest of his life behind bars as a cripple, Lonely believes. Pushing the sorrowful reflection aside, Lonely returns to being the cold-hearted detective he is.

He then inspects the back alley street, making sure no one witnessed the incident. The alley is empty and free from any prying civilians.

Lonely hears another burbling cry emerge from Gary. Hardening himself, Lonely raises his arm and places the mouth of his steel gun on Gary's head.

In the chaos of his pain, Gary feels the cold gun touching his skin. He wants to scream out in protest, but Gary's blood-filled throat won't allow it.

A million thoughts flash in his head.

Gary doesn't want to die like this, the same way his parents had died: by the hands of a red-eyed creature.

No, this can't happen, not this way! Gary thinks. He also reflects on how Melody will cope if she receives a call to the morgue to identify his body.

That vision tortures Gary's mind.

Lonely then squeezes the trigger.

Gary is killed instantly.

The small bullet hole doesn't even bleed.

"There...I helped you, kid. It's over now," Lonely states weakly.

Gary's empty, lifeless eyes stares at Lonely hauntingly, accusingly at his murderer. The stare actually frightens Lonely, causing the cop to quickly head back to his vehicle.

It was for the better, Lonely keeps telling himself in his head, trying to rid his conscious of the nagging guilt Lonely is beginning to suffer from, trying to justify the execution.

He blames Gary for the misfortune while driving away.

Ten minutes passes at the scene of the incident.

No one comes to the aid of Gary's dead corpse.

No one.

Except a fly...

Trying to find a meal for its maggot offspring.

But as the fly softly lands on the eyelid of its children's meal, the back alley street fills with a terrifying scream. Gary awakens from the inescapable depths of his own death.

Eyes begin to blink.

Breathing becomes stronger.

The shattered bones in Gary's chest are now like fire that intensely burns his insides. The excruciating pain stimulates every nerve in his being, forcing Gary to struggle to be free of the metal wreckage that confines him, punishes him.

Screeching sounds of metal enters his ears, causing Gary to believe that he's hallucinating from the shock of his injuries. Instantaneously, the wrecked vehicle Gary drove begins to move, bending, and tearing itself apart, freeing the tortured man from his hellish confines.

With a tremendous surge of power, the crashed car tears in two halves, easily as onion paper, before flying fast in opposite directions from one another.

Gary's limp body falls onto the ground, as the car pairs crash several feet away from him. While lying on his back, Gary's eyes widens in disbelief, because of the bizarre event.

As he tries to move, something strange begins to transpire. The unimaginable pain that Gary originally felt begins to subside, becoming more tolerable by the second.

The bullet that's lodged inside of his brain, start to move, as though Gary's flesh wants to be rid of its intrusion. Suddenly, the slug falls from the small wound it created, and the hole closes. It begins healing itself, as well as the rest of Gary's crippled body.

Becoming more aware of his rejuvenating state, Gary rises off of his back, turning on his hands and knees. Gary soon vomits blood from his lungs, causing his muscles to tighten in spasms.

Gary's eyes then falls upon his torn shoulder, which has a sharp, jagged bone pointing out of his flesh. He gazes in bewilderment, as Gary's skin begins to grow over the bone, before pulling it into its rightful place.

Sweating profusely, Gary trembles, more out of fear and amazement than anything else. He crawls to the brick wall and uses it to pull himself up. Gary's balance is held on shaky legs, as he touches his wet face with disbelief.

I'm suppose to be dead.

Gary knows that he should be lying in the wrecked car, now torn into two parts, with a piercing bullet in his skull.

But he isn't.

The pain is now gone, Gary's body is miraculously restored of all that ailed him moments before.

A strange vibration soon filters throughout his physical form. Haunting memories swiftly flashes into Gary's mind at the pace of an epileptic seizure, rocking his foundation to the core.

Recollections of a sharp knife entering his chest when Gary was a newborn, a wound that should have killed him, come about. He then remembers seeing his baby brother, Andrew throat being slit, and the Vowdun witch, who changed into that unearthly creature.

Gary also sees visions of that blinding light, the light that came from the wicked being, which did more than heal them. Gary now realizes that it had changed he and Andrew somehow.

Thoughts of waking up in the backseat with Andrew by his side, who was still peacefully asleep, comes to Gary's mind. The Vowdun, the creature it had become in the hut, calling out to him silently that night is remembered.

Gary even recalls his parents not seeing the creature's glowing red eyes ahead in the road, and waking up Andrew, as their mother and father argued inside the car. The horrid memories of the vehicle haphazardly crashing into the creature, and being able to only save his baby brother, lastly forges into Gary's head.

Up until this moment, standing alone in the darkened back alley street, Gary finally realizes that it was he who created the sphere that shielded himself and Andrew from the fires; Gary, being very young at that time to understand his new, strange abilities.

Putting the puzzle of his past together, Gary now begins to make sense of the memories. He comes to the conclusion that the Vowdun had altered Andrew and him in some way, making them beyond human; giving the two gifts beyond their understanding.

Gary then gazes at one of the demolished halves from the wrecked car, knowing now that he tore the vehicle apart. He slowly raises his hand, pointing at the remains. Gary begins to concentrate, envisioning the wreckage rise from the ground; feeling as if he's connected to the remains by some invisible force.

The wreckage moves a little, surprising Gary that it budged at all. Then, to his amazement, the demolished halve suddenly rises from the street, to height of twenty feet.

Gary gasps in shock, losing his concentration, and the torn metal falls awkwardly, landing back onto the street with a thunderous crash.

A white spark soon ignites the gas in its tank, and it explodes, sending sharp fragments flying in Gary's direction. Fearfully, he covers his face, causing a reaction in his mind to emerge.

Gary's hands begin to brightly glow with a radiant, royal blue fire, and a translucent blue sphere appears protectively around him, crackling with electrical current.

The debris from the explosion burns to nothing, when it comes into contact with the orb Gary manifests by accident. As he uncrosses his arms, Gary realizes that what surrounded him is the same bubble that protected he and Andrew as children.

Gary stares at the burning flame that flows from his hands in astonishment. He then calms his thoughts, and the fires and orb vanishes.

Flames from the explosion now reaches up the wall, making shadows dance in the back alley street. Gary finds himself laughing insanely.

He soon realizes that these are the gifts the Vowdun witch had given him; the price his parents paid for long ago with their lives.

Testing his newfound abilities, Gary makes himself slowly levitate from the ground. Soon after, his body swiftly shoots off into the night sky at a blinding velocity, heading for a distant location.

Gary now knows his life will never be the same again.

* * * * *

On *Wall Street* in *New York City,* a being of incomprehensible power grins, baring its sharp fangs; knowing that one of its chosen has awakened to its gift.

Gary Romulus has no idea of his planned purpose, or the dynamic future that is in wait for him.

FIVE

Two weeks passes since Andrew's meeting with Alberto McKoon. He's now explaining what transpired at the meeting to Yoshi Hiro, the head of the *Japanese* division of Lortech, and best friend to Andrew's deceased father.

Yoshi flew in from *Japan* the day before, to consult with Andrew regarding a bothersome situation. Yoshi is like an uncle to him, furthermore, Yoshi wanted to visit Andrew, and report directly on the latest developments of Lortech's overseas lab.

Andrew sits on his *Italian* leather sofa in the living room of his posh, triplex penthouse apartment, located on the *Upper East Side* of *Manhattan*, reviewing the classified documents Yoshi offered.

"I believe that the situation can be handled by other means, Andrew. Alberto McKoon is not a man who offers mergers out of friendship," Yoshi adds.

Andrew raises his eyebrow.

He knows Yoshi means other than the words he speaks.

"I already handled his request, Yoshi. I politely told him to go to *Hell.*"

Yoshi chuckles; slanted eyes now opens brightly.

"Your father, GOD bless him. He was correct in choosing you to take over. Anybody else would have probably taken McKoon's offer, out of fear of retaliation."

"What retaliation? He is no *threat!*" Andrew states in a tone accented with bravado. Yoshi's facial expression now becomes dull and serious.

"McKoon's a dangerous man, Andrew, in the past he has had men killed. Even though the authorities don't have a chance to prove it, I know better; your father knew this, also. This is the *real* reason why I came to visit you in person."

Andrew listens intently to the older *Japanese* man, Yoshi continues.

"I will never hide anything from you Andrew, especially now. The power we hold in this world makes us targets—I will not even allow McKoon to try to harm you. I want his motives to end before they even begin."

Andrew now becomes troubled by the sullen expression that masks Yoshi's face.

"You have a solution to this problem I gather, Yoshi?"

"Yes I do. You are the head of Lortech, Andrew. This position requires you to make decisions beyond to so-called moral obligations to society, and this *must* become your standard...I can send someone to dispose of McKoon."

Andrew catches his breath.

Yoshi's blatant offer startles him.

"Yoshi, you're suggesting an assassination?"

"Yes I am. I have someone who is very professional and efficient in his work."

"I don't want the man killed."

The elderly *Japanese* man pauses for a moment; Andrew now sees Yoshi's eyes twitching rapidly.

"Listen to me. Lortech is the prize, Andrew. McKoon will try to eliminate you in *any* way he's capable of. No matter if you realize it or not, McKoon has declared war on you, and you *must* react appropriately."

"But I—"

"There is *no* time for buts, Andrew!" Yoshi blurts, cutting off Andrew's words. "I can send someone to terminate your rival. It will be clean, and it will never come back to you."

Andrew becomes captivated at how easily Yoshi Hiro speaks of assassinating another man, yet, still has his own reservations.

"You mean your best, Yoshi, but it's too soon to make that assessment," Andrew says, causing Yoshi to sigh.

Andrew truly admires and respects Yoshi, ever since he was a child. Yoshi always spoke to him as though Andrew was his equal.

Now offering to terminate the rival industrialist, Alberto McKoon, only makes Andrew feel more assured that he isn't a wrongly place inheritor of his father's corporation. Rather, Andrew is a man handling Lortech's great responsibility with ease.

"I see. I will not press you, Andrew, but if you do decide, you will let me know, yes?" Yoshi questions.

"Yes, I will."

67

Leaving the subject alone, Yoshi begins briefing Andrew on the documents that are spread on the oval glass table beside the two.

* * * * *

Acres of long, hazy grass sways in the gentle breeze of April's wind. The sun burns in the clear sky above, its golden shine illuminates the meadow with splendor.

Gary remembers coming to this area as a child when he was in foster care. For the last two weeks, Gary has found shelter in an abandoned farm in upstate *New York,* away from people, where he hones his newfound abilities.

Gary raises his right hand.

He stares at it with fascination.

Concentrates....

Shortly after, blue fire quickly emerges around Gary's hand. The blazing flames seem to be flowing from his skin, but it doesn't burn Gary at all.

It still mesmerizes him to witness the display of his powers. Gary lifts his arm even higher, and the blue fire changes into a pure, white flame.

Struggling to control the creation, Gary releases it, causing hot white flames to shoot out into the sky, with a dazzling array of energy. The fire vanishes as Gary calms his thoughts. He recently practiced this act many times, now beginning to get the hang of it.

Soon, Gary's feet rise from the grassy earth, and he glides through the meadow at a slow pace. If anyone could see him, they would surely believe that they're seeing a ghost.

Gary now understands why he possess the strange powers, his oddly enforced memories of the night Gary's parents were murdered, has shed light on the terrible dilemma.

Having to face the countless nightmares over-and-over again, allows Gary to remember that night in full detail. He remembers why his father brought his family to *Haiti*—there, receiving the blessings of the Vowdun witch, who'd given Gary his abilities.

Does Andrew also possess such gifts? Gary thinks.

All of his life, Gary has felt unwanted and worthless. Now having special powers, things are different.

Nothing will ever be the same.

Gary's body soon pauses, as he sits down in the grass. Gary quickly learned earlier this week that his extraordinary powers drain him of energy; migraine headaches are common after he uses them.

Turning his head sideways, Gary focuses on a blade of grass that's close to his face. He studies its small contour, then, with a single thought, the top of the blade splits off.

Gary makes it hover, before diligently placing the newly cut blade of grass back upon its incision, using his mind to hold it still. The blade of grass looks as if it wasn't severed.

A stinging pain is felt behind Gary's left eye, and the grass falls softly to the earth. The irritated nerve soon subsides; he lifts his head to face the open sky.

Gary feels peaceful, with a full embrace of comfort for the first time in his life. Yet, Gary is still baffled by the events that transpired two weeks ago.

His body has healed from the mortal wounds that claimed Gary's life in the terrifying car crash, and from what the cop had done to him.

Gary has resurrected from death.

He knows this, but still doesn't comprehend the full measure of his regeneration. Gary eventually reflects on the morning when he cut his hand on the shattered glass from Melody's mirror.

Gary's mind, he believes, made him imagine that his finger had healed. After all of this, Gary knows that he didn't hallucinate that morning—the small wound actually healed.

If I tell Melody about my powers, she will believe I'm crazy! Gary thinks as he laughs to himself. Gary then imagines how Melody's face would look if he used his special abilities in front of her. *Melody then will have to believe me.*

That is, if she will ever forgive Gary for the way he treated her. Gary frowns, wishing that he could turn back the hands of time, to change that moment. He loves Melody and she loves Gary, that's all that matters.

I've done the time, and my life of crime is over. Black can go to Hell! Gary thinks to himself.

This time, things will be different, because of what he possess. Gary now can give Melody anything she dreams of. In death he found rebirth, and now, Gary's dormant gifts are awakened to a new dawn.

The face of the cop who shot him fuses in Gary's brain. He wants to make the detective pay for what he's done. Gary is determined to seek revenge—if he ever sees the pig again, Gary will crush his skull. But, this isn't his main agenda.

First, Gary will reunite with Melody and make things right with her. Then, he will tell Black that his gig is over—no more robberies, no more stealing cars.

Gary doesn't care how Black will take the news.

As the scenarios run through his mind, thoughts of Andrew are pushed aside. Gary is content with the belief that his long lost brother is gone forever, and that there is no reason to dwell on false hopes that he will find Andrew.

Gary had given up on that idea years beforehand.

Little does he knows Andrew's destiny is already at pace with his own. The evil creature that had changed both siblings already deemed it so.

No longer fearful of his nightmares, Gary now accepts the morbid dreams. They are the key to unlocking his understanding, of what the Vowdun had done to him.

*   *   *   *   *

Melody is feeling more edgy and troubled as of late. The time is one o' clock in the morning, and her shift at the hospital is over. Melody fumbles through the last of her duties and clocks out.

When she gets into her car and adjusts the rearview mirror, Melody notices the heavy bags underneath her beautiful brown eyes, a sure sign of anxiety. Melody hasn't seen or heard from Gary since the morning she told him to leave.

The heated argument they had, tears Melody up emotionally. She didn't deserve the way Gary treated her, the awful things he'd said to her, but since it's been days since Gary hasn't returned home, Melody begins to worry.

In the past when the two had their feuds, it was common for Gary to disappear for a while, eventually returning home, bringing Melody gifts and apologizing to his heart's content; until she forgave Gary for whatever he'd done.

His bark is always worst than his bite, Gary being like a playful puppy to Melody, yet, one with teeth of a pit bull.

Gary should've come home by now...something's terribly wrong, Melody thinks. Her mind conjures all types of scenarios to explain her lover's vanishing—each situation makes Melody sick.

She feels that her brother, Black has something to do with Gary's disappearance. Melody now silently vows that if Black has harmed Gary in any way, she will make him pay.

Visions of Gary being dead, rotting body lying somewhere secluded, makes hairs on the back of the Melody's neck stand on end. She immediately dismisses the idea; Melody won't bring herself to face that awful reality, until she has proof. Melody has to see if Gary is dead before accepting that horrible fate.

"Lord, *please* let him be okay," Melody whispers while driving. She turns up the volume in her car to drown out her saddening fears. *"Come Back To Me"* by *Janet Jackson* plays on *98.7 Kiss FM,* and Melody tries hard to relax, but the lyrics effect her emotions. Melody's eyes begin to water.

Using her free hand, Melody wipes the salty substance away to clear her vision. Deciding it's a mistake to listen to the tune, Melody turns the radio off.

She now makes up her mind. Melody can't bear anymore guessing of why Gary is missing. Determined to find her man, Melody straightens her manner, pulling her emotions together.

Even though she despises the place, Melody heads for Black's club. Her temper begins to rise; Melody will confront her brother and find Gary by any means.

A half hour later, she pulls her car over and parks on a curb next to Black's club. Melody quickly gets out of the vehicle, and angrily slams the car door.

Swiftly, she advances through the crowd of patrons who wait patiently to enter the establishment. Brown's eyes widens when he catches sight of Melody walking towards him.

"Hey Melody. What in the *hell* are you doing here?" Brown questions, turning away from the clubber he's checking for weapons.

Melody doesn't look at Brown.

She raises her hand to silence the bouncer.

"Brown, I'm *not* in the mood for any *shit!*" Melody retorts as she enters the club. Brown, still surprised by her visit, notices Melody's demeanor; he refuses to bother her.

The man Brown is checking taps him on his shoulder, causing Brown to turn and stare at him.

"Aye, man, why the *hell* does that *bitch* get in before us? You *fuckin'* her?" The guy jokes, making his two friends beside him laugh. Brown grits his teeth.

A powerful, sharp blow lands on the right side of the comedian's face. Before he takes another breath, Brown breaks the man's jaw—the clubber's body falls to the concrete street unconscious.

The man's two friends shut up immediately, not only in shock, but also in fear, as Brown now stares them down.

"Get this stupid *motherfucker* out of here and hit the bricks!" Brown orders while raising his muscular arm, showing the men his large balled fist. "Before this brick hits you!" Brown continues.

Moving quickly, the two men lifts their injured buddy and scampers away.

"Next time, tell your boy to *watch* his mouth!" Brown adds as he returns to his duty; Brown carefully eyes the group until they're out of his sight.

The strong odor of mischief within the club makes Melody utterly disgusted. She tries her best not to make eye contact with any of the clubs workers or customers, as Melody ventures to the stairway leading to Black's office.

When she makes it up the path, Melody spots Mex, a guard standing on-duty by the doorway, smoking a cigar filled with weed. When he notices Melody, Mex chokes on the smoke, surprised by her presence.

He reaches out and grabs Melody's arm before she can enter Black's office—Melody instantly yanks her arm free.

"Don't you *ever* touch me!" Melody yells at Mex. He puts on a fake smile, unbothered by the outburst.

"Melody, what's the deal, baby girl? You ready to give me some of that and leave that lame, Exodus alone?" Mex says nonchalantly before palming Melody's left cheek.

Melody's lips tightens while hearing his rash comment, suddenly, she slaps Mex's face. He instantly becomes enraged, yet, before Mex can retaliate, Melody slips into her brother's quarters.

Black's face lights up when he sees his sister standing in front of his desk, Melody now breathing erratically.

"Nice of you to visit me, sis. You lookin' for work or somethin'?" Black asks coldly.

"Where the *hell* is he?" Melody retorts.

"Where's who?"

"Don't play games with me, Black. I know you did something to Gary, you *dirty* bastard!"

Black stands up from his seat.

He stares at Melody in anguish.

"Don't come in here askin' me where that *nigga* is, I don't keep tabs on him. You're the one who's *fuckin'* Exodus, so *don't* come in my spot actin' like you own it. I haven't seen him in two weeks."

Melody doesn't believe Black.

She never does.

Melody feels in her heart that Black has something to do with Gary's sudden disappearance.

"You're lying! I swear to GOD, if you hurt him, your going down, Black."

"I told you I haven't seen that *motherfucker,* now get the *fuck* out of my club!" Black demands.

Melody doesn't move.

"Gary showed me the money you gave him. Why couldn't you just leave him alone this time? Gary doesn't *need* to be like you. Everything you touch dies—Gary is *not* like you!" Melody screams.

Black's face contorts in rage.

"What the *fuck* do you mean, he's *not* like me? I've known Exodus longer than you have, Melody. He's nothin'…a worthless piece of *shit!*

"You're standin' here, tryin' to convince yourself that I must've done somethin' to Exodus, because he ducked out on your *ass,* well boo-hoo. You better wake the *fuck* up, Exodus probably took my money and skipped town.

"Don't get mad at me because you're lonely…that's what the *fuck* you get for sellin' your heart to a thief. Go ahead and call the cops on me, 'cause when I get out, your ass *will* be missin' just like Exodus. NOW, GET THE *FUCK* OUT OF MY CLUB!"

Black's disrespectful words brings tears to Melody's eyes, yet, he becomes fed up with his sister's accusations. As Melody begins to reach into her back pocket, Black looks at her peculiarly.

Distraught, Melody pulls out a small .22 automatic pistol, startling Black; he leaps back as Melody aims the handgun at his head.

"I'm *sick* of you," Melody pleads, moving her aim to Black's slow movements. He panics because of Melody's emotional state, which is more sensitive now, being that she has a gun.

Black now holds his hand out, trying to ward off any bullets that may be fired: "Calm down, sis...calm down," Black quietly suggests, trying his best not to get shot.

"No, I won't. It's *all* because of you."

"Melody...nothin' is wrong with Exodus. He might be at your apartment right now waiting for you. Melody, please stop this, I'm your brother for GOD's sake."

"NO!"

Black carefully moves closer to Melody, trying his best not to antagonize her, continuing to speak in low tones.

"Exodus was locked up for a year, Melody, he needs time alone; that's all. Just think about it...I swear on our mother's grave I haven't seen Exodus, *please* put the gun down," Black negotiates nervously.

"Did you kill him, Black?" Melody cries, her face having perspiration and tears. She wants to believe Black. Melody also wants to believe that Gary is at her apartment waiting for her, but the image of his dead body haunts her mind, making Melody's heart cold.

"DID YOU KILL HIM?" Melody cries out again.

"No. No, Melody, I didn't," Black answers solemnly, his vision locked on the pistol. Melody then hears the office door click, briefly turning to see who's coming in.

Reacting instantly, Black takes full advantage of the opportunity, grabbing the gun with his left hand before throwing a quick uppercut to Melody's midsection.

The hard blow knocks the wind from her lungs, causing Melody to fall down to the floor in the fetal position. She hugs her stomach, now exploding in pain, before gasping for air; Melody then feels her chest convulse.

Black looks down at Melody in bitter rage. What she did is unforgivable in his eyes. Black then delivers a brutal kick to the side of Melody's face—Melody now falls flat on her back with horrendous force of the attack.

"Don't *ever* pull a *fuckin'* gun on me again, *bitch!*" Black grits through his teeth.

Blood slowly leaks from Melody's mouth, as she lays limp, racked with pain. Mex, standing at the doorway, looks on silently at the battery. The savage attack reveals Black's psychotic temper—he glares at his bodyguard.

"Get this *bitch* the *fuck* out of here," Black coldly instructs. Mex follows his order, lifting Melody off the ground. As the guard holds her in his arms, Black grabs his sister roughly by the hair, and harshly stares in her swelling face.

"Now look at you…all *fucked* up. Tell that *nigga,* Exodus, to get my money and my car to me when you see him, or I'll *kill* both of you."

Melody can't understand Black's words, her disillusioned mind is in turmoil; trying to make sense of the agonizing pain that wracks her chest and head. Black quickly pushes her face away from him.

Mex leaves the office with Melody, broken in his arms. Black now disgusts him, seeing what Black has done to his own sister, who's unconscious.

Already aware that Black is indeed crazy, Mex questions further the state of Black's mental health; witnessing Black brutally beat Melody inside of his office, as if she was an enemy.

It was beyond anger.

It was simply barbaric.

Mex carries Melody past the prying eyes of the club's patrons, and out the front door. As soon as Brown sees the condition Melody's in, he grows frantic.

"WHAT THE *HELL* HAPPENED, MEX?" Brown asks, taking Melody from Mex's arms and into his own.

"She pulled a gun on Black, so he attacked her," Mex replies.

"Nah, man, this is *fucked* up!" Brown responds, as he gazes at Melody, who still is fully unconscious. The stocky bouncer becomes mortified as he views Melody.

"Mex, I'm taking her to the hospital."

"Brown, we got a club to run. Black's not—"

"FUCK BLACK! DO YOU SEE WHAT HE DID?" Brown shouts as he walks away from his post, heading to his car. He holds Melody carefully in his arms.

Black shouldn't have done this, Brown thinks to himself. He then puts Melody in the back seat of his *BMW* and drives off, making sure to keep an eye on her at all times; as Brown races to the emergency room.

SIX

Holding the beautifully wrapped dozen of red roses in his hand, Gary contemplates what his first words will be to Melody, as he rides up the elevator. Gary laughs and shakes his head, silently practicing the lines.

How can I explain my newfound abilities? ...How will Melody react if I take her to the roof, leap off suddenly, and remain suspended in air? Gary thinks.

Gary then imagines how Melody would smile if he did such an act. That brings a sense of enjoyment to him. When the elevator reaches its destination, Gary steps out doing a jig, as he approaches Melody's apartment door.

Gary fumbles with his spare key before putting it into the slot. After he turns it, Gary frowns suspiciously, realizing that the door is already unlocked. He quickly reverses the direction of the key, carefully entering the apartment.

Searching the area with his eyes, looking for Melody, Gary soon hears a noise coming from her bedroom—low thumping sounds, as though someone's walking around.

Gary remains silent.

He reaches into the back of his waist, and retrieves the handgun he kept since the night of the car crash. It's uncommon for Melody to leave her apartment door unlocked, causing Gary to feel a sense of danger.

While taking a mute breath, Gary grips his handgun. He braces himself for whatever, whoever is in the bedroom. Forcefully, Gary kicks in the door, and aims at the first thing he sees moving.

Brown nervously jumps away from the opened dresser he's fumbling through. He's more surprised than startled to see Gary, who has his eyebrows raised in disbelief.

"Brown, what the *fuck* are you doing here? And why are you searching through Melody's shit?" Gary questions, still pointing the gun at the bouncer.

"Exodus, *boy* am I glad to see you! Where the *hell* have you been? And put that gun away—stop that *bullshit!*"

Gary has second thoughts about giving into the bouncer's request, but realizes that he doesn't need the gun to protect himself anymore. Old habits die hard—Gary puts the gun back into his waist.

Brown sighs in relief and speaks: "Something happened to Melody last night, she's in the hospital. I'm here looking for her Social Security Card."

Instantly, Gary feels grief rising from his stomach.

"What happened to her?" Gary asks immediately, moving closer to Brown. Brown's eyes slowly fall to the floor, he holds back from speaking.

"I SAID WHAT THE HELL HAPPENED TO HER!" Gary's voice rises angrily.

"Melody came to the club looking for you, she thought that Black did something to you. You know how emotional Melody gets about you."

Brown then pauses, trying to find the right words for what he has to tell next: "...Black told her he hadn't had contact with you, but Melody didn't believe him, so she pulled a gun out on Black. He got the gun away from Melody."

The grief grows more, like a sickening virus in the core of Gary. Brown reads the turmoil upon Gary's face as he continues.

"...If I was there, I wouldn't have let Black put his hands on her—that's my word!"

It feels as if that bullet had once again, tore through Gary, but this is agony that will never heal.

"He...he beat her?" Gary mumbles, as his voice fails.

"Yeah, man, she's in a coma. That's why I need Melody's Social Security Card. That *coward,* Mex saw the whole thing—he didn't try to stop it," Brown growls.

Gary's sullen sadness is beginning to mix with morbid anger—he refuses to allow himself to shed tears. Brown places his right hand on Gary's shoulder, trying to show him that he too, knows Gary's state.

Yet, Gary walks away from Brown with forced steps. He goes into the kitchen and jumps on top of the counter. Gary quickly finds Melody's Social Security Card above the cupboard, where she always hides such documents.

Brown's worries grows, watching Gary move mechanically back down to the floor. Gary then walks up to him wide-eyed, holding out his hand to give Brown Melody's Social Security Card.

Brown sees fire in Gary's eyes, as Gary speaks through clenched jaws.

"Take me to her, now!"

*　*　*　*　*

The study bleeps of a heart monitor are the only sound that's heard, in the grieving quiet of the hospital room. Gary sits by Melody's bedside, softly caressing her limp left hand, as if he can touch Melody's soul.

It feels as if Gary's heart is ripped from his chest as he looks at her. Tears roll freely down Gary's cheeks, as he views Melody's bandaged face. Her right eye and cheek are swollen beyond recognition, but to Gary, Melody is still beautiful as ever.

Breathing devices are placed in her nose and mouth to assist in Melody's shallow respiration. Earlier, The doctors told Gary that she suffers from blood clots in her head from massive head trauma, and that three of Melody's ribs are broken. When Gary asked when would she awake from her coma, the doctors told him that they're uncertain if Melody ever would.

Now, Gary blames himself; believing that if he'd never left her apartment that morning when he said those things to Melody, that none of this would've happened.

Lost in the battery of emotions, Gary doesn't notice that he's been sitting in the chair for the last five hours, staring at Melody without ever blinking. Hoping that she'll awaken from her coma, Gary wishes that it were all a bad dream, a nightmare that has started, the day he was released from prison.

Reality tears apart that delusional gesture.

Melody, Gary's true love, the only person that ever cared about him, is now broken, like a priceless painting that can never be put back together again.

Gary's jewel is shattered.

For a moment, his desperation grows—Gary thinks that he can use his powers to help Melody. Yet, Gary doesn't possess the gift to heal others, only to destroy.

Melody loves Gary so much, that she attempted to murder her own brother, Black for him. She'd tried to and failed. The guilt of knowing this is unbearable for Gary, it's like a permanent, non-repenting sin that accusingly clings to him.

Yet, Gary feels that he isn't the only one to blame; rather, someone else has to be punished for the barbarism.

"Yes, punished," Gary silently vows, letting vengeance override his mind. He has the power to avenge.

Gary starts breathing heavily.

He thinks about the punishment...

Black's image comes to mind.

Rage explodes throughout his being.

Soon after, Gary calms himself, stands up and bends over to kiss Melody's forehead; Gary having dry, chapped lips.

"I'm going to make everything better, Melody, you'll see. I promise," Gary pleads to Melody, needing her forgiveness.

Melody doesn't answer.

She probably won't speak again.

Won't ever kiss Gary back with her soft lips.

Never hug and embrace him into her warm body...

Again.

Gary's face contorts, he's bordering on breaking down, as the full magnitude falls upon him. Even though Melody's body is alive, it's as if she's gone from Gary.

Forever.

He gently rubs Melody's palm on his cheek: "Don't leave me, Melody, come back to me."

No answer.

Carefully placing Melody's hand upon her stomach, Gary slowly turns away from her. As he walks to the exit the hospital room, Brown steps in front of Gary, knowingly. He looks up at Brown, pure hatred masks Gary's face.

"Don't do it, Exodus. I know what you're planning—you won't be any good to Melody dead. This happened because of you, so I'm not going to let you throw your—"

Brown's misunderstood sentence is abruptly halted. With surprising speed, Gary places his gun on the bouncer's temple. He holds it steady, fighting himself not to squeeze the trigger. Brown stands frozen, with the knowledge that he's about to die.

Clenching his jaw muscles, Gary controls his fueling madness. Melody isn't far away from the two, and if Gary blows Brown's brains out, more guilt will overwhelm him. After all, it was Brown who brought Melody to the hospital, he being the one who saved her life.

Gary soon removes the gun from Brown's head; to Brown's relief, Gary gives it to him.

"I don't need it anymore, I don't need *anything* anymore," Gary hisses.

Brown hears the pain in Gary's voice. He steps aside, letting Gary quickly leave the room. Brown also watches on as Gary violently shoves someone who's in the way of his path.

What Brown doesn't notice are Gary's fists being so tightly clenched, that his palms starts to bleed.

*　*　*　*　*

The smoke from Black's *Cuban* cigar gently rises to the ceiling of his office. He casually takes another tote and breathes out slowly, letting the flavor marinate for a moment. There is no guilt in what Black did to his sister, Melody.

No remorse.

He's now angry that Brown didn't show up for work after the incident. Mex told him about the bouncer's comment, and Black decides that he will discipline Brown at the first opportunity that presented itself.

It's three in the morning, and the pace of the club is still strong. Only the more money to get, like a powerful addiction.

Black puts the cigar in an ashtray on his desk momentarily, as he bows his head, snorting one of the several lines of cocaine on the mirror that lies in front of him.

Black yawns...

Stretches.

Falls back lazily into his chair.

Black now wonders if he should tell Mex to send up one of the girls, for his *own* sexual amusement.

The door to Black's office clicks and slowly opens. His dilating pupils strain to see who's coming in. A warm pool of blood then trickles into the office, spreading out on the floor, as if someone spilled a bucket of it.

Black's wicked eyes widens in horror, staring at the crimson liquid that's also splattered on the office door. He wants to believe that the cocaine he ingested has given him some kind of hallucinating effect.

Gary soon steps through the doorway without a drop of blood on his clothing. Moments before, he snapped Mex's body

81

like a twig, before tearing the guard's corpse apart without making a sound.

Black quickly reaches into a desk drawer and pulls out a nine-millimeter handgun, silencer attached to its nozzle, before standing up. As Gary walks to the far side of the office, Black aims the pistol at him—Gary doesn't worry about the gun.

"Why did you *beat* Melody like that, Black? She's your sister!" Gary spits coldly.

"She pulled a gun out on me because of your stupid *ass*. What the *fuck* was I supposed to do, let Melody kill me?" Black shouts back, his gun hand begins to tremble slightly. "Don't *come* in here judging me, or else you might end up like her. Now, where's my car, Exodus?"

Black's eyes move from Gary to the door, then to the floor. The blood is still there—it isn't his imagination. Black then stares back at Gary.

"What the *hell's* goin' on, Exodus? Where's that blood comin' from?" Black questions, fearing the answer. Gary refuses to tell him; Gary's face twisted in sheer rage.

"Melody was right, Black, you're nothing but a heartless *bastard;* you don't deserve to live!"

"What, *nigga?* I made you!" Black retaliates. Gary shakes his head.

"You *made* me? I have nothing of worth from you. The only person that made my life worth living is in a coma because of you, and now, you're going to *suffer* for what you've done."

Black laughs at the threat, "You talk a lot of *shit* for someone with a gun pointed at him. You're not a *fuckin'* hero."

"Go ahead then, pull the trigger!" Gary barks. His disregard to the death threat infuriates Black. Without wasting another moment, Black's finger squeezes the trigger.

The hammer of his gun pulls back, springs to hit the back of the bullet, but something strange happens. The hammer freezes in place, just a moment away from its intended target.

Black's eyes widens in shock!

He tries to pull the trigger again.

The hammer doesn't budge.

Gary then raises his right arm and opens his hand. The pistol Black is holding immediately bolts from his own hand, as if pulled by an invisible force. It quickly twirls through the air until it lands in Gary's grasp.

Before Black can comprehend what just happened, Gary shoots off two rounds. The bullets tear through both of Black's kneecaps, permanently disabling the cartilage and bone.

Black falls to the floor.

He's screaming and writhing in pain.

Blood squirts from the fresh bullet wounds.

Gary ignores Black's loud cries.

Now drops the gun.

Approaches the wounded man.

Black glares at Gary in outrage.

"YOU SHOT ME, *BITCH!*" Saliva spews from Black's mouth, as he squirms in his own crimson fluid. "I'LL *KILL* YOU!"

A sinister grin appears on Gary's face, before he levitates Black's crippled body from the floor with his mind. Gary then walks up to him, and maliciously grabs Black by the throat.

As Gary holds the helpless man, the terror within Black grows, because of the supernatural events transpiring. He can't believe that something other than the strength of Gary's arm is holding him off the floor.

THIS CAN'T BE REAL! Black's panicking mind screams, he now being stricken with torture. *IMPOSSIBLE!* Black soon looks into Gary's eyes and sees a blue eerie vapor coming from the man's sockets, as if they're burning.

"You don't deserve to die by a gun. I'm going to prepare you for your journey to *Hell,* Black. You're going to burn."

As Black now realizes what's happening, an intense, overpowering fear embraces him. He believes an evil demon has arisen from the depths of Hell to claim him, before thinking Gary's an angel of death.

"You're...you're-the-Devil!" Black proclaims, his words vibrating through his constricted throat.

"Maybe I am," Gary whispers.

A blue fire intensely burst forth from Gary's hand, which envelopes Black's whole form.

Black doesn't feel anything at first.

Then immense heat rises.

Followed by the burning.

Black screams horrendously!

His clothing and skin sizzles!

Both charred away, until burning flesh is left.

Gary watches on with no compassion, as Black's bulging eyeballs begin to boil; organs now popping from their sockets like overcooked boiled eggs. Gary refuses to call off his powers until Black is no more. Soon after, Gary drops the burnt remains and views the destruction he caused.

Black will never lay a finger on Melody or anyone else again. The only pity Gary feels is, regretting killing him so fast. Gary now wishes he'd tortured Black slowly, maybe for a couple of days, in order to savor the moment. But, being enraged caused Gary to use his abilities to the extreme.

Turning away from the dead, Gary makes his way to the closet where he witnessed Black get the handgun he'd given Gary weeks prior. As Gary opens the door, he sees many guns lined against it. Gary isn't interested in the weapons; he's more attentive to what's in the safe.

With a gestured thought, the safe's metal door bends from its hedges, and crashes into the opposite wall outside the closet. Gary notices that he's becoming more powerful than before when he first learned of his powers. Gary no longer has to concentrate strenuously to move objects, he now thinks briefly, and things move at his will.

Soon after, Gary looks into the broken safe, seeing stacks of bills and jewelry. Believing that the contents will be useful, he grabs a suitcase near the desk and takes all that's inside.

Leaving the office to make his way out of the club, Gary feels distraught. The perversions that surrounds him, no longer gives Gary a sense of lust; rather it disgusts him to the pit of his stomach.

No one heard what transpired, due to the loud music blasting out of the club's speakers. As Gary exits the club, he stops abruptly, freezing for a moment. A stormy wrath suddenly awakens in Gary. Using his mind, Gary shuts and permanently welds the club's front door.

There are three hundred people in the club, and Gary cares for none of them. With just another thought, the building begins to shake, as though an earthquake has begun.

Club patrons inside are caught by surprise by the sudden tremors that start off weak, soon becoming stronger. Objects fall from the walls, which crack at their foundations. Gary concentrates harder as he makes his way across the street, refusing to gaze upon the destruction he's creating.

Inside, clubbers begin running to its doorway, crying in terror, no longer entranced in their perversions. Manically, they shove each other and pull at the door, screaming loudly, while scampering on top of one another for freedom.

The door won't open.

Gary's deaf ears ignore their cries.

Compassion doesn't exist.

The building comes collapsing down.

Crushing and killing the many people inside.

Gary slowly shuts his eyes.

He hears the thundering crashes and destruction.

Gary has great power to kill and destroy, but no power to save the woman he loves. As the tremors quietly die, so does a part of Gary's soul.

Immediately, Gary leaves the carnage, without taking a glance at the anarchy he created.

SEVEN

So peaceful it is, Andrew thinks to himself, while standing in the back wing of his mother's estate in *East Hampton, New York.* He then reflects on the digital conference he had with Desmond Jones, the head of the excavation team Andrew had sent into Lortech's diamond mines in *Libya, North Africa.*

There, Desmond told him an extraordinary story about what's written on the tomb's coffin. It's engraved in *Arabic,* reason being why Andrew couldn't understand the message when he found the tomb. The corpse inside the coffin name was Bakarot.

The message indicates that he was the first and only to rebel against the Etherea, his master, Lord Moon. All of this fascinated Andrew, because Desmond could find no historical records of those names. Also, what the archeologist told him next, really puzzled Andrew.

He said that Bakarot and his armies of the Jinn Legion rose up against their master, because they'd found out the truth of the coming of darkness, born the Lord Moon.

The ethereal struck down all of Bakarot's enemies, and the few that lived had buried him alive, with the blessed staff that was once given to the warrior, by the Etherea, Lord Moon—the cherubims, AU and AG, whom the staff of the lord controlled. It was the Etherea who had forged the staff from Bakarot's own power.

After Desmond told the story that's written on the tomb, he questioned Andrew if he'd taken anything from the mausoleum. Andrew lied and told Desmond that he hadn't.

What then bothered the archeologist was the fact that his carbon dating devices went haywire when he tried repeatedly to find the date of the tomb. Soon after, Andrew told Desmond that anything that he found was his to have, before abruptly ending their conversation.

The story had intrigued Andrew, for whomever it was that had created the staff and the two supernatural beings it controlled, had a superior intelligence than even modern man.

Andrew was also content with the fact that he's now the one in possession of them all.

But for now, the story Desmond Jones told him will be his personal knowledge, along with the staff and metallic statues.

Andrew soon pushes his thoughts of the meeting aside. He closes his eyes and fills his lungs with the fresh air around him. The pink glow of the sun through Andrew's eyelids is tranquil. He slowly exhales when hearing approaching footsteps behind him.

Valerie Taylor now smiles at Andrew as glances at her. They hug warmly, and she kisses Andrew on the cheek.

"How was your trip to *Africa?*" Valerie's question brings another fleeting smile to her son. Andrew ponders on how to tell his mother about the extraordinary event that happened.

"…Very mind-altering. In fact, it opened my eyes anew," Andrew simply answers. The two then sit down at nearby seats, and Valerie instructs her maid to get them something to drink.

When she turns back to Andrew, Valerie notices the worried glint in her son's eyes, something she is all too familiar with raising Andrew as a child.

"Are you alright, Andrew? You seem bothered," Valerie states inquisitively.

"No, mother, Lortech is under control."

"I'm not talking about that. In fact, I know that Lortech is the least of your problems. You have the intelligence to succeed in anything you put your mind to."

Indeed Andrew has problems; yet he refuses to confess to his mother.

Valerie purposely pauses as the maid comes, holding a serving plate with a pitcher of iced tea and two glasses, which are quickly filled. Delicately, Valerie takes one of the glasses and sips very little of the liquid; Andrew refrains from drinking.

"…Have you heard from Sharon lately?" Valerie adds, strategically. A light frown immediately appears on Andrew's face.

Sharon must've told mother about my refusal to give her funds for the foundation. She knows that mother will easily try to persuade me to make a different decision.

"…Yes, I've spoken with her about 'Shattered Dreams', and I declined to help Sharon," Andrew tells truthfully.

"I'm not talking about her foundation. Son, you have to learn to stop jumping to conclusions so adamantly."

Valerie's voice is soft and kind as always. Andrew has never witnessed his mother lose her cool; it's as if Valerie always remains in control of her moods. The only time Andrew can remember her crying was at his father's funeral.

Valerie soon reaches into her pocket and retrieves her sunglasses, protecting her eyes from the gleaming sun.

"Son, I know the relationship between you two has gone sour, but Sharon is doing something positive with her life. I'm not trying to force you into doing anything, but, I believe you should set your feelings aside and help her."

Valerie is very fond of Sharon, hoping someday that she will be the mother of her grandchildren.

"Mother, Sharon's trying to accomplish a task that's futile, by wasting resources on a program that in the end will fail," Andrew defends.

Eyes hidden by her sunglasses, Valerie stares at her son. She recognizes the look on Andrew's face: his mask of stubbornness.

"Do you honestly believe that, Andrew?"

"I do," Andrew answers flatly.

"Well, so be it," his mother adds. "I guess I've just wasted two-hundred thousand dollars for a lost cause. Your dear old mother must be *losing* her mind." Valerie's statement is flared with sarcasm, scolding Andrew.

"Stop it. You're not losing your mind at all, mother, and you're not going to make me feel guilty."

Valerie grins, reaches out and softly palms her son's hand, causing Andrew to look directly at her.

"Look at you, my only child who's now a man. I can still remember when you were very young, and how you used to get angry because people felt that you were alone," Valerie says kindly. "To other people, your intelligence frightened them, they were scared of you. You were in college when other kids your age were in grade school. Remember how you used to cry on my shoulder about that, Andrew?"

"I don't know why you're bringing that up."

Andrew's voice is breaking because of all the painful memories. It's all too familiar to him, how others would point at Andrew and stare, because of his genius. How the whispers burned into Andrew's mind. Even now as he sits by his mother, Andrew finds himself staring out blankly.

Valerie witnesses his discomfort: "Yes, you do remember."

"Why would you bring—I"

"Because I'm trying to make a point, son," Valerie stops Andrew from talking by interjecting. She already knows what he will say.

"Andrew, when people shunned you because of your mind, Sharon accepted you wholeheartedly. She wasn't scared of you, nor intimidated. Sharon loved you, and she still does. You just refuse to see that."

Valerie now raises her arm and caresses Andrew's face.

"I know your father left you with great responsibility, but you are *worthy* of it. So don't let Lortech cloud your vision."

Mother is right.

All of Andrew's life, he felt like an outcast; mocked by his peers since the age of five. None of the other kids wanted to be around the prodigy that knew it all.

Even Andrew's schooling was hell, because everyone was much older than him, which made Andrew exceed further. He accomplished his higher education quickly, to be away from the scornful whispers and hateful stares.

Andrew's own hatred consumed him; it caused Sharon to be repulsed by his arrogance. Andrew blames her leaving him as Sharon's envy of his status, but the truth of the matter is that, Andrew changed from when she first fell in love with him.

Andrew now removes his mother's hand from his face.

"You're correct, mother, I will give Sharon a call."

Valerie smiles.

"Enough talk about me, how have you been?" Andrew questions, trying to change the subject of the conversation.

"I've been doing the best since your father's passing, but I will *never* get over his death, never," Valerie states, feeling saddened—the memories of her husband's demise.

She then pauses momentarily, catching her breath before again speaking.

"...Life must go on, I know that David would want me to be happy."

Valerie takes another sip from her glass, letting the cold tea dance on her taste buds before swallowing.

Andrew's now concerned about his mother. She's been a widow for seven short months. Valerie is strong, but Andrew can tell that her mourning is as strong as the day his father died.

"Mother…mother I know it hurts, but father lives on in both of us," Andrew says comfortingly. For a moment, Valerie says nothing; she only stares at the green landscape.

"…You're right, Andrew," his mother finally whispers, Andrew's words has sparked energy into Valerie that lifts her up. "That reminds me, I'm going to have a fundraiser here soon for Sharon, and I would like for you to be here. After all, you are a promising young bachelor."

Andrew sighs. Valerie continues.

"Hush, boy. You're a healthy young man, and you should be thinking about finding a wife."

I'm *only* twenty-three."

"You're no average twenty-three-year-old. You may fool someone else with that, but I'm your mother. I know that you have the maturity of someone twice your age, and to add to that fact, *when* will you bless your dear old mother with grandchildren?"

There it is again, that sarcastic tone that rings a bell in Andrew's head to give in to her wishes.

"Stop saying you're old, and stop manipulating me," Andrew says playfully.

They both laugh.

As their joy heightens, the small cell phone in Andrew's pocket rings. He brings the device to his ear: "Yes?"

"Mr. Taylor, this is Michael Masters, I'm sorry to disturb you at the moment, but there's something I need you to see at the lab. It's KD-49."

"I'll be there immediately," Andrew answers before hanging up. Valerie is still venting the last of her laughter when her son stands up.

"Mother, I have to go."

"So soon? My *poor* son is being worked to death," Valerie says; as Andrew bends down to kiss her good-bye.

"I'll be at your banquet, so I can give you many grandchildren," Andrew jokes. "I love you."

"I love you, too, sweetie," Valerie answers as Andrew departs.

Three minutes passes, and Valerie continues to think about Andrew. She loves him as if Andrew were from her own womb. He has become the child that Valerie always wanted.

I am his mother...even if...

Valerie's thoughts now refrained, but she finds her strength. It's unknown to Andrew that he isn't her biological child. Valerie promised herself that she would never reveal this secret to him.

Andrew's toddler years warned Valerie that the revelation could have dire consequences.

Andrew's my son, Valerie thinks, as she takes another sip of her iced tea.

*   *   *   *   *

Deep within the sublevels of the Lortech tower, its AI and cybernetics lab remains hidden from the rest of the building, like a rare jewel. Andrew Taylor stands firmly beside Michael Masters, viewing a large, 60-inch, closed-circuit flat screen, displaying the experimental project that's taking place.

Karen Scott, the scientist in charge of KD-49's creation and test, sits at one of the many computer consoles; analyzing the fast-paced data that KD-49 feeds her. Andrew watches the mobile weapon with unsympathetic eyes; his moral demeanor is unaffected.

Half of the screen shows the half-human/half-machine's form, strapped down to a vertical steel table with metal harnesses, restricting any movement whatsoever. KD-49's copper metallic limbs encase its deadly offline weaponry.

The cyborg's human skull is fused with reinforced steel to prevent any damage to its most vital organ, the human brain; the main reason the whole AI project is so successful. It was grown from human fetuses produced in the lab.

All diligent actions were taken to insure the AI's completion before Andrew even owned Lortech. Masters had briefed him on the groundbreaking creation months beforehand.

"Mr. Taylor, sir, I believe we have a problem with KD-49's assessment grid. The chip in its head makes the subject compliant with our orders we instruct him."

"Let's not be humane here, Karen, it's a machine," Andrew interjects, cutting down the scientist's words. Karen is dismayed by his comment.

"Well, sir, KD-49 has a problem with analyzing non-threats."

"I don't understand. If it's on a mission to terminate hostiles, then it's doing what it was created for."

Masters, looking at the screen, listens to Andrew openly. He witnessed the simulated mission earlier before Andrew arrived. Masters shakes his head and speaks: "Mr. Taylor, I think you should see how the cyborg reacts in a simulated mission before you make an assessment. Karen run the program," Masters orders.

The scientist nods and begins typing into the computer. Half of the monitor goes blank before a jungle landscape appears. It looks so real, no one can tell the difference between what's authentic or not in the digital environment.

"I'm now loading a simulated combat mission on a virtual reality program," Karen indicates, as she lowers her head and speaks into a microphone that lead to the room the cyborg is stationed in. Two other scientists stand quietly next to KD-49, measuring its heartbeat and brain activity.

"Load KD-49's simulation input, I'm running a test," Karen instructs.

A scientist in the room lifts a circuitry wire and opens a compartment in KD-49's shoulder, quickly attaching the jack before he steps back: "KD-49 is ready for the system; proceed with program."

Andrew is already predisposed with the cyborg's capabilities; still, he remains anxious to witness the experiment. No trace of Andrew's eagerness shows on his face.

"The opposite screen will display the mission through the eyes of the cyborg. I'm downloading a program in which KD-49 will terminate his target," Karen states.

"Proceed, Karen," Andrew orders.

The virtual reality simulation is breathtaking. The details are so keen, that anyone watching will believe they're viewing something that's actually taking place. The plant life, even the sounds of the insects make it realistic.

KD-49 moves stealthily through the jungle environment, until it comes upon what seems to be a hangar, having twenty armed guards moving outside its perimeter.

A small cube with a photo of the cyborg's target appears on the side of the screen, giving KD-49's point of view. The cyborg quickly analyzes the faces of the twenty guards and finds no matches.

A long, thin, silver blade extracts out of KD-49's left forearm, as it arranges its strategy. The screen then displays five guards who are huddled together. At rapid speed, the cyborg rushes towards the group from their blindside.

Before one of the five guards turned around, KD-49's sharp blade swiftly slashes through all of their bodies, killing the group simultaneously.

Then, its vision locks on a nearby light tower, counting one guard on-duty. Out of the cyborg's shoulder, a small, high-powered laser shoots out a fine ray of red light. The projectile goes straight through the tower man's forehead, sizzling his brain. The guard falls silently.

Without pausing, KD-49 locks in on ten more targets, firing off rapid shots within three seconds.

All are killed.

Out of the darkness, one of the guards catches the cyborg offhand. Before the man is able to warn his troops, KD-49 grabs his head and grotesquely crushes the guard's skull. Aware of its mistake, the cyborg emits a radio scrambling signal, blocking out any threat of communication. Soon after, KD-49 violently annihilates the last three troops and approaches the main hangar.

Switching its vision to heat detection, allows the cyborg to see who's in the building, giving KD-49 a count of four more hostiles. It then scans for weapons, finding only one of the antagonists armed.

A compartment now opens on the cyborg's thigh—KD-49 retrieves a small explosive device, placing it on the hangar's front door. Using a pipe, the cyborg then climbs to the roof of the building, as a fifty-second countdown initiates.

KD-49 then perches itself directly above the group. When the door explodes, the gunman fires at the debris. The cyborg shoots another laser through the wooden ceiling—the heat-searing ray tears through the gunman's heart.

Andrew smiles at the intended kill. Using the art of surprise on its target amuses the businessman. Andrew further watches the simulated mission, as KD-49 uses the weight of its body to crash through the rooftop, landing in front of its main target.

Positive identification confirmed.

The cyborg's blade extends, as it slashes downward vertically, dismembering the man in half. High-pitched screams coming from the screen's speakers are heard throughout the lab, as KD-49 sights the last two surviving members.

Andrew's eyes widen as he sees a simulated woman holding a newborn child clutched to her bosom; she looks terrified of the cyborg.

Andrew's upper lip quivers, he becomes mortified when KD-49's targeting signal aligns on the woman and child's heads.

"STOP THE DAMN PROGRAM!" Andrew shouts. Karen, startled by his reaction, immediately hits a computer key that halts the simulation. Andrew begins to breathe harder—the simulation seems so real to him.

"WHAT THE *HELL* IS WRONG WITH THE DAMN CYBORG, KAREN? THE WOMAN AND CHILD WERE NON-THREATS!" Andrew yells. Masters becomes intrigued by Andrew's distressed behavior.

"I was making appoint, Mr. Taylor. KD-49 is supposed to be devoid of emotion and adamant of orders we feed it. It has a human brain, but no concept of humanity. All it knows is how to terminate its missions' objectives. Look on the screen."

Andrew views the side of the monitor that displays where the cyborg is bound and hooked into the system. He then sees a sickening hint of a smile upon its synthetic face. Andrew almost refuses to believe what he sees, but nevertheless, KD-49 is smiling.

"It displays some sort of emotion in completing its task—I don't fully comprehend this behavior," Karen explains.

"Fix it, Karen!" Andrew replies.

"How? All of this is experimental. We can store massive amounts of information in the cyborg's human brain, but we have no control over its emotions," Karen clarifies.

Andrew's brows furrow in frustration. He can't figure out the reason why the simulation makes him so upset. After all, KD-49 did complete its programmed mission with the greatest of ease.

If there are civilians around when the cyborg is on a mission in the real world, then they will be as guilty as the cyborg's targets. That isn't Andrew's problem to deal with; it's the military's black ops and the NSA issue.

Andrew looks back at the screen. KD-49's prosthetic skin is still pulled back in a frozen smile. Andrew clenches his teeth.

"Karen, give KD-49 electrical shock treatment to the pain receptors of its brain," Andrew says calmly. The female scientist wants to reject his proposal; instead, Karen turns back to her console.

"Yes, sir," Karen whispers while typing into her keyboard.

Masters stands in silence, observing the president of Lortech. The cyborg did its job, and the thought of it killing the woman and child does not affect Masters in the least. He raises his piercing blue eyes to the screen, just as Karen administers the instructed punishment Andrew ordered her to do.

As the strong electrical current runs through KD-49's brain, its copper metallic body tenses. Although its cybernetic frame feels no notion of pain, the jolt of electricity to its neuro-sensors becomes a quick dose of agony.

The surge now ceases, and the cyborg goes back to its normal sentinel position. The twisted smile is no longer visible. Andrew sighs, knowing the multi-million dollar Lortech creation now understands its punishment.

Andrew also knows that torture is a great tool used to manipulate every beast that walks the face of the earth; tormenting KD-49 into submitting to his will.

"The problem is fixed. Do the same every time that behavior arises, until the cyborg learns it's unwanted. Then move on to the final trials and get it prepared for action."

"But, sir I—"

"Do it!" Andrew immediately interjects. The scientist obeys and continues her work.

Andrew then rotates and begins to leave the lab—Masters follows him. A surveillance computer rapidly scans both men's eyes before the elevator door opens. The two enter somberly.

As the elevator ascends to its destination, Masters speaks: "Andrew, can I be frank with you?"

Andrew gives Masters a look of sarcasm: "When haven't you been frank, Masters?" Andrew responds with a slight grin.

"Well, during the simulation I noticed your anger..." Masters pauses for a moment, expecting Andrew to disagree. No arguments come from him, so Masters continues: "KD-49 is the perfect soldier in all manners. Karen believes the cyborg's behavior is defective, but as you witnessed, whatever emotion its brain felt, didn't interfere with the virtual mission. Why did you

95

get upset when KD-49 was about to terminate the woman and child?"

"I didn't get upset."

Andrew lies.

Masters knows better.

"If you say so. I believe the cyborg was correct in deciding to terminate the last two survivors, therefore there would be no witnesses to verify its presence," Masters deliberates to his younger superior.

"Perhaps you're right, Masters. I'm new to all of this, and it takes getting used to."

"I understand," Masters adds, as the elevator's doors opens to the top floor.

Both men immediately walk to the doors of Andrew's office. After Andrew scans his hands and eyes, he types in a code on the scanning device on the wall—the doors open.

AG and AU stand unmoving, as Andrew sits at his desk; Masters is unaware of the two metallic statues' abilities. Like everyone else, he thinks Andrew had them forged as a statement of his wealth and power.

Like so many others, Masters is tragically wrong.

"How has the stem cell research progressed, Masters?"

"Our *European* developers have informed me of a rather new approach they have. Their lab has developed capabilities to generate stem cells into new organs within weeks. After their human trials, we're going to influence the FDA, for *American* purposes."

"Very well, Masters," Andrew now concludes.

Soon after, Masters exits the office, and Andrew stands up from his chair. He approaches the large ceiling-to-floor window that gives beautiful views of *New York City*. The warm sun shines through the glass, giving the office an abundance of natural lighting.

Andrew, once again, thinks about what he saw in the cyborg's simulation, the vision of the woman holding her baby flashes in his mind. When it happened, Andrew felt the odd impression that it was he whom the woman held in her arms.

Why? Andrew ponders.

He soon rejects the self-pity. If Andrew is to run Lortech as his father intended, there will be no times for doubts, or guilt of what the company creates.

EIGHT

Melody's apartment is silent.

So silent, that it seems like the void of sound has absorbed all of Gary's senses and destroyed them. He just finished taking a shower, staying in so long, that Gary's fingertips are wrinkled.

Gary tried to wash away the scent of death he inherited the night before. The screams, the lives Gary has taken, the morbid images—all which he refused to watch when Gary demolished Black's club, now plays heavily in his mind.

Opening Melody's closet somberly, Gary begins deciding on what clothing to wear from the many outfits she bought him, prior to Gary's release from prison; pulling out a baggy pair of *Levi's* blue jeans, with a matching blue hooded sweater.

Fully dressed, Gary catches himself running his hand over a pillow that Melody has slept on.

Gary brings it to his nose.

Inhales…

Smells her alluring scent.

Gary's eyes begin to water with bitterness of great sadness. He tries to suppress the emotion by placing Melody's pillow back on her side of the bed. Gary then stands up.

The suitcase of money and jewelry he took is now placed in the corner of Melody's closet. Gary hopes that somehow he can buy a miracle and persuade the doctors to give her better medical care.

But the wish fades.

Gary soon leaves the apartment and makes his way to the hospital.

* * * * *

One hour passes.

Once again, and forever if need be, Gary sits beside his beloved, Melody, with her hand in his palms.

Gary watches Melody fight for her life.

With every second that passes, he hopes that Melody will show some sign of life: a winking eye, a movement of any kind, but none has come.

Gary waits for three hours…

If Melody does awaken from her dark depths of unconsciousness, he wants to be the first person she sees; Gary wanting Melody to know that he's safe, and remains by her side.

Lost in memories of Melody, Gary reflects on the moment that they first met, and how she rejected him. At first, Melody was reluctant to get involved with Gary, because of his affiliation with her brother. But he persisted in chasing Melody, despite Black's warnings. In time, she finally broke under Gary's charms.

At age fifteen, when most their age didn't have intimate relationships, the couple fell in love. Even as Gary continued to do crimes for steady income, Melody still clung to him, giving Gary hope and faith—something he'd never known in his tough childhood.

Gary becomes startled when feeling a slight touch of pressure on his shoulder. He turns his head and sees Brown standing above him.

"I saw what happened to the club on the news this morning. It's a tragedy when things happen like that," Brown states with his eyebrows arched.

"Yeah…a tragedy. I guess GOD works in mysterious ways."

"I can't argue with that. Exodus, you know they didn't find Black's body in the wreckage."

"I don't *think* they ever will," Gary proclaims coldly, putting Brown's suspicions to rest. Brown carefully retrieves a nearby seat, and sits next to the couple.

"I guess I'm out of a job…I'm not even going to ask you how you pulled it off, but you were a *little* extreme, Exodus."

Gary stares sternly at Brown—a disgusted frown appears on his face.

"What he did to Melody was extreme," Gary hisses. Brown doesn't argue with him, in a way, he feels that Gary is right.

"Melody's like a sister to me, Exodus, I would've killed Black myself if I had the chance."

Gary is silent.

Brown feels his desolation.

"Listen, Exodus, I know that you're hurt. The doctor told me you've been in here for three hours—you look tired. Maybe you should take a break, get some fresh air, some coffee. I'll be here with Melody."

Gary stares into Brown's eyes pleadingly. The puffy bags underneath his eyes, exposes the battery of stress Gary endured, since his release from *Rikers Island.*

"You really think I should?" Gary whispers, causing Brown to nod his head approvingly. "What if she wakes up?" Gary hopes.

"I'll be right here, I'll let Melody know that you're here. Okay?"

On shaky knees, Gary rises, leaving Brown with Melody.

* * * * *

For twenty minutes, Gary ventures away from the hospital, like a zombie detached from the world around him. He comes upon a newsstand and gives the cashier a ghostly glance.

"I need a pack of *Newports.*"

"Five bucks," the *West Indian* cashier states.

Gary tosses a twenty-dollar bill on the table: "Give me two."

After taking the money, the cashier turns his back and goes to the far corner of the booth, in search of cigarettes. As the man retrieves the products, Gary studies several magazines on display, interested in purchasing one to read, for when he returns to the hospital.

Gary reads the titles: *The Source, Playboy* and *Essence.* None holds his attention, until he sees one that draws him in, like a fawn caught, frozen in the headlights of an oncoming vehicle.

Gary picks up *Fortune.* On the cover is a photo of a Black man who smiles confidently. He's wearing a black, three-piece power suit, having his arms crossed. To Gary, the guy on the cover looks like a typical sellout, the type of Black man who thinks he's better than the rest of the least fortunate.

Gary studies the man's face.

Chills shoots up his spine.

Flashes of images quickly runs through Gary's mind.

The man's face is so similar to his own.

Suddenly, Gary throws the magazine down as if it's burning his hands.

"Your cigarettes, sir," the cashier says while holding out his hand.

Gary doesn't respond.

His mental capabilities are somewhere else other than the world around him—it's locked in the recess of Gary's mind.

Soon...*Gary is no longer standing in the street, he's staring upward at an all too familiar face, while being held in the arms of his crying brother. Gary sees the third silver eye in the middle of his older sibling's forehead. The stench of burning flesh of his parents fouls the air he breathes, but Gary's not afraid.*

"Mommy and daddy are gone now," Andrew told him twenty years ago. *"I'll never leave you."*

HE PROMISED!

But his brother lied.

Andrew did leave Gary.

Left him alone with terrifying memories.

The cashier now notices Gary's body trembling, as though having a seizure.

"Hey, mister, are you alright?" the cashier shouts.

The vision of the past leaves Gary as fast as it came. He stands again in the present, gazing at the magazine cover he held with trembling hands.

The photo of the Black man on the cover eerily moves, and stares hard into Gary's eyes, as if alive. In the middle of the man's forehead, a bloody third eye opens. The man no longer smiles; instead, he has a scornful expression that frightens Gary to the core.

Instantly, Gary shuts his eyes tightly, not wanting to see the evil face on the cover of *Fortune.*

"MISTER!" The cashier at the newsstand shouts, causing Gary to quickly snap out of his delusion. Both men look at each other worriedly.

"Do you want the cigarettes or not?" The cashier now asks, growing impatient. Gary quickly glances at the magazine cover once more. He's startled, noticing that the image he saw moments before is now gone. The cover photo is as normal as when Gary first viewed it.

Examining the cover closer, he reads the headline, which is in bold letters, *"ANDREW TAYLOR: THE MAN OF THE TIME."*

Without looking at the newsstand man, Gary picks up his two packs of cigarettes, turns and begins to walk away. "I'm taking the magazine, too, keep the change," Gary states, leaving with the publication in his grasp.

"Kids...they need to get off those *fucking* drugs," the cashier snickers after Gary departs.

Gary now believes he's found the answer to the nightmares that has tortured him since childhood. He discovers the person who'd deserted him, abandoned him.

Now, with nothing to lose, Gary is drowned in the determination to prove his past. A tremendous rage reawakens, as he thinks about when he and his only brother, Andrew will meet face-to-face.

*   *   *   *   *

When Gary returns back to the hospital, he assures Brown that he's feeling much better, in which Gary lies. He then sits back into his chair, and carefully watches Melody's condition.

Shortly thereafter, Brown excuses himself and leaves the hospital, promising Gary that he will return tomorrow. Once again, Gary finds himself alone with Melody.

Of all the things GOD can curse me with, it has to be punishing solitude!

His sight then falls upon *Fortune* magazine. Gary begins to slowly read the article on Andrew Taylor. It tells a successful story of corporate power, how Andrew inherited Lortech from his deceased father.

Gary feels repulsed as he reads on, knowing that his brother's life has been one of privilege, while his own life has been of degradation and struggle.

The situation now becomes clearer. Andrew must have been adopted, but the article gives no mention of such an indication. When Gary had first set eyes on the magazine, instantly he knew that the man on the cover was his long lost brother; especially after seeing his first name in print—Andrew being the name their biological mother had given his older brother at birth.

Gary grows angry—the revelation of Andrew's wealthy lifestyle tears him. Deep inside, he's scorned with the thought that he was taken away from Andrew, and Andrew never tried to find him.

For twenty years, the person Gary sought was right under his nose, here in *New York City* at Lortech. The contrast to what he now thinks about Andrew is between hatred and envy.

The night of the car crash had revealed to Gary that he was unlike other people, he discovering that he was far more different.

The Vowdun witch changed me, so Andrew must be different, too! Gary reasons. The third eye he'd stared into that night, long ago in *Haiti* was the clue.

A scenario now runs through his mind. Gary thinks about how Andrew's character might be: high and mighty.

Probably never suffered a day in his life! Gary believes.

A grim smile grows upon his face. Gary knows he's extraordinary, no longer considered "a nobody", having abilities that no ordinary person else can comprehend: the gift and the curse of the Vowdun.

Gary's blood begins to boil.

I'M GOING TO MAKE ANDREW SUFFER! I WANT TO HEAR HIM CRY OUT IN PAIN! NO ONE WILL STOP ME! NOTHING WILL, NOT EVEN DEATH!

How bittersweet it will be for Gary to witness Andrew scream out in agony. Andrew's wealth and corporation won't be able to save his life, nothing will.

Killing Black was for Melody, but Andrew is a different vengeance. The bare anticipation of it all, now leads Gary to a growing blood lust.

"Excuse me, Mr. Romulus, visiting hours are over." Gary hears the voice of a nurse who stands at the room's doorway. He gives Melody one last glance.

Gary then makes a silent prayer, begging for her to come back to him. Soon after, Gary promises that after he deals with his own brother, that he will never kill again.

Leaving the *Fortune* magazine behind where he sat, Gary believes he doesn't need it anymore. It gave him all the information he needed.

Yet, what the article didn't give Gary was the truth of his brother's past, and the forgotten life that Andrew wasn't aware of.

NINE

Rain falls from gloomy grey skies, as *Heaven's* tears of sorrow, washes *Earth* with mourning. The storm comes suddenly, cooling the city with its cold waters. People race up and down the streets, avoiding the rain and strong winds it brings with it.

Standing outside Lortech's tower, Gary ignores the downpour, with his face hidden by his drenched hood. As pedestrians walk steadily by him, some wonder why the young man is staring up at the building with such distaste, and disregard for the weather.

Gary is being drawn into an awareness that's beyond natural. He can sense a single presence within Lortech's corridors. The aura of Andrew Taylor is now sought and found, by his long forgotten brother.

Gary can't wait a second longer. His body levitates from the ground at a fast velocity, knocking over a nearby patron that passes him by.

*   *   *   *   *

Stationed at his desk, Andrew is studying sensitive documents that Yoshi Hiro gave him days before. He's reading a particular section that bothers him. It reveals a treatment for skin cancer Andrew's *Japanese* counterpart has been developing for several decades.

In the course of trying to find the cure to the cancer, Lortech has created a virus named, Chronos, that attacks melanin in the skin. When a person has a certain level of the substance, the Chronos virus makes the skin deteriorate, eating the outer layers grotesquely. Then it works its way deeper into the muscle tissue and vital organs, until the infected is dead.

Andrew closely studies the photographs of a scientist who'd accidentally been exposed to the cancer. He was contained in a unit for a four-week period, until the Chronos virus had run it's full course.

Andrew was appalled when Yoshi described the scene in person. The young entrepreneur learned in his earlier years while studying science and medical practices that, many grave sacrifices and untold horrors were done in the name of medicine, for the "betterment" of humanity.

Luckily, the *Japanese* division of Lortech has fully contained the melanin virus. It can't be used as a means for military usage, because of it's dangerous potential. Andrew now wants to get word back to Yoshi to destroy it as soon as possible, to prevent any further incidents.

Andrew turns to another file. On the cover page it reads: *"CROSS-GENOTYPE PROJECT"*. He begins to examine the file, unaware of the presence behind him. Outside Andrew's window, Gary studies the man's office, hovering silently, as though a ghost arriving on the winds of the past.

Gary stares menacingly through the large glass window. His lips are curled in an animalistic snarl, as he quickly takes in the features and contents of the room. Becoming envious, the gold and silver statues disgusts Gary—the fortunes his brother possesses.

Andrew, with his back still turned to Gary, reading the documents on his desk, is unaware of the immediate danger that hovers, just a few feet behind.

It's time, Gary believes, *time for you to suffer!* He then raises his arms and points his palm to the glass, now concentrating.

Slowly, Andrew raises his head from the papers he's viewing, when he hears a low-thumping sound, coming from behind him. Andrew rotates his chair to inspect his office.

A gasp escapes his lips when Andrew sees the image of the hooded man outside of his window. The metallic cherubims follows Andew's movements, sensing the fear coming from their "Messiah".

Before Andrew can fully comprehend what he's seeing, the window begins to crack suddenly, glass now shattering into his office. In a state of panic, Andrew darts out of his chair, reaches into a compartment inside of his desk, and retrieves a handgun, leaping over the desk for protection.

Gary grins, because of his brother's cowardly action, before allowing himself to float into the office—Gary holding several fragments of glass in the air, with the powers of his mind.

"Don't hide, Andrew! You can *never* hide from me again!" Gary spits. Andrew, hearing his name said, rises to his feet. Andrew is awestruck witnessing Gary before him, hovering off the ground; thousands of broken pieces of glass floats along with Gary.

"THERE YOU GO!" Gary blurts in a frightening tone.

With a thought, glass shoots in Andrew's direction. Wide eyed, he crosses his arms above his face for protection.

"GOD, help me!" Andrew screams.

Now, Gary becomes surprised, as AU leaps in Andrew's path. The glass fragments flies towards statue, and shatters into even smaller pieces, harmlessly falling from the cherubim's metallic body.

The sentinel has to be robotic, Gary thinks. AU barely catches the movement of his brother, who tosses his handgun to AU's counterpart. When AG catches the weapon, it begins firing mercilessly at Gary.

A translucent blue sphere appears around Gary, electrical currents crackles outside the orb. Bullets from the gun incinerates upon colliding with the sphere.

The sight of the blue orb bewilders Andrew. Something now triggers in his mind, making Andrew feel as though he'd seen it before.

Gary's mind races, as another thought manifests. AG's feet lift from the ground, as if it's being caught in the grasp of invisible hands. AG struggles to break free of the hold, but it's of no use.

AG's body is swiftly hurled through the shattered window—the living statue falls to the city street below, along with the cold rain.

Horrified by the strange abilities of the unknown intruder, Andrew tries to hit a button on his desk phone to alert security.

Gary catches his attempt.

AU deflects Gary's attention by rushing towards him.

Gary smiles.

Not worried about AU's attack.

The blue sphere radiates even more, as AU jumps at the illumination. The cherubim reaches out its hand, coming within inches of the orb. Gary's confident that the limb will burn to vapor, but to his surprise, AU's melting hand punches through the sphere.

Defensively, Gary moves his head back before the molten hand could scorch his skin. He immediately used his mind to push

AU away, pushing with such a force, that the cherubim speeds through the air. Andrew ducks, nearly missing a collision with the living statue.

AU's form violently crashes through the office door, and collides through the building's interior. The cherubim then slams through one last wall, on the opposite side of the building, before falling freely to the street; hundreds of feet below—like its counterpart.

The amazingly destructive force Andrew witnesses, leaves him paralyzed in fear. He gazes into the hateful eyes of Gary, as the younger sibling removes the hood that covers his head.

"W-What? What do you want?" Andrew stutters, trying to make sense of the intruder's abilities.

Gary feels as powerful as ever, as he gazes at his cringing brother. Gary lifts his hand, and a white flame manifests, "I want to see you *suffer,* brother."

Before Andrew's eyes can adjust to the glowing flames, Gary points his hand in Andrew's direction. A stream of white fire shoots at the older brother. The manifest fire bears into Andrew's chest, causing him to scream in agony. His internal organs incinerates as the fires tears through his body, before punching out of his back.

The flames vanishes, along with Gary's protective sphere, as Andrew's lifeless corpse falls to the floor; Andrew now having a hole in his torso the size of a basketball. The corpse hits hard onto the floor—Andrew's eyes wide open in sheer terror, staring at his executioner.

Gary's feet come gently to the ground, as he ceases levitating. He somberly approaches Andrew, studying the grotesque scene. Andrew's flesh is burnt so severely that no blood escapes the gaping wound. Gary now bends his legs and grabs at Andrew's collars, pulling him face-to-face.

"Get up, coward, you can't die," Gary growls at Andrew.

He shakes Andrew's head.

Tries to get a reaction.

But none comes.

Gary doesn't want his vengeance to be over, but he knows he's immortal, now guessing that Andrew has the same ability.

Using his thumb, Gary rubs Andrew's forehead, seeking the third eye he'd stared into, the night their parents died.

Andrew's tight skin hid nothing.

"GET UP, ANDREW, THIS IS *NOT* OVER!" Gary demands.

The corpse Gary holds in his hands does not move.

Andrew is in fact, dead.

Instead of the angry glare he had seconds before, Gary's eyes now softens. A doubt enters his mind: *Maybe this isn't Andrew. Or is it? ...Why doesn't he move? The Vowdun had given us both of her gifts...it's impossible for Andrew to be dead.*

The empty gaze of the corpse's eyes stare back hauntingly at Gary. *Maybe Andrew isn't immortal,* he thinks, as the feeling of guilt overwhelms Gary again; plagued with the idea that he's now the murderer of his own brother.

All I wanted to do is make him suffer, make Andrew beg for his forgiveness...but now he's dead.

Gary continues to hold Andrew.

With his free hand, Gary closes Andrew's eyes, and lays his dead brother's body down on the floor.

"What have I done?" Gary whispers to himself, as he turns away from Andrew, walking towards the broken window he demolished. Gary can't bear to look at the mangled corpse any longer; he can't face what he's done.

Standing at the window, Gary's eyes searches down towards the streets, looking for the metallic being he tossed out of the building.

If Gary had looked in Andrew's direction, he would've witnessed the wound in his brother's torso rapidly healing, regenerating all that was destroyed in the attack. He would've also saw Andrew's eyes had opened again.

Instead, he stares down at the tremendous crack in the sidewalk. AG's motionless form lies in the center of it. Pedestrians gather around, gawking at what they believe is a plain statue. Gary's eyes are locked on his destruction, until he hears a distant thumping sound, coming from above. Gary raises his head and sees a helicopter, lowering itself to the window.

Michael Masters is returning from a meeting with members of Lortech's board. Upon arrival, he and the helicopter's pilot witness both of Andrew's statues crashing out the building, which also causes a spectacle aboard the aircraft.

Masters orders the pilot to maneuver to the side of the tower where Andrew's office is, instead of the building's roof. Masters sees the shattered window, and a man who isn't Andrew staring at him. Immediately, Masters call in to security, sending a team to Andrew's office.

Masters now tells the pilot to move closer to the building, pulling out his handgun while opening the helicopter's door. Masters aims the nine-millimeter at the unknown intruder. Amused by what he sees, Gary raises his hand, focuses his powers; with every intention to crush the helicopter like a can.

A strong hand grabs the back of Gary's head, making him lose his train of thought. Before Gary can use his abilities to defend himself, Andrew slams the front of Gary's skull into a nearby wall. His face slides down on it, leaving a trail of blood. Gary then falls limply on his back, unconscious.

The helicopter hovers dangerously close to the broken window. A brisk breeze enters Andrew's office, as Masters jumps into the building, risking death. He lands hard, rolling over to his feet. The chief of Lortech's security soon aims his gun at Gary's downed form.

Andrew stands over Gary, breathing harshly, shocked. He can't take his eyes off of his almost assassin. Yet, Masters is more interested in the two burnt ovals in the front and back of Andrew's suit.

"Mr. Taylor, what happened?"

"I believe someone failed in their attempt on my life!" Andrew says, suspecting his rival, Alberto McKoon, because of his attacker's phenomenal abilities. He then touches his muscled mid-section in awe, remembering the agony he endured, yet the attack seems surreal to Andrew, as if he hallucinated what the intruder did to him.

"What happened to your suit?" Masters questions.

Andrew is puzzled.

He pushes the troubling memories aside, snapping to attention; ignoring Master's question.

"I want this man contained in the lab, and kept under sedation before he has a chance to wake. Use KD-49's serum. I want to find out everything about his biology. Perhaps Taterax has just handed us their most prized creation. Have someone retrieve AU and AG before this commotion gets out of hand, and becomes too public for our own good," Andrew instructs.

"AU and AG?" Masters asks bewildered.

Andrew gives him a stone glare: "My statues!" he adds, as a security team enters his office with weapons drawn. Andrew then shakes his head in disgust of their lateness.

If not for the resurrection that he isn't aware of, bringing him back from death, Andrew would already be lost.

TEN

Darkness....

Darkness light can't penetrate.

Lost in an empty abyss of nothing.

A void of vacancy...

Not cold.

Nor hot.

Empty.

A maddening deprivation from the world...

"A-R-R-R-R-R-R-R-R-R-R-R-R-R-G-H!"

Gary screams out in rage.

His shrieks are silent in the strange world of nothingness where he's imprisoned. But this was like no other prison Gary had ever been to.

He can't feel his body.

Can't hear his heartbeat.

Gary knows he's alive, somehow.

He's alone in a hellish chamber of no images.

No inhabitants.

Alone.

With only his sadistic mind...

"HELP M-E-E-E-E-E-E-E-E-E-E-E!"

No help will come.

The void has none to give.

"His brain waves are spiking!" Karen Scott states, as she monitors Gary's condition.

Gary is stationed in the same room KD-49 was in earlier today. Andrew now observes his attacker, peculiarly on the giant screen.

Gary is stripped down, naked.

A state-of-the-art virtual simulator is worn on his head, preventing Gary from seeing or hearing anything in the outside world. Many wires are injected into his veins, feeding him nutrients, along with a steady dosage of KD-49's serum, which halts the use of Gary's nerves; giving him no feeling of his body. Other devices are strapped to his genitals and anal cavity, disposing of any discharge.

Andrew is fascinated by the young man Lortech's security team has now captured, witnessing Gary's capabilities earlier up close and personal; Andrew believing that he was sent by Alberto McKoon.

Andrew wants to find out how Taterax possess such technology, to allow Gary to levitate, and move objects without touch. Yet, Andrew's bothered by the fact that the subject made him "believe" he was dead; Andrew still trying to find logic in what he experienced.

Andrew remembers feeling the flame, and as the agonizing torture arose—everything went black. The next thing he recalls is awakening, seemingly unaffected by the flames.

Prior to this, Andrew recalls the intruder staring at him out the window, their scuffle, and Andrew taking advantage of the situation, bringing Gary down.

But there's the evidence of the suit he's wearing—the burnt oval holes are in the front and back of Gary's suit.

Real evidence, but how?

Regaining his focus, Andrew watches the biological charts on Karen's computer screen.

"What do you mean his brain waves are spiking? Is something wrong?"

"The environment I programmed is blank. The subject is in a state-of-shock, sir. Maybe we should—"

"Maybe we should what, Karen? Stop the drugs and take off the *damn* helmet? I've seen what this guy can do, and I'm *not* willing to take that chance. I want you to find out how he's able to do the things he did."

Karen now hits a command on her computer's keyboard, and it shows a display of Gary's brain.

"I believe I already have, sir, before you came down here, or I might just have found the origin of it. I've scanned his whole body, and I'm currently working on his DNA; he has no cybernetics. It seems he's basically human, but look here sir."

Karen enters another command, and the computer monitor enlarges the section she indicating.

"It's his temporal lobe, sir."

Andrew studies the monitor eagerly, until he notices what the scientist is trying to show him.

"Is it me, or is something wrong with the computer chart?" Andrew questions, baffled by what he sees.

"No, Mr. Taylor, it's real. The subject's temporal lobe is *four* times larger than the average Homo sapiens. This might be the origin of his abilities," Karen tells, she being fascinated with the find.

With her brilliant scientific research, Karen is well aware of the mysteries of the brain, and she's come to learn that the temporal lobe is one of its greatest secrets.

Andrew, who is now perplexed, looks at Karen with a confused expression upon his face, thinking that Taterax has such technology to alter humans in such a way.

"I viewed the security cameras," The scientist begins, reflecting on seeing Gary rise from the ground outside of Lortech's tower. He moved so fast, the cameras barely caught the ascending to Andrew's office. What transpired within the confines of the office is a different matter, being that Andrew doesn't allow any cameras in his private space.

"...And what I've seen, has me lead to determine that the subject possesses psychogenic capabilities above normal humans. If it weren't for the serum and the virtual simulator, he would be tearing this lab apart!" Karen adds.

"Psychogenic? So you believe the abilities originate from his mind?" Andrew asks.

"In theory, it is possible, Mr. Taylor. Some scientists state that we use a very small percentage of our mental powers, but this subject has abnormal growth in his temporal lobe. As you know, sir, our corporation is in the business of making the impossible possible, through our developments."

Andrew listens carefully to the scientist as she continues.

"I've also taken the liberty of checking the subject's fingerprint on the national databanks," Karen adds with a smile. She now hits a few more keys, and the screen brings up a mug shot, along with the captured specimen's birth date and police records.

"Now, this *doesn't* make sense. Car theft, gun possession and drug sales? It must be wrong." Andrew states, confused by the rap sheet he reads. *Why would Taterax use a twenty-one-year-old criminal to assassinate me, let alone give him such abilities?*

From what Andrew gathers, the police records doesn't fit the description of the man who attacked him, Gary, having such amazing power.

No, it has to be false, Andrew thinks again. He looks at the name on the screen. It reads, *"Gary Romulus, a.k.a. 'Exodus'"*.

"This is *ludicrous,* it *can't* be true."

"We can find out if it is, sir. It says that Gary Romulus was released from *Rikers Island Prison* barely three weeks ago. We can do a background check," Karen offers.

Andrew rubs his left thumb and index finger on his upper lip, trying to systematically analyze what has happened to the man, who's strapped down like a guinea pig in the containment room. Andrew wonders if Taterax experimented on Gary, using the man just to assassinate Andrew.

How? ...Why? It's too risky.

Soon after, he glances at the screen, and then at Karen, who watches Andrew intently, waiting for an answer.

Andrew thinks about what Gary said, and how he knew his name. This isn't what really bothers Andrew though, what haunts his mind is the other thing Gary mentioned: *"You can never hide from me again."*

It's as though the subject knows me personally, and there was envy in his tone. Assassins don't envy their targets, Andrew thinks.

Karen's computer screen suddenly blinks and changes, showing a warning of Gary's erratic brainwaves.

"Sir, the subject is going mad in there. Maybe I should download an environment program, to give his mind some stimulation. If I keep the program on deprivation too long, he's liable to become schizophrenic," Karen states concernedly. By the tone of her voice, Andrew senses that Karen is sympathetic to Gary.

"No you won't, his mental health is a chance *I'm* willing to take."

"But, Mr. Taylor, he's *not* a cyborg, he's human!"

"That depends on your *perception* of this matter," Andrew adds coldly, remembering the scorching heat he felt at the attack. Karen composes herself.

"I'm going to have someone investigate this Gary Romulus—I want a *full* background check! I want to know where he was born, the names of his parents, grandparents and siblings, if he has any. I *have* to know every detail of Gary Romulus' life, before I believe this person truly exists."

Andrew begins to walk away from the control deck, but Karen stops him by grabbing his left wrist. Andrew rotates to face her, as the scientist removes her glasses.

"Give me a moment, sir. I think I have a better solution." Karen pauses briefly, curiously gazing into Andrew's eyes. "...I can interface you into his virtual world, so you two can be face-to-face, so to speak. Within the simulation, you can ask the subject any question you want, and I can monitor his readings, to ascertain whether he's telling the truth or not. I can make him believe he's back in the real world, so the subject will feel secure.

"Also, by using the simulator, you will be perfectly safe, because his abilities will not work in the program. If you give me a couple of days, I can have the interface ready," Karen suggests, still holding on to the Andrew.

For a second, by the glance of Andrew's eyes, she believes he'll be open-minded to the experiment. But Karen's hopes quickly fades, when Andrew yanks his arm free of her grasp.

"I don't *need* to speak with that monstrosity, Karen. He nearly *killed* me! After I find out who this man is, and how Taterax developed him, I'll have *all* the information I need. The subject will be dissected and put on ice for further study, like guinea pig it is; understood?" Andrew spits.

Karen is appalled, because of his lack of compassion. She finds herself avoiding Andrew's stare, gazing at the floor.

"Understood, sir."

Andrew gives Karen one last glance before proceeding out the laboratory. The scientist is unsettled, as she sits back at her console.

The readings of Gary's brain bother Karen. They're so chaotic, unlike the calmness of KD-49's brain, which has no inkling of humanity. Gary's human after all, and the deprivation simulation is driving him insane.

Karen knows that if she doesn't do something, his mind will shatter like broken glass in a few short days. If that happens, Lortech will surely lose the subject. Karen has seen it happen hundreds of times with the simian test subjects.

She has made up her mind. Karen respects Andrew and the position of power he holds, but she knows that he's letting his anger over Gary's attempt on his life, cloud his better judgment.

Karen's diligent hands begin furiously typing on the computer's keyboard. The scientist downloads a more suitable environment, one that won't put as much strain on Gary's distraught thoughts.

"It's for the better," she whispers. As the program runs, Karen's mind is already plotting on a way that she can communicate with Gary Romulus.

* * * * *

Gary still yells out in desperation within the black abyss, where he is held captive. Shortly, his surroundings suddenly change. A stunning, golden light makes Gary shut his eyelids, as his irises adjusts to the rays of what appears to be the sun, shining brightly above him.

Gary raises his hand to cover his face, and for the first time since he awakened in this unbelievable nightmare, Gary notices that he has a body; one with no physical sensation.

Instinctively, Gary pinches his skin with his right hand.

It doesn't sting.

Gary doesn't even feel pressure from the ground he now stands on. He searches the area surrounding him. It appears that Gary's in a forest. He now even hears birds singing, and the chirps of an insect, letting Gary know there's life in these woods.

It's all too strange.

For a moment Gary wonders if he's truly dead, but before Gary couldn't die—can he now? The memories of what happened before Gary enters this strange world, surfaces.

He'd broken the metallic statues in Andrew's office, before using his powers to burn a hole through Andrew's chest. Gary remembers how he waited for him to revive, but Andrew didn't.

Gary also remembers how he was about to take down the helicopter, until someone grabbed him, pushing Gary's head into the wall before he retaliated. Gary has no recollection after that moment, nothing.

"Maybe I'm dead," he says out loud, not hearing his own voice. Gary now concentrates, trying to lift his body from the ground. His powers don't work. Disappointed that his supernatural abilities no longer work, Gary gradually begins venturing into his surroundings, not knowing where he will end up.

Gary's ignorant to the fact that the world around him is nothing more than digital information, while in the real world, being strapped down to a metal table.

* * * * *

Karen Scott continues inspecting Gary's brain activities. They're calming to a normal range. The scientist smiles pleasingly.

* * * * *

A total of two hours pass since Andrew's first encounter with Gary. The repair crew, escorted by a security team, is leaving his office, just as Andrew steps out of the elevator.

Michael Masters greets him when Andrew walks into the room, that hours ago, almost was Andrew's grave. The living statues, AU and AG, lie in the middle of the floor on their backs, unmoving. The beings were retrieved, immediately after the threat of Gary Romulus was eliminated.

Masters studies the president of Lortech closely, bewildered by the unexpected events that has unfolded.

"I don't know where to start, Andrew, this is unbelievable," Masters remarks.

"Karen is studying the assailant as we speak. Did anyone get hurt when the statues hit the streets?"

Masters shakes his head, "No. It did startle some civilians though. I already have our public relations team feeding the media a story about a freak-renovation accident. And if that isn't suffice, we'll just have to make a donation to the mayor, so he'll forget about the fiasco."

"Very well, Masters. The name of the attacker is Gary Romulus."

"How did he *do* this?" Masters questions awkwardly, reflecting the scene of the office a few hours earlier.

"Karen has a theory that he used his mind. The subject has abnormal growth in a certain section if his brain. My guess is that he's one of Taterax's creations, and they're the one's who sent him here to kill me."

As Andrew speaks, Masters can sense the anger in his tone. He watches as Andrew approach his statues, Andrew kneeling beside them before he continues.

"I want you to find out who this Gary Romulus is. Karen will fill you in on the information she has. I want you to learn everything, and *anything* you can about him, Masters. I need to know *every* detail of his life, down to if he pissed in the bed. If Taterax has more like him, they have a major advance over us," Andrew hisses.

Masters places his hand on his boss' shoulder, causing Andrew to look up at him.

"Okay, Andrew, I will get back to you when all this is accomplished," Masters says before leaving the office. Once alone, Andrew's attention falls on his cherubims lying motionless. The only damage retained is AU's melted arm.

Andrew reaches down.

Touches AU's limb.

He's awestruck when it begins to change into the living liquid that Andrew saw when he first discovered the being. Suddenly, Andrew remembers his conversation with Desmond Jones, and the story the archeologist told him. Again, Andrew is fascinated to know the origin of who created the cherubims.

"AU? ...AG?" Andrew stammers, as he watches AU's gold hand reforming itself, back to the original forge. AG soon rises miraculously to his feet—AU now does the same.

Andrew stares at them with admiration, before hearing that familiar, simultaneous voice: *"What is your will, Messiah?"*

He doesn't answer.

Instead, Andrew reaches into his jacket pocket and grabs his cell phone, dialing out to his aging friend. The phone rings four times before it's answered.

"Greetings Yoshi," Andrew says in *Japanese.*

"Andrew, son, I'm pleased to hear from you so soon."

Andrew pauses before speaking. He contemplates on the grave decision he's about to make.

"...Yoshi, I've reviewed the documents. I want you to dispose of the melanin virus, before any further outbreaks occur."

"Understood."

"Also, I've made a decision about your offer." Yoshi fully comprehends what Andrew means. "Activate the termination!" Andrew blurts, voice now stricken with anger.

On the other end of the line, Yoshi Hiro nods his head in agreement: "It shall be done," Yoshi answers, in a way that shows no reaction to the magnitude of what Andrew requested. "Is that all?"

"Yes."

"You have chosen the right path," are Yoshi's last words before he hangs up.

Andrew closes his eyes and grimaces.

The trauma of events has caused him to suffer a migraine. The pain is most felt in the middle of Andrew's forehead. The troubling thought of what Gary did to him returned.

Andrew opens his shirt.

Exposes his bare chest.

Index finger inspects the skin.

I felt those fires burn me—I saw the smoke marks in my suit when it happened.

Then there were the wounds. Andrew wonders if Gary has caused him to hallucinate the events, in order to torture his mind, but why?

It no longer matters. Andrew is alive, and soon his corporate enemy will be dead: *Alberto McKoon will pay for what he did!*

There's no turning back from this. Andrew realizes, that in war, death *is* an intimate partner. He can't allow any more attempts on his life, especially by creations of Taterax.

*   *   *   *   *

An hour later, Andrew leaves the Lortech tower, to go to his penthouse in *Manhattan,* for much needed rest. He believes that a couple of hours of sleep will relieve his mind of the stress that plagues Andrew.

Tomorrow, Andrew hopes that he'll be in control of his life, knowing how Taterax created Gary Romulus, and continue to successfully run the corporation his father intended him to do.

Fate instead, will hold a more devastating blow for Andrew, one that will come as a ravenous storm—swallowing, before leaving an aftermath; which will never be recovered.

ELEVEN

Domna Kenshu waits patiently in the shroud of night, to perform his duties. It's been three days since Yoshi Hiro gave the *Japanese* assassin orders to kill Alberto McKoon. Domna doesn't want his employer to wait another day before he accomplished the termination.

Today, he stakes out the complex of McKoon's mansion in *White Plains, New York*. The bodyguards are all accounted for; Domna knows their shifts and how they search the grounds.

Wearing black, tight-fitting clothing, with a gun strap holding a .38 caliber handgun, silencer on it's nozzle, Domna moves silently through the perimeter, with the slyness of a panther. He's extremely careful not to trip any security alarms that will compromise his concealment.

Once Domna is close enough to the mansion, he quickly scales a wall that leads to the balcony of McKoon's master bedroom. It's risky, but it's a chance the man is willing to take.

He peers through the windowpane and sees McKoon's sleeping body, covered by ruffled blankets. Domna takes a fleeting glance at his watch—it's 3:45 AM. He has a full fifteen minutes before the security makes their hourly rounds, more than enough time to put a bullet in the head of the CEO of Taterax's skull.

Easily, Domna picks the multi-locked door, making precautions not to wake his target. The assassin pulls his gun from its holster, and silently approaches McKoon's bed. Domna doesn't notice his nostrils widen, as McKoon inhales the foreign scent within his home, as an animal notices its prey.

McKoon lies on his back, with his head slightly turned in the man's direction. Domna raises his gun, bringing the nozzle within inches of his target's skull. In the moment of accomplishment, between the seconds of life and death, McKoon's eyes open.

Startled by not only being discovered, but also noticing the strange shape of McKoon's irises, Domna immediately squeezes the trigger.

It's too late.

119

McKoon moves swiftly, grabbing the man's wrist, making the bullet miss its intended target. Domna tries to forcefully punch McKoon with his free hand, as he's thrown off-balance by the man who's twisting his wrist.

Suddenly, McKoon leaps out of his bed, causing Domna to bend over. The pressure McKoon puts on the assassin's arm, causes Domna's limb to stick out straight in the powerful hold.

He now grits his teeth, and fights back the urge to scream, as McKoon brutally uses his forearm to strike down between Domna's elbow.

The hard blow cracks the man's arm in half, a broken bone tears out of Domna's flesh. Blood spills out of the wound, trickling to the glossed wooden floor, along with the assassin's handgun.

Pain rings through Domna.

His eyes become bloodshot.

In a fit of anger, McKoon pulls hard on the injured limb, before Domna's thoughts can recover from the shock of his injury. Swiftly, McKoon now smashes Domna's face into the bedroom wall; the assassin immediately sees a flash before falling to his knees, in a chaotic jumble.

Floating visions dance, as Domna soon feels McKoon's large hands run through his hair. Domna's hair roots tighten, before McKoon forcefully turns his head to the left.

Driven by determination, Domna grabs the eleven-inch knife that's strapped to his thigh. He believes he can still succeed in terminating his target.

Domna, focusing all of his strength in his only useable arm, rotates wildly and breaks free of McKoon's powerful grasp. The assassin now swipes the blade at the man's neck. McKoon quickly ducks, avoiding the knife, retaliating by delivering a sharp, uppercut punch to the assailant's chin.

The blow stuns Domna!

He doesn't have a chance to react as McKoon clutches the knife-wielding hand, twisting Domna's arm behind his back. The assassin is soon slammed hard onto the floor, as he lies in his own blood.

With a grim push by McKoon, Domna's left arm pops out from his shoulder socket. The assailant, once again, fights back the overwhelming urge to scream, now pinned to the floor, crippled beyond recuperation.

McKoon quickly twists his fingers into the Domna's hair, pulled the man's head back, causing Domna's neck to strain unnaturally.

"I smelt your scent as soon as you came into my bedroom—who sent you?" McKoon hisses.

If Domna wasn't lying on his chest, with his diminishing sight staring at McKoon's bed, he would be able to see the eyes of the man he was sent to kill. Domna would also know that McKoon is beyond *anything* that he can comprehend.

Yet, it's too late, far too late.

If Domna had known, he would've never taken the job.

"GO TO *HELL*, WHITE DOG!" the assassin growls in his native tongue in defiance.

"*Japanese,* huh?" McKoon taunts.

Using his unoccupied hand, McKoon retrieves Domna's silver knife. He admires the reflection of light that sparkles from its sharp edge. McKoon then places the tip of the blade on the assassin's neck. Domna inhales, in the anticipation of his death.

"I will ask you *again,* who sent you?" McKoon orders.

Domna refuses to respond.

He will not cower in the threat of his demise. Domna already has failed the hit, to also give information, will forever bring shame upon him.

McKoon isn't amused.

He now removes the blade from the assassin's neck, and brings it to Domna's back, just between his shoulder blades.

McKoon coldly drives the knife into Domna's spine.

For the first time, the assassin screams hellishly, as McKoon quickly rips the knife downward, until he reaches Domna's lower back.

"I can torture you *all* night if I choose to," McKoon spits, as he furiously flips Domna over. "Then, I'll *cut* off your balls!"

Domna's eyes widens in shock.

His terror grows more when he stares at McKoon's face, the man who causes him such agony. McKoon's skin complexion is extremely pale, so white, that it appears as if he's dead. McKoon's brows are arched insanely, but the most terrifying feature is his crimson-colored eyes.

They aren't human.

They're the eyes of a serpent.

Domna believes what he sees is not a man, but rather a demon.

The assassination is botched; Domna can no longer move his arms, nor legs. There's no chance of escape it seems.

But there is one.

Domna feared of this ever happening, yet, he has no other choice. Using his tongue, the assassin mercifully pushes off the cap of his left molar, freeing a pill Domna never wanted to use. He can already taste its chalky bitterness.

Forcing himself to do the unthinkable, Domna swallows a cyanide capsule, says a silent prayer.

"BAKIMA!" Domna soon shrieks, as his throat is constricted from the poison's immediate effect. Breathing now shallow, Domna smiles. His vision soon fades, as the cold blanket of death embraces him.

McKoon notices the lack of strain in the assailant's movements. He bends down closely atop of Domna, feels for a pulse. There is none.

In a way, McKoon admires the assassin's restraint from giving up his employer, but just by the language Domna had spoke, added to McKoon's suspicion of who sent him.

Knowing full well of his provocation of Andrew Taylor is most likely the reason. But McKoon also feels that Andrew doesn't have the stomach to order the botched hit: *It has to be someone else within Lortech.*

Someone who McKoon is aware that came to *America* a few days ago—Yoshi Hiro. McKoon now grins decisively, as he firmly grips the knife in his hand.

Andrew made a mistake in ordering the termination of the president of Taterax. It is not a man who he tried to have killed, but the leader of a cabal of unimaginable power.

The bedroom door soon opens slightly ajar. One of McKoon's most-trusted bodyguards, Loki steps in. The man glares intently towards his leader—Loki isn't bothered at all by the gruesome scene.

"You handled that well, McKoon. I can't believe the assassin truly thought we would let him get that far unnoticed," Loki grimly states.

McKoon's eyes lifts to the man: "Sometimes the spider must abandon his web. Once Lord Moon allows us, Andrew

Taylor and all that his father created, will be annihilated by the Jinn Legion."

"So be it," Loki adds, as he leaves the bedroom, quietly closing the door behind him.

Left alone in darkness, McKoon commences to his mayhem. He mercilessly slashes the throat of the corpse below him, over and over, and over again.

TWELVE

"Andrew…Andrew I want you to know before I give you these documents, that what I've uncovered is wholly confidential. It took some diligent research, but…" Masters says before pausing. His demeanor is somber and distant, as though he can't continue.

Andrew's left eyebrow rises in suspicion, because of the man's odd behavior. It has been nearly a week since he gave Lortech's Chief of Security orders, to investigate the background of Gary Romulus. Now, Master's stand gazing at the floor of his office, holding a briefcase tightly in his hand.

"What is it, Masters? Continue," Andrew says worriedly.

Masters gives Andrew a frozen stare, before approaching the newly installed marble desk. He slowly places the briefcase atop the structure.

"Sir, Gary Romulus is real, his identity has been confirmed through several sources, but, in the process of discovery, I came across some rather bizarre findings."

"Well, what is it?"

As Andrew asks the question, he notices that Master's lip begins to quiver. Masters then presses the two locked mechanisms on his briefcase before pulling it open.

"Andrew, in my *sincerest* regards, I'm asking you to forget about these documents."

"Are you *insane,* Masters? You're asking me to just up and forget, or disregard the possibility that I might find out who that *abomination* is that we have in the lab?"

"With all due respect, sir, I am," Masters answers back sternly, with a glare that brings a morbid feeling over his superior.

"I can't do that, Masters."

Masters breathes out harshly, almost angrily: "It's your call, Andrew, but be warned, you will *not* like what you find. Once Pandora's box is opened, it can never be closed."

Masters then turns the opened case to Andrew before leaving the office hastily. Andrew's eyes follow him the whole way. He's awestruck by the things Masters said, as if he was trying to give a warning.

It would be highly doubtful for Andrew to just turn his back on the findings of the origin, of the man who almost killed him, using abilities no other human on earth possesses to his knowledge. Andrew has to find out why and how.

His attention falls on the large amount of papers before him. At the very top of the stack is a copy of Gary Romulus' birth certificate. Andrew reads every detail.

Gary's father is Wilfred Romulus, his mother—Marylyn Frazier Romulus. Gary was born in *New Rochelle, New York.* Andrew removes the birth certificate from the top of the documents and studies the next page.

It's an adoption document from the Kennedy Adoption Center of *New York.* A photo of a four-month old baby is on the top left corner—the picture is of Gary Romulus. Andrew carefully reads the document. It states that Gary's parents died in a car crash in *Port-au-Prince, Haiti.* Andrew is intrigued, he keeps on reading, until Andrew comes across something that startles him.

The document states that Gary Romulus' only living relative is Andrew Frazier. At first, Andrew pays no mind of the fact, until he studies the age and birth date of Andrew Frazier.

His heart skips a beat.

Gary's brother has the same birth date as my own.

A cold sweat begins to bead on Andrew's forehead.

...The attacker did refer to me as "brother".

Something at the time Andrew interpreted as slang.

"It *can't* be," Andrew whispers to himself. For a moment, the president of Lortech's hand refuses to move, as if he understands why Master's didn't want to give him the documents in the first place. Conquering his fears, Andrew turns to the next page, wanting to dismiss what's becoming an insane thought.

His pulse quickens.

Andrew views the next document...

Towards the top left side of the adoption form is a photo of a three-year-old child. The little boy's young rounded face makes Andrew want to tear his eyes from it. The adoption form states: *"Andrew Frazier. Father: unknown. Mother: Marylyn Frazier Romulus".*

Andrew forces himself to read on.

By the time he gets to the last line, Andrew's eyes water with conflicting emotions. The document is legitimate and notarized, but to Andrew, sitting down gritting his teeth, a wave of rage overwhelming him, can't believe what he's read.

At the bottom of the adoption form indicates the adoptive parents: *"David and Valerie Taylor"*.

A guttural scream loudly wails throughout Andrew Taylor's office, a scream so agonizing, it comes from the deep, naked core of he who unleashes it.

The scream turns into a cry of confusion, a cry of anger. It's the cry of a man, terribly shattered by his own opening of Pandora's box. Andrew feels the sorrow of a king, one who was truly born a peasant.

* * * * *

One level below Andrew's office, Masters rises from his chair when he sees the president of Lortech storming down the corridor, heading for his office. Masters notices that Andrew's holding the briefcase he brought to Andrew, two hours prior.

Andrew bursts through Master's door.

Violently slams the briefcase atop of his desk.

"What the *hell* is this, Masters, some sick *fucking* joke?" Andrew snaps. By his remark, Masters can tell that the documents have enraged his superior; watery, glazed eyes of Andrew, clearly reveals his pain.

Masters himself had uncovered all of the information. He went over every last detail from start-to-finish, even using some of his tactile influences to find out some of the things that were classified.

Every step had taken Masters deeper-and-deeper into the investigation, until he had to face the saddening truth of his employer's past. Something Masters didn't want to believe.

"I'm sorry, Andrew, it's not a joke. I wish it were, but it's not." Masters says as calmly as possible in the troubling situation.

Andrew rushes at him, unexpectedly knocking the older man off his feet; Master's back crashing into a nearby wall. Andrew now has him pinned, clutching both of Masters' collars tightly. He can feel Andrew's knuckles pressing painfully into his shoulder.

The angry attack catches Masters off-guard; he has never seen Andrew in such a chaotic state of emotional distress.

"Did McKoon put you up to this? ...He sends one of his experiments to try to *kill* me, then for some sick, perverted reason, he forges documents to get me to believe that, that thing in KD-49's lab is my brother!" Andrew hisses.

Masters is beginning to feel lightheaded from the lack of oxygen to his brain, his eyes widens as he speak: "Listen to yourself, Andrew, you sound crazy. Why in the *hell* would I do that? My loyalty was to your father and his corporation, now my loyalty is to *you,* and only you, not him. Just calm down and pull yourself together."

Masters is first ignored, but soon after, he feels Andrew's grip loosen. Finally, as Andrew becomes aware of his actions, he lets go Masters entirely. Masters then takes a step away from Andrew and smoothes the wrinkles in his shirt.

"I *personally* did the research and investigation you ordered me to do. If I'd known that it would've lead to what I found, I would've turned my back on it."

Andrew's cold stare follows Masters' every move.

"This can't be true, Masters. I—"

"Andrew, I interviewed the employers where Gary Romulus and..." Masters pauses for a moment, not knowing how to say his next sentence, "...and you were adopted. It checked out. I'm *sorry* that you had to find out something like this in such a way."

"You're wrong, this is some *cruel* setup from someone who's out to *destroy* me, and they tricked you, too!"

"I only wish that were true, Andrew. I've seen the records. I—"

"SHUT UP!" Andrew demands. He doesn't want to hear anymore. Andrew wants to believe that this is some sort of horrible nightmare he'll soon wake up from. But that won't happen. His new reality is now like a chasm, ready to pull him in more.

Soon after, Andrew forces a weak smile, trying to avoid showing his true distress. It doesn't work.

"I know what to do, I know how to prove these documents are wrong, you'll see," Andrew then states, while removing the briefcase from Masters' desk. Andrew's last comment is more like a threat to prove his identity.

Masters watches on as Andrew hastily leaves the office. Andrew is someone who's always cool, calm and collected—a prominent reflection of the twenty-three-year-old man's genius. He always wise beyond his reasonable years.

Masters has just witnessed the frustration of his employer's youth and weakness. If Andrew had turned around for a second, he would've seen the slight hidden smile on the Masters face.

* * * * *

It's 9 PM, and Andrew's chauffeured limousine now drives through the front gates of his mother's *East Hampton* estate. He notices that many vehicles are parked on her property. At first Andrew is surprised, until he realizes it's the day of the "Shattered Dreams" fundraiser.

A valet opens the doors to the vehicle and greets Andrew with a friendly smile, one that Andrew ignores, as he enters his mother's home.

Andrew hears violins playing a rather calming symphony. Many of the event partakers respectfully give their "hellos" to him, while others, wonder why Andrew isn't dresses appropriately for the occasion.

He rudely ignores them all, as Andrew desperately searches for his mother, with the conviction that she can clarify the outlandish documents in the briefcase he clings to.

Through the crowd, Andrew finally catches his mother's eyes, and when Valerie Taylor sees her son she smiles, gesturing for Andrew to come to her.

Valerie, standing next to Sharon Puwa, is engaged in what seems to be an interesting conversation. Andrew approaches Valerie. He tries to smile, but finds he can't, no matter how hard Andrew attempts.

His mother knows that something's wrong.

Not only is Andrew in his business attire holding a briefcase, but his eyes are red and swollen also, as if Andrew had been crying, or fighting back the urge.

Sharon can also sense her former lover's distraught nature. Disregarding her last meeting with Andrew, she kisses his left cheek.

"Andrew, are you okay? You seem to be ill," Sharon states. Andrew gives her a fleeting glance, before returning his attention back to Valerie.

"Mother, I need to speak with you."

"Then speak, dear," Valerie says frankly.

"No, mother, I *need* to speak with you privately," Andrew says in a pleading tone that his mother notices.

Valerie now hands Sharon the champagne-filled glass flute that she's drinking from: "Pardon me, Sharon. I'm sure we'll finish our conversation before the night is over," Valerie assures apologetically.

"I'm sure we will, Mrs. Taylor," Sharon adds, as Valerie and Andrew walk away.

Andrew leads his mother up the stairs, and into a quiet bedroom in the west wing of her home, where they won't be disturbed by anyone. Andrew shuts the door and faces Valerie, with him having a look of urgency upon his face.

"Son, are you sure that you're not ill? It's highly unlike you to behave in such a manner," Valerie indicates, as she places her palm on the right side of her son's cheek. Andrew's skin is extremely hot, as if he has been jogging, or doing some other form of exercise.

Andrew casually removes Valerie's hand, and places the briefcase he has been holding on a nearby dresser.

Andrew takes a steady breath before opening it...

Doubt, bombards his power to move.

How can Andrew dare question his birthright that he isn't the child of David and Valerie Taylor? They *are* his parents, the ones who raised and guided him to become the man Andrew is today. He now feels it's wrong to do so, but the malicious documents has already destroyed Andrew's ego.

"Andrew, is there a problem at Lortech that you want to discuss with me? I'm your mother, dear, you can tell me anything. ...I remember when your father had problems at the corporation. There were things that he told me, and I always counseled him to the best of my abilities. That always use to help your father, so tell me, dear, maybe I can help you," Valerie says, while sitting on the bed; now bothered by the whole scenario, as she looks at her son's back.

Andrew doesn't face Valerie.

His eyes are tightly shut, but even that can't stop the tears that escape them. Andrew opens the briefcase and retrieves the adoption forms of Gary Romulus and Andrew Frazier.

"Mother...there is something that I *have* to ask you, I just *have* to know if it's true," He states while closing the briefcase. Andrew then approaches Valerie with his arms outstretched, holding the papers—his mother has no inkling to how damaging they are. She takes them from Andrew's hand, and sees the tears that are rolling down his cheek.

"Andrew, why are you crying?" Valerie asks worriedly.

Andrew wipes his face: "Mother, just *please* read the documents, I have to know," he pleads.

Valerie does so, lowering her sight. Instantly, Valerie feels sickened with grief, now realizing what she possesses in her grasp: the adoption sheets of Andrew from the Kennedy Adoption Center of *New York.*

Valerie painfully reads the first page. Inside she wants to burst into tears. For what Valerie held is something that she never wanted Andrew to know, not this way. It's something his mother couldn't bring herself to tell him, but now Andrew knows.

He sees how Valerie reacts as she reads the document—Andrew doesn't know what to make of her body language.

Is mother upset because she's holding false documents? ...Or is it because she knows it to be true? Andrew thinks, praying silently that the documents are false.

Valerie reads the next sheet.

Her eyes widen.

It's the record of Gary Romulus: a brother, twenty years ago, Valerie was never told he had. Andrew mother takes a deep breath, trying hard not to show her inner-emotional state. Valerie places the papers by her side, now finished reading them both. She stares at the ground blankly, not knowing what to say.

"Tell me they are false, mother," Andrew barely says in a whisper. Valerie raises her head to face him.

"Where did you get these, Andrew?" she questions, not wanting to tell him the truth.

"Are they true?" Andrew begs.

Valerie slowly rises from the bed, feeling as if she will lose her strength and fall. Valerie approaches Andrew, wrapping her arms around his shoulder as she hugs him tightly. So tightly, Andrew now can feel her abrupt breathing, as Valerie, the woman he's always known as his mother, set free a river of tears.

Andrew opens his jaw before closing his eyes. Before Valerie can speak, Andrew knows the grim answer he so desperately sought.

"I'm so…I'm *so* sorry, Andrew," Valerie confesses, "I just wanted to protect you," she says and cries. Andrew becomes rigid and numb. As Valerie releases her hold, she gazes into Andrew's watery eyes.

"Why didn't you tell me?"

"I couldn't, I didn't want to, Andrew, especially knowing what happened before we adopted you...I didn't want to hurt you," Valerie tells.

She now wipes the tears from Andrew's cheeks. He clearly sees the pain in Valerie's features; mascara now beginning to run down her face. Valerie is as hurt as Andrew, if not more.

"When you first came into me and David's life, you were so traumatized, because of what happened to your biological parents. Andrew, you became catatonic. I felt so *helpless,* watching you as a three-year-old child being so fragile—you didn't respond to anything. David thought that we'd made a mistake at first, but we both loved you, we *couldn't* give up on you; not for a moment."

Andrew frowns as Valerie continues to speak.

"The psychiatrist warned us that you might not ever come out of the state that you were in, and that we should try other forms of treatment, such as medications, and other therapies to bring down your psychological wall. But I would hear *none* of it! I told them to go to *Hell!*" Valerie says angrily, as the memories surface.

"Andrew, for three months I took care of you. I was by your bedside day and night, praying that someday, you would show some sign of life—a movement, a word; anything to show me that a soul was alive inside of you. The doctors said I was being too objective, but I *knew* you were fighting to come out, Andrew. I *didn't* give up on you—how could I? Then one day, I got an answer to my prayers."

Valerie turns and makes her way to the window.

She opens the curtains.

Admires the stars gleaming in the night sky.

Andrew watches Valerie silently, seeing a smile emerge upon her face, as she reminisces the past.

"It was on a night like this one, Andrew. The sky was clear, but it was winter, and snow was all over. I was sitting by your bedside, reading a story from one of your children's books David had brought for you. I'd dozed off in the morning hours—I guess those books had rather put me to sleep. Later I'd awaken, and was still sitting in that chair, something that had become all too familiar with me.

"I'd wiped the sleep from my eyes, and sitting there in that bed smiling at me was you. At first, it scared the *hell* out of me, and then I thought that I was still dreaming, until you hopped right out of your bed, into my arms. You were full of energy, and you hugged me. I'll *never* forget the words that came out of your mouth: *'I love you, mommy, thank you.'*

"When I heard those soft, kind words come from you, I hugged you so close to me, Andrew, and I cried so much that day, more than I *ever* cried in my life. You should have *seen* the look on David's face when he came home, seeing you running up to him with such a beautiful smile. Yes, GOD did answer my prayers."

Andrew walks up to his mother, and views the stars with her, as she continues.

"The doctor told us that we should never try to get you to remember what happened to your parents, because it could cause you to revert into a severe relapse. I could *never* do that to you. It was if I bore you from my womb, Andrew, *you* became the son I always wanted. And your achievements only made me more proud to be your mother. Andrew…I apologize for keeping such a secret from you, I was wrong, so wrong," Valerie weeps, bowing her head as she cries even more.

Andrew reaches out and gently touches his mother's chin. He softly raises Valerie's head, so that they see each other eye-to-eye. The shock Andrew initially had when he first discovered the secret, is no more as heavy as the sadness that consumed him, before Valerie told Andrew the whole story.

"You weren't wrong at all, mother, you did so much for me. I *am* your son, and you *are* my mother, no matter what. You did what was best—I know that now; please don't be hurt."

Andrew now kisses Valerie's cheek, holds her.

"There's just one more thing I have to ask you mother, and we can put this all behind us."

"Ask me anything, son, I'll tell you," Valerie promises, feeling relieved of the exposed secret she thought would follow her to the grave.

"Why did you pick me instead of Gary?"

"Andrew, I swear, we didn't know. They never *told* us that you had a younger brother. If I'd known, I would have adopted you both. I would have *never* separated you two," Valerie says truthfully before continuing. "Maybe we can find Gary, now that you and I know. It's not too late to find him."

These words haunt Andrew.

How can he tell his mother that he already found Gary? Or rather, Gary has found Andrew, and has tried to kill him? How can Andrew also tell Valerie that he now has his own brother, Gary captured, who's being studied like an animal at the Lortech lab?

He can't.

"Maybe I can find him, mother, and you're right, it's never too late."

Valerie smiles faintly under the circumstances.

Andrew has always thought of her as being a strong woman, now, more than ever, he thinks that she's the strongest woman he's ever met.

The room door now opens.

Andrew and Valerie turn their heads and see Sharon.

"I'm sorry to intrude, but," Sharon says and halts when she sees the look on Valerie and Andrew's faces, noticing that they both seem saddened. "…I apologize. I just wanted to see if you both were okay," she then confesses, moving closer.

"Don't worry about it, Sharon. You're welcomed in any of my rooms, in any of my homes," Valerie assures, putting on a friendly grin. "After all, we're just mother and son reminiscing about our family," Valerie adds while nodding at Andrew, who smiles back in return.

"You're absolutely right. Are you going to be alright, mother? I'll end the gathering if you want me to," Andrew suggests.

"No, I don't want to stop everyone from their fun. You just go on home and get some rest, surely you need it," Valerie now gestures.

Andrew gives his mother another warm hug. He then retrieves the adoption papers from the bed, placing the documents back into the briefcase.

"Andrew, stay for a while," Sharon proposes when he walks by her. Andrew turns to look at the woman—Sharon now places her hand upon his shoulder.

She wants to forgive Andrew for the things he said to her in their last meeting. Sharon doesn't care that he refused to make a donation to her foundation. Sharon knows in some way, at this moment, that Andrew needs her, just as he did when they were children.

Andrew's face is now very close to Sharon's. If he moves any closer, Sharon will kiss him.

She wants to.

Sharon wants Andrew to know that she never stopped loving him. If only Andrew had given Sharon the slightest hint of warmth, she would've passionately kissed him.

Yet, Andrew's drained from the incredible revelations he's had in the last four hours. Even though Andrew can see the approval in Sharon's eyes, he just can't give in to her.

"I wish I could stay, Sharon, but it's best I leave. I have some urgent business to attend to in the morning," Andrew lies.

Before Sharon can say anything more, he leaves the room, holding the briefcase Andrew arrived with. Sharon stares at his fleeing back until Andrew disappears down the hallway, and down the stairs. Her attention turns back to Valerie, who's standing silently.

Sharon slowly approaches the older woman, gazing at the extent of her sadness. She then hugs Valerie sympathetically, not aware how the sadness came about.

"You okay, Mrs. Taylor?"

"Yes, honey," Valerie lies. It will take more time then Valerie knows to move on from her son's discovery. "How's the fundraiser?"

"It's doing well. Let me fix your make-up, and you can see for yourself," Sharon offers.

Valerie soon sits down in front of the beveled glass mirror in the bedroom, looking at her reflection, as Sharon fumbles around in her own handbag, looking for her make-up compact.

"I'm going to take care of you, Mrs. Taylor."

"Please, call me Valerie, Sharon. I've known you since you were a baby after all."

Sharon feels a small joy entering her heart when she hears Valerie's words.

"Come on now and fix me up, darling."

"I sure will. I'm a *fashion* designer, so you *know* you're in good hands," Sharon states proudly.

"Perhaps some day you'll be much more. I'm hoping my daughter-in-law," Valerie adds.

Sharon smiles at her inclination.

The two stare at each other momentarily. Then, out of nowhere, both women begin laughing.

THIRTEEN

Tragedy is that of the soul to bear, Andrew thinks to himself, as KD-49's Anasthesea serum is injected into his veins. There have been a few great discoveries within a short period of time, that it leaves Andrew with the desire to just breakdown and lose himself.

The time of tears has ended.

Now it's time for Andrew to use his intelligence, and find a meaning to make sense of an irrational world.

He's studied all the information he has on his brother thoroughly. So much, that Andrew remembers each line. Record wise, he knows Gary's history, but truth of the matter, Andrew is unaware of who his brother is entirely; mainly how Gary came to possess those magnificent abilities.

There's no record of that.

As the serum rushes through Andrew's circulatory system, it begins to take effect immediately. Andrew no longer feels the pressure of sitting in his chair—his body is now numb of physical sensation.

Andrew has chosen this path. It's something he feels he has to do, or else Andrew's life, and who he actually is, will mean nothing. Gary knows who Andrew is, and has found Andrew after twenty years, but how? Andrew is now driven to find out. He needs to know everything Gary has knowledge of.

Everything.

Knowledge is power, yet ultimate power means unlimited danger, a risk Andrew is willing to take decreases that danger, as much as possible.

Gary's criminal record also leads Andrew to other information, and an unfamiliar name: Melody Black.

The serum now forces Andrew to reflect on the past, and how he loved playing chess, especially as a child with his father; despite the fact of now knowing David Taylor isn't his biological father—although Andrew still thinks of the man who raised him as just that.

Andrew also has found out that his father had abandoned his biological mother, Marylyn before he was even born. There's no signature of his father on the birth certificate, that knowledge doesn't bother Andrew, now feeling that his only blood relative is, unfortunately, strapped down naked on cold steel, in another sector of the lab.

Andrew's mind now drifts back to the game of chess.

The game is like life.

It has its ups and downs, its sacrifices and victories. You have to learn to master the game to outwit your opponent. One also has to develop intuition to know what the person sitting across from you will do, before that person even knows.

David Taylor was Andrew's opponent. When he first taught him the game, Andrew was only five. For three months, his father would beat him at each match. After that, Andrew won every game they played. Often Andrew's mind would be occupied with other things, such as science; nevertheless, he always won.

Karen Scott now places a sticky heart monitor device on Andrew's chest, with similar devices on each side of his forehead. Andrew can't feel it clinging to his skin. The serum has taken its full effect.

Continuing to ponder, Andrew also thinks about how he hates when he can't find the answers to puzzles, frustrating Andrew to the point where he can't sleep. Andrew always wants a solution to everything, and if he can't develop one, Andrew stubbornly comes to the conclusion that one doesn't exist.

Chaos is reckless and without intelligence.

Chaos has no solution.

But chaos remains in perfect harmony with order.

That was the reflection of Andrew's life the day Gary stormed in and tried to kill him, with powers that Andrew couldn't fathom the origin of.

Many thoughts jumble in Andrew's head, he has to sort them, make order of them—order and chaos.

Two weeks ago, hours after Valerie revealed that the adoption documents were true, Andrew headed straight to the Lortech lab, where Gary was being kept in stasis. At first, Andrew wanted to have him killed, so he could hide the truth of his past. Yet, Andrew found that he couldn't give the order.

Instead, Andrew stood there, troubled, staring at his younger brother, whose mind had been trapped in the limbo of simulation. Shortly afterwards, Andrew checked Gary's readings, finding that they weren't as erratic as when he was first detained.

Going against her better judgement back then, Karen told Andrew that she'd changed the simulation environment, so that there would be less strain on Gary's mind. Unbeknownst to Karen, he thanked her silently, and was more than agreeable with the scientist's decision.

Andrew also asked Karen about the technique she could develop, in order to communicate with Gary. During that time, Karen once again, told him the full details of what she could try in theory.

Minutes later, Andrew had a meeting with Michael Masters, fully knowing that the head of Lortech's security and information was a great asset to his company. He took a huge gamble by threatening Masters with the loss of his job and benefits, if he'd ever disclosed any information about Andrew's adoption to anyone.

Masters knew that legally, even though Andrew wasn't David Taylor's biological son, that Andrew was still the president of Lortech, and there was no challenge to the fact. He promised to take Andrew's secret to his grave. After that and other crucial issues were taken care of, Andrew decided to make the toughest decision he'd ever made in his life.

During Andrew's first week of ever touching a chessboard, David Taylor had told him: *"The number of pieces left on the board means nothing. Even if you're left with only two, it is still possible to beat your opponent, as long as you think deeply about your moves. You could still topple an empire."*

Andrew now has all of his pieces set-up.

It's time to witness how his new opponent will play.

The opponent: Gary Romulus.

Prior, Andrew studied every detail of his brother's life, and was planning to use the knowledge to his full advantage when communicating with Gary, during the simulation.

Karen uses a medical flashlight to inspect Andrew's irises.

"Are you ready for interfacing, Mr. Taylor?"

Andrew nods his approval, causing Karen to lift a silver metallic helmet off of her desktop.

"Remember, sir, when in the simulation program, the helmet will scan the electrical output of your brain, so you can move freely. I'll be watching you and the subject's interaction on my computer monitor. Whenever you want me to pull you out, I will, okay?"

"Okay, Karen."

Before she can put the helmet on his head, Andrew stops her. The scientist sees a worried look upon his face.

"Do you want to abort this plan?" Karen asks concernedly.

"No. I want to continue. I just want to say that, I'm glad you're on my team, just in case something goes wrong. I wanted you to know that."

Karen is surprised by Andrew's reply. He never congratulated her on any of her achievements. Karen smiles and touches Andrew hand.

"Thank you, sir, and I promise you, everything will be safe and secure. Let go of your doubts."

Andrew gestures her to attach the helmet, and Karen carefully does so. Not wasting another moment, she straps his legs and arms to the chair Andrew's seated in.

As the large helmet comes over his head, Andrew's vision is lost in darkness. He can't hear any noise in the lab, nor his panicked breathing. Gary had endured this same type of deprivation, this dim, silent death of the real world; Andrew's heartbeat rapidly increases, as he thinks about this somberly truth.

Earphones soon come on.

Andrew now hears his heavy breathing.

"All systems are go, Mr. Taylor."

"Confirmed, Karen."

It's much better since he can hear once again. Andrew slowly relaxes, eyes remaining wide-opened; searching for anything besides the black wall he seems to be imprisoned within. His irises dilate because of the lack of a light source.

"Karen, I see nothing, it's not working."

"I haven't downloaded you into the system, sir. I will give a countdown when the system is ready, okay?"

"Affirmative."

Karen now punches in the commands into her computer, initiating the simulation.

Gary has been in his own dream world for the last three weeks. Karen ran several tests on him, trying to desperately find the origin of his unique abilities. Besides the abnormal growth of

Gary's temporal lobe, she couldn't find any other indication of where his powers came from.

Secretly, Karen admired Andrew for personally taking the risk of finding out the source. What she didn't know is that, Andrew is after something far more detrimental, namely, the answers to his questions of his own past.

A bleeping sound comes from the computer.

Karen instantly looks at her screen.

The program is ready.

The scientist pauses for a moment...

Looks at the biological monitors of Andrew and Gary.

Both are stable.

Andrew's heartbeat beats faster...

He's nervous, and has every right to be.

Other than that, all systems are a go.

Karen bows her head to the microphone on her desk.

"Mr. Taylor, all systems are ready for initiation," she says calmly, now waiting for a reply.

"I'm ready, Karen."

Although the words come from Andrew's lips, he doesn't know what they mean, or what he's ready for.

It's mind-boggling to fully understand.

Andrew's drive has taken him this far, there's no turning back after the point of no return. Or is there?

He won't allow himself to do that. It will be cowardly if Andrew did so. Questions will eat his conscience alive, if Andrew allowed his doubts to conquer the search for the truth.

"Initiating countdown."

Andrew's heart beats even faster. He sees a small, white, circular dot that's in the distance ahead.

"Ten, nine, eight, seven."

As Karen counts down, the light in the distance appears to grow, and speed towards Andrew, as if it will smash into him.

It's not real, Andrew tells himself.

"Six, five, four."

The light is coming quicker, racing towards Andrew.

IT'S NOT REAL!

"Three, two, one, converging systems."

The awesome blaring light consumes Andrew in its glorious illumination. He shuts his eyelids for protection.

But the bright light still blazes through.

FOURTEEN

It takes a few moments before Andrew's eyesight returns to normal. He finds himself staring down at grass, bent down on his knee, feeling nauseated by the ordeal. When Andrew hears birds chirping and the sound of crickets, he knows that Karen has succeeded in interfacing him into the system.

"Mr. Taylor?"

Andrew hears her voice, but doesn't answer at first, fearing that he'll vomit.

"Mr. Taylor?" Karen repeats.

"I'm okay, Karen," Andrew answers, breathing harshly.

"You should get up now, you have company," the scientist warns.

Company? What the hell? Andrew thinks. He begins to raise his heads, and is caught off-guard when he sees Gary staring down at him, with an expression of pure hatred locked upon his face.

"I *knew* it!" Gary hisses, before throwing a hard, brutal kick to Andrew's face. Andrew's body is thrown backwards because of the attack—he involuntarily falls on his back.

Although the kick would've caused serious damage in the real world, in the simulated program, Andrew feels no pain at all. He's fully aware that none of it is real, in which Andrew can't be physically harmed. Gary has some inclination of the strange environment, but he doesn't know the full measure.

Andrew now tries to retaliate, but Gary lands a swift uppercut to his jaw, knocking Andrew back to the ground. Gary leaps on top of him, and immediately begins strangling Andrew. Little does Gary know that it has no affect on his brother's breathing capacity.

"What have you done? Tell me, you piece of *shit!*" Gary shouts. He grips Andrew's throat tighter. Andrew glares at Gary, who's on top of him. Gary has so much hatred within, that it scares Andrew.

"DIE! ...WHY WON'T YOU DIE?" Gary pleads, as his eyes begin to water. He now notices Andrew's face. It isn't the face of a man being strangled, as Andrew's face is calm and serene.

"Why do you want to *kill* me, Gary?"

Gary coils back for a moment when he hears Andrew's voice.

Why isn't Andrew gagging? How can he even speak with his throat constricted? IT DOESN'T MAKE SENSE! Gary thinks to himself.

"Why do you hate me?" Andrew speaks again.

"SHUT THE *FUCK* UP AND DIE!"

Andrew looks at him, seeing Gary's desperation.

"No. I will not," Andrew calmly states.

In one swift movement, he grabs Gary's arm, turning it, as Andrew rolls to his side. Gary's virtual body is pinned to the ground with his arm locked.

"Stop this madness! You want to *kill* me for something I'm not even aware I did, why?" Andrew demands.

Gary doesn't answer.

He only strains to be free of Andrew's hold.

"Mr. Taylor, sir, I think I have a solution," Karen says. Andrew is the only person in the simulation that can hear her.

"What is it, Karen?"

Gary doesn't know whom Andrew is speaking with—he doesn't care.

"Well, sir, I need you to let go of him, and take a step back," Karen implies.

"Are you *crazy,* Karen, what are you planning to do?"

"Trust me, sir. If he attacks you again, just stay totally still. I have an idea."

Andrew now goes against his own judgement. Karen has brought him this far, and she is after all, the creator of the program. Grudgingly, Andrew releases his hold and steps away from his brother, He waits for whatever the scientist has planned. Gary soon stands up, grinds his teeth, and quickly runs at Andrew.

"Karen!" Andrew calls out.

"Don't move," the scientist orders, as Gary pulls his arm back, ready to strike Andrew.

Andrew closes his eyes, and Gary's fist collides with his jaw. There's no power behind the blow, it's as if a feather bounced against a brick wall. Gary throws more punches, one after the other, on different places of Andrew's body.

None have any effect.

Andrew finds himself smiling, because of Karen's plan. The scientist modified the program, so that Gary's strength is useless.

"Thank you, Karen."

"No problem, Mr. Taylor."

"What the *fuck* happened?" Gary questions, bewildered by the alteration.

"Your persistence in trying to harm me is futile, Gary. Now let's talk," Andrew proclaims.

"Talk about *what?*" Gary spits, growing more enraged.

"I want to know why you tried to kill me, when I've never done anything to you. And I want to know how you got your abilities?" Andrew says truthfully.

Gary is disgusted by his brother's arrogance: "MAN, FUCK YOU!" he shouts in defiance.

Andrew shakes his head.

"Who sent you? Was it Alberto McKoon who gave you the order to kill me?" Andrew interrogates further.

"I don't know any *goddamn* Alberto McKoon!"

"You're lying," Andrew retaliates.

"No, he's not, sir. I'm scanning Gary's heart rate and nervous system, he's telling you the truth," Karen interjects. Andrew hears her but doesn't reply.

"Then why do you want me dead?"

"BECAUSE YOU ABANDONED ME!" Gary scowls and shouts.

Andrew is taken aback by Gary's reply. Andrew's face now has a blank expression, caused by the simplicity of his brother's confession.

"You grew up with *everything* you ever wanted, everything you *needed*, but you *never* searched for me! You promised to never leave me, Andrew! YOU PROMISED!" Gary tells, as the emotional pain begins to surface. Andrew hears the turmoil in his younger brother's voice.

"Gary…I didn't even know I *had* a younger brother, until you found me. I didn't even know I was adopted."

Now *you're* the one who's lying. How could you forget? Don't you have the nightmares, the same nightmares that have *haunted* me all my life? They remind me of what happened to our parents, what happened to us!" Gary shouts.

Andrew takes a step closer to Gary before speaking: "I have documents of what happened to our parents. They died in a car crash in *Haiti.*"

"No they didn't! They were *murdered* by the Vowdun witch!"

Andrew stares blankly at Gary...

In all of his brother's records he studied, gave no mentioning of mental illness, but the statement Andrew just heard made him suspect otherwise.

"Listen to yourself, Gary. A *witch* killed our parents? *Witches* don't exist."

"It wasn't a witch. It was a *fucking* monster, or something! I can't explain it, but it happened. I remember, why don't you?"

"I can't remember anything before I was three years old."

"I don't give a *shit* if you think I'm crazy!" Gary defends himself.

Andrew doesn't reply to his profanity.

"How did you get your abilities, Gary?"

"Look, man, *shit*...the witch did it. She changed you and me somehow."

"I don't possess the abilities you do. I'm not like—"

"Yes you are," Gary interjects. He then raises his hand, and places his index finger in the middle of Andrew's forehead. "You had the third eye, Andrew, I remembered it from when I was a toddler, the night our parents died. We were in that car and you carried us out. There was a third eye in the middle of your forehead," Gary recounts.

"That's *ludicrous.*"

"Is it? Then explain why you're alive. I burnt a hole in your chest the size of a basketball, yet you're still here, aren't you?"

Andrew remembers his first encounter with Gary. He recalls how fire emerged from his brother's hand, and the agony Andrew felt when the flames came at him.

But it had to be a hallucination. Gary had to have tricked me, Andrew thinks to himself, although Gary tells him otherwise.

"I grew up with *nothing,* Andrew, then when I learned about my powers, I wanted to make you pay. I *fucked* up when I let my guard down."

Andrew is still digesting the bizarre account of what happened to him in his office that day, when he notices that Gary is quickly walking away. Andrew immediately snaps back to attention.

"Where are you going?" Andrew asks curiously.

"I don't know, I've been *stuck* in this forest so long, it's just more-and-more forest; like I can't escape this *shit!* I don't even know if this is all real—maybe it's just another nightmare that I'll wake up from. I'm used to it," Gary replies.

Andrew runs and catches up to him. "You're right, Gary, it's not real, none of this is" Andrew admits. Gary pauses.

"What?"

"You're in a simulation, Gary, a made-up world."

"I done heard it all. Get the *fuck* out of my way."

"I'll prove it," Andrew states, standing firmly in Gary's way.

"Karen?"

"Yes, sir."

"I want you to alter this environment. Change it into the sector where the body is being held. Can you do that?"

"I can, sir, but do you think it's wise to do so?"

"Please, Karen, just do it."

"Yes, sir."

After the deliberation, Andrew faces Gary. He's being reckless, Andrew knows this, but he feels it's the only way to persuade Gary.

"Gary, I'm willing to make amends for whatever wrongs I've done you."

Gary eyes Andrew cautiously as he continues.

"I've been brought up in a life of privilege and power, and now, I can share it with you."

Andrew smirks at Andrew's proposal.

"I don't need *shit* from you, I have powers that you don't, and I *intend* to use them against you, once I'm free of this nightmare!"

Andrew is becoming frustrated because of Gary's show of arrogance. He begins to walk away from the aggressive sibling, ready to pull out of the simulation—Andrew stops abruptly before speaking again.

"You believe your abilities make you unstoppable, *no* one in this world is unstoppable, not even me…. Gary, I read about what happened to us that night in *Haiti,* and I have some information that will interest you."

"Oh yeah?"

"Yes. It seems you do have another living relative other than me—your father, Wilfred Romulus' mother. Her name is Doris Romulus, she's your grandmother, and she's still alive and well."

"Andrew, you're trying to *trick* me!"

"Am I?"

"That's all people like *you* do is lie!" Gary is conflicted by the information Andrew reveals.

"That night when our parents died, Gary, Doris Romulus was the one who first met the authorities that found us. She tried to keep you and I, but being that we were *American,* your grandmother couldn't. That's why you and I were separated in the adoption.

"If they would've let her keep us, we would've still been together. You and I can still find Doris Romulus together, Gary, once you drop this *death* sentence you have against me!"

Andrew's words are getting through to Gary, but Gary still holds the hatred that's firmly planted in his heart.

Suddenly, the scenery of their surroundings begins to change. There is no more sun, no more greenery. The forest is completely gone. A sharp contrast instantly causes both men's eyes to strain. Four large walls appear with lots of heavy, rusted, steel machinery attached to them.

In the center of it all, right in front of the brothers is Gary's true body. He's spread eagle in tight metal constraints, with many types of wiring attached to him. Gary gasps in disbelief, as he runs towards the image of himself.

"WHAT THE *HELL* HAVE YOU DONE TO ME?" Gary screams.

"I did what I had to do, in order to stop you from posing a threat to me. It's up to you to decide what happens next," Andrew says frankly.

"YOU *FUCKING* BASTARD! YOU EXPECT ME TO *BELIEVE* ANYTHING YOU SAY AFTER WHAT YOU'VE DONE?"

"I've done nothing to harm you, Gary, you're just in stasis for the time being. Even though you've tried to *kill* me, I'm trying to *help* you, can't you see that?" Andrew scowls furiously.

"Gary, there are people in this world who would do *worse* to you than this, out of fear of the abilities you possess. They'll treat you like a lab rat, which is what I intended to do, until I found out that you're my brother. I can help you, Gary, only if you let me."

Andrew's voice becomes emotional as he speaks. The magnitude of it all is affecting him; even Gary can feel Andrew's distress.

"I don't know who I *am* anymore. I *just* want to know, and only *you* can help me, don't you see that?" Andrew cries. "The only link I have to my real past is you, I *can't* lose that!"

Gary becomes disturbed because of Andrew's plea. He no longer has the presence of someone Gary loathes. It's truth that comes from Andrew's cries that changes Gary's perception— Andrew not remembering the remarkable events of their past. The saddened face Gary now sees, reminds him of an earlier time in his life.

The night that the Vowdun murdered their parents, Andrew had carried Gary from the burning wreckage, crying, just as he's doing now.

How can Gary condemn him if Andrew truly doesn't recall that night? It will make Gary just as much as a monster as the one who'd smashed into that car, and murdered Wilfred and Marylyn Frazier Romulus that horrendous night.

Andrew now has his head pointed downward, sulking. Andrew believes that he's failed, and will never get the answers to the questions of his life. Gary approaches him, looking knowingly into Andrew's saddened eyes.

Eyes reflecting a pain, Gary had known all of his life.

"Andrew…Andrew I'm…what do you want me to do?"

Andrew can't believe his ears as he hears these words. Andrew gently touches Gary on the shoulder, takes a relaxing breath, and tries to regain his composure.

"All I'm asking for is for you to trust me, that's all."

Gary nods agreeably.

"Karen, end the program and bring us both out," Andrew instructs.

"Are you sure, sir? He might be bluffing," the scientist gestures.

"I'm willing to take that chance, Karen."

"Affirmative."

The scene immediately dims, as if it's being consumed by shadows. Both brothers keep their eyes locked on one another, as the virtual world vanishes into nothingness.

Darkness....

FIFTEEN

Gary's irises shrink as the virtual helmet is removed off his head. The bright, illuminating lights in the lab have momentarily blinded him. Gary soon hears the whirring motors of the table he lays on, as it turns downward, Gary faces the ceiling.

"Release the locks."

He hears a voice say.

It's the voice of Andrew.

The solid metal straps around Gary's arms, ankles and neck rapidly retracts.

Something is still wrong—I can't feel my body. My sense of touch is still gone...IT'S A TRICK! Gary thinks, assuming Andrew is trying to deceive him into believing he's free of the digital prison. Yet, there's one sure way he can find out of he's truly out of the program.

Gary slowly raises his back off the metal table, and sees Andrew standing at a closed doorway with two other male scientists wearing white robes, that reminds Gary of doctors. Sitting at a nearby computer terminal typing, is a woman who stops what she's was doing, and stares at Gary strangely.

Unexpectedly, Gary furiously hops off the table, startling everyone in the room. He angrily points an open hand at Andrew, causing Andrew to believe that he's made a terrible mistake in freeing Gary. Andrew now unwillingly, levitates from the floor.

He struggles to be released, as the invisible force tightly clutches his neck. Andrew gasps, as he begins to choke, Gary smiles victoriously, staring at the bulging eyes of his brother.

"Who's got the upper hand now, you dirty bastard?" Gary boasts.

Andrew tries ending what's happening, but the grip grows tighter. The other two scientists rush towards Gary. With one fleeting thought by Gary, they're thrown back forcefully; both men slam into a wall before falling limply to the floor.

Karen stands up from her terminal, and Gary instantly points at her with his free hand.

"Don't move, or I'll *snap* your neck like a *fucking* twig!" Gary warns.

Karen is frozen with fear.

Her eyes desperately watch Andrew, noticing he's suffering, before diverting her attention back to Gary.

"Please, Gary, please! He's your brother!" Karen pleads.

"That *bastard* did something to me! I *can't* even feel my body, so *don't* 'please' me!"

"It's the serum that has made you numb, the effects will wear off soon! Andrew hasn't done anything to you!"

Gary ignores her, as he glares into Andrew's bloodshot eyes. Something inside of Gary is driving him to murder his brother.

"I...I trusted you," Andrew gags, voice now failing.

"That's funny, because I *never* trusted you," Gary taunts wickedly.

Karen wants to scream out her protest. She wants to stop the madness, even if it puts her life in jeopardy. Karen hits a key on her computer.

Gary sees Karen's action. He's about to harm the woman, but the laboratory doors suddenly burst opened. Gary's prepared to mutilate anybody who enters, until he sees a figure walking in, wearing blue jeans and a white shirt. The individual also has a bandage wrapped around the top of their head.

Gary stares intensely into the eyes of the person who steps in, they're the eyes of someone he thought he would never see again; eyes that make the concentration Gary's using to focus his powers cease.

Andrew instantly falls from mid-air, hitting the floor hard on his hands and knees. He heaves and strains as Andrew inhales, bringing the denied oxygen into his lungs now.

Gary's eyes begin to water, with a sorrow that aches his weary heart, as the face of an angel stares back at him.

"Gary?" Melody says softly, as she approaches him; Gary stands silently with quivering lips.

He can't believe his vision.

In Gary's mind he tells himself: *This can't be,* until Melody caresses his cheek with her smooth right hand. Tears begin to stream down the young woman's face.

"Melody?" Gary forces himself to say, causing Melody to smile sadly.

"It's me, baby," she assures, before kissing Gary softly on the lips.

"I...I—"

"S-h-h-h, it's me."

Gary carefully brings Melody to him and hugs her tightly. He sobs, as Gary holds Melody in his arms.

Karen runs over to Andrew who is still recuperating. The scientist helps him to his feet. Andrew is light headed, and a bit shocked by the attack. His eyes fix angrily on Gary. Andrew begins to approach him, but Karen stops Andrew.

"No, Mr. Taylor, you shouldn't. I think Gary's finally gotten the message—look," Karen explains. Andrew now observes.

Gary, standing there naked with Melody, buries his head on her shoulder, as he weeps. The scene stops Andrew indeed. The angry glare in his eyes slowly but surely fades, as Andrew calms himself.

"Maybe we should leave them alone for the time being. Perhaps it's better if we do," Karen suggests. Andrew nods.

He takes in the sight one last time, before he and Karen escorts the other two scientists out the laboratory room, leaving Gary and Melody alone.

"I thought I lost you. I thought Black had did something to you," Melody confesses, as Gary carefully touches her face.

"I just made a mistake I shouldn't have...I-I love you, Melody," Gary struggles to say.

"I know you do, Gary. Your brother had his people operate on me, in which they said that I had a blood clot in my brain. Karen is the one who made me better. Gary, I didn't know you had a brother," Melody adds. Gary smiles.

"I really didn't know I had one either, but that doesn't matter now. All that matters is you." He kisses Melody again, deeper and more passionate than he's ever done before.

Andrew helped Gary, giving his brother back the one person Gary couldn't have ever gotten back himself: Melody. At this moment, as Gary thinks about it, his animosity towards Andrew doesn't matter anymore.

"You alright, Exodus?" says a low and deep voice. Gary looks over Melody's shoulder and sees Brown entering the lab, carrying folded garment bag over his arm, and a pair of shoes.

The two men shake hands, surprised to see each other.

"I told you I'd take care of her, Exodus."

"You did, big bro," Gary replies to Brown.

Brown's eyes slowly inspect the area. To him, the lab's environment is like a scene out of the old *Frankenstein* movie.

"Yo, I don't know how y'all know these people, but they got some *major* paper, having all this *shit!* And why the *hell* are you naked, Gary?"

Gary laughs at Brown's comment, as he begins to feel the pressure of Melody's soft touch.

SIXTEEN

As Gary rides up on the elevator within the Lortech tower, he feels awkward wearing the suit Brown has given him. The bouncer stands beside Gary, trying to hide his own grin, smirking at Gary being uncomfortable. Prior to Gary getting dressed, Brown tells him that Andrew wants to meet, so Gary brings Brown along.

He then explains to Gary, how Andrew's medical and science team, lead by Karen, removed Melody from the hospital, and took him with them when Brown tried to fight the scientists.

Brown also informs Gary how Andrew explained to him prior that he's Gary's brother, and that Andrew could help Melody, none of which the bouncer believed at the time. It took three days for Melody to revive after the surgery, in which moments ago, she and Brown were finally able to visit Gary.

Now, Gary and Brown stand nervously silent, as they ascend to Andrew's office. Melody stayed behind in the laboratory with Karen. Gary didn't want to leave her, but Melody assured him that she's safe. Gary could tell by Melody's slow movements that she's fatigued, so he didn't argue; in addition to Karen promising Gary that Melody was okay, and would be well taken care of, in the short time he would be gone.

The effects of the body-numbing serum that was in Gary's bloodstream are now gone. He still has his powers, which relaxes Gary's troubled thoughts; Gary having the idea that he's in no threat of anything. His only worry is Melody's health.

The elevator door opens. Three well-suited guards who are armed greet Gary and Brown. One guard gives directions to Andrew's office. Brown and Gary glance at each other before proceeding to meet with Andrew.

Andrew stands wearily inside of his office, as the two enter. At this point, Gary can easily attack Andrew if he wants to, but there's no need or want for that. After all, Andrew has given him a second chance with Melody; Gary couldn't harm the man who saved her life.

"Gentlemen, welcome to my office. I believe you've been here already, Gary," Andrew says condescendingly at his desk, as

AU and AG stands next to Andrew, silently observing Gary and Brown.

Gary looks around, noticing that there have been changes. He then looks at Andrew and speaks: "Andrew, I didn't mean to attack you down there, it's just...I didn't know if I could trust you."

"There's no need to apologize. I'm *assuming* that you're no longer interested in taking my life?" Andrew questions, not really expecting an answer.

"No-no, I'm not," Gary stammers.

"What is he *talking* about, Exodus?" Brown asks, bewildered by the conversation.

"Nothing, Brown, just a big misunderstanding, that's all," Gary answers. Gary's eyes don't waver from looking at Andrew, who also seems relatively calm, after what Gary did to him.

"Yo, I can't believe this guy's your brother?" Brown blurts out.

Before Gary could reply, Andrew speaks, "Yes, it's true, but, I only wished we'd met under better circumstances," Andrew states, truthfully. "But none of that matters now, all that matters is where we go from here," he continued.

Gary now feels uneasy by Andrew's inclination.

"I mean no disrespect, Brown, but could you step outside for a moment? I would like to speak with my brother privately."

Brown curiously looks at Gary.

Gary nods his approval.

"Just give me a second, Brown, and I'll be back out there with you," Gary promises.

Brown touches Gary on the shoulder for assurance before leaving the office. The two brothers don't speak until the office doors hisses shut, locking them both in. Gary now eyes the two metallic sentinels that are beside Andrew.

"I thought I broke them. What are they, robots?" Gary asks.

"Truthfully, I don't know the answer to that question. I'm more interested in finding out who I am, and who you are."

"Andrew, I told you who we are, and that someone killed our parents in *Haiti*. No, it wasn't a person. I don't know *what* that witch was, but it murdered them, and changed us," Gary tells, while seeing the blank expression on Andrew's face.

"If you could remember what happened, you would know that I'm not making any of this up, Andrew."

Andrew listens intently to Gary. He opens up a briefcase on his desk, retrieves a small file, and hands it over to Gary.

On the document's cover is a photo of an older woman. She's light skinned, has jet-black hair, and supple cheeks. Her slanted hazel eyes almost make the woman look *Asian* in appearance.

"That photograph was taken twenty years ago, Gary. It's a photo of your grandmother. She's still alive and lives in *Haiti*."

Andrew sees Gary's eyes water, as he stands there still, studying the photo, securely holding it in his grasp.

"I'm leaving to go to *Haiti* tomorrow, Gary. I'm going to find out what really happened to our parents. I'm going to visit your grandmother, and I hope that you will join me."

The sentence lingers in the air for a few moments before Gary speaks, "...I can't. Melody, she...she needs me," he rations.

"I understand, but just consider this. My medical staff is at your girlfriend's every whim right now. Melody will still need a few weeks to fully recover from her operation, and she's better off being right here now."

"I still need to be by Melody's side, Andrew. I almost *lost* her!" Gary defends, adamantly.

"That's your choice," Andrew whispers. He respects Andrew's loyalty for the young woman, but he needs him.

"I read up on your past, Gary. You've been committing crimes since you were a little boy. I can't, and I won't, condemn you for what you've done in your past. I didn't live the life you did, so I can't fathom what you've faced. But now I know that you're my only brother. And even if you don't want my help, I'm always here to give it to you. If you chose to believe it or not, I'm very honorable."

"What do you mean by that?"

"I've taken it upon myself to transfer funds to you and Melody Black's new bank accounts. There's five million each for the both of you."

Gary becomes rigid as he listens to Andrew, not liking what he's hearing.

"I don't *want* your money, I'm *not* a parasite."

"I never said you were. You have a strong will, Gary. People who are strong are never parasitic. You're my brother, and

I need your help, more than you need mine. There are answers to questions that you and I both need, waiting for us in *Haiti*. I can feel it. Will you help me to find those answers?"

"...I'm not just going to give in to your needs, Andrew."

Andrew becomes disappointed. He can still feel Gary's defiance, just like Andrew didn't want to accept that Gary, who tried to kill him, was his long lost brother.

Gary soon places the photograph of his grandmother, Doris Romulus, back on the desk.

"I...I can't, Andrew," Gary states flatly.

"I respect your decision, but I want you to know that I'm here for you. I'm getting on that plane tomorrow, with or without you—I hope that it's with you."

Andrew's breathing increases as Gary turns and heads for the door. When Gary gets to the entrance, he pauses with his back facing Andrew. The photograph of his grandmother soon lifts from the desk, and floats into Gary's hand.

Andrew is surprised for a moment by the eerie display of his brother's supernatural abilities, powers that Andrew wants to find out how Gary acquired—another reason Andrew wants to visit *Haiti*.

"I'm keeping this," Gary indicates, without turning back to look at Andrew. He then puts the picture into his pocket, and calmly exits the office as the doors opens.

Grief has stricken Andrew.

Gary refused his offer.

Andrew thought he would win this "chess game" with what he did and offered Gary but, he's wrong.

This is not a game.

Andrew makes up his mind. He won't let anything stop him from finding out he and Gary's past. *Gary ran away from the idea...maybe it's the pain he's experienced in life,* Andrew believes. Gary needs more time to heal.

Tomorrow, Andrew will be on his way. He will make the journey alone if he has to.

It's Andrew's to make.

* * * * *

Gary's eyes wander blankly, as he feels the warm caress of Melody's left cheek against his skin. The couple is sitting side-by-side atop a glass desk, in a sector of Karen's lab.

156

About twenty-five yards away, Brown is being fully entertained by a computerized game of *Solitaire,* the scientist downloaded for him. Brown's constant laughter reflects that he's more of a kid than a grown man, one who can become fiercely violent, at the drop of a dime.

Gary tells Melody about his brother's offer—she listens intently. Melody's head lies upon his shoulder, as she palms his hand comfortingly.

"Why won't you go, Gary?" Melody questions.

Gary becomes bothered that she asks. He can't, nor he won't leave, because of Melody. It pains Gary to even think about it! Gary reaches into his pocket and pulls out the photo of his grandmother. Melody takes the picture from Gary's hand and looks at it.

"She's beautiful. What's her name?"

"Doris," Gary answers. "Andrew thinks that she knows what happened to our parents. That's the real reason why he wants to go to *Haiti.*

"Do you want to know, too?"

Gary's thoughts pause.

The expression on his face tells it all.

But Gary's words hide his wants.

"The past is the past, Melody. Besides, I don't want to leave you. I almost *lost* you the last time I did, because I was only thinking about myself. That's something I will *never* do again."

Melody squeezes Gary's hand.

Turns his face to hers so their eyes can lock.

"Gary, this woman is your *grandmother.* She's a part of you, just like your brother. Remember how you used to tell me how you *wished* your mother and father were still alive? You told me that your life could've been different, and better, *if* they were here. Now, you do have a family, go visit her, Gary!" Melody exclaims.

"No, Melody."

"…What do you mean, no? Like you said before, when you left me, you were thinking about yourself. The reason I went to Black's club was for *you!* I was thinking about what he could've done to you. I was ready to *kill* him for you, and Black hurt me for that, hurt me badly."

"I'm sorry, Melody. I should have—"

"Don't be sorry. God paid him back for what he did to me. Brown told me that the club caved down on him," Melody tells, with a hint of anger in her tone.

"What I'm trying to say is, your brother is *not* Black, so don't *treat* him that way! He's your own flesh and blood, Gary, so is the woman in this photo. Don't turn away from this chance, *don't* turn your back on finding your family."

Gary can't help himself from holding back the smile on his face. The young woman who he stares at is so strong. Melody's will is one of the things Gary always admired.

"I understand that you don't want to leave me here in this condition, I don't want you to leave either. But this is something that I can't stand in the way of. Karen has already told me that she'll have to monitor me for a few weeks anyway."

Gary's lips moves as if he's about to speak. Melody silences him by placing her index finger on Gary's lips.

"Go. I want you to. I will be here when you return, Gary. I trust these people. Karen over there saved my life. Besides, Brown will be here to protect me, won't he?" Melody says with a slight laugh, gesturing to the burly man.

When Gary sees how Brown is reacting to the video game, he laughs also. Gary soon returns his eyes to Melody.

She knows me so well, it's as if Melody can read my mind. Melody is unselfish in what she thinks is right, she always is, Gary thinks.

Melody brings her lips to Gary's head and kisses him tenderly: "Things are going to be alright, Gary. They'll work out for the better, I know they will," she breathes into his mouth.

Little does Melody know that, things will drastically change: for the better, and for the worst.

SEVENTEEN

It's seven in the morning, and a limousine driver chauffeurs Andrew onto the airport's runway, to board his private company's jet. The vehicle drives directly to the plane's boarding stairs.

When the chauffeur opens the door, Andrew steps out and briefly pauses, before ascending the stairway. He thinks about his brother, and doesn't feel right about making the trip alone.

Gary told Andrew what he believed happened in the past, but the story isn't one Andrew takes for being accurate. Gary was merely a baby when their parents died, so Andrew can't take his story as gospel.

Andrew's mind is bombarded with that thought, also thinking that if it weren't for Gary, Andrew would have no idea that he's *not* the person Andrew was raised to believe he is.

Andrew now walks up the final step with his head down low, head filled with many questions, Andrew hopes that soon will be answered

Before entering the jet, Andrew sees a speeding, black *Lincoln Town Car,* coming down the runway—it's his own. The vehicle halts. The door opens. Gary quickly jumps out.

Andrew smiles, as Gary ascends the stairs towards him.

"I'm glad you changed your mind," Andrew states.

Gary doesn't respond.

He ignores Andrew's comment, and enters the plane, causing Andrew's smile to vanish, because of his brother's rudeness.

Andrew then realizes that, it doesn't matter what he do to please Gary, because his younger brother will always hold animosity against him. The only thing that matters now is that Gary is present, and ready to take the trip to *Haiti;* willing to take an unknown journey.

Andrew soon enters the jet after Gary, and the door closes—locks and seals.

*   *   *   *   *

It's an hour into the flight before Gary finally speaks: "How do you *know* that my grandmother is still alive?"

His words startle Andrew, who's becoming accustomed to Gary's silence.

"Well, to give proper credit, all of this is possible because of you, Gary. After I found out who you were, and that you were my brother, I did a thorough background check on every aspect of your past.

"It all began to come together, like pieces of a jigsaw puzzle, one piece at a time—our parents' death, the adoption. Then, I found out about Wilfred Romulus' mother, and how she tried to keep us with her. The *Haitian* authorities didn't let her. A man named Louis Petitehomme, provided me with that information.

"His father was part of the people's army at the time our parents died, so he had clearance to the files; for the right price I provided. You will meet Mr. Petitehomme when we arrive, Gary."

The industrialist pauses, and takes a sip of the fine white wine he's drinking before continuing. "...They rushed us back to *America,* because of our parents' death. I'm hoping that your grandmother will provide us with the real answers to how they died; a car crash can't be probable."

Gary sneers at Andrew's theories. He knows all too well how his parents died, and why. The nightmares that haunted Gary all of his life thus far, will never let him forget.

"You think you're *so* smart, *don't* you? How would you know that they *didn't* die in a car crash?"

"Gary, honestly, do you really believe our parents would leave us alone in *Haiti,* to go out on a drive? The documents state that the authorities found us next to the remnants of the collision—it doesn't make sense. I—"

"We were in *that* crash, and the Vowdun witch *killed* them! I remember what happened, and I'm *telling* the truth!" Gary reveals.

Andrew is baffled by the sudden outburst. He remembers Gary saying the same thing in the simulation. Andrew thought his brother was delusional then, but Gary confirmed it again: *"The Vowdun witch killed them!"*

Andrew doesn't want to cause further strife between he and his brother. He then takes a more rational approach, "I'm not saying that I don't believe you, Gary, but you were just three months old. How could you remember what happened?"

Gary lifts his index finger, and a small blue flame emerges from it.

"The same way I remember how I got these powers!" Gary answers with conviction, as the fire dies out. "It's *you* who can't remember Andrew, not me! The first time I used my powers is when we were in that crash.

"I protected you, but I didn't save our mother and father. How could I? I didn't even understand what I had. Andrew, you used your powers, too. You had a third eye—"

"A third eye?"

"A third eye in the middle of your forehead! After that night, my abilities were dormant, until..." Gary pauses. He now has a distant gleam in his eyes, as Gary reflects on that tragic night. "...Until I got into an accident, and got shot. I guess that's what triggered it to awaken."

Andrew intertwines his fingers, intrigued by what's being told to him. "You were shot, Gary?"

"Yeah, I was. And for a second, I think I was actually dead. But now that I think about it, I don't believe I can die, neither can you."

Something about the look and glare in Gary's eyes, when he just spoke, frightens Andrew to the core.

"I-I-I don't...I don't have your abilities, Gary." Andrew stutters, as he refuses to comprehend what he's being told.

"Yes you do. I burned a *hole* in your chest. I *killed* you, Andrew, but you came back, just like I did. I think your powers don't show, because you don't want them to. Maybe because you can't...or rather you won't remember what happened that night in *Haiti*. The power are inside you hidden somewhere."

Andrew is extremely bothered by what Gary says. He now remembers the story that Valerie told him about his past, and how whatever Andrew witnessed when he was younger, had put him in a trance state, in which Andrew became catatonic.

Andrew begins to have second thoughts about making the trip. But, it's too late to turn back now.

Gary gets more comfortable in his seat. He closes his tired eyes, feeling a drowsiness overcome him.

"Andrew, wake me up when we get there, and if you see me fighting in my sleep, wake me immediately. I might make a mistake and *blow* this whole plane apart by accident.

His comments make Andrew choke on his wine. He then hears a small chuckle from Gary.

"Don't worry. Like I said, we can't die. Maybe that's what needs to happen for me to prove it to you."

Gary now yawns before falling asleep.

EIGHTEEN

Lortech's private jet lands in the capital of *Haiti, Port-au-Prince* at 8 PM. Andrew and Gary exits the jet, now greeted by Louis Petitehomme, who was already informed that the two would be arriving. One of Andrew's associates advised him about the man, and last week, Mr. Petitehomme provided vital information that Andrew needed, for a price. Now, he's to be Andrew and Gary's guide, in the land that's foreign to both brothers.

Mr. Petitehomme's thick accent is understandable, and his slightly humorous comments about *Americans,* loosens both brother's tension, as he drives Gary and Andrew to what's considered an upscale hotel for the night.

The room Andrew acquires has an adjoining suite, and is deemed to be a luxury suite. Not by Andrew's standards. Gary on the other hand, highly enjoys the room, considering why he came to the country in the first place.

Neither Andrew or Gary leaves the hotel tonight, and after Mr. Petitehomme brings them more suitable clothing, not only for the climate, but to fit in better with the natives, both brothers retire to their separate quarters for the evening.

Andrew notices that Gary has been quiet since they arrived. The young man is his brother, but Andrew knows it will take much more time before Gary can truly consider him as family; no matter what material privilege Andrew can bestow in Gary's life.

Yet, Andrew has saved Melody. That act changed somewhat of how Gary views him, which is a start. Tomorrow, Louis Petitehomme will bring the two to visit Doris Romulus, Gary's grandmother.

Maybe she'll be able to place the shattered pieces of our lives back together, and then I can make sense of this newfound madness, Andrew thinks to himself, as his eyelids grow heavy. The entrepreneur soon drifts to an uncomfortable sleep, in the balmy climate of his room.

Across the hall, Gary stands wide-eyed, staring at the luminous moon outside the window. It glows in full bloom, reminding him of the last time he was in Haiti, and the night Gary's parents were murdered; by a creature that changed his life forever.

Gary balls his fists in frustration.

Sweat beads forms on his forehead.

Gary doesn't want to sleep, fearing that he will relive those horrible events of his past, a past his brother can't, or won't remember.

Gary now wonders how that can be. He himself was just and infant when the murder happened, yet Gary remembers every awful detail of that dreaded night.

He's anxious to visit his grandmother with a thirst for urgency, for the reason why his mother and father had to die. Gary also wants to go back to the hut of the Vowdun witch that has caused all his suffering, and tear her apart!

Gary's a grown man now, who wants revenge on the monster who's caused this great pain, with death.

The young man soon fights the urge to sleep as best he can, twisting and turning in the king-sized bed—Gary's teeth clenched in anger. Later, in the waking hours, sleep overcomes him.

At this time, the familiar past returns in Gary's dreams, changing it into a horrific nightmare.

Gary is not afraid.

Hatred and rage overrides all emotion.

He now mumbles in his sleep.

This morning, Andrew awakens from his sleep on sweat-stained sheets. He can't recall what he was dreaming about, only that he woke up, gasping for air, as if Andrew was drowning. As he gets out of bed to open the room's window blinds, to Andrew's surprise he sees Gary, sitting in a chair intently staring at him.

"You're up early," Andrew says, not betraying his own awkwardness. Gary's eyes quickly follow Andrew's movements.

"Yes, I am, and I'm ready for our trip," Gary answers, with a menacing frown upon his face. Andrew then glances at the clock on the wall: 7 AM.

"Our escort should be here in an hour, Gary. I'm going to take a shower. Maybe you should order something to eat, you must be hungry."

"No, I'm not."

Andrew nods, before walking towards the bathroom. Suddenly, he freezes in place, being held by an invisible force. It keeps Andrew from moving an inch. He strains to free himself, but to no effect Andrew's trapped.

It's Gary's powers.

"You don't believe me, do you, Andrew? I told you the truth about the witch, about what happened to our parents, but I know deep down inside, that you still don't believe me," Gary says calmly, not watching what he's doing to Andrew, who's now beginning to panic in Gary's psychogenic restraint.

"You said you wouldn't *hurt* me!" Andrew implies through clenched teeth.

"I can't hurt you. I already told you that. Now answer my question," Gary demands. Andrew isn't assured by his brother's inclination.

"It's not that I don't believe you, I'm scared to find out the truth. And even though you have those special gifts, Gary, I know that deep down inside, you're scared, also."

As those last words grunts from Andrew's lips, he's released. Andrew then immediately turns and glares at Gary angrily: "Don't ever—"

"I promise, I won't," Gary interjects, knowing what his brother would say.

Feeling the sweat run down his form, Andrew storms inside of the bathroom and shuts the door, leaving Gary to regret his action.

Gary is so powerful, that he doesn't realize how easily he can humiliate, and abuse others.

* * * * *

The drive from *Port-au-Prince* to the town of *St. Marc,* forty-five miles from the capital, is long and quiet. The only occasional conversation comes from Mr. Petitehomme Louis, who's driving the vehicle to the home of Doris Romulus.

Every now-and-then, Andrew speaks with the *Haitian* guide, only to take his mind off of Gary, who's sitting in the backseat; with his eyes locked on the back of Andrew's skull.

A half hour later, Gary notices the incredibly lackluster change of scenery. He's first aware of it when they left *Port-au-Prince,* but now, it's even more prominent. To Gary, what he sees here is as familiar as the place he had struggled in, to survive as a child.

This is the ghetto.

It doesn't matter if it's *Haiti,* or *Harlem,* the aura of poverty permeates from what Gary sees.

Andrew is quite shocked by the sights, also. People are walking barefoot; some of the children's clothing are ragged and torn, as if their attire had been passed down for generations.

Andrew has never seen anything of this nature, up close and personal before. It appalls him!

"Please tell me that Doris Romulus doesn't live here, Mr. Petitehomme?" Andrew questions while frowning.

"Not here, sir. We have one more mile to go, but I must tell you, it is very much the same," the guide warns.

Andrew hears Gary snickering at Mr. Petitehomme's reply.

Where did Andrew think she would live, somewhere comfortable like him? Gary spitefully thinks.

Andrew now glances through the rearview mirror.

He sees Gary staring back at him.

The same ghostly way he had this morning.

So much hatred still exists within Gary.

Andrew now believes his brother will *always* resent him.

The vehicle pulls up near what appears to be a shanty. Behind it is a beach and the clear-blue sea. The waters crash on rocky cliffs. It's in sharp contrast to everything else about the area.

Andrew quickly steals another glance in the mirror. He sees what appears to be sadness in his brother's eyes. Gary now is biting his bottom lip.

There's a child outside of the shack, chasing a mud-covered pig. She immediately stops her playing when she sees the car stop in front of the property.

Is this the place, man?" Gary asks, speaking for the first time since they left the hotel. Andrew and their *Haitian* guide, turns in his direction.

Mr. Petitehomme smiles, "Yes, it is, sir. Are you ready to meet your grandmother?"

Gary doesn't answer. Instead, he opens the passenger side door and steps out, Andrew and Mr. Petitehomme follows his movement.

The little girl reaches into her waist and pulls out a self-made slingshot. She loads it with a small rock, aiming the weapon at the unfamiliar three men, whom she'd never seen before. The child's lips pull back in a defensive snarl, causing the three strangers to pause.

"WHO ARE YOU PEOPLE?" she demands in her *Haitian* dialect. Mr. Petitehomme takes a step towards the girl, and she aims at his chubby face.

"I SAID WHO ARE YOU PEOPLE? I SWEAR I'LL SHOOT YOU!" the little one threatens in her native tongue.

Gary finds himself admiring her protective nature. He can snatch the slingshot from the young girl by using his abilities, but truthfully, Gary wants her to shoot the guide in the face for a laugh.

Mr. Petitehomme smiles at the little girl, before talking to her in his native tongue. Andrew tries to understand what is being said, but the *Haitian* dialect of *French* is confusing him. Gary and Andrew watch silently, as the little girl's frown now leaves her face. Soon, she lowers her weapon, and begins pacing backwards to the shanty, until vanishing inside the shack.

"What did you say to her, Mr. Petitehomme?" Andrew questions.

"I told her that you and Gary were the grandchildren of the woman who lives in this house. The young girl's a bit high-spirited, but I convinced her. Come on, let's go see, Ms. Romulus," Mr. Petitehomme gestures.

The three men begin to approach the home, but abruptly stops in their tracks again, when the door to the home becomes slightly ajar.

Gary gazes in anticipation, when a pair of hazel-colored eyes cautiously peeks out of the crack. His pulse races quicker when the door suddenly slams shut. Gary's heart erupts with disappointment and sorrow. Andrew immediately reads the emotion on Gary's face, before turning to Mr. Petitehomme with a frown.

"What is this, Mr. Petitehomme? It can't be the right home." Andrew says to the guide, who's just as puzzled as him.

"It's the right home," Gary whispers, as he stares at the ground.

"How could you possibly know this?" Andrew asks.

"I saw her eyes, Andrew, I saw her eyes," Gary proclaims. The growing sadness takes the strength from his voice. "We made a mistake coming here."

Gary not only saw his grandmother's eyes, he felt her presence ever since they'd arrived on the property. Gary kept it to himself, fearing that this would happen.

She rejects me, Gary thinks.

"I refuse to believe that, Gary. This can't—"

Before Andrew was able to complete his sentence, the door of the shack unexpectedly opens, silencing all three men.

Standing there with the little girl they encountered earlier is an elderly woman. Her long, jet-black hair, flows to the small of the woman's back. In her hand is a photo. Her eyes stare hard at the three men before her, before the woman examines the photo.

Gary sees the old woman's eyes water, in which tears now falls from them. His mouth opens; Gary tries to speak.

No words escape.

The woman approaches the group, now just inches away from Gary and Andrew. Her warm palm touches Gary's face, as she tries hard to fight back the tears.

"Gary?" Doris Romulus whispers, before turning to his brother, smiling, "Andrew?" Her arms reach out, now wrapping around Gary and Andrew's shoulders, pulling them together in a tight embrace, as she cries out, "My grandchildren come back to me," the elderly woman says in broken *English.*

Mr. Petitehomme watches on in silence.

Gary's eyes are tightly shut, as tears roll down his face. The tremor of emotion even strikes Andrew.

She said 'grandchildren', not 'grandchild', Andrew thinks, as the woman's words sink into his head.

As Doris releases her hug, she tries her best to remove her Gary's tears.

"Don't cry. Here," Doris says to her grandson, while handing Gary the photo in her hand.

Both Gary and Andrew eye the image. It appears to be old, but still holds the clarity of when it was taken two decades ago. For the first time, the two brothers lay eyes on a photo of their family, together.

Wilfred Romulus stands on the right with a then, three-year-old Andrew, sitting upon his shoulders. Marylyn Frazier

Romulus stands by them, with Gary, their newborn baby in her arms—the mother's holding Gary's head for support.

Their mother is beautiful. What's more, is the image of a happy family; something that no longer exists. Andrew has absolutely no memories of when it was taken, but he knows, beyond a shadow of a doubt that it's him; the others in the photo are his forgotten family.

"Your father sent it to me before...before—"

"We know what happened to our parents," Andrew assures Doris before politely interjecting, now receiving a strange stare from Gary, who knows Andrew can't *fully* imagine what their parents suffered.

Doris wipes away her tears, before taking both of her grandchildren's hands. "Come, come into my home, we have a lot to talk about," she includes with a smile, despite the mixture of joy and sorrow. The old woman now leads the three men into her impoverished home.

The little girl, who threatened the men earlier, gives Doris a puzzled look.

"Don't be afraid, Anea. These are my grandchildren, my family, little one," Doris tells the girl in her native language.

Anea grins before stepping into the elderly woman's home. Andrew, Gary and Mr. Petitehomme follow behind.

NINETEEN

"I'm sorry for what happened to your mother and father," Doris states apologetically, as she begins to light several white candles in her home. Doris soon serves the three men each a cup of hot tea. Andrew and Gary had been speaking to their grandmother for a few minutes before she offered her apology.

"You're not responsible for what happened to them. I remember that night, it had nothing to do with you," Gary defends.

"My grandson, in ways that you don't know, I am responsible for what happened to your parents. And what I fear has happened to the both of you," Doris confesses while taking a seat.

Andrew listens intently, watching Doris' face now changed from bliss to grief, now mourning. She takes a sip of the vaporous, peppermint tea she's holding, and sighs, as a faraway gleam comes to Doris' eyes.

"When my son, Wilfred, was very young, he got into a terrible accident, out there by the rock cliffs on the beach. Wilfred was hurt so badly, and I knew if I didn't get help or do something, he would probably die; or be crippled for the rest of his life. I had no other choice, I didn't want my son to die before I did."

Anea stops Doris from speaking momentarily, as she sits in the old woman's lap. Doris runs her fingers through the little one's kinky hair. Mr. Petitehomme soon smiles at Anea.

Andrew takes in the sight of the scenery, which seems to draw him in. *Maybe it was the calm candlelight,* he believes.

Gary sips his tea silently, not knowing what his grandmother will say next. Gary desperately wants to know how she can blame herself for his parents' death.

"So what did you do? How did you save him?" Andrew questions.

Doris, still playing in the young girl's hair, answers in such a calm manner, "When I was young, about Anea's age, my mother told me something that her mother had told her, when she was a child. My mother said that there was a very powerful Vowdun who lived not far from here."

Doris' statement instantly bothers Andrew and Gary. She sees the puzzled expression on Andrew's face.

"A Vowdun is a witch, Andrew, someone who retains the magic, and rituals of our African ancestors. When Wilfred was hurt, I brought him to see the Vowdun."

"And she healed him?" Gary asks.

"Yes, she did. In one day. The Vowdun's magic fascinated my child. Wilfred told me that someday, he would bring his firstborn child to receive the gifts of the Vowdun. I warned him, threatened Wilfred not to, but he didn't listen to me." Doris tells, her voice straining with emotion.

"Grandma, are you okay?" Gary asks worriedly.

"Yes. Yes, I am." Doris controls her distraught mind and continues.

"Once my mother had told me about the son of an *African* chief, who the Vowdun cursed with immortal life, only to haunt him for the rest of his days. My mother said that the chief's son now hides in the shadows, fearful that the Vowdun will claim him.

"You see, no one knows how long the Vowdun has lived, or what she really wants. I took a chance with Wilfred's life, and in turn, he took a chance with the both of yours—after I'd warned him not to."

Gary isn't bitter at the story his grandmother reveals. He's actually now relieved, fully knowing the fact that the witch had killed his parents, and that the creature did exist—Gary understanding at this point that his nightmares are real, and that he isn't crazy.

Gary moves his chair closer to Doris, who reaches out and gently squeezes his hand.

"Twenty years ago, when you all arrived here in *Haiti,* I had a nightmare, something inside me knew that something was wrong. I awoke in the middle of the night. I knew something was *terribly* wrong.

"I put on my robe and ran to the Vowdun's hut. My heart was beating in my chest so hard I thought it would burst. The sun began to rise when I got halfway to where the Vowdun lived. I cried out at what I saw.

"There were police, and a car that looked like it had burned, and that is when I first saw you two, my grandchildren.

Andrew, you were holding Gary so tightly, the police thought you were crazy," Doris states while gazing at Andrew.

"Your parents' bodies were in that car. I tried to tell the police that you two were my grandchildren, but they wouldn't give the both of you to me, because of the fact that you were *American.*

"They sent you back to *America,* despite the fact I was your grandmother. My heart was broken, the only thing that kept me sane, was knowing that you were together. And now, I know that you are alright, because you've come back to me. Bless your souls."

Gary and Andrew look at each other. They hadn't been together at all. Their distant lives had made them total strangers, until recently.

"I knew the Vowdun had done something to the both of you. Your mother and father died in that car, but the both of you hadn't. I asked myself why a thousand times."

"Maybe it was so that someday, we can be with you," Gary interjects, causing his grandmother to smile.

"Maybe so, grandchild, or maybe you and Andrew have a deeper purpose."

Andrew listens to Doris' tale with an open heart, and it troubles him.

Maybe the Vowdun is the source of Gary's abilities, but it doesn't explain why I don't possess those same gifts, Andrew reasons. Now he's fueled with more questions than answers.

Andrew believes that science can do the impossible, but feels there's no such thing as magic—believing magic only to be, what a person couldn't understand.

While rationalizing his Doris' story, Andrew glances at his watch: *9 PM.* He's surprised that time passed so quickly.

"It's getting late. I should retire back to the hotel until tomorrow," Andrew states. Gary turns his back on his brother.

"You can do what you want to do, but I'm staying here, if it's alright with you," he retorts before looking at his grandmother for confirmation.

Doris nods her approval, as Andrew rises. He approaches the old woman, and she hugs Andrew.

"Thank you," Andrew says, before taking a step away from Doris. She instinctively grabbed his hand; Andrew and Doris' eyes now meet.

"Andrew, you *are* my grandson. I know how you must feel. But believe me, I love you *just* as much as I love your brother. Do you understand?"

Andrew sees the sincerity in Doris' eyes.

"Yes, I do."

She soon lets go, and Andrew and Mr. Petitehomme leaves the shanty. As the tour car's engine starts, tears begin to well in Gary's eyes.

"What's wrong, Gary?" Doris asks.

"...It's just after all these years, I thought I was crazy. And now...now..."

Gary pauses. He reflects on his life, and the things that he'd done, even after knowing about his abilities.

Anea comes off of Doris' lap, and goes to pat Gary on his head. It causes him to gaze at the young girl's face. Anea smiles awkwardly, so does Gary.

"I know what you fear, Gary, and I know that you're strong enough to face what's to come," Doris says, as she watches Mr. Petitehomme's car's drifting taillights. "You have to be strong for your brother, and help Andrew find himself, as you already have. You both need each other."

"But he hates me."

"No, no he doesn't. Andrew's just scared, and he has every right to be."

* * * * *

As Andrew rides with Mr. Petitehomme back to the hotel, he's in deep thought about what Doris Romulus told him and Gary. Gary has never met his grandmother before today, yet he and Doris' story, of what transpired twenty years ago is the same.

The Vowdun, is it true? Andrew questions. *Did my mother and stepfather make a deal with a witch?*

It has to be something else that gave Gary his abilities, but even Karen Scott's brilliant mind, can't find the answers to the origin of Gary's powers. Andrew himself can't do the special things his brother does, and Andrew wonders why?

Again the story of the Vowdun plays through his head.

There can be no other answer.

Andrew begins to feel a sense of guilt. He's going back to sleep in a luxurious hotel, while Gary and the woman who called Andrew her grandson, will sleep in a poverty-stricken shack.

173

It isn't right at all.

But Andrew has never suffered such harsh reality.

He's special.

Upper class.

Elite.

A shocking thought now comes to Andrew. He wasn't born of the elite. Andrew once had a family that was poor, and if it weren't for the night his parents had died, he would probably still be poor.

It's a night Andrew has no memory of, but Gary does.

Why can't I remember, Andrew thinks to himself.

Maybe his conscience refuses to.

The car soon pulls in front of the lavish hotel, and Andrew gets out. Now, another strange feeling hits him. Andrew feels like he isn't supposed to be here, believing that he's suppose to be in the shack—with his family.

Tomorrow, Andrew plans to try to make up for his lack of compassion and understanding, if Doris will allow him to. What Andrew doesn't understand is that, the only thing Doris wants is for Andrew to realize who he *truly* is.

TWENTY

This morning, Gary awakens with a cramp in his lower back. He's in a small room in his grandmother's shack, in which Gary grew accustom to, when he drifted off to sleep last night. Gary now notices that there are no beds in the shanty. Doris just sleeps on a sheet, which seems harsh for such an elderly woman.

Gary soon ventures into the kitchen where Doris is busy cooking scrambled eggs for breakfast. She turns to him, and greets Gary with a warm smile. He returns one instantly.

"Good morning, Gary. Did you sleep well?"

"Yes, I did," he tells truthfully, despite the diminishing pain in his back. "Where's the little one?"

"Anea is out by the beach, trying to catch seagulls to eat. I told her to stop doing that, but Anea can be difficult at times," Doris says before sighing, as she puts half of the scrambled eggs from the frying pan on a plate. She then hands the plate to Gary, who begins eating the dish immediately, enjoying the taste.

"Why does she live with you?" Gary questions.

"I knew Anea's parents. They died of AIDS a few months ago, and I didn't want her to be alone," his grandmother answers. Doris now places the rest of the eggs on another plate, and sits down beside Gary. "Why haven't you told me about your gifts?" she asks, nearly causing him to choke on the eggs Gary's eating.

How did she know? he thinks. "I haven't—"

"I know, you haven't told me. I know what the Vowdun does, grandchild. She changes people…I know many tales of that *witch's* poisonous powers, stories that are too *frightening* for me to believe!"

Gary stares at Doris, having a blank expression upon his face, baffled that the woman knows more about him and the Vowdun than he does.

"I…I don't really understand it. I can move things, cause things to happen with my mind. Andrew said that it's called psychogenic."

"Oh, and what about your brother?"

How can I answer my grandmother?

Gary knows that Andrew came back to life, after burning a hole in brother's chest. He also ponders on telling Doris about Andrew's third eye that Gary had discovered, the night their mother and father were murdered. Gary then contemplates on even sharing the truth about his own nightmares.

He looks at his grandmother and speaks cautiously, "If Andrew does have any of the Vowdun's gifts, he hasn't shown any signs of it."

Doris now places two glasses of goat milk on the table.

"Or maybe Andrew doesn't realize he has them," she offers.

*　*　*　*　*

After eating, Gary makes his way to the beach, where Anea is busy launching small pebbles at squawking birds. She hands the slingshot to Gary when he approaches, as an invitation for him to try. He laughs and gives the homemade weapon back to the little girl, who frowns at Gary's denial.

Noticing that Anea is upset, he kneels down and picks up a stone from the sand. Watching in fascination, the young girl witnesses Gary open his palm, and to Anea's amazement, the rock rises and floats, inches above his hand.

Gary immediately places his index finger to his lips, making a shushing sound, as if Gary's now a magician, doing his own private magic show for Anea. He stands up, and suddenly, the pebble quickly shoots away over the waters of the beach.

The small projectile smacks into the heads of three, unsuspecting, flying seagulls, causing them to freefall. Before their feathered bodies could hit the waters, Gary focuses his powers, and brings the dead birds in front of the wide-eyed girl.

Astonished, Anea gazes at the seagulls, before diverting her attention back to Gary, who's standing beside her.

"Don't tell anybody. It's magic!" he says dramatically, grinning from ear-to-ear. Mouth now ajar, Anea picks up the prize, and races back to Doris' home, in anticipation of telling on her grandson.

Gary isn't surprised by Anea's reaction. He makes his way back to the home too; ready to offer Doris an explanation. Gary then notices Louis Petitehomme's car driving up.

Andrew gets out of the car and goes straight to the trunk, where Mr. Petitehomme is already opening it. Inside are two boxes, filled with an assortment of canned goods, Andrew purchased for Doris; wanting to do something for her, hoping he isn't being too assertive in the process.

Andrew sees Doris standing outside her home, with Anea jumping up-and-down, excitedly telling the elderly woman something, while holding what it looks like to Andrew, a few dead birds.

He's now glad that he decided to make the purchases. Soon, Doris greets and kisses Andrew on the cheek, and he smiles back at her. To Andrew, the woman seems happy, something he himself couldn't fathom being, living in such harsh conditions.

Gary even has a smile on his face when approaching the group, something that Andrew hasn't seen, in the short amount of time that he's known his brother.

"What's in these boxes?" Doris questions.

"Some canned goods, I thought they might help."

"I see. Well, take them in the house," she politely directs. Andrew and Mr. Petitehomme do as they're told, before shortly coming back outside.

"I want to take you two somewhere today. There is something I have to show you both, because I think it's right," Doris announces.

"What's that, Grandma?" Gary asks.

Doris gazes at him with weary eyes, as if she can't answer. She rotates and goes to Mr. Petitehomme, saying something in her native tongue, in which Gary nor Andrew understands. The *Haitian* guide nods a yes to Doris, and she begins to approach his car.

"Your driver will take us. Please, come," Doris insists.

Andrew and Gary give each other a puzzling glance, before following the old woman.

Soon after, the vehicle drives away. Mr. Petitehomme chauffeurs with Andrew in the front passenger seat. Gary, Doris and Anea, are in the back. The young girl curiously questions Gary about his "magic"; in a language he now has no hopes of understanding. Gary hears his grandmother chuckle, because of Anea's continuous banter.

"What is she talking about?" Gary asks.

"She's asking if you can make her fly," Doris translates.

Gary now beams, "As high as you want to go."

Doris smiles at his remark, before translating to Anea.

Thirty minutes into the drive, Gary notices a change in his grandmother's mood. Her facial expression is emotionless and distant.

Andrew observes the change in scenery. They're no longer on paved roads, but rather on dusty hillsides that seem desolated; as if no one lives where they're heading.

Gary feels a sudden chill run up his spine. A flashing image of the moment his parents died comes to mind. Gary's throat becomes constricted, and he breaks out in a cold sweat.

Gary now turns his head to gaze at the dusty road, feeling an eerie, growing fear, until feeling the touch of Doris' warm hand; causing him to look at her.

"We're almost there, Gary," his grandmother alerts him, as if sensing his panic. Gary remains calm with Doris' words. She and her younger grandson now knows that they just passed the site, where Wilfred and Marylyn Romulus died twenty years prior.

After another thirteen miles, the car stops.

"We are here," Mr. Petitehomme states. Doris opens the door after lying Anea's sleeping body, down in the seat.
The elderly woman begins walking in the grassy land silently. Both brothers get out of the vehicle and follow her.

Their grandmother soon halts, when she comes to a dusty patch in the field. Andrew watches Doris, as she stares sternly at the ground below her.

"Why are we here?" Andrew asks.

"This is the place where your beloved parents brought you."

Gary takes in the view of the whole area. More haunting visions resurrects in his mind.

"She's right, Andrew, I remember this place," Gary indicates. Andrew gazes at him before looking back to Doris, in which her eyes are beginning to water.

"It was here, this *damned* place!" she hisses angrily. "*This* is where the Vowdun witch lived. After your mother and father died, and the police took the two of you away from me, I came out here with my *machete* in my hands. I came to *kill* the Vowdun...but the witch was gone, as if never existing.

"After all those years of what she did to my son, his wife, and you—she was gone. I brought your parents remains out here and buried them, to show the Vowdun my *hatred* for it. I wanted the Vowdun to know what it did, to know that I will *never* forget or forgive it!"

Tears are rolling down the woman's face as she speaks. Doris' voice reflects the extreme disgust and anger that boils within her. Both Andrew and Gary can feel Doris' distraught heart.

The elderly woman angrily looks to the sky. Its billowing clouds don't fear her anguish.

"DO YOU HEAR ME, VOWDUN? I HATE YOU!" Doris cries out before falling to her knees, on top of her son and daughter-in-law's grave.

Gary kneels down next to his sobbing grandmother. His arms wraps around her, as Gary wishes that he could take away Doris' pain.

Gary has relived that nightmarish evening when his parents died, repeatedly; believing that he alone, only knows what he's suffered. Yet, here is the woman who also had felt Gary's pain, just as much as him.

Gary now whispers to Doris that he's sorry, for something he hadn't done. Andrew joins their embrace, also, while Mr. Petitehomme, who's pained by the emotional scene, flees back to the car.

Andrew is beginning to understand and accept, what has happened in the past. Even though he has no memories of the events of his childhood, Andrew still feels the great loss of his parent nonetheless. He holds his grandmother and brother in the sad embrace, sharing their sorrow.

"It's alright now, grandma, our family is back together again," Gary says sympathetically, wiping away Doris' salty tears.

Andrew's eyes catches Gary and Doris' eyes.

"Yes, we are a family. I won't let *anything* change that. Never," Andrew promises.

TWENTY-ONE

Andrew dials a number on his cell phone, hearing it ring three times before getting a response on the other end.

"Hello?" says the soothing voice.

Andrew clears his throat before speaking: "Hello Sharon, it's Andrew," he answered, almost expecting Sharon to hang up. She doesn't.

"Hi Andrew. Where are you? I've been trying to get in touch with you for weeks."

"I'm on vacation in *Haiti*."

"*Haiti?*" the woman stammers. *Haiti* is not a place Sharon would imagine Andrew vacationing at.

Andrew takes a sip from the bottled water he's drinking before responding, "I wanted to call to thank you for being honest with me about my behavior."

"Andrew, you sound troubled. Are you okay?" Sharon asks, hearing the strain in her ex-lover's tone.

"I'm fine, Sharon. I'm feeling better than I've ever felt in my life."

"I'm glad to hear that."

A small group of children run by Andrew, wearing tattered, unkempt clothing. Even though he knows how terribly poor they are, the kids seem joyous.

Andrew now reflects, *I could've once in my life, been one of those kids.*

"Andrew? ...Andrew, are you there?" Sharon asks, breaking his thoughts.

"Yes, I'm here. Sharon I want to make a donation to your 'Shattered Dreams foundation'."

"You do?"

"Yes, I do. I'm giving you ten million, and if that's not enough, I'll donate more." Andrew now hears Sharon's slight gasp through the receiver.

"Andrew, what made you—"

"I've grown up, Sharon," Andrew interjects, answering as if he knew what the woman would say. "I've changed."

Holding her phone, thousands of miles away, tears now roll down Sharon's face: "Andrew, I've missed you, the person you were before the corporation."

"I'm back, beloved."

"Come home, Andrew, I've missed you *so* much."

"I am, Sharon, that's a promise."

After a distant goodbye, Andrew hangs up and turns towards Doris' home. A week has passed since he first landed in *Haiti,* with his long lost brother.

Andrew doesn't feel the same as he did when he'd first arrived. The revelations of Andrew's past have humbled him somehow, more than he realizes. Now, it is time, time to tell his grandmother he has to go.

Andrew has to return to Lortech and uphold his responsibilities, one that can't be avoided. He owes it to Valerie, and to David, the man who raised him.

He soon notices Doris watching him through her window. The woman smiles, causing Andrew to wave back at her.

Bless her heart, he thinks. If it weren't for Doris, he and Gary's past would've been lost.

Now it's time to take care of their future.

* * * * *

Alberto McKoon stands regally, surveying the panoramic view of *New York City's* skyline from his ceiling-to-floor office window. The entrepreneur's hands are crossed below on his lower back, and McKoon's teeth grits, because of the swift internal-to-external metamorphosis, that grows from within.

He shuts his aqua-blue eyes from the vision before him...and when they reopen, the eyes no longer reflects anything remotely human.

"The world has been ruled by the hidden since the dawn of time, and the unknown's strength, comes from its ability to remain unseen, within the darkness. Of course you know this."

McKoon waits for a brief moment before continuing.

"...The Jinn Legion's power comes from the eternal one, Lord Moon, that is where our knowledge and power resonate. This Andrew Taylor is not *worthy* of the power he has with Lortech, and I feel it is time for it to be taken!" he hisses.

"That is *not* your decision to make, McKoon," a strong voice projects. The president of Taterax now turns to face one of five men, standing within his office. Michael Masters meets McKoon's glare with the disgust of his own.

"You have *no* right to speak, Masters."

"Who are *you* to tell me what to do, McKoon? You *think* that you lead the Jinn, but if David Taylor was alive, you would be *nothing!*" Masters retaliates.

McKoon sneers angrily before going to his seat, never once letting his serpentine eyes leave Masters.

"I beg to question where your loyalty lies, Michael. You were *second* to David Taylor when he ruled the Jinn Legion, and his employee for years. But now, you are the *subordinate* of his son, excuse me, Taylor's orphaned *bastard* boy!" McKoon chuckles, now adding insult to his newfound knowledge, of Andrew Taylor's childhood. Masters gave McKoon the information before even disclosing it to Andrew.

"Watch your tongue, McKoon!" Masters demands, balling up his fist tightly.

"Andrew Taylor must be *killed,* Masters! He and his corporation are a threat to the Jinn!"

"No! What Andrew Taylor *really* is, is a threat to Taterax. You want him terminated for your *own* greed, McKoon!"

McKoon swiftly stands up.

Slams his fist hard atop the desk.

"How *dare* you, Masters! He sent someone to *kill* me!"

"Yes, Mr. Taylor did, and you provoked him. I'm not afraid to admit I admire him for that," Masters says, grinning.

A white-haired man quickly moves to Masters—Loki. The bodyguard pulls out his gun, and places it on the back of Masters' skull, causing his insidious grin to fade.

"Put down you gun, Loki! You won't dare kill me!" Masters demands. Loki doesn't listen.

"I said put—"

Before Masters could finish his words, an amorphous shadow quickly races across the room. Loki has no time to react, as a long, fleshy vine shoots out of the shadows, and crashes into the man's chest. Loki slams hard into the wall, before falling to the floor unconscious.

McKoon's eyelids widens, as the form of his master, Lord Moon emerges from the void.

"ENOUGH!" the creature screams.

Masters, along with the others in the office, crouches down on bent knees, before lowering their heads in the presence of their lord. Its black, scaly skin reflects the office lights, as the beast's glowing, red eyes, falls on McKoon.

McKoon's heart rate speeds up in terror!

"I will *destroy* you *all*, if need be!" Lord Moon states.

"Y-Yes, my lord," McKoon stammers.

"Andrew Taylor will be judged in due time. I and I alone, will decide when," the beast informs the group. A slime-coated tentacle soon slithers from the creature's towering frame. It touches Masters' skin, who lifts his head to face his lord.

"You will return to Taylor and remain loyal, despite McKoon," Lord Moon instructs to Masters. "And you," the eternal creature's begins with cold stare towards McKoon, one that sends a shiver up the president of Taterax's spine, "you will *not* pursue this matter any longer, until *I* give the order! UNDERSTAND?" its voice screeches.

"I understand, my lord," McKoon quietly replies. Lord Moon's evil, piercing eyes, looks through his minion for a moment longer, before the creature suddenly vanishes.

Masters stands, and gives McKoon a fleeting smile, before leaving the office along with the others. The boiling contempt inside McKoon pulls him to a depth of malice, that can't be contained much longer.

He looks at Loki, who's still lying on a broken heap on the floor. *Andrew Taylor will die!* McKoon thinks.

One way or another, the president of Taterax will have to pay for his transgression.

* * * * *

"Doris, there's something I want to ask you," Andrew says to the elderly woman, who's standing by her window. Doris turns to face him.

"Yes, Andrew. You can ask me anything."

The look on her face makes Andrew bow his head, as he goes to sit down before speaking again.

"I'm leaving tonight. I have to return to *America,* I have responsibilities that I can't leave unattended. But, I want you to come with me. I have associates that can make it possible." Andrew pauses, trying to read the expression on Doris' face. There is none.

Andrew continues, "I...I am a very wealthy man. I can take care of you in *America*."

"Andrew, I understand what you're telling me, and I am grateful for having such a giving grandson, but I have to decline your offer."

A flood of disappointment washes over the young man.

"Why?" Andrew questions, not wanting to believe that Doris refused. He can't fathom how she could decline.

"Andrew, I was born here, in this country of poverty. This place that I know appalls you, is a place that I find joyful memories and bad ones. It's a part of me, and I could never leave it. *America* is a strange place for me... It's just like me asking you to stay here forever, I would never do that."

Doris' words strike Andrew. At first he fights them in his heart, but, as Andrew thinks about the woman's spirit, he accepted Doris' remarks wholly.

The old woman now approaches Andrew, kissing him in the center of his forehead. Andrew soon sees Doris' warm smile.

"I respect what you've said, and I'm thankful for your wisdom, grand...grandmother." It's the first time Andrew called her that, and he truly meant it.

"I'll be here whenever you need me, Andrew, you can count on that."

Shortly, Gary and Anea steps into the home carrying grocery bags. The two just returned from the market. Gary looks at Andrew, before quietly taking out what he purchased. Andrew now goes towards him.

"I'm leaving tonight, Gary, you are free to come with me, if you want—I"

"I'm staying. It's too soon," Gary retorts and turns his back.

"I respect your wishes. I'll give you my cell phone, and you can call my office when you're ready. I'll send my jet to come get you," Andrew says while facing Gary's back.

Gary doesn't answers. Andrew has found out in the short time he's known him, how difficult Gary can be. Andrew chooses not to force him to leave. Doris now steps in between the two brothers.

"Goodbye grandmother, I'll visit you again soon, this I promise." Andrew pledges. He kisses Doris, and places his cell phone on the table before finally leaving her home.

184

Doris' hand now touches Gary's shoulder, stopping him from putting away the remaining groceries.

"Gary, you remind me so much of your father."

"Do I?"

"Yes, you do. He was defiant and headstrong, just like you."

"Why would you say that about me?"

"Hush, child, I know what you hold inside. You don't open yourself to your brother, because you think Andrew will betray you."

Gary's eyes meet Doris'. She's telling her grandson the truth about how he honestly feels, emotions that Gary has harbored.

"You don't realize it yet, but someday you will, Gary. Andrew needs you, just as much as *you* need him, no matter how hard you try to deny it. Go back to *America* with your brother, you're all he's got," Doris says sincerely.

Gary now fights his emotions, as Doris brings him to her, hugging her grandson tightly.

"I will be here whenever you need me, Gary. And I want you to bring your girlfriend you told me about on your next visit. I need to meet the woman who will someday bring forth my great-grandchildren," the elderly woman adds with laughter, bringing a smile to Gary's face as their embrace ends.

"GOD *bless* you, grandma," Gary says from his heart.

"GOD blessed me the day you were born. Now go catch up with your brother, Andrew, the car hasn't left yet," Doris indicates, as caresses his right cheek.

Gary gives his grandmother one last embrace, before he retrieves the cell phone, and heads towards the front door. Yet, Anea now stands in front of Gary, blocking him from exiting. Gary bends down, and gazes at her sad, beady eyes.

"Where are you going?" his newfound friend asks curiously, in a language Gary doesn't understand; but Anea's message is clear to him—she's hurt.

"He's going back to *America,* child. Don't worry, he'll be back," Doris tells the girl in her Haitian dialect.

Emotionally distraught, Anea pitifully looks back at Gary, who doesn't want him to leave. Her tiny arms tightly wrap around hiss neck, and Anea sadly sobs her distress. Gary hugs the girl back, trying his best to make the pain go away.

185

"I'll be back soon, Anea, I *promise,*" Gary pleads. Anea lets go of her "magical" friend, and wipes her face as best as she can.

"I will never forget you!" Anea blurts out in her native tongue. Gary rises and pats her on the head, smiling, even though he's as hurt as Anea is.

He takes in one last glance of his grandmother and the little girl, who both has grown fond of him, in the week Gary has been in *Haiti.* Forcing himself, Gary leaves the home.

Andrew is sitting in the backseat of Mr. Petitehomme's car, when he sees his brother approaching. It surprises Andrew when Gary gets in the vehicle and sits down beside him.

Andrew looks at his brother intently…

Gary returns his stare…

"Are we leaving or *what?*" Gary asks aggressively, startling Andrew. His brother doesn't question Gary's sudden change of heart. Instead, Andrew faces forward.

"You heard the man, Mr. Petitehomme. Take us to the airport."

TWENTY-TWO

The flight back from *Haiti* has been a solemn one. Both Andrew and Gary have learned so much about the origin of their past, yet, they still remain relatively strangers to one another.

Andrew believes it will take more time for Gary to accept him, and Andrew himself, is still not connected to his brother. Gary's supernatural abilities, also continues to bother him.

After the jet lands, the two men proceed down the aircraft's stairs, and head towards the two limousines that awaits them. Brown, acknowledging Gary by waving his hand in the air, sits on the hood of one of the vehicles, with Melody standing poised beside him. Gary flashes his friend the peace sign, and winks his eye at Melody, who's now smiling.

She's wearing a turquoise sundress, a matching scarf wrapped around her head, with a pair of hot pink sandals that shows the *French* pedicure, on Melody's pretty toes. Gary grins and approaches her. Melody's smile melts his heart, and Gary now can tell that his girlfriend is almost fully recovered from her surgery.

"How was your trip, Gary?" Melody asks, wrapping her arms around Gary's shoulders.

"Good. It was good," he repeats. "I'm just glad to have you in my arms again," Gary whispers, now giving Melody a quick kiss.

Andrew peers through his sunglasses at the couple, as he stands outside the awaiting door of his limousine.

They truly are in love, Andrew thinks. Both Gary and Melody radiates something he's lost, a long time ago. While glancing over Gary's shoulder, Melody sees Andrew staring at them.

"Look at your brother, Gary. How can a man with so much money, seem so sad?" she gathers. Gary turns in Andrew's direction and sees the same.

"I don't know, Melody. Honestly I don't," Gary answers.

Andrew halts his driver and goes to approach the three. He stops right in front of the group, and offers his hand to Gary.

"I wanted to tell you that I'm sorry I wasn't in your life, Gary. Maybe me being with you could've made things differently. I will try my best to be there for you from now on, if you let me. I know that we're brothers but, I want to be your friend," Andrew states, still holding his hand out.

Gary can't see his brother's eyes through the dark sunglasses, but if he could, Gary would see the saddened eyes Andrew's tinted lens hides. He takes Andrew's hand with a firm grip, surprising his older brother, as Gary pulls Andrew to him, giving the man a hearty hug.

"Remember what grandma said. We're family, bro, and nothing's going to change that," Gary whispers to Andrew. He's finally accepts Andrew wholly, something that the Andrew needed most of all.

Gary lets go of his brother, and Andrew nods to him before walking back to his limousine.

"I'm coming to check on you as soon as I can," Gary says, waving his brother off. Brown, Gary and Melody watches, as Andrew's vehicle departs.

"This is like a dream, baby," Melody says while grabbing Gary by his hand.

"I know what you mean, Melody," Gary replies.

"No you don't, but I'm going to show you," she adds, pulling her boyfriend into the limousine.

Brown chuckles, as he gets in and closes the door.

* * * * *

As Andrew enters the complex to his penthouse suite, the security guard at the front desk informs Andrew that he has a visitor waiting for him.

As Andrew asks the guard who it is, he tells the industrial that the guest didn't reveal his name, but has full clearance to Andrew's suite, because of the keycard the visitor has; one of two Andrew was given, when first leasing the place. Andrew knows exactly who it is before he entering the elevator.

Yoshi Hiro is sitting in the living room, awaiting Andrew. One of his bodyguards stands firmly beside the elderly *Japanese* man. Yoshi is seated with his left leg crossed over the right, in which his right hand holds his bamboo walking cane.

188

As Andrew enters the triplex apartment, he smiled a greeting, in which Yoshi doesn't return. Instead, the old man stands and approaches the president of Lortech.

Andrew bows to Yoshi respectfully, and Yoshi's free hand, palms Andrew's shoulder. He now sees a troubled look in the elder's eyes, assuming whatever Yoshi came to visit for, won't be good news.

"How was your trip, young one?" Yoshi asks.

"Enlightening," Andrew replies.

"I had to come see you as soon as I heard you were coming back from *Haiti*. Why were you there in the first place?" Yoshi asks inquisitively.

Andrew can't tell him the truth, as it's too soon for anyone to know the origins of his past; which even bothers Andrew. It's something he will keep hidden for the time being, Andrew believing that it's the best thing to do.

"I'm thinking about opening a Lortech branch there in a certain sector. It can benefit us, and at the same time, boost *Haiti's* economy," Andrew lies.

Yoshi raises his left eyebrow peculiarly. He refuses to question Andrew further about his trip, besides, that isn't the reason why Yoshi is here; the old man's reason for visiting being far more grave than Andrew can expect.

The two men sit down, and Yoshi motions his bodyguard to bring him the briefcase he's holding. Afterwards, the guard departs the penthouse, standing on guard in front of the suite, leaving the two men alone.

"I'm sorry, Andrew. Son, I have failed you miserably," Yoshi says while whispering.

A grievous stone strikes Andrew's heart: *Failed me? Failed me how?* Andrew ponders. There can only be one answer, a task Andrew has given the *Japanese* man, more than a month prior.

"What happened, Yoshi?"

The elderly man's eyes seem to weigh his soul. "The assassin, somehow he was caught. I would've never believed that he would fail, but he did."

"How?"

"I received the assassin's dismembered head at my home, so I suspect that he told McKoon who sent him. That is the only

189

way he could've known it was me. The *bastard* cut off his head!" Yoshi tells, now full of disgrace, as his eyes falls to the floor.

"McKoon must know that I gave the order, Yoshi."

"No. Not even the man I sent knew it came from you." Andrew's worries increases, as he realizes his own accusations started it all. Andrew had let his anger cloud his better judgement. The meeting with McKoon last month angered him, so when Gary attacked Andrew in his office, displaying those strange abilities, he'd blamed McKoon.

It was Andrew who gave the orders. As it turns out, it was a disastrous mistake.

"But I fear there may be other matters. McKoon may be getting information from other sources close to you," Yoshi states. Andrew remains silent, as Yoshi opens the briefcase he brought with him.

"For years I've had an inside man at Taterax, one who's given me and your late father, information about McKoon. I had to give this to you myself. Andrew, we have serpents among us, and I fear we have already lost," Yoshi says while handing Andrew a brown envelope, in which he immediately opens.

The president of Lortech's eyes widens, when he gazes down at the contents within. At first Andrew is shocked, then he feels betrayed, which now is growing into fury.

"Michael Masters is *not* who he seems to be," Yoshi adds, as Andrew looks at several more photos of his chief of security and information, appearing with the president of Taterax, Alberto McKoon.

"I can't *believe* this," Andrew strains, as his thoughts are in jumbles. The photographs alone are enough to damn Masters. There's no conviction of why he would be possibly having meetings with McKoon, and to make matters worse, Masters knows all to well about personal affairs dealing with Andrew. Mainly of his true parents, and Andrew's strangely gifted brother.

"They *both* must be dealt with immediately!"

"I agree, Andrew," Yoshi sighs. "Son, I am becoming too old for such betrayal."

Andrew clearly views the fatigue on Yoshi's aging face.

"No, Yoshi, this is something *I* will deal with myself. This is the reason I am the president of my father's corporation. I will show you I am worthy."

"But—"

190

"Alberto McKoon has knowledge of your involvement in the attempted assassination. You need to disappear for a while, until this is over."

Yoshi's face masks his disapproval, but Andrew is correct. McKoon can be conspiring the *Japanese* man's death at this moment for all they know. Andrew will leave nothing to chance.

"Find sanctuary, understand, Yoshi?"

The old man nods his head before speaking, "The informant I have inside Taterax, his name in Ong Mra. I will instruct him to answer to you directly now, I suppose he will be of help."

"He will be, Yoshi."

Both men now rise, and Andrew shows Yoshi to the door.

"Be safe. I do not wish to see you come to harm," Andrew says. The elderly man smiles.

"I will, young one. My spirit will be with you," Yoshi adds, as he meets his bodyguard outside the door.

As Andrew is alone, he glances once again at the photos. They are like nightmares to him. Never would Andrew have thought that Masters would betray him.

The evidence lies before Andrew.

Regardless of how personal his relationship is with the man, Andrew is now fueled with bitter rage to *kill* Masters himself!

TWENTY-THREE

"IT'S BEAUTIFUL, ISN'T IT?"

Melody's question still boggles Gary's mind, as he overlooks the wonderful view of *The Village* in *Manhattan,* from the extravagant, duplex penthouse apartment in *SoHo,* where Melody has brought the young man and Brown. Crystal chandeliers sparkle upon the twenty-foot ceiling high above the trio's heads, and expensive home decorations surround them.

Melody's delicate fingers, touches her lover's chin, which she now pushes upward to close Gary's wide-opened mouth. He's awestruck. Gary looks at his girlfriend, a bit confused of the situation.

"Melody, how did you—"

"Your brother, Gary, he paid for all of this—for us."

A frown of doubt appears on Gary's face: *Why? ...Why would Andrew do this?* Gary doesn't like the idea of it, *Andrew should've told me!*

Yet, Gary now realizes that if his brother did tell him, he probably would've just declined.

"Gary, *this* is what I've always *dreamed* about!" Melody says, grabbing Gary by the hand, quickly leading him to other parts of the luxurious suite. He follows Melody quietly, as she guides Gary upstairs, leaving Brown alone in the lavish foyer area.

Melody brings Gary to the top floor, but stops abruptly when she feels the tension in his arm. Melody suddenly stares into Gary's eyes, noticing for the first time since they entered the home that he's unhappy.

"Is something wrong? Please tell me, because it's written all over your face, Gary."

"Melody...I don't know how to say this but, I don't think we should be here."

"Why not, Gary?"

Gary can't answer.

He can't explain to Melody that, by accepting what Andrew has given them, reminds him of the offer from her dead brother, Black.

"It just doesn't *feel* right Melody, I've only known my brother for a short period of time, and he's *giving* us all of *this?*"

Melody's palms touches the sides of Gary's face. She now brings hers close to his cheek, that Gary can feel Melody's breath.

"Maybe you're right, Gary, but maybe this is what GOD intended. You've been struggling for *so* long, baby, we both have. Now, we've finally got a break. For a second, *just* for a second in time, let's enjoy our life, and not *worry* about tomorrow."

Melody's lips touches Gary's as they kiss passionately.

"Damn, I love you," she breathes into Gary's mouth, before Melody's hand quickly fumbles to open the door of the master bedroom room they're in front of.

Her hand finds the doorknob Melody searched for, and she immediately pushes the door open. Gary unlocks his lips when the huge bedroom door swings open. He smiles, as Gary now views the opulent room.

"Besides, if you decide that you want to turn this apartment down, I have to make love in here at *least* once," Melody jokes, causing them both to laugh.

Gary steps into the room, and doesn't stop until he comes to the balcony that leads outside. The warm sun shines brightly, as Gary opens the sliding *French* doors, and walks onto the balcony.

His hands grasp the steel railing, and Gary slowly views the city below. The scenery is amazing to him, something truly to behold. Melody steps out behind Gary, wrapping her arms around his back. The cool wind caresses their bodies.

"I can't believe this," Gary whispers.

"I couldn't believe it at first, either, but the world is now ours," Melody hints, as she rests her chin upon Gary's shoulders. "Damn, I love you."

"Melody…there is something I have to tell you, but you have to promise that you won't freak out."

Melody raises her chin, and Gary rotates to face her. She gives him a puzzling stare, "What is it?"

"There's something about me that you don't know… something that I didn't know myself, until recently."

"Don't tell me that you're dying!" Melody shouts and her face frowns.

"No silly, that's not it, but you *have* to promise that you won't freak out."

"Just tell me, Gary!" his girlfriend demands, growing frustrated.

Gary places one hand on the banister, and takes a look down at the city streets. He soon glances back at Melody with a mischievous grin on his face.

"I can show you better than I can tell you."

Melody instantly gasps in shock, when the love of her life, jumps over the railing into a deadly freefall. She leans over the edge of the balcony, and screams out in terror: "G-A-R-Y!"

Melody continues calling out his name frantically, peering through teary eyes at the busy streets below. She soon turns away, as Melody sees Gary falling fast, now wanting to believe that it's a nightmare she's having.

WHY WOULD GARY JUMP TO HIS DEATH WHEN WE NOW HAVE SO MUCH? THIS ISN'T REAL! Melody thinks, as she cries with her eyes tightly shut. The young woman now falls to her knees and sobs uncontrollably.

THIS ISN'T REAL!
...THIS IS A NIGHTMARE!
WAKE UP, MELODY!

Gary focuses his mind as he falls. Suddenly, the young man's body levitates upwards at an incredible high speed. Gary now flies above the balcony he just leapt off of, and his heart skips a beat, now realizing what he did.

Gary wanted to surprise Melody with his special abilities, yet the sight he sees, makes Gary regret in going too far. Soon after, he lands lightly back onto the balcony, and kneels beside his love.

"Melody? Melody, I'm sorry," Gary offers. Melody now opens her eyes, and gasps when seeing Gary next to her.

"How?" she says in awe. At first, Melody is relieved that he's alive, but begins to angrily swing her closed fists at Gary.

"DON'T DO THAT TO ME! DON'T...how?" Melody shouts before mumbling, as Gary grabs her flailing arms, and brings Melody to him in a warm embrace. She sobs uncontrollably into Gary's chest.

"Why did you *do* that, Gary?"

"I won't scare you like that again, I just wanted to show you."

"Show me what?' Melody whispers.

"Look, love," Gary says calmly.

Melody observes, and immediately clutches on to him tightly, realizing that her feet isn't on the floor. Melody now floats in Gary's arms.

"THIS IS IMPOSSIBLE!" she claims.

"It is possible," Gary assures Melody. "I have these abilities. I've had them since I was a kid, but didn't know until recently."

Melody is still taking in the incredible fact that she's floating. The young woman turns her head to look up at Gary, and he gently wipes away Melody's tears.

Gary, the man who holds Melody tightly, is the love of her life, whose powers doesn't scare her, now filling Melody with awe.

"There's a lot I want to ask you, Gary...this is all so strange."

Gary smiles, "I will answer everything, Melody. I don't want to keep anything from you. I—I"

Melody silences him.

Without warning, she kisses Gary.

Forgetting all about the sudden shock.

Sharing only with Gary: a moment of *absolute* magic!

TWENTY-FOUR

Michael Masters is in the middle of a board meeting, discussing the benefits of Lortech's latest developments in biotechnology, when he spots Andrew quickly approaching his office through the glass door.

Masters smiles at his superior, yet, it soon fades, as he notices the mean expression on Andrew's face. The president of Lortech now violently shoves the doors open, causing everyone in the room to pause, now staring at Andrew in shock.

"This meeting's over! I want everyone out!" Andrew demands.

Masters gives Andrew a quizzical glance, "I'm sorry, Mr. Taylor, this is an important meeting."

"Maybe you all didn't *hear* me, I want everyone out!" Andrew orders a second time, not letting his sight leave the man who he suspects is betraying him.

One-by-one, among appalled and hidden whispers, the board members exit the room. Andrew doesn't speak again, until he's sure that he and Masters are alone.

The older man slowly approaches Andrew: "Mr. Taylor I—"

"Be *silent,* Masters, I *don't* want to hear you!" Andrew spits. "I've just returned from *Haiti,* and I've had time to clear my head. I've decided to terminate your employment here at Lortech!"

His statement is like a smack in the face to Masters, who's now startled by Andrew.

"What the *hell?* You *can't* do that to me, have you gone mad? Is this about your brother?"

Andrew rushes towards Masters, catching himself at the last moment poised to strike the now ex-chief of security.

Andrew's muscles are tense with fire.

He points his finger an inch away from Masters' face.

"Don't you dare, Masters! I have *proof* of your meeting with Alberto McKoon. There's no telling *what* this corporation has compromised because of you!" Andrew barks.

The accusations hit Masters to the core.

196

"You're wrong, Andrew."

A sharp punch now hits Masters' mouth, causing him to stumble back. Andrew feels the pain in his knuckles immediately, clenching his hand tighter, yearning to strike Masters again. Masters soon grabs his face with his right hand, to ease the pain of Andrew's unexpected punch.

"You've betrayed Lortech, you've betrayed my father, and you've betrayed me! I would have *never* suspected you. How could you, Masters?" Andrew asks through his constricting throat.

Masters spits blood from the newly formed cut in his mouth before he answers: "There are things that you don't know, Andrew, things about your father, and Lortech! Things that you'll wish you'd *never* have unlocked, if only you knew! I tried to *protect* you!"

A grim smile now appears on Masters' face, and for a quick second, Andrew swears to himself that he sees something strange about the man's eyes.

"You *can't* fire me! I'm *too* much of an asset to you and this corporation!"

"You're a cancer, Masters." Andrew interjects. "If a body has cancer in its arm, you *remove* it, so the body can survive. Masters, I will have you watched to the point that, you will not be able to take a *shit* without eyes on you. Anymore attempts to disclose *any* information about Lortech's projects to anyone, and I'll freeze *all* of your funds, you'll be broke. I'll make it to the point that you won't exist. Now, get the *hell* out of my building!"

Masters is furious!

Andrew makes powerful threats, ones that Masters isn't sure he can initiate.

Clutching his jaw, Masters approaches the door.

"You're making a grave mistake."

"AM I?" Andrew answers sternly. He watches carefully, as Masters exits his former office. "One more thing. If you have any more meetings with Alberto McKoon, I promise, I will have you *killed*."

Masters didn't look at Andrew when he said those last words. Instead, Masters leaves the office silently.

TWENTY-FIVE

Ong Mra is a genetic researcher at Taterax's Sector 7 department. His intelligence and service are profound, so it's of no surprise when he receives a call to have a meeting with president, Alberto McKoon.

On the elevator ride up to McKoon's office, Mra feels uneasy. He loosens his tie, imaging that the fabric is restricting his breathing. Mra has no idea what McKoon wants, but Mra has no choice in the matter. If McKoon wants to have a meeting with one of his researchers, then it will happen, no questions asked.

Mra's ever-growing nervous demeanor comes from something else entirely. His secret *is* the reason, newly formed beads of sweat forms on Mra's forehead. Mra's trying to calm himself with the knowledge that, McKoon will never know of his true intentions, working at Taterax.

The elevator stops.

The doors open.

A security guard escorts the silent researcher down the hall, and into the office of McKoon. As the doors slams shut, Mra's curious eyes search the president's spacious office.

McKoon sits at his throne, stone-faced. His hands are interlaced, covering the bottom of his face. A man is standing behind McKoon with his back turned to them, staring quietly out of the giant windows; admiring the morning's skyline. Mra can't see the man's face; nevertheless, a haunting feeling now embraces the researcher.

"Please, Mr. Mra, come closer. I have something that I need to urgently discuss with you," McKoon says calmly. Mra complies with his boss' wishes, sitting down in the seat closest to McKoon.

"Thank you for having the time to meet with me, Mr. McKoon. I must admit that, I am a bit surprised, though. What is it that you would like to discuss?" Mra offers, fighting the urge to squirm in his seat. Mra then steals a glance at the man who's still staring out the window; the man's pose doesn't waver.

"I'm interested in your progress. You're a formidable asset to this corporation, and that fact doesn't miss my eye," McKoon states with a smile.

Mra clears his throat, trying to keep his focus on the president of Taterax in front of him. "Well, sir, we're making strides in our implications of genetic therapies and—"

As Mra speaks, the man standing by the window finally turns around, causing Mra to pause when he sees his face. McKoon notices the gleam in Mra's eyes when he sees Michael Masters—McKoon now interrupting the researcher's speech.

"I apologize for not taking the time to introduce you to one of my business associates."

Masters grins, and extends his hand to Mra.

"Have you two ever met?" McKoon asks.

"No, no we haven't. My name's Ong Mra, and yours?" Mra questions. His nervousness shows clearly on his face, and Masters feels it when he shakes Mra's sweaty hand.

"I think you do know my name," Masters points out.

"How could I?"

Masters' grin vanishes.

Both men's stares seem to burn into Mra, as he pulls his hand away from Masters.

"As I said before, Mr. Mra, you *are* a valuable asset to this corporation, and with that, comes a price. Are you *willing* to pay that price?" McKoon questions inquisitively, before standing.

A bead of sweat runs down the researcher's head.

Do they know my secret? Mra thinks. *They have to know, why else would I be here?*

As Mra now stares into the eyes of his boss, he sees something that terribly scares him. Both Masters and McKoon's eyes suddenly change.

They're no longer human.

The eyes are animalistic in appearance.

Mra quickly jumps to his feet, with his heart beating rapidly inside his chest. Mra immediately steps back from McKoon and Masters, unable to comprehend what he's witnessing.

"The lord knows *all* secrets, Ong Mra. Knows your betrayal, knows your fear!" McKoon hisses. Mra darts for the office door, as he hears McKoon's eerie voice.

A bulging, slime-coated tentacle, reaches out from the shadow on the wall, and snares the researcher, quickly wrapping around Mra's body. It constricts his movement, gripping tightly to Mra's struggling muscles.

He wants to scream...

But the enormous pressure keeps Mra from breathing.

The giant vine now twist, bringing Mra face-to-face with the hideous form it's attached to.

Large, red, serpentine eyes, glares menacingly, at the human it has in its grasp. The creature's mouth now opens, bearing multiple rows of flesh-tearing fangs. Ito Mra, it's like staring into darkness, darkness that's infinitely evil, and terrifying alive.

"You will become one with my Jinn, your betrayal will be forgiven," comes the blood-curdling voice of the creature.

Mra's blood-shot eyes widens, as he sees its mouth open wider. The researcher hears the buzzing of insects, and what looks to be a mad swarm of bees, emerging from the rancid bowels of the beast.

The angry group of insects begins to attack Mra's head. He gasps and chokes, feeling the agony of the bees, entering his orifices. By the hundreds, they violently force themselves in Mra's ears, mouth and nose, causing him to gag, as tears falls from the man's eyes.

The vicious intrusion into Mra's body, as well as the swarming cloud the bees create, as they make their brutal journey, cause the captured to cease breathing—Mra now only tasting the bile intruders, feeling the agonizing pain, as they violate him.

The eternal one drops the researcher on his hands and knees, as the last of the swarm makes their way, into the depths of Mra's body. When the bees' invasion ends, he gasps for the denied oxygen, before vomiting on the floor.

Mra's whole form is on fire, as the transformation is complete; the insects inside of him have merged with Mra's entire being. Soon, the pain ends, now replaced by a great sense of power, as a dark, menacing force embraces him.

Mra now hear voices that aren't his own...

It's a communion of others, others like Mra.

Who understands and submits...to the dark denomination.

Mra glances upward, watching the world through his now serpentine eyes. He sees the true, unbridled forms of the two men, who once appeared human to Mra. The researcher soon gazes at the creature he will now, and forever, call his lord.

"Now, you are one," Lord Moon declares. Mra grins forebodingly before answering.

"Yes, Lord Moon. The Jinn Legion are one."

Mra is now, as so many before him throughout time, one who shares the flesh of the eternal one.

The man is now an avatar of the Etherea.

Known as Lord Moon.

* * * * *

Cold sweat drenches all over Andrew, as he awakes. His heart is pounding fast in his chest, and Andrew trembles, as if frightened by whatever jarred him from his sleep.

A dream?

Rather a nightmare, one that Andrew can't remember, now that he's conscious.

Andrew looks at the clock: *9 AM.* He slept late, because yesterday strained him: the exhausting trip back from Haiti, his enlightening meeting with Yoshi, and having to fire Masters, who Andrew believed was loyal to him.

The industrialist spent the rest of yesterday, and the waking hours of the night, reprogramming security and access codes, in his office at Lortech. When Andrew finally returned home, the fatigue left him with nothing more than the urge to sleep.

Now, Andrew still feels groggy and shaken, as he makes his way to the shower. The water refreshes Andrew very little, whatever he dreamed, is still bothering him. Andrew can't recall a single image, yet the panic still lingers dreadfully.

Soon after, he gets dressed, and prepares to return to his daily duties at Lortech. Two armed security guards, awaits Andrew in the lobby of his penthouse. They soon escort the entrepreneur to his limousine.

Andrew now knows, with all the sudden transformations in his life, that he will have to strive even *harder,* to control Lortech.

Andrew owes it to the man and woman who raised him.

* * * * *

Gary stands next to Melody while holding her hand, on a sidewalk in the *South Bronx*. Across the street are demolished bricks, of what used to be a club, Melody's brother's strip club. With much guilt, the young man decides above all else, that he has to tell his girlfriend, the truth about Black's death.

"Why did you bring me here, Gary? You know I hate this place."

"Because you need to know the truth about what happened, Melody, even if you decide to leave me for what I did. You have to know the truth," Gary states, with his eyes staying locked on the debris while speaking.

"Did you *blow* up that building, Gary?"

Gary doesn't answer...

"Did you?"

Gary takes a deep breath, still refusing to let his sight wander from the demolished building.

"When I first found out about my powers, I got scared, Melody, and became desperate. I needed time to be alone, to figure out what it was that I possessed, and to find out where the abilities came from. I went upstate, and had some time to learn how to control them. I left for two weeks.

"When I came back, Melody, you were gone. I'd found Brown in your apartment, and he'd told me everything—how you'd thought Black did something to me, and the way you'd confronted your brother, as well as what that *bastard* did to you," Gary's voice begins to fade, as the memories arises and pains him. Melody recognizes her boyfriend's turmoil.

"When I saw you in that hospital bed on the edge of death, I was so *fucked* up, Melody. I wanted to trade in my *life* for yours—I wanted to die! It was *my* fault, it was because of *me* that you almost died!" Gary admits, as his sorrow is immediately replaced with rage. Melody feels the muscles in her lover's arm tense, as Gary continues.

"With *all* of my powers, I was unable to save you, you being the *only* person who gave a *fuck* about me, the only one that I love. But there was one thing I could do, one thing that GOD couldn't even *stop* me from doing!"

"Gary, stop, I don't want to hear anymore. You don't need to—"

"Yes, I do, Melody, you have to know," Gary interjects, as he turns to face Melody for the first time, since they had

202

arrived to *The Bronx*. "I came here, and entered the club with one goal. I *killed* Mex by tearing him apart, then I found your brother, Black, and made him burn, Melody. I wanted Black to *pay,* to feel the *fucking* pain he gave you!"

Gary now sees the horror growing in his girlfriend.

"That wasn't enough, Melody. When I left the club, I'd locked everybody inside. I wanted to destroy *everything* that was a part of Black. I brought the building down, and killed everyone inside. I heard them screaming, Melody—I killed them."

The young man's horrible tale causes Melody to take a step back. There's something about Gary's demeanor that frightens the young woman.

"What do you think, Melody? Am I a monster? ...I don't deserve you, not after what I've done."

Gary bows his head, and stares at the concrete below. He's ashamed, feeling as though he's condemned. Melody's hand softly touches Gary's face, and he raises his head to face her.

"I don't think that you're a monster, yet, I know you've made a mistake. You were hurt, Gary, just as I was. Whether what you've done was right or wrong, I'm not going to judge you, Gary—because I love you. I forgive you for what you've done."

Gary bites his bottom lip, fighting back the tide of anger that emerges, with the recollection of that night.

"Thank you, Melody. You don't know how much that means to me," Gary answers, feeling a burden leave his soul.

"I do, Gary," Melody admits, as she takes his hand, and leads Gary back to the limousine they arrived in.

Gary believed that his confession would damn him in Melody's eyes, yet she understands and forgives Gary. Melody doesn't want to leave him, nor does she thinks that Gary's a demon, as her brother, Black had called Gary; the night the young man killed him.

Shortly afterwards, Melody dozes off to sleep in Gary's arms, as they drive away. No matter how powerful he's becoming, Gary's cursed gifts doesn't scare the young woman, as Melody truly knows what lies in his heart.

TWENTY-SIX

Andrew instructs the limousine driver to stop at the main entrance of Lortech's tower, instead of entering the building's parking lot like he usually does. One of the entrepreneur's personal bodyguards, exits the vehicle first, and holds the door open for Andrew, as the other sentinel comes around the sidewalk from the other side.

The president of Lortech doesn't take three steps, before a sudden commotion breaks out.

Ong Mra waits at the building's entrance for Andrew to arrive. He strains while charging towards the three men, as Andrew and security exits the limousine.

One of the industrialist's protectors notices the fast-approaching man, and instinctively withdraws his weapon, causing his partner to protectively step in front of Andrew and do the same.

Now, Andrew is stunned, until realizing what has brought about his guards' action. He sees one of his security men quickly restraining an unfamiliar pedestrian, grabbing Mra in a tight chokehold, and immediately placing the mouth of his gun on the man's right temple.

Mra has a crazed expression upon his face.

Sweat pours down heavily from his head.

White spittle drips all around the man's lips and chin.

A sick twisted version of the guy Mra was hours ago.

"Sorry, sir. Looks like we got some sort of drug addict. Probably just out of his mind. We'll have him arrested," one of the guards assures.

Andrew breathes a sigh of relief.

The problem isn't as serious as he thinks.

Andrew begins to walk away.

The constrained man struggles to speak:

"Wait. Wait, Mr. Taylor, p-l-e-a-s-e!"

Andrew continues on walking.

"You might not know who I am, but my name is Ong Mra!" the man soon yells.

The industrialist immediately halts. *Ong Mra,* Andrew suddenly recalls what Yoshi Hiro told him.

Andrew rotates.

Takes two steps closer to Mra.

The man's blood-shot eyes are wide.

As if Mra's heavily under the influence of drugs.

"What did you say your name was?" Andrew asks.

"Ong Mra. Please, listen to me, Mr. Taylor—your life is in danger!"

Andrew is now bothered, he motions for his guard to release the man. The protector complies.

Mra takes a deep breath.

Wipes the foam from the corners of his mouth.

"Alberto McKoon, Michael Masters—they're planning to *kill* you! Destroy your corporation! I had to warn you, they're part of something I *never* imagined."

"What are you talking about?" Andrew questions.

Mra wipes the thick snot that's dripping from his nose.

"The Jinn Legion, I can *f-e-e-l* them inside of me. I can't control it, they're taking over. Lord Moon, it's…it's," He now struggles to speak, but finds he doesn't have the power.

Mra's words don't make sense to Andrew.

The strange man sounds delusive and insane.

Andrew palms Mra's shoulder.

Mra now freezes…bows his head.

Turns upward, and glares at Andrew crazily.

Andrew frowns at the sight of Mra's condition.

"What did they do to you?" Andrew probes.

A maddened grin suddenly appears on Mra's face.

"THEY SET ME F-R-E-E!"

Before Andrew can react, Mra opens his mouth, revealing large, jagged fangs. The man moves fast towards Andrew, and the guards attempt to protect their superior, but can't react in time.

Mra suddenly sinks his sharp teeth into Andrews' neck, with his jaws closing with such pressure, that the blood shoots out of the industrialist's wound, and splatters on the sidewalk.

Andrew's eyes widens in shock and terror!

One of his guards quickly places his gun on the back of Mra's skull, and pulls the trigger. The gunshot is so close to Andrew's face, that he can smell the burning gunpowder, as he and Mra's lifeless body, falls to the ground.

Andrew instinctively grabs the bleeding wound, and warm blood trickles through his fingers, staining his suit. The second guard helps his boss to his feet, as the other who shot Mra, turns the man's body around.

"I'm sorry, sir, I wouldn't have—"

"I DON'T WANT TO *HEAR* YOUR EXCUSES!" Andrew orders, angrily staring down at the dead man, peering at Mra's opened mouth. The man's teeth doesn't appear as they did seconds ago, they're now normal. Andrew's mind searches for some rationale of what he'd seen.

There is none.

"Sir, we need to get you to the hospital," a bodyguard suggests to Andrew.

"No, not until I find out what's going on. Get me to the bio lab and alert the proper authorities. Too many people just witnessed this."

"Okay, sir."

One of Andrew's protectors quickly escorts the president of Lortech into the building, while the other phones the local police.

Andrew reflects on the look on Ong Mra's face, his erratic behavior, and what the man told him about McKoon and Masters.

It's as if he was infected with something…

Andrew's first priority is to find out that the latter isn't true. Then, he will make sense of the strange encounter, and find out what was done to Mra.

Andrew soon has a growing suspicion that: *Everything is going to get much worse….*

*   *   *   *   *

Two hours later, Andrew sits silently in his office, viewing three LCD computer screens on his desk. Scientist, Karen Scott took samples from Andrew's wound earlier, and patched him up, when Andrew first entered the building.

She also told him that no infections were found, or any traces of pathogens in Andrew's blood sample. But Karen warned him that she needed clearance from the proper authorities, to further analyze Ong Mra's corpse. Andrew told the scientist that he would get it done.

After the cleaning and patching of his wound, Andrew finds himself, replaying the things Mra said to him, and reliving the moments, of what Andrew recently witnessed. Mra blew his cover, warning Andrew about Michael Masters and Alberto McKoon. The man said that they'd planned to kill him, and destroy Lortech, but what Andrew doesn't understand, is when Mra started babbling about the Jinn Legion and Lord Moon.

Andrew thought that Mra was talking madness, until recalling that he'd heard the names before. Now, Andrew watches the data Desmond Jones had provided him two months ago. On one screen is the photo of the coffin the entrepreneur had found, and on the other monitor is Desmond's translation.

Lord Moon and the Jinn Legion are names used in the translation, names Desmond told Andrew that he'd never heard in historical context.

How could Mra have any knowledge of it? Andrew thinks: *It doesn't make sense!*

The tomb had been hidden in the mines for an undetermined amount of time, no one knew about AU and AG but Andrew. Desmond and his team are the only ones aware about the mines.

I wonder if Masters somehow found out about the two supernatural beings, and has told McKoon...

The idea plays in Andrew's head, he has to find the connection. Ong Mra told him too little before attacking Andrew—Mra, the only person who could've made sense of the puzzle, who's now dead.

...What did they do to Mra to put him in such a state? Andrew continues to ponder.

"Mr. Taylor, someone is here to see you," comes over the speakerphone at his desk.

Andrew touches the "speak" button: "I don't want to be disturbed at this time, tell them to reschedule."

"But, sir, the man is from the FBI, he says his name is Richard Banker. He wants to speak to you about the incident this morning."

Andrew's raises his eyebrows.

Presses a command button on the computer keyboard.

It flips around in front of him.

Three computer screens folds into the marble desk...

Unseen.

"Let him in," Andrew instructs.

The industrialist braces himself.

Andrew's office doors opens.

In walks an older White man that appears to be in his fifties. His face is sullen, and the man's eyes droop low, giving the expression that he's tired.

"You must be Andrew Taylor—I'm agent Banker," the FBI agent states, holding his hand out in greeting.

Andrew doesn't oblige.

"My secretary has already informed me of who you are, but I don't understand why you're here. I believe my security has already notified the local police about the incident," Andrew tells, clearly showing the fact that he doesn't like the fact that the FBI is getting involved.

"They did indeed...not very much on details anyway." The FBI agent reaches into his pocket, and pulls out a pen and a small writing pad. "It says here that, the assailant, Ong Mra attacked you, so one of your men shot him in the head."

"That's what happened."

Banker continues, "Why would someone risk attacking a man, escorted by two armed guards? Did he know you, Mr. Taylor?"

"The man knew my name, said he had something to tell me that was important."

"Did you know the assailant?"

"No," Andrew lies.

Banker jots down something on his pad, "Would you mind telling me what the attacker had to tell you that was so important?"

Andrew thinks fast. He won't allow himself to reveal his business to the FBI agent, but, there's something that Andrew will let Banker know, a fact that even bothers him.

"The man told me that someone called the Jinn Legion and Lord Moon were going to destroy me."

Banker stops writing.

"I'm sorry, could you repeat that."

"The attacker warned me that the Jinn Legion, and Lord Moon would destroy me."

"That sounds very *odd*, Mr. Taylor. Have you heard of these people before?"

"No, I was hoping that maybe you could enlighten me. Do you think the man was talking about terrorists?"

"If he was, I've never heard of them. Maybe the attacker was crazy, what do you think?"

"I believe he was," Andrew says, before standing up. "After the man said that he attacked me, he bit me in the neck." Andrew touches his neck to emphasize.

"Looks like a nasty wound, maybe you should go to the hospital and get it looked at."

"My staff has already tended to my needs. Is there *anything* else you want to ask me?" Andrew says hastily.

"I think that's it."

"Then I have a question for you."

Banker shrugs his shoulders while putting the items in his hand, back into his pocket. "What is it?"

"I still can't figure out what business this is of the FBI."

Banker smiles. "I'll answer that. When a man of importance, such as yourself, is attacked right in front of a building he owns, in such a way, red flags go up. We've been watching you, Mr. Taylor, since you've inherited your father's corporation. Someone of your age shouldn't be in a position of such...such—"

"Power?" Andrew says, cutting off the agent's words.

Banker hesitates. "...Well, I was going to say—"

"Good *day,* Agent Banker," Andrew interjects, angering the agent with his arrogance.

"Good day to you, too, Mr. Taylor."

Andrew coldly watches the agent, as Banker leaves his office. Andrew soon goes to his window, looking at his own reflection.

The entrepreneur pulls the bandage off from his neck. Andrew now knows, just as he has an hour ago, that the wound is now smooth skin. The evidence to what happened to him, when Andrew first arrived at Lortech, is gone, without a trace.

"Mr. Taylor, I'm sorry to disturb you again, but I have a call from Valerie Taylor, she sounds upset."

Andrew places the bandage back on his neck, ceasing his floating thoughts, as the industrialist sits back at his desk.

"Put her through on a secured line."

"Yes, Mr. Taylor."

As the phone clicks over, Andrew already has a firm idea of what his mother wants.

"Andrew, are you there?"

"I'm here, mother, I'm alright."

"Good, baby, good. I just heard what happened on the news. Those *crazy* drug addicts, I heard he attacked you."

"He really didn't get a chance to, my guards kept me safe."

"That's good news. Why didn't you tell me you were back from your trip, I've been worried about you, especially because of the last time you visited."

"You're right, I apologize."

"I want you to come see me tonight, Andrew. I just have to see you, with all of this *madness* going on."

"I was coming to see you tonight, anyway. I'll be there."

"Promise me you will."

"I promise," Andrew answers, knowing full well how determined the woman can be."

"Okay then, I want you to be safe, son, I love you."

"I love you, too."

With that, the phone call ends.

Andrew believes that Valerie is right, spending some time with her, if just for a conversation or two, will give him back the normalcy he needs to regain his sanity.

Andrew also faces the assumption that Gary is right: *"I do possess some strange gift.* His rapid healing from the wound Ong Mra has inflicted only heightens the fact. Out of all the scientific marvels, and creations Andrew has witnessed working at Lortech, he finds that his past is the greatest mystery of it all.

When Gary attacked Andrew when they first met, the entrepreneur didn't accept the magnitude that he'd healed from those fires, believing that somehow, what happened could be explained.

Now, Andrew doesn't feel as though any of his childhood was that simple, nor will his adult life be.

TWENTY-SEVEN

The sun settles, and nightfall comes. Gary decides that he wants to spend the evening back at the penthouse with Melody. The couple dines on steamed shrimps and lobster tails, which Melody knew he would like. After their meal, the two sit on the living room couch, sipping champagne.

Afterwards, Melody lies comfortably in Gary's arms, as they watch *Friday* on their *Sony* 60-inch, plasma flat screen television. The drinks make Melody and Gary more relaxed, and soon, they find themselves laughing at the movie they view; as if the drama that crept into their lives recently, is now gone.

Gary watches the young woman's gentle smile, in the darkened room. He absolutely loves Melody, who now cradles onto him. The young man soon realizes that he never thanked Andrew for saving her life. Without Melody, Gary would have no reason to live. Now, everything seems perfect. Gary has found peace, and it's to be cherished.

"Melody?" Gary says softly.

Smiling because of the humorous movie, Melody turns her head to face him: "What's up, Gary?"

He slowly runs his hand through Melody's short hairdo.

"I've been thinking about some things. My brother told me that he put millions of dollars in our accounts."

"Andrew did do that, Gary."

"Well, you and I have spent most of our lives struggling to make ends meet. We've never had a break until now, and I…" Gary pauses, trying to find the right words. "…I want to see the world with you. Melody, I want us to spend the rest of our lives happy. Let's get married, have some kids—let's leave *New York,* and build a foundation together."

Melody's smile grows wider, as she takes in her boyfriend's suggestion. "You *really* want to have kids, Gary?"

"I want to spend my life with you, Melody. I've known that since the first time I met you," Gary confesses.

Melody's hand caresses his chest, and her eyes begin to moisten. "Okay, Gary, but your brother?"

"I'll always know where he is. Andrew's my flesh and blood, but you, you're my heart."

Gary wipes away Melody's first budding tear, and she now pulls his face to hers. They begin to kiss, and Gary unnoticeably uses his powers, gently floating he and Melody to the bedroom, as though it's the most natural thing to do.

When their bodies touch the king-sized bed, Melody unlocks her lips, noticing the change of environment. She grins mischievously.

"Gary, how did we get here?"

"Who cares, let's make babies," he jokes.

Melody laughs, as Gary grabs her playfully.

Soon, they make passionate love, without a care for the outside world; Melody and Gary love as though it's all they know. When their bodies become exhausted, both Gary and Melody sleep in each other's arms.

It's a prelude of love, as strong as the chaos to come.

*　*　*　*　*

In the subconscious world of dreams, Gary finds himself in a frightening familiar place. He watches the flickering flames from the single torch, outside the Vowdun's home. Gary's back in Haiti again, in the blackness of night.

Alone.

Off in the distance, he sees two bright lights in high beams, from a car that's coming closer to the area. The vehicle stops thirty yards away from the witch's hut.

The car door opens, and out comes Wilfred and Marylyn Romulus with their two children. When the Vowdun emerges from her home, Gary sees the fear in his mother's saddened eyes. His pulse begins to race, now realizing that this nightmare is far more different from the others that Gary has had, throughout his life.

He isn't reliving the nightmare as the newborn baby he was when the incident really happened; instead, Gary is now a grown man, viewing the surreal, upsetting dream as it's taking place.

Gary gasps as he sees his younger self and brother being taken into the Vowdun's lair.

I can't let this happen again! I can change it this time! *Gary thinks to himself.*

In desperation, he quickly sprints towards the witch, running past his mother and father, who don't even notice his presence.

Gary now runs faster.

"N-O-O-O-O-O-O! I WON'T LET IT HAPPEN AGAIN, YOU HEAR ME, WITCH?" he calls out. Surprisingly, the Vowdun turns around and sees Gary. Her sulky, yellow-colored eyes, beam at the charging man, before they flash and change to crimson.

The witch lets go of Andrew's small hand, and raises her hand, the Vowdun's palm now facing in Gary's direction. A horrid grin shows on her old, aging face.

"You will never stop me!" the witch hisses.

As Gary is mere meters away from the vile woman, an immense flash of light, burst forth from her hand, with a force so great, it sends Gary flying high and fast in the air. He soon crashes down hard on his back, winded, as Gary's chest burns in pain.

He coughs up blood from his mouth, and struggles for oxygen. Full of rage, Gary soon stumbles awkwardly back to his feet, ready for battle, but when his vision clears, nothing is there, except the flaming torch.

The hut, car, Vowdun and Romulus family are all gone. Gary is once again, alone, in the desolate Haitian land. Boiling in anger, he unleashes glowing fires from his hands. It flickers wildly around Gary's tightly balled fists, but ceases to harm him in any way.

"COME OUT, WITCH! I KNOW YOU'RE THERE, I CAN FEEL YOU! I'M GOING TO KILL YOU, YOU FUCKING COWARD!" he cries out, eyes swiftly darts back-and-forth.

Suddenly, two vine-like tentacles come racing out of the darkness, and before Gary can react, they rapidly wrap around his fiery hands, causing Gary's powers to cease. The tentacles soon bind around the whole of his arms, until they're at Gary's shoulders, squeezing his muscles tightly.

It's as if Gary is in the deadly embrace of two large snakes, the young man now being Gary captured. He now hears and feels his bones, as they pop out of Gary's shoulder socket as he's being lifted.

Gary screams out in agony!

Out of the shadowy night comes the creature, standing at nine-feet-tall, covered by a large black cloak, in which all that can be seen is its horrid, gruesome face. The limbs that grips Gary mercilessly, brings him to the body that they're attached to.

The young man's watery eyes stares into the large, glowing, red serpentine eyes, of the beast who had changed him; the monster Gary remembers the witch had become when he was an infant.

Gary grits his teeth, fighting the excruciating pain, as he views the true form of the Vowdun—the monstrosity that hides behind the witch's wrinkled flesh.

Gary now isn't afraid—he's enraged. The young man quickly gathers saliva in his mouth and spits at his nightmare. The beast with its hellish voice, chuckles.

"YOU KILLED MY PARENTS! I'LL DESTROY YOU FOR WHAT YOU DID TO MY FAMILY, FOR WHAT YOU DID TO ME!" Gary retorts.

"BE SILENT, MY CHOSEN! ACCEPT WHAT YOU HAVE BECOME, THE GIST I HAVE GIVEN YOU AND YOUR BROTHER, IS FAR GREATER THAN THE SOULS OF THOSE DEAD!" the beast screeches.

"YOU GAVE US NOTHING BUT MISERY!"

"I'VE GIVEN YOU BOTH A PART OF MY ETERNAL ESSENCE. THAT IS SOMETHING THAT YOU WILL NEVER ESCAPE. YOU TWO ARE MY SEEDS, MY SONZ OF DARKNESS!"

"WE WILL NEVER BE A PART OF YOU!" Gary growls. Even with the incredible amount of torture he's receiving, Gary's thirst for revenge is far greater.

"YOU WILL ACCEPT YOUR DESTINY, MY CHILD, OR FACE DESTRUCTION BEYOND YOUR IMAGINATION. WHAT I HAVE GIVEN YOU, MY CHOSEN, CAN'T BE TAKEN BACK."

"FUCK YOU!"

The creature's face snarls at Gary's defiance. "IF YOU WILL NOT TAKE HEED, THEN BEHOLD." The tentacles turns Gary away from the eternal one, and the young man's eyes widens at what he sees.

His young brother, Andrew now appears naked and battered, surrounded by horrific, animalistic creatures, with the likeness of the beast that Gary captured. Andrew is helpless in their savagery.

"STOP THIS! STOP IT!" Gary demands.

"NO, I WILL NOT! ONLY HE CAN!"

Gary watches on, as one of the terrifying creatures, slowly sinks its teeth in Andrew's neck, and horrendously tears the young boy's throat out. Andrew haphazardly falls to the ground while bleeding heavily. The young boy now tries to crawl away from the creatures, as the Earth quickly swallows Andrew's blood.

Afterwards, Andrew's blood-shot eyes meet Gary's, who now hears the young boy's gurgling plea: "STOP THIS, VOWDUN!"

The giant creature doesn't answer, as the monsters surrounds Andrew's form, attacking him by viciously tearing Andrew apart.

Gary's eyelids shut tightly, as tears fall from them. He desperately tries to block out the gory scene, yet Gary can't shut out the loud, terrifying sounds he hears during Andrew's brutalization.

Instantly, everything becomes silent.

"NOW DO YOU UNDERSTAND, CHOSEN? YOU WILL KNOW NOTHING BUT SUFFERING, UNTIL THE END OF TIME," the Vowdun's eerie voice says to Gary.

Gary's body moves wildly as he screams: "I'll KILL YOU! I'LL KILL YOU ALL!"

* * * * *

Melody gets out of bed as Gary thrashes in his sleep, becoming frightened by the things she hears Gary screaming. Melody now stands next to the bed, watching him suffer with the nightmare Gary's trapped in.

Soon, the young woman gathers enough courage to get on top of him, and holds Gary tightly, pleading for him to wake up. Melody wants her lover to be free from whatever hell torments him.

Suddenly, Gary's screaming and punching ends, and he stops fighting. Cautiously, Melody slowly raises her head to look Gary in the face. She's taken aback, seeing that he's now was awake and watching her calmly.

"You okay, baby?" Melody whispers.

"No, Melody, but I will be."

Gary gets out of bed, and stands up, causing his girlfriend to wonder what scared Gary so much in his sleep. He walks to the balcony door and opens it. The nightly air breezes through the room as Gary enters the balcony. Melody immediately gets up and follows him.

"Tell me what's wrong, Gary."

"It's my brother. I can't explain it, but I know Andrew's in trouble. I have to help him right now, I know it."

Gary palms the left side of the woman's cheek warmly and turns to look at her: "I have to help him."

Melody clearly sees his worries.

"Stay here, Melody, and call Brown. Only let him in."

"But, Gary, how—"

"Please trust me."

"I do trust you."

Gary gives her a heart-warming smile. Then, without warning, he quickly leaps off of the balcony. Melody carefully watches, as Gary descends to the streets below, in a death-defying freefall. She doesn't turn away, as Melody did the first time, instead, she watches her lover in awe.

Gary opens his mind as he falls, just as the young man did when first felt Andrew's presence that day when he stood outside the Lortech tower. Gary allows the invisible link to expand beyond the boundaries of the city, and it fully awakens with him.

Melody now sees a blue orb surrounding Gary's body, and like a shooting star, he swiftly flies back into the night sky, and off into the distance; at such a fast speed, that within seconds, Gary's gone from her sight.

TWENTY-EIGHT

The weather cools, as rain clouds builds in the sky. Andrew drives up to the front gates of his mother's *East Hampton* estate, alone. The huge, steel gates opens, and he enters. Despite what happened earlier today, Andrew doesn't bring security, nor informs anyone of where he was going tonight.

Andrew soon sees a parked car that he doesn't recognize, as the young man parks his *Range Rover* in front of the main doorway of his mother's home. Maria, a maid who has worked for Valerie for years, warmly greets Andrew.

"Hello Andrew, may I take your coat?" she asks, having a light *Spanish* accent.

Andrew smiles as he enters the doors, giving his coat to her. "Thank you, Maria. Where's my mother?"

"She's in the West game den with company. I believe she's been waiting for you," Maria tells, as she walks away with Andrew's coat snuggled in her arms.

Andrew soon heads towards the den. As he approaches the doors, the young man hears Valerie speaking with someone. Andrew opens the doors, and is startled to find who his mother's company is.

Michael Masters smiles, while holding a drinking glass in his hand, as Valerie makes her way to her son.

"Dear, I'm *so* glad to hear you're safe," Valerie says, as she warmly hugs and kisses Andrew. She looks at the bandage on his neck and lightly touches it. "These maniacs in *New York,* the mayor should have them all put in prison."

"I'm alright, mother, I swear," Andrew says, never letting his sight leave Masters. "Why is he here?" he adds, Andrew hiding his displeasure as best he can.

"Oh, Michael's one of the reasons why I needed to speak with you, son," Valerie answers while sidestepping Andrew, before closing the den doors for privacy. "Andrew, I'm troubled by your actions as of late. Is it true that you *terminated* Michael's employment at Lortech?"

"Yes, it's true, mother. Yet, you shouldn't trouble yourself about that, I have very legitimate reasons."

"Andrew, I'm sorry, but I have to know more than that. Michael has worked for your father's corporation for decades, without any prior incidents, and now, you want to *fire* him?"

"I'm afraid he's becoming paranoid, Mrs. Taylor. Maybe he's beginning to show signs of stress," Masters interjects, fueling Andrew's hidden anger.

"Shut the *hell* up!" Andrew shouts, surprising Valerie with his sudden outburst.

"Andrew! What's *wrong* with you? Michael also said that you hit him yesterday morning, in addition to telling me that you've been lacking in your responsibilities at Lortech, and…that you met your brother?"

Andrew's eyes cut to his mother.

"You're becoming so isolated, and secretive lately. Why haven't you told me about Gary?"

"I was in time, mother, I just needed time."

Andrew sees the look of worry in his mother's eyes, before she goes to stand next to Masters on the other side of the room.

"I own thirty-five percent of Lortech's stock. I believe you should inform me when you want to fire employees, Andrew, ones who are an asset like Michael. He was a friend to your father," Valerie states.

The flickering flames from the fireplace, dances in the shadows of the room.

"Mother, Masters has deceived us. He's betrayed our family and father's corporation."

"Son, why do you make such accusations?"

"Because I've seen proof with my own eyes. I had an informant watching Masters. He's been having meetings with Lortech's competitor, Alberto McKoon, disclosing *GOD* knows how much, of our corporation's intelligence.

"This morning, my informant came to me frantic and hysterical—I thought the man was drugged. It's the same man who attacked me earlier, mother. He wanted to warn me, saying that Lortech and I were in danger. The informant also rambled something about Lord Moon and the Jinn Legion."

Valerie is taken aback by what Andrew is telling her. It sounds so strange and bizarre, that the woman wishes to herself that she'd never asked. Valerie now rotates to face Masters, with a pleading glance, "Is this true, Michael? Have you put our corporation in jeopardy?"

Masters refuses to respond.

"GO AHEAD, TELL HER THE TRUTH! WHAT IS THIS JINN LEGION AND LORD MOON? WHAT DOES IT HAVE TO DO WITH YOU?" Andrew yells, as his temper rises by the second.

"Tell me, Michael, what have you done?" Valerie insists.

Masters raises his right hand, and rests it upon the woman's shoulders, his eyes saddened. "Forgive me, Valerie." He then raises his left arm and bends it. "Please, forgive me."

A sharp bone that transforms into a blade, sudden rips out of Masters' elbow, and he violently plunges it into Valerie's chest, until it exits her back.

Andrew's heart leaps in his chest, as he sees his mother's blood dripping off the blade's point, Valerie's eyes widens in shock and horror.

"N-O-O-O-O-O-O!" Andrew screams, as he darts across the room to his mother.

The bone that turned into a blade retracts back into Masters' elbow. Andrew quickly jumps, and catches Valerie before she hits the ground, as blood spurts from the gaping wound in her chest.

"MOTHER! MOTHER, HOLD ON!" Andrew loudly cries out, pressing his hand against his mother's chest, trying to stop the flow of the blood.

Valerie's eyes are distant and fading. The blade cut through her heart, and she now vomits bloodied secretions.

"MARIA! MARIA!" Andrew soon calls out. He's so concerned with his mother, who's dying in his arms, that he doesn't realize Masters has left the room. The maid immediately comes running into the den, as she gasps in horror at the mortifying scene. Andrew looked at Maria.

"Call the ambulance, call them, now!" he demands. The maid wastes no time in doing so.

"Andrew," Valerie whispers, barely making a sound. Her son gazes down to her, as tears of agony streams down his face.

"S-h-h-h, don't talk. You're going to be okay, mother."

The woman now reaches up with her bloodied hand and touches Andrew's saddened face: "I...I love you...son." Valerie smiles before grimacing.

"No, no, no, N-O-O-O-O-O-O!"

Her hand falls away from his face, and Valerie lets go of the last breath she would ever take.

"Wake up, mother!" Andrew begs hopelessly.

The woman's eyes are blank and empty.

Andrew clutches her tighter before screaming out in sorrow. He then lifts Valerie into his arms, and lays his mother's body on a nearby sofa. Andrew closes her eyes, and kisses his mother's right cheek.

It's now that he realizes, that Valerie is gone.

Forever.

The woman who loved and raised him is dead.

The overwhelming sadness he experienced vanishes, as Andrew soon thinks about the one who took his mother away from him. All of the young man's emotions are replaced by an all-consuming wrath. Masters has done this unspeakable act, and he will surely pay.

Andrew gets up, and races to the mansion's doorway. He opens the main door, seeing what he believes is Masters' car start up, and begins to head towards the estate's gates. With all his might, Andrew chases the vehicle.

"I'LL *KILL* YOU!" Andrew shouts loudly, as his muscles tenses.

The main gates open, and three other vehicles pull into the estate. The drivers soon park, as Andrew comes within twenty yards of Masters' car, which has now stopped.

The driver's side door opens, and Masters steps out holding a *Glock nine-millimeter.* Without warning, he fires. Andrew immediately feels the slug tearing into his stomach. He stumbles, but continues to advance. Another shot rings out, and Andrew falls.

He clutches his midsection, as Andrew curls into the fetal position, fighting the growing agony. He hears more car doors open and shut, and also hears approaching footsteps coming towards him.

Shortly, Masters brings his fingers through Andrew's hair, pulling his former boss' head back, in order for Masters to face him.

"You *bastard!*" Andrew hisses through clenched teeth. It's now that he stares into the serpentine, inhuman eyes of Masters.

"I tried to protect you, now you lose, Andrew. Everything."

Masters places the mouth of his handgun on Andrew's temple. He then looks at one of his men, who have arrived in one of the three vehicles. The man nods his head, and goes to open one of the vehicle's trunks. Masters' soldier then unlocks the weapon, and lifts its targeting mechanism, pointing it to Valerie's home.

"I want you to see this before you die," Masters indicates to Andrew.

Masters' soldier quickly activates the weapon, sending off a missile with a smoky trail, speeding rapidly towards the mansion.

"N-O-O-O-O-O-O!" Andrew cries out.

The missile hits its target, and explodes into a fury of fire, destroying the estate.

"The Jinn Legion is beyond you. By tomorrow, Lortech will be nothing! I'm going to take all the data, Andrew. Then, I'll track down that *abomination* you call your brother, and kill him! Or give him to Taterax to be dissected, and find out what makes him tick. You're finished, and David Taylor's legacy of the Jinn shall be in its rightful place," Masters tells Andrew venomously.

Immediately after, he hears harsh laughter coming from Andrew's mouth, which made him come closer to Andrew.

"What's so funny?"

"I promise you, you're going to *die* for this, Masters," Andrew retorts, before spitting in Masters' face. Feeling disgustingly insulted, Masters immediately pulls the trigger...before releasing Andrew's lifeless skull.

Masters quickly gets into his vehicle now, as well does the other men. They drive off, as the fires light up the night's sky. Andrew's dead body lies motionless, just yards away from the total ruin of Valerie Taylor, and her home.

Masters shows no emotion in his vehicle, leaving the chaos he's brought about.

* * * * *

Soaring high above in the night, Gary soon sees the roaring flames of where he's being brought. He panics, realizing that his link to his brother is somewhere near the fires, and begins to descend from the sky, as Gary now sees Andrew.

He lands swiftly and runs to his brother's side. Blood slowly pools around Andrew's body, causing Gary to become dismal. Instinctively, he bends down, examining what happened, seeing the gunshot wound in Andrew's head, and the blood oozing from his stomach.

Gary's too late.

"I'm sorry, man, I'm *fucking* sorry," Gary stammers. His nightmare is now real, and just as in Gary's dream, he can't do anything to help save his brother.

Gary fights back the tears, as he bends his knees and lifts Andrew into his arms.

"I know you're not gone. Can you hear me, Andrew? ...Open your eyes...you can't die, remember? ...WAKE UP!" Gary pleads.

Suddenly, he hears police sirens approaching the demolished home.

"You're going to be alright, you hear me?" Gary reassures. A translucent, blue orb surrounds the two, sparkling brighter than the stars, hidden by the clouds in the sky.

Gary now flies off with his dead brother in his arms.

TWENTY-NINE

Death...it isn't pleasant. Nor opposing, as so many believes. There's no transcending. No embracing peace.

Andrew Taylor's conscience is in an empty void of blackened shadows between the world of the living, and the garden of the dead; trapped, reliving the horrible moments of Valerie Taylor's murder, and his own.

The Jinn Legion, Ong Mra has warned me about it.... It isn't the words of the translation on the tomb.

Andrew now reflects on the bone that extracted from Michael Masters' elbow, how it impaled deep into Valerie's chest. He soon ponders on the man's horrid, red, serpentine eyes that stared at him, before Masters took Andrew's life.

Masters isn't human, he's a beast—similar to the vision of what Mra was, just before he attacked me earlier today. Now everything is lost: my mother, my father's corporation, even my very own life, no longer exists! ...Then why am I having these thoughts? Andrew comes to realize. *It's like I'm conscious with nothing, but this purgatory void that's embracing me...*

...A-R-R-R-R-R-R-R-R-R-R-R-R-G-H!

He screams out in his prison, a maddening, desperate cry. Andrew yells until he feels something—a sudden strange, warmth, touching his cold outer shell.

This isn't the first time Andrew has had this weird experience. He remembers his first encounter with Gary, when the young man shot an inferno of fire through Andrew's chest. That was the first time he tasted death, and even then, a warm, almost benign power, brought him back from the void. Andrew dismissed it the first time, rejecting the notion that he was dead, but it's happening again.

Now, Andrew fights against the darkness, clawing his way back, back to the place: the ever-willing plane of existence called life. The fuel of vengeance, now feeds Andrew's hunger in the battle.

*   *   *   *   *

Gary stands by the bed he just laid Andrew on, with Melody holding him cautiously. She's horrified—her boyfriend returned ten minutes ago with his dead brother in his arms.

Brown, who immediately came to the apartment when Melody called him, is also standing in the room, awestruck about the fact that Gary has a dead body in the room, looking at it, instead of calling an ambulance. Brown also still can't figure out how the young man got back into the penthouse without him knowing.

"How did you know, Gary?" Melody asks inquisitively, bothered by the turn of events.

"I dreamt that Andrew was in danger—I just knew."

"But you were too late.... He's dead, Gary. I'm sorry," Melody assures, burying her head into Gary's chest.

He feels soon the young woman's wet tears on his skin, as Melody begins to sob, not only for her, but also for Gary; knowing how he can hold back his emotions. Gary now caresses Melody's back, and to her surprise, he simply smiles.

"It's alright, Melody, Andrew won't be dead for long."

Melody almost chokes when she hears the young man's comment, and the expression on Gary's face, now makes him seem even more bizarre. He then nudges Melody, and points his finger in Andrew's direction before speaking.

"If you don't believe me, then look for yourself."

Melody is now convinced that Gary is losing his mind.

She forces herself to face Andrew anyway. He's dead, gone, and Melody thinks Gary can't accept it, feeling that he has finally snapped.

"Andrew's dead, Gary, you *have* to face it!" she pleads to Gary's rationality.

"No, he isn't. Look closer and you will see." Gary hasn't faltered from his determination. Melody turns away from him, and her wide doe eyes once again, falls upon Andrew's dead corpse.

Seconds later, she proceeds to leave the room and call the ambulance herself, but Melody notices something strange happening, something that wasn't there the first time she examined Andrew.

The bullet is now coming out from the middle of Andrew's forehead, as if something is pushing it from the wound.

Melody shudders, as the bullet falls from the wound entirely. She focuses even more.

Brown's face is cloaked in amazement, momentarily thinking he's hallucinating, as the bullet wound is growing, smaller and smaller.

All three watch on, as the other two bullets come out of the dead man's body. Shortly, the wounds vanish, leaving stains of dry blood, where seconds ago, the holes were embedded.

Suddenly, Andrew's chest jumps, as his denied lungs eagerly feasts on oxygen—Andrew's body now shooting upright, and his eyes opening.

Melody, shocked, by the resurrection, instantly passes out. Gary catches her limp body in his arms, as Andrew's eyes quickly dart back-and-forth, immediately taking in his surroundings.

"What the *fuck* is going on, Exodus?" Brown whispers.

Gary smiles, ignoring his friend, "Welcome to the world of the living, Andrew," Gary states to his brother who's revived.

Andrew turns to face Gary. His mind is racing with a thousand thoughts, but he asks one question, as he stands up: "How, how did I get here?"

"I brought you here. I had a sense that you were in trouble, so I found you, the same way I found you when we first met. I was too late, you were outside of a house that was on fire, when I found you dead," his brother answers.

Andrew touches his stomach, recalling the pain from his wounds. He's fully healed.

"I was dead, now I'm alive?"

"Did you see it, Andrew? Do you believe me now?"

"Who? Did I see who?"

"The Vowdun, the witch," Gary replies, hoping that Andrew will finally remember his clouded past.

"No. A man did this to me. He betrayed me, and murdered my mother."

"Andrew, our mother died twenty years ago."

"I'm talking about the woman who raised me," Andrew confesses through grinding teeth. Flashed images of Michael Masters soon comes to mind—the way he killed Valerie, and the vision of Masters' serpentine eyes; evil, inhumane eyes, Andrew saw before the man shot him.

"We have to get *out* of here! I have to get you somewhere safe, so they can't find you!" Andrew states, with panic in his voice.

"Who?" Gary questions.

"The Jinn Legion! You're in danger, Gary! We have to get out of here before it's too late!"

"You're not making sense, Andrew."

"I know I'm not, but please trust me, Gary. You're all I got left."

Gary now sees something in his brother's eyes that troubles him. Gary nods his head, and follows Andrew as he leaves the room. Gary holds Melody in his arms, and looks at Brown.

"Are you coming or not?" Gary asks his friend.

Brown is still amazed at what he witnessed.

"I'll be *damned* if I'm not!" the man answers.

THIRTY

Sharon was sound asleep before receiving Andrew's phone call—the man now sounding frantic and nervous, as he asks for the woman's urgent help.

Something is wrong, horribly wrong with Andrew, Sharon thinks.

Andrew asks her if some friends of his can stay at Sharon's place until the morning. He doesn't say why, but Andrew's serious. Sharon couldn't refuse him, no matter what's going on, she loves Andrew too much.

It's thirty minutes later since the phone conversation between Andrew and Sharon has taken place, and she continues to stand by the front door, waiting, until a car pulls up in her rain-drenched driveway. Sharon opens her door, wearing a black silk robe with a matching teddy. She approaches the car, as all four doors opens.

Andrew is the first to greet Sharon. He hugs the woman, and she sees the sadness in his eyes.

"Andrew, what's wrong? I need you to tell me, I want to help."

"You're helping so much by doing this for me, Sharon."

Andrew lets go of Sharon, and points to the rest of the people he's arrived with.

"Sharon, this is Melody, my soon to be sister-in-law."

Melody gives Sharon a small wave, as she's tired and spent, because of everything that's happening.

"This is Brown, and this, this young man, is my brother."

"Brother? You don't have a brother, Andrew," Sharon replies.

"It's a long story, one that I will tell you at the appropriate time," Andrew states.

Sharon now gazes at the four people standing in front of her home. "Well, alright, let's get inside, everyone, and get out of this rain," she states warmly.

Brown is the first to inside the house, as Gary now whispers something to Melody, and kisses her goodbye. Tears falls from Melody's eyes, as she enters Sharon's home.

"Thank you, Sharon, this means so much to me," Andrew says. He then turns to walk away from her, and Sharon quickly pulls Andrew back to her, bringing him in close.

"I don't know what's going on, Andrew, but make sure you stay safe," Sharon advises before kissing Andrew. Shortly after, Andrew unlocks his lips, and stares at her, surprised by Sharon's actions; the woman's soft, sweet lips now makes Andrew's heart pound faster.

"I will," he promises, before rushing back to the car.

As Andrew restarts the car's engine, a knock comes at the driver's side window. Andrew looks up at his younger brother's face, and rolls down the window.

"Move over, Andrew, 'cause I *know* I can drive better than your boughie *ass!* Plus, I don't want to hear Brown's mouth if you *fuck* up his car."

Andrew pauses. "…Look, Gary, you don't have to come, this is my fight," he says concernedly. Gary bites his lip.

"We're *fucking* family, man! Your beef is *always* my beef, so move the *fuck* over!"

Gary's defiance causes his brother to smile. Andrew does as the young man requested, and Gary takes over the driver's seat.

Sharon watches silently, as the vehicle drives away. She's well aware of the dangers the brothers are about to face, because the danger was part of her, as it's part of *all* those of the Jinn Legion. Sharon's love for Andrew, can't stop her from what she knows have to be done.

It's what Lord Moon wants…

And Sharon *can't* go against its power.

No one can!

Thunder now begins to roar.

Sharon closes her door.

* * * * *

A jet-black Bentley quickly drives up to the sidewalk near the main entrance of Lortech's tower, followed by five vans, all arriving at a screeching halt.

Masters steps out of the car, and makes his way to the entrance of the building. He stops at the main door and looks down at his watch: *3 AM*. Masters immediately smiles as he types in his security code and is denied access.

Yesterday, Andrew worked fast in changing all the passwords, after he fired Masters. *The Boy*, Masters secretly refers to his former superior in his mind, *is predictable, but now he's dead, and I won't let nothing stand in my way!*

Two security guards approach the glass doorway; one now speaks through the intercom: *"Good morning, Mr. Masters, what seems to be the problem?"*

"My codes are being rejected by the computer, maybe it's the storm that's affecting the system."

The security guard nods his approval. The other sentinel goes behind his desk and types into the terminal to electronically open the entrance. Masters soon steps inside, and walks behind the guard who first greeted him.

"I'm sorry for the inconvenience, sir, this never happens," the security man offers.

"I'm sure it doesn't."

Masters sneakily pulls out his handgun, which has a silencer on its end. He ruthlessly shoots the sentinel in the back of the head—the guard never had a chance.

The other watchman, sitting behind his desk, quickly reaches for his weapon, shocked by what's happening. A bullet bolts in the middle of the second guard's face, and his body falls hard to the floor.

Masters quickly moves behind the desk with the calmness of a natural-born killer. No alarms are tripped, which means the rest of Lortech's security is unaware of the situation. The man now types security codes into the computer terminal, and the main entrance doors of Lortech's tower opens.

Fifty paramilitary-armed soldiers of the Jinn Legion, rush into the building, soon pausing, waiting now for further orders. Immediately afterwards enters two well-dressed men, who arrived in the same vehicle as Masters appear—Alberto McKoon and his personal bodyguard, Loki. McKoon stares at Masters while Loki smiles.

"Wonderful, Masters, I never believed this could be so simple. But with Andrew Taylor dead, the sky's the limit," McKoon says happily, with a sparkle of glee in his eyes.

"Not entirely. Because of the hour, there is less security, yet I'm opening all access to the building. I want Team 1 to take out the remainder of security in Sector 3—you should be able to take them by surprise. Team 2, and Team 3, head to the research centers in Sector 4 and get what we came for—leave *no* witnesses!" Masters orders, as he types quickly into the computer.

"McKoon you're with me, along with your guys. In order to get the access codes to the international Lortech database, we're going to have to get into Taylor's main office, or all of this will be for nothing."

Masters comes from behind the desk, and tells some members of the squad to remove the guards' dead bodies thats lying on the floor, and to take their place.

"So it won't be as easy as I thought," McKoon mildly states.

"It never was," Masters answers, as the armed men spread out to obtain their missions.

Masters goes to an elevator with three other soldiers.

McKoon glances at Loki and nods.

Loki understands his boss' gesture.

McKoon quickly joins Masters inside of the elevator.

*   *   *   *   *

Karen Scott came to work at 2 AM this morning. It isn't odd for her to do so, being though the scientist's work and genius mind, keeps Karen locked in her developments and discoveries at Lortech; this being the capacity of the scientist's life.

Karen is well into her analyzing cyborg, KD-49. The project is nearly complete, and she's proud of it, Karen being the head of the team that created the monstrosity, for the black ops of the United States Military. Yet, the scientist would've never dreamed that her life is, at this moment, in danger.

The computer screen Karen is viewing goes blank, and a sign comes up that reads, *UNAUTHORIZED PERSONNEL IN SECTOR 4.* She immediately types into her computer, and watches through a surveillance camera, which now causes Karen to gasp in shock, as she witnesses several armed men, gunning down her fellow scientist and researchers.

Karen's pulse quickens, realizing that they're advancing down a corridor that leas to the lab she's in. The scientist alerts Lortech's security team on her computer, and is ignored. Quickly, Karen overrides the cameras that views their station, and becomes horrified by the vision on her screen: bodies are torn apart, blood is splattered on the walls and pooling on the floor.

All of Lortech's guards are dead.

Karen begins to panic—her mind is racing with the thought that soon, she will inevitably share their fate.

Immediately, Karen gets up from her seat, and makes a dash for the cybernetics sector, as she reaches into her lab coat, and retrieved a small cell phone.

Karen quickly uses the speed dial.

Her eyes begin to water.

The phone rings three times...

No answer.

She presses the speed dial button again.

Karen's slim hope is already beginning to fade.

Her heart paces faster!

Karen now hears gunshots blaring at the lab's entrance.

* * * * *

Gary is driving at an extremely fast pace of one-hundred-and-ten miles per hour, and he becomes jarred by the ring of Andrew's cell phone. While speeding, he takes a quick glance and sees his brother reach into his pocket to retrieve it. Andrew now accepts the call, and hears harsh breathing on the other line.

"Hello?" Andrew greets.

"Hello...Hello sir, this is Karen Scott. I-I don't know what's happening."

Andrew listens to her pleading voice."

Karen, calm down. What's wrong?"

"There are soldiers killing *everyone* in the building. I can't get out. They're almost in the lab."

Andrew's eyes widen!

Masters wasn't lying when he told Andrew that he would destroy Lortech, it's actually happening. Now, One his head scientist is in danger, and people are dead.

"Karen, *listen* to me, I want you to find a place to hide so they don't find you. I want—"

Andrew hears a loud explosion over the line, and the phone goes dead. He grits his teeth in anger. Gary, who dares not to take his eyes off the road, listened to what his brother was saying while one the phone.

"BASTARDS!" Andrew growls.

"What's happening? Fill me in!" Gary inquires.

"The men who tried to *kill* me now have Lortech under siege!" Andrew hisses.

"It won't be long, Andrew, we're almost there," Gary assures. Both brothers fall silent, as the vehicle races down the street, with Lortech's tower being just twenty miles away.

* * * * *

The cell phone falls from Karen's hand, and breaks into pieces when it lands on the floor, as the laboratory's doors are blown in. Loki enters the lab first with his weapon drawn, having ten armed men follow him in.

Karen stands up from the spot she's in, and darts for the room containing the cyborg, KD-49. All of the men fire their guns at the fleeing woman, as Karen quickly opens a door, and shuts herself in, as it automatically locks upon Karen's entry.

The scientist views the offline monstrosity. Karen is now desperate and terrified, feeling that the soldiers can take her life at any moment. She runs to the computer terminal and begins typing furiously—KD-49 being Karen's only option, believing that the cyborg will help her survive.

Outside the room, Loki is also typing on a computer. He knows what the scientist is trying to do, and he won't give Karen a chance to save herself. Loki overrides the locks for the door.

Karen's heart quickly paces, as she hears the whirling of machinery coming from KD-49. It's like the awakening of a giant, a savior for the scientist's life. KD-49's eyelids opens, and it stands from its steel bed, as its metal shackles unlocks.

Karen smiles, as hope stirs inside of her chest.

Suddenly, the doors to the room burst open! Karen turns to see Loki, the white-haired man, who leads the soldiers into the lab. He tosses two silver metallic objects into the room, and shuts the doors, which automatically relocks.

Karen looks at the two objects, yet doesn't even have time to react. The devices explode in an incredible blast, killing the prolific scientist, and destroying her cybernetic creation.

THIRTY-ONE

Four armed security guards stands at Lortech lobby entrance. After the company's security team was massacred, four of the Jinn Legion's soldiers disposed of their bodies, and dressed in the guard's uniforms, as they watch the main lobby's post; posing to fool any unsuspecting Lortech employees that might show up.

Gabriel Nunez, the team's leader, now watches contently through the glass doors, the downpour of raindrops, and flashes of lightening outside.

Soon after, the windows begin to shake and thump louder, in which Gabriel thinks it's because of the powerful wind that's picking up steadily, since their arrival. The windows now begin to quake even more vigorously. All four men watch in fascination, as the glass walls and doors begin to crack.

Suddenly the destruction shatters inwardly. Broken shards fly at a high velocity toward the four soldiers, who stand helplessly, as the glass tear through their bodies, dismembering limbs; body parts fall to the floor, and blood pools from the lacerated men.

Immediately after, Andrew steps into the lobby. His eyes views in awe at the death his brother just caused. Andrew knew they weren't his employees, not only because of Karen's phone call, but also by the number of men standing on post; the lobby never having more than two security guards at a time.

Gary has no pity for the slain, especially knowing what the men did to his brother, and to Valerie Taylor's home. Andrew also told him what Masters did to his adoptive mother, and for that, Gary will make sure, if he has the chance, to kill Masters and his men them horribly.

Andrew walks behind the security desk and begins typing. The information he seeks is given. Fifty-three unauthorized occupants, including the dead men in the lobby, are in the tower. Five are outside the doors of his office, and the rest are throughout the sublevels of the research center and lab.

"Where's the scientist who called you?" Gary inquires.

"Karen is in Sector 4. After that explosion I heard, I don't know if she's dead or alive."

"But it says that she's down there, right?" Gary asks urgently.

Andrew bends down and retrieves two *Beretta 93R* handguns and some clips, high-powered, automatic weapons that are used for war.

"Karen's down there, right?" Gary repeats.

"Yes, she is, why?"

"Karen's the one who performed the surgery on Melody. She saved her life, and I *owe* it to Karen to try to save hers."

Andrew stands up and views Gary with a growing respect. It's the young man's choice to make, and in no way can Andrew stop him. "Hit buttons 'eight', 'nine', 'one' in the elevator, it should take you to that sector."

Gary nods. He walks into one of the elevators, wondering what he's about to face. Andrew now stands at the entrance.

"Gary, there are armed men down there, so be careful. I'm going up to my office, meet me up there after you find Karen."

Gary hits the three digits that Andrew instructed him to, and a light smile comes upon his face. "Andrew, I'll be careful, you just don't get killed again," Gary nervously jokes before the door closes.

Andrew soon steps into another elevator and checks the ammunition of his twin handguns. A dark cloud falls over him. Andrew's grip tightens, as well as his jaw.

Michael Masters will die by his hands, he thinks, *by any means necessary!*

* * * * *

Melody sleeps lightly in the bedroom Sharon offered her. It's a hard feat to accomplish, after what she witnessed earlier tonight. Melody now awakes from her short slumber, as she feels the pressure of another person's body at the food of the bed. Melody groggily gazes at the silhouette of a woman.

"I'm sorry to have awaken you, Melody. I just couldn't rest," Sharon says to the young woman. Her back is turned to Melody, so she can't view Sharon's face.

"Are you ill?" Melody asks.

"You can say that. You see, I have this dilemma, Melody, that I have to face, and I have no other choice but to do so."

Melody slowly reaches for the lamp switch on the nightstand beside her, all the while, keeping her sight on Sharon.

"Maybe you can tell me what the problem is, or the dilemma that you're facing."

"I could...but that will only place fear in your heart."

Melody becomes troubled by what Sharon is saying. She turns on the lamp, giving light to the room. Sharon still doesn't turn to face her.

"Why would I fear your problem, Sharon?"

"Because, Melody," Sharon whispers with her voice sounding different. Sharon finally turns her head in Melody's direction, and the young woman's eyes widen, as she sees Sharon's face.

The fashion designer's once beautiful features, are now a mask of contorted horror. Large jagged teeth lines Sharon's mouth, as her bestial eyes burns into Melody before she speaks.

"...YOU HAVE TO *DIE!*"

Sharon raises her right hand to reveal flesh-ripping talon claws, and Melody loudly screams out in terror when Sharon leaps at her.

* * * * *

Brown shoots upright out of bed when he hears Melody's shrilling shriek. He runs out of the guestroom and into the direction it's coming from. Alert and frantic, Brown bursts into the room, and is shocked by what he sees.

Sharon is on top of Melody, who's desperately holding the beastly woman's wrists. Brown eyes the claws that are extending from Sharon's hands, and her horrid face. It's as if he's awaken into a nightmare. Without wasting a moment, Brown rushes at Sharon, forcefully tackling her off the bed.

Melody struggles to get up, before her hands quickly fumble through her pocketbook that's on the nightstand, as Sharon and Brown crash into the wall. The collision cracks the foundation, and the two fall to the floor.

Sharon moves with the grace of a panther, prying herself away from Brown's hold. The man now rises and throws a powerful right hook, smashing his large fist into Sharon's jaw.

Bone cracking is now being heard, as Sharon's jaw bends horrendously under the impact of the hard blow, yet she doesn't fall. Brown is sickened, hearing the popping of bone, as Sharon's jaw snaps back into place. A grotesque smile slowly appears on the gruesome woman's face.

"Care to try again?" Sharon hisses. Disgusted by her horrid form, Brown swings again. Sharon ducks the blow, and her talons cut across his stomach, slashing through Brown's flesh.

The sharp pain instantly causes him to palm the wound and bend over. Brown fights the excruciating aching in his bowels, as he soon stumbles two steps forward.

Suddenly, Sharon's claws cuts across Brown's face, and the burly man falls to the floor. Brown tries to focus through hazy vision, but the beastly woman stands on top of him, ready to strike once more.

"GET...GET AWAY FROM HIM!" Melody demands.

Sharon's hair tosses, as her head whips upright. Melody now has a pistol pointed at deadly aim, right in front of the horrid woman's face. Sharon's nostrils widen, as she walks away from her wounded prey, with slow, graceful steps.

"DON'T *FUCKING* MOVE, OR I'LL *SHOOT* YOU! I *SWEAR* I WILL!" Melody threatens Sharon.

"You must *die,* love, Lord Moon demands it. Do not fear death," Sharon hisses, as she moves closer to the bed.

"I SAID DON'T *MOVE,* SHARON!"

"You won't kill me, it's not in your nature. But it *is* in mine!" Sharon snaps. Her mouth now widens, and more fangs appear. Sharon attempts to leap on the bed.

Melody squeezes the trigger!

THIRTY-TWO

Gary steels his nerves as the elevator halts. He immediately manifests the blue sphere, surrounding his entire body as the elevator doors open.

A hail of bullets rings out!

Ten troops fires at Gary, the unexpected visitor. Loki stares with fascination at the magnificent blue orb, as he fires.

Gary doesn't even flinch.

The intensified heat radiating from the protective sphere destroys the projectiles, as they make contact with the orb. He now focuses on the men in the corridor, and begins to levitate out of the enclosed space of the elevator, burning a perfect circle in the elevator's entrance. Soon after, Gary raises his right hand, and points in the direction of a soldier.

Psychogenic fires ignite in Gary's hand, as an inferno of white flames shoots straight for his target. The fires burn through the man's chest, before Gary singes away the head of a soldier standing behind the burning warrior.

Loki's crimson, serpentine eyes widens, as he witnesses the strange abilities of the young Black man.

"FALL BACK AND REPOSITION!" Loki soon shouts, before darting down one of the many corridors of the sector.

The soldiers begin to disperse in different directions, while continuing to fire from their weapons. Many of the men are conflicted with the thought of what they're now facing.

Gary's anger is growing rapidly, which seems to heighten his special powers. He stretches out both of his arms, and hones in on the four different directions the paramilitary soldiers are running in.

"YOU *FUCKING* COWARDS THINK YOU CAN ESCAPE?" Gary growls. The flame immediately conjures from both of his hands, growing wildly.

Loki desperately searches for an exit. He spots an air ventilation hatch, and reaches into his coat for one of his explosive devices created at Taterax—a combination of two deadly, volatile chemicals. Loki finds one and hits its activation

237

switch. Angrily, he grits his teeth and throws it in Gary's direction.

Gary now feels the strength of his powers building up, as he effortlessly unleashes them, sending four searching beams of light to quickly shoot down all four corridors.

Horrid screams fill the halls, as flesh burns away from the Jinn Legion's soldier's bodies, Gary's fires having the intensity of a nuclear bomb.

The small device that Loki tossed underneath the translucent orb ignites, causing an explosion that ripples throughout the halls.

* * * * *

Michael Masters, Alberto McKoon and three of the Jinn's soldiers stand outside of Andrew Taylor's office doors, which are electromagnetically sealed, reinforced with ten inches of titanium steel. Andrew had the doors reinstalled when Gary attacked him, and smashed the gold metallic statue through the building. It's an installment Masters is well aware of.

The men just easily killed three guards who secured the floor, yet the trouble lies in actually gaining access into Andrew's office. They can't blow through the steel, and Andrew's retina and fingerprint scan, along with the access codes, are needed. Masters believed that he had the access covered, when he programmed overriding codes in the system months prior. Once again, Andrew had foiled his plan by rebooting the system yesterday.

McKoon is growing extremely impatient as time passes. Masters pays no mind to him, as he goes through the hundred of command codes to override the system.

I know this building better than Andrew ever could! Masters thinks. *It would've made things much easier if I'd just cut out Andrew's eyes, and chopped off his hands when I had the chance!*

"What I *don't* understand, Masters, is how you let a *child* outwit you," McKoon blurts out, trying to insult Masters.

Masters now stops typing.

He raises his head from the laptop computer screen.

Angrily glares at McKoon.

"The doors will be open in *five* minutes, McKoon. If you say *one* more word to me, I will *remove* your head from your neck," Masters promises.

Too much is on the line for Masters to endure the taunts of the Jinn Legion leader, Masters being the one who betrayed Andrew and Valerie Taylor. Just hours ago, he murdered the Valerie, the wife of the man who was once the Leader of the Jinn Legion, when he lived. Back then, Masters was loyal to David Taylor—today he isn't anymore.

Masters has done all of these acts of deception for McKoon's gain, and for this he despised himself. In his heart, Masters wishes that it was McKoon who was dead, that wish will have to wait another day.

Suddenly, Masters, along with the other men, becomes startled as they hear the chime of the elevator. They all turn and watch in preparation, as the elevator door opens. The soldiers target their weapons at the entrance. The doors now open fully, and everyone's tension fades, as they see that no one is inside.

Unexpectedly, Andrew quickly enters from the door of emergency exit stairway, with two guns blazing in his hands. He fires rapidly, running fast towards a column in the hallway.

Masters freezes as he sees Andrew's face. A bullet now tears through his shoulder, and the force knocks Masters off his feet. He grimaces, grabbing the fresh, painful wound.

McKoon grabs Masters and drags him to a safer position inside the hall, as the other three soldiers returns fire.

"I thought you said he was dead, Masters!" McKoon yells.

"It's impossible! I *killed* Andrew Taylor myself—it *can't* be him," Masters shouts over the blaring gunfire.

Andrew hears what he says, before turning from behind the column, and aiming at one of the advancing soldier's head. Andrew fires four shots—he immediately sees the man going down, before quickly retreating back behind the column.

"I'm not dead, Masters! You *killed* my mother, and I'm going to make sure that you *die* right now—you, McKoon, and the rest of the Jinn Legion!" Andrew yells, as he reloads his dual guns.

Masters stands up when he hears the threats. Using his only working arm, Masters retrieves his gun.

"I don't know who the *fuck* you *think* you are, but you're the only one who's going to *die,* Taylor!" Masters spits.

Andrew comes from behind the column shooting, now running towards his office. Whirling bullets comes at Andrew, hitting him twice by, as the young man falls by his office door.

Andrew bares the pain...

Keeps shooting...

As the computer system now scans his eyes.

McKoon growls in frustration, as he witnesses Andrew dropping the gun in his right hand, as he places his fingers onto the screen; *ACCESS GRANTED* it reads, and the office doors hisses open.

"N-O-O-O-O-O-O!" McKoon barks, charging towards the opening, as Andrew limps and falls into his throne. Through blurred vision, Andrew spots his two sentinels standing on post.

"AU, AG, HELP ME!" he pleads.

Both turned to Andrew and simultaneously say: *"Whatever you will, Messiah."*

* * * * *

Breathing heavily, Gary mentally pushes hundreds of pounds of debris from the explosion off of him. His nose is bleeding, a sign that Gary's powers are under strain. He has never expelled so much of his abilities in such little time. Now, Gary is finding out the repercussions of doing so.

Slowly, he struggles back to his feet, and begins to venture into the demolished corridor. The young man immediately remembers where Karen Scott's lab is. Gary is drastically alert as he finds the lab, seeing that there are no doors.

It looks as though someone blew their way into the area. Andrew did say he heard an explosion.

Gary walks cautiously into the laboratory. It's not the sterile-clean, mechanically-ran place he remembers. Sparkles of electricity comes from torn wires and appliances, and computers are smashed and bullet ridden.

"Karen! Karen, where are you?" Gary calls out.

Silence is his answer.

Gary sees the door to the room where he was once contained and studied by the scientist. He runs to it, and opens the door. The pungent aroma is the first thing that hits Gary, a scent that's becoming horribly familiar—burning flesh.

He gasps with grief, realizing that the blood-splattered stains on the wall are those of Karen. Gary soon sees the remains of her cyborg, KD-49. Its arms are still moving, but the rest of the cyborg's body is defunct.

Staring at the gruesome scene, the young man suddenly hears footsteps, many of them, coming from behind him at the lab's demolished entrance. He swiftly whirls around, as twenty red targeting beams falls upon his form. Gary bares his teeth, as he glares at the soldiers.

"You *motherfuckers* just don't learn, don't you?" His nose begins to bleed again, as the blue sphere surrounds his frame. "I'm going to *teach* you!"

The orb, with Gary inside of its core, flies towards at the gunmen.

The soldiers open fire.

* * * * *

AU, the gold metallic cherubim statue, grabs the hand of its master, and quickly pulls Andrew away from the office entrance. AU eventually lets him go when Andrew is safely behind his desk. The industrialist tosses his gun to AG before pressing a device on his desk.

"Initiate voice protocol."

"*Yes, Mr. Taylor,*" says the computerized voice from the computer's built-in speakers. Three monitor screens rise from compartments on Andrew's desk, and the front compartment of it flips over before the man, now revealing a keyboard.

AG stands on-guard at the door with the handgun Andrew given to the being, aimed and ready. As a soldier comes in front of AG, the man receives an unexpected surprise. The silver being shoots the startled gunman down, not wavered by any forms of fear or compassion.

Andrew becomes startled a bit, hearing the first round of gunshots, but regains his composure quickly, ignoring the throbbing pain in his leg from the bullet wounds that are inflicted upon him. Andrew begins to rapidly type in the command codes needed, in order to succeed in what he's planning to do.

Masters and McKoon both witness AG gunning down the soldier who approached it, as they immediately find cover.

"What the *hell* is that?" McKoon now questions in disbelief.

Masters has some suspicions about why Andrew has the two metallic statues in his office. They serve a purpose in which the man now understands. He believes that they're cyborgs, prototypes of the KD-49 that Andrew kept for himself. Masters vile eyes quickly glances at the last of the soldiers.

"Engage the enemy!" Masters orders. The warrior stares back at the man, puzzled, until Masters grabs the soldier's collar, pulling him in closer.

"I said engage!" Masters shouts.

The Jinn Legion soldier has no will to refuse, even knowing that he's walking into a certain death, also realizing that if he refuses the command, the will be killed anyway. As the warrior approaches the sentinel, Masters marches directly behind him.

AG turns in their direction and opens fire.

Masters jumps defensively to the left of the soldier. A sharp bone that transforms into a blade, extracts from Masters' elbow, causing the weapon to cut through the nozzle of AG's gun, rendering the firearm useless.

McKoon now takes advantage of the situation. Using his incredible hidden strength, granted to him by Lord Moon, McKoon rushes at the living statue and swings. The charging causes a loud thud, as McKoon's fist collides into the cherubim's head, knocking AG off its feet.

The silver metallic statute goes sliding backwards into Andrew's office, causing Andrew to pause at what he's doing. Shortly after, the entrepreneur watches in disbelief, as Masters and McKoon now enters his office.

While inside, McKoon's suit soon tears at the seams. The man's built frame becomes overly massive, as McKoon's transforming, awakening the dark gifts that are within his DNA. McKoon's face now appears deformed, and his barrel chest breathes harshly.

AG rises, prepared for whatever is to come, as AU joins the being at its side, ready to defend Andrew, their "Messiah".

"I don't know how you're alive, but *this* time, you're *not* going to *trick* me!" Masters spits.

"It's *over*, Masters…. You *murdered* my mother, *destroyed* my life, but you *won't* get what you came for!" Andrew adds vengefully.

"You have no mother, and Lortech is *not* yours. It was owned by David Taylor, a man who was *not* your father!"

"SHUT UP!" Andrew snaps.

"You see, David Taylor was one of *us,* so this corporation belongs to the Jinn Legion."

"LIES!" Andrew screams, after hearing Masters' ugly words. The man took great pleasure in just telling Andrew what he knows, Masters feeling as if killing Andrew at this point will be all the more satisfying.

"AU, AG, KILL THEM, KILL THEM BOTH!" Andrew orders. The two cherubim charge at Masters and McKoon, with the intention that Andrew so greatly desires.

THIRTY-THREE

Broken bones, dismembered limbs and charred corpses, surrounds the area where Gary stands. White smoking vapors rises from his hands, as Gary calms the storm in his mind. Each and every one of the gunmen who attacked him is now dead.

Karen is gone—Gary's too late to save her.

Andrew won't stand a chance if he has to face as many soldiers, Gary thinks to himself, gathering that his brother may be in the same danger, as he swiftly sprints down the hallways of the sector. The young man needs to get back to the elevators, so he can be with his brother.

But Gary's head now throbs...

He's suffering from a migraine.

Gary soon stumbles.

His eyes now fall on the debris from the explosion earlier, indicating that Gary's close to the area. As the young man makes another turn, he sees the flickering lights ahead from the wrecked elevator he came to the sector in. Gary now allows his pace and begins walking.

He soon pauses, noticing a slight change in the illumination around him. The lighting is becoming increasingly darker. Gary's blood quickens in his veins, as he no longer sees the light coming from the elevator.

Gary now stares into pitch-blackness. Something he's seen a very long time ago. It's the same darkness his parents had drove into, one that tragic night in *Haiti.*

Two large, slanted red eyes, glows in the distance, as Gary's fear suddenly alters into anger.

"FINALLY DECIDED TO SHOW YOURSELF, WITCH, INSTEAD OF HIDING IN MY NIGHTMARES? I *KNOW* YOU'RE BEHIND THIS!" Gary shouts.

The shadow remains silent.

"SEE WHAT I DID TO YOUR *FUCKING* MEN? NOW IT'S *YOUR* TURN!"

"My chosen," the creature's horrid voice hisses. A twisting tentacle now reaches out of the darkness, like a cobra striking out.

244

Gary's thoughts are inflamed. Using the debris around him, he mentally throws projectiles at the oncoming appendage. The sharp, jagged bricks, tears through the limb, and cuts it off from its hidden body.

The creature screams!

The shadow vanishes.

The towering, grotesque form is now visible.

Its widespread shoulders and thin frame broadens, as the beast stakes its clawed feet into the ground. The monster's mouth opens, and sharp fangs extend from its gums.

Gary stares hard at the creature's jet-black, scaly skin that ripples over its body, as he musters a malicious smile, his burning blue sphere soon surrounds him, and Gary's hand bursts out white flames.

"THERE YOU ARE!" Gary shouts, aiming his right arm in the direction of the monstrosity, unleashing fires. The inferno races at the creature.

Lord Moon sees the fiery illumination, and quickly extends its clawed hand. An invisible force halts the flames, just inches away from the beast's palm.

Gary is in shock, witnessing what's happening, who now amplifies his effort. A vile grin immediately appears on Lord Moon's face, amused, as the creature focuses its omnipotent powers, and pushes back Gary's fires, reversing its direction.

The young man lets out a piercing cry, as the skin on Gary's arms suddenly sizzles and burns. Immediately after, the flames ceases, and Gary grabs his scolded flesh, falling to his knees.

"I'm intrigued with how powerful you've become in such a short time, my child. Yet, you will come to learn that you're *not* ready," Lord Moon states.

Gary hears the monster, as he experiences the unbearable pain it inflicts. The young man goes to touch his horribly burned arm, and recoils when his contact rubs off his own flesh. With jumbled thoughts, Gary glares up at the giant beast that murdered his parents.

"I'M *NOT* YOUR CHILD!" he defiantly yells. Lord Moon laughs at his agony, and begins approaching the fallen man, Gary hears the loud stomping of its feet.

His mind quickly grabs at the broken bricks around him, and thousands of shards flies at the creature, spinning with deadly accuracy. They tear through Lord Moon's frame, also boomeranging back, slashing more through its flesh.

The eternal one instantly stumbles under the assault, but focuses its tremendous power, as the flying bricks soon explode into harmless dust.

"Your tricks don't amuse me," Lord Moon says, as Gary rises. His shifty eyes glares at the creature, and suddenly, the area around the two quakes, with tremors that grows stronger by the second.

"I WILL *KILL* US BOTH IF I HAVE TO! WE'LL BE BURIED ALIVE!" Gary spits, as blood now runs out of his nose, and Gary's mind begins to strain.

Lord Moon feels his power, the strange, supernatural power it had given the young man when Gary was a child. The creature's shoulder suddenly tears horridly, as the walls around them crack. The pain seems to pleasure the eternal one, as much as it displeases the sensation.

Gary Romulus, it seems, is worthy of the essence the beast had given him, worthy of the destiny of the *Sonz of Darkness.*

Several slimy snake-like tentacles, worm out from the monster's flesh, elongating, preparing to attack, outside of Gary's orb. Each limb has ten glowing heads attached with opened mouths, and the flesh of the monster's shoulder soon regenerates.

Gary grimaces in pain.

He feels a building pressure, pushing upon his protective sphere from all directions. The tremendous force grows even more, and becomes extremely overbearing. Blood slowly trickles from Gary's eyes as he pushes back. The young man then falls to the floor, and his vision fades.

Gary's mind is being overtaxed.

Lord Moon senses his weakening and reacts.

The snake-like tentacles sway around Gary's orb, unleashing beams of energies that punch through Gary's sphere. The rays rip into his body, and Gary rolls over on the ground, wracked in sheer turmoil. The wounds from Lord Moon's attack leaves smoking holes all about Gary, and his glowing orb vanishes.

"YOU WILL *NEVER* DEFEAT ME ALONE, MY SON! YOU ARE *NOT* READY FOR YOUR DESTINY!" Lord Moon proclaims.

Rapidly, the monster's mind reaches out to Gary and throws him to the ceiling. The young man's spine snaps in two, as he instantly feels the shock of the collision, Gary now brutally falling back onto the ground.

"LEARN THIS LESSON WELL, SHED YOUR HUMANITY!" Lord Moon instructs. Crimson tears continue to roll down Gary's emotionless face, as he's stricken with pain.

I failed...it's over.

Flashes of memories now haunts Gary's mind: the terrible way his parents had died by the creature standing above him, and the nightmarish dream Lord Moon constantly sent Gary about murdering his brother, Andrew.

I can't win...my parents won't be avenged! I've loss— Andrew will, too, Gary adds to his thoughts before closing his eyes, accepting whatever further tortures Lord Moon has in store.

Shortly after, out of the deepest chasms of Gary's pain, he hears his grandmother words in his head: *"You have to be strong..."* Gary remembers her telling him he had to be strong for he and his brother. Now, a woman's image comes to Gary, one who he can't let die, or ever lose again.

"Melody?"

Lord Moon hears its now broken, defeated chosen speak a name.

"MELODY!"

Gary's eyes opens, as the memories of the woman he loves, fills his heart with hope.

The creature soon sees a flicker of light around Gary's body, and it slowly steps back, as the magnificent blue sphere, once again, surrounds Gary's form.

The young man now uses his mind to raise his body from the ground, now turning to face the eternal one. As Gary hovers, his eyes illuminates with a white glow, as vapors escapes from them.

"YOU *CAN'T* BE VICTORIOUS ALONE, MY CHOSEN!" Lord Moon threatens.

"I don't intend to," Gary retaliates. He then flies at the creature, and collides into its chest, pulling Lord Moon off the ground. The two violently crash into the small space of the wrecked elevator.

Before the beast can react, the enclosed space explodes with a white flash that climbs upwards, melting everything in its path.

*   *   *   *   *

The force of a powerful blow to Masters' mid section cracks three of his ribs. The man's legs are weakened, as the gold metallic being in front of Masters, prepares to deliver another strike.

McKoon, now fully transformed, due to the altered DNA inside of him, grabs AG by the throat, and lifts the silver cherubim off its feet. McKoon now throws AG into his counterpart, giving Masters a chance to recuperate.

"Use your communion, Masters!" McKoon demands. Masters has taken too much damage to ignite the metamorphism; Masters will die if he tries to endure the change.

McKoon now glares at Andrew and begins to approach him. Andrew sees the monstrosity McKoon has become, as he reaches into a desk compartment to retrieve his gun. Andrew rises, and aims his nine-millimeter at McKoon, before glancing at the three computer screens. The program he activated is only eight-five percent complete, in which a few more seconds is needed for completion.

"Looks like you're a *victim* of your own experiments, just like Ong Mra was," Andrew retorts.

"You *fool!* I am perfection—my lord has blessed me. The Jinn Legion is beyond your comprehension!" McKoon barks, taking another step forward.

Andrew pulls the trigger repeatedly, and watches as bullets quickly tears through McKoon's frame; causing him to stumble back until the clip of Andrew's gun is empty.

McKoon's dry, chapped lips peel back a haunting grin, one that strikes to the core of Andrew's heart. He advances again towards Andrew.

"Program complete. Password needed."

Andrew, Masters and Mckoon now hear the computer's voice, Andrew grins.

"Messiah," Andrew states.

"Accepted."

Wobbling to his feet, Masters fears what has been done.

"The Jinn Legion will get *nothing!* The virus I pre-programmed will devour and infect everything in the system, even I can't stop it," Andrew indicates to Masters and McKoon.

"You *idiot!* Lortech will be *destroyed!*" Masters scowls, causing Andrew to give him a fierce stare.

"When you decided to *betray* this corporation and my family, you already left me with nothing!" Andrew replies.

McKoon, enraged at what he's hearing, rushes at Andrew. AU collides with McKoon, slamming them both into a wall. Andrew takes full advantage of being saved by AU. He limps from behind his desk and places his hand on a nearby wall, which is actually a hidden screen.

Andrew states his name and the panel rises, in which he grabs the staff hidden within. Andrew quickly motions for AG to attack Masters, and the cherubim do so immediately. Andrew hears the cracking of the two men's bones, as he steps out of the office, leaving AU and AG to handle Masters and McKoon.

Using the staff as a walking stick, Andrew makes his way to the elevator, until he hears a slight rumbling that's growing louder. Andrew's eyes widen, and his irises shrink instantly, as the elevator explodes in a searing white flash, knocking him off-balance.

The bright light dims, and soon fades away altogether, as Gary violently comes hurling out of the elevator's shaft, and through the closed elevator's doors; crashing to the floor a couple of yards away from his brother.

Andrew quickly approaches him, and turns Gary's body over, repulsed at what he sees. Half of Gary's body is singed, burned beyond recognition, and he gasps for air, almost nearly dead.

Through hazy vision, Gary sees his brother. Blood now clogs his throat as he struggles to speak: "The witch...the Vowdun is here." Gary clutches Andrew's shirt tightly, "It's over. It's..." his grip loosens, Gary falls unconscious.

Andrew's thoughts now races.

The incredible agony his brother suffers, causes Andrew to wonder what could've done this. He's frantic, as Andrew takes off his jacket and wraps it around Gary. He now looks at the demolished elevator his brother flew through, and sees something strange.

Hundreds of slimy snakes slithers through the opening Gary made from the closed elevator doors. The bizarre appearance makes the hairs on the back of Andrew's neck stand on end. Using all of his strength, he lifts Gary into his arms, leaving the staff, and heads in the opposite direction of the elevator. Andrew soon spots the doorway leading to the roof, feeling that it's their only escape now.

The helicopter! Andrew thinks. He places the palm of his hand on the scanner, and the door automatically opens. Bracing himself, Andrew begins to climb up the stairs with Gary in his arms, step-by-step; not allowing the brutal bullet wounds in his leg affect him.

As Andrew arrives at the top of the stairs, he doesn't waste anytime in pushing the door open. The brisk breeze fills his lungs, as his eyes quickly examines *New York City's* skyline. Heavy rain pours down on the two, as Andrew carries his brother towards the lone, unmanned helicopter.

I know how to fly it—I just need to get to it. Then all of this will be over! Andrew thinks to himself, *Gary and I can face the Jinn Legion another day!*

Suddenly, a glowing ray of energy, shoots from behind the brothers, and heads for the helicopter. Andrew is immediately blown off of his feet, and he and Gary's bodies haphazardly hits the ground, as the helicopter unexpectedly explodes into a great ball of fire.

THIRTY-FOUR

Andrew's teeth grits, as his head lies on the watered ground of the roof. Tears well up before slowly falling down the sides of his face. Andrew now struggles back to his feet.

"N-O-O-O-O-O-O!" he desperately screams into the night sky, and it loudly thunders back at his plea. Andrew turns to face the roof's entrance where light is now emerging. He sees McKoon first, and now a wounded Masters, coming through the doorway with another white-haired man, whom Andrew has never seen before—Loki.

Andrew lifts Gary back into his arms, and on trembling legs, he steps back to the edge of the tower's roof. The fire from the burning helicopter flickers off the reflective watered floor around them. Gary soon stirs in Andrew's grip. His right eye flutters open, and the young man sees the three men. Andrew eventually hears his brother's weak moan.

Andrew left the ornamented staff that controlled his metallic protectors, AU and AG, now there's nothing standing in the other three men's way, Andrew regretfully believes.

"WHAT ARE YOU WAITING FOR? COME FINISH WHAT YOU STARTED!" Andrew calls out in defiance. He now hears a small chuckle escape McKoon's throat, yet, none of the three men moves in the slightest.

Snake-like tentacles begin to come out of the doorway, the same way Andrew saw them come through the elevator. Andrew braces himself, as whatever it is that inflicted the incredible damage to Gary, has now come upon the roof.

Andrew's eyes widens in horror when he views the gruesome creature's form. It stands nine-feet-tall, and its body is black and terribly deformed, appearing arachnid. Andrew looks down at Gary and meets his brother's glazed eye.

"It's the Vowdun," Gary whispers.

Using the last bit of strength he can muster, Gary surrounds he and Andrew with his blue sphere. Andrew becomes surprised by the illumination. Something about it feels so familiar to the man. Andrew gazes at the crackling, electrical currents, that moves outside of the manifestation.

"Be gone, my Jinn!" the eternal one demands to the three men beside it. Andrew watches as, McKoon, Masters, Loki, vanish one-by-one from his sight. Andrew now becomes even more frantic, as his vision locks back on the monstrosity before him.

"What *are* you?" Andrew questions.

"I am *all* that you will come to know, my child. *All* that you are, and what is left of you and your brother. You are my chosen. You will fulfill what destiny I have given you!"

Andrew shakes his head, trying to block out what he's hearing and seeing. He takes another step back at the edge of the roof, ready to die, before experiencing anymore of the agony that has entered his life.

Andrew glances at Gary, who now also stares back at him blankly. It all feels as if Andrew has done this before, holding his younger brother in his arms, as the strange, blue orb surrounds them. Andrew glimpses once more at the monster. It's menacing, glowing, red eyes, now seems to capture him, as Andrew helplessly becomes lost in them.

The heavy, falling rains begins to slow in their descent to earth. Time seems to slow its pace, as Andrew's mind is at a standstill. Everything around him takes on an evanescent quality, and gradually vanishes from his sight.

Andrew soon gazes down at his arms, and realizes Gary is no longer present. He looks back at the beast, and sees a being of pure light.

Andrew is in another time.

Another place.

Where he is only conscious.

Now, Andrew is slowly being drawn into the light, and instantly feels its omnipotent energy, one that's alive and individual, in this strange plane of existence.

These are memories, which are not Andrew's own.

He suddenly knows the name of the conscious energy— Etherea. It exists in a perfect balance of its solitude, in the universe.

...A great catastrophe immediately takes place, as a nearby brilliant star, bursts its incredible energy, before transforming into a giant black hole. It consumes everything it can, and pulls the Etherea from its balance, sending the omnipotent energy into the universe, when the worlds were young.

The chaotic impact sends tremendous ripples throughout the planet, causing an extinction of the majority of the planets inhabitants. The dust and debris from the shock, blankets the planets ozone, plunging the world into total darkness....

Andrew's consciousness now understands, and experiences how the Etherea traveled across boundaries of time and space, until it collided with the world that would come to be called Earth. A forgotten wisdom is awakening within Andrew, as he's being fed the incredible knowledge.

He now knows that as the Earth healed, the Etherea became flesh, trapped in a plane of existence, from which it couldn't escape.

Time begins to speed in Andrew's mind. He witnesses how new creatures emerge as the solar system's sun, once again, shines on the planet.

Then comes the birth of mankind.

At that time, the Etherea had begun to despise all life, and this world that had become its prison, hating the inferior creatures the planet had given birth to. The Etherea wanted to die, to become nonexistent, to reach chasm of darkness, of nothingness. It wanted to escape.

Andrew is aware of the Etherea's twisted plan, as if it's his own, that rises from the Etherea's bitterness and misery.

The Etherea had shared its ominous flesh with those it deemed worthy of man, making them stronger, and more vicious; giving them the ability to change their forms.

These were the original nine tribes of the Jinn Legion. They would all come to call the Etherea, Lord Moon, and it would become their god. After the Jinn's numbers had grown, Lord Moon pit them against each other to see who was the most destructive of them.

Horrifying wars had taken over the lands of the Earth, and out of them came the warrior king, Bakarot, who ruled over all of the Jinn. Lord Moon was pleased by the vicious nature of man. The Etherea had formed four weapons from its eternal energy: the ornamented staff, and two unstoppable cherubim for which it controlled, AU and AG. The last of the weapons was the golden sword, which raped the life force of those it slain—it was called Nazareth.

The Etherea had given these tools of its destruction to its follower, Bakarot. It then had given the warrior king a vision that his own god would destroy the world.

Bakarot and his army of men rose up against their alien god, and all but few were destroyed in a day. Those who'd survived, buried Bakarot alive, along with the staff, and the two metallic beings it controlled. The remaining had returned to their god, Lord Moon, and the Jinn Legion lived on, in the cabals of coming civilization, from generation-to-generation. That battle had taken place ten thousand years ago.

The Etherea had grown even more malicious, seeing that its plan had failed, one that couldn't be destroyed. As time moved on, its insane mind had conceived another plan. The Etherea would share its essence, its eternal energy with four of the seed of original man.

Andrew soon sees the Etherea's first chosen, one who had large, jet-black eyes, and dragons upon his skin. He was the son of a Zulu chief in Africa, his name was Sha—the Etherea called him Attila.

Fragments of the past begin to shatter, as Andrew is given the vision of the second chosen, while seeing the place where the Etherea had tortured him for nearly a century. He was named, Koshat Otemi.

Time begins to bend, and once again speeds, as Andrew now is given the origin of the Etherea. He knows of the Jinn Legion, they are not like the chosen.

The chosen are immortal.

They shared the pure essence, the eternal life force of the Etherea—it was fused into every molecule of their existence. The Jinn Legion only share its grotesque flesh, which was merged into their DNA.

Everything ceases.

...Andrew's surroundings alter to a more recent time.

He is young again.

Andrew sees his real parents, and his baby brother, Gary, who he loves; one who Andrew also thinks has a big head.

He remembers.

A door is opening in Andrew's mind.

The Vowdun witch is the Etherea; a being that needs the last of its chosen.

Andrew cries out, as he witnesses what happens to Gary as a child, by the hands of the Etherea; Andrew now feeling the agony of having his own throat slashed.

Now comes the sharing of the essence.

The chosen are now complete.

The crash, Andrew's real parents' death, and Gary protecting him from the fires, Andrew recalls it all. He now remembers crying that night, and making a promise to Gary.

Andrew now remembers everything.

He sees visions of a near future, and the coming war.

Andrew knows his destiny.

He's the beholder of the gift and the curse.

Andrew is one of the Sonz of Darkness.

* * * * *

Gary watches through hazy vision at Andrew.

His brother's eyes are closed.

Distant.

As if Andrew's in a trance.

Soon, Gary sees something appear in the middle of Andrew's forehead.

A tear of blood forms.

Weakly, Gary reaches up to touch it. From the tear a slit forms, as though Andrew is cut in the area. The skin in the middle of Andrew's forehead opens, revealing a third silver eye.

Gary smiles as the tear of blood runs down Andrew's cheek, falling into the palm of Gary's hand. Andrew's other eyes opens, wide and fierce. They're filled with an ageless knowledge. Andrew glances down at his brother, and gives Gary a slight smile.

"Everything is going to be alright, Man-head," Andrew says, referring to Gary by his nickname he'd called him as a newborn.

Gary, lying limp in Andrew's arms, knows that he finally reached his real brother. Shortly after, all three of Andrew's eyes glare at the eternal creature in front of him.

"Yes, my chosen. You have foreseen your destiny," Lord Moon hisses.

"I have foreseen it, Etherea. I promise you, you will *die!*" Andrew proclaims.

"Then let it begin."

Tentacles tears out of the eternal one's flesh, and their tips begin to illuminate. Beams of raw energy shoot out of them, punching through the roof's ground.

The intense power the creature unleashes, rams through each level of the building, traveling lower-and-lower into the tower's structure. As the beams hit the building's foundation, they bring on an enormous explosion of unfathomable power, which climbs up each level of Lortech's tower, annihilating everything in its path.

Andrew stands firm, as the roof of the tower shakes in tremors, as its foundation crumbles. He takes one last glance at the Etherea, and lightly steps off the tower, falling to the city streets with his brother in his arms. Instantly, Andrew opens his mind, using his long, dormant abilities.

Several feet below their descent, a giant black hole appears, rapidly opening wider, as it's a portal to a predestined location. Andrew and Gary falls into the limbo, just as the extreme power of the Etherea unleashed, climbs up to last of Lortech's tower and blazes.

New York City's streets are terribly blinded in a wave of rushing dust and debris. Hundreds of pedestrians will die before the chaos is over.

The Etherea's loudly twisted laughter can be heard, with the deadly rumbling of Lortech's falling tower, for miles around.

THIRTY-FIVE

One week later...

"FBI sources say they are still baffled by what could have caused the explosion here at the Lortech Tower, in Manhattan's downtown Tribeca district, but they have released a statement, indicating that, 'Andrew Taylor, president of Lortech, told them of an unknown terrorist group called the Jinn Legion, were threatening the industrialist.' They may be responsible for the tragedy, yet authorities have no further evidence supporting the allegations.

"Strangely enough, Valerie Taylor, the mother of Andrew Taylor, mansion in East Hampton, New York was destroyed, earlier the night of the explosion. It is believed that Andrew and Valerie Taylor are deceased, victims of any two of the incidents. Andrew Taylor's remains still have not been found, but may be among the hundreds at the explosion site. That's all for this hour. This is Dali Well of Channel 8, World News reporting. Good day."

Gary turns off the portable television that's resting by his chair. He slouches back into the seat, as the radiant sun shines brightly on his face. Gary now hears seagulls calling in the sky above. He covers his brow with the palm of his hand, trying to catch a glimpse of the flying birds. The silhouette of a woman standing beside him, blocks Gary's vision.

"Enjoying the view?" Melody asks, comfortingly.

Gary pulls her towards him, and Melody sits in his lap. She kisses him deeply, and when their lips unlocked, Melody gently caresses Gary's face.

"Your brother went out of his way for this," she says, admiring the beauty of the seventy-foot yacht they're on.

"We do need a vacation, don't we?" Gary states.

"Yes, we do," Melody answers, as she rests her head upon his chest. "I just wish Brown was here to share it with us," the young woman adds. It's clear that what Melody experienced, still haunts her dreadfully.

Gary is thankful to have Melody, and he prays for Brown, the man who saved her life, twice. Yet, there's no way to thank him.

When he and Andrew escaped through the portal his brother created, the two went to Sharon Puwa's home. Gary and Andrew found Melody in a room, clutching tightly to Brown. Unfortunately he'd bled to death in her arms. Sharon also was dead, as her body was sprawled upon the guestroom's bed, Sharon having a bullet in her head.

Last week, Andrew told Gary that when his dormant powers activated, that he knew Melody was in danger. Andrew also told Gary an abundance of other news days ago, that the information actually gave him migraine headaches. But Gary thanks GOD that the woman is now safe, and in his arms. Gary has not lost what he holds dear to his heart.

Andrew on the other hand, has lost everything: his adoptive mother, ex-lover, friends, and even his corporation. Andrew also doesn't seem as though he's the same person, who he was, before that tragic night.

At times, Gary feels haunted, just by looking at his brother's face, believing that Andrew is a completely different person, now that he has his memories back.

Gary soon turns to watch Andrew, who's standing by the bow of the ship, talking to an elderly *Japanese* man, who Andrew tells Gary is his friend.

"I'm *greatly* sorry for your loss," says Yoshi Hiro, as he looks at Andrew with terribly saddened eyes.

"My mother's soul is at rest, Yoshi. I thank you for your friendship, when I was in need," Andrew replies to the old man. "I'm giving you full ownership of Lortech," he adds, shocking Yoshi.

"But, Lortech is yours, your father—"

Andrew's eyes now cut across to Yoshi, seeming to silence him.

"It's for the better. That will make it easier for me to strike back at my enemies. Lortech has suffered a major blow, and I believe you are the man who can bring it back to its former glory. It's what my father would've wanted."

Andrew's words are striking into the pit of Yoshi's thoughts, more like controlling.

"Now rest, Yoshi."

Thank you, Andrew," Yoshi answers, as he slowly walks away from the younger Black man.

Now alone, Andrew spots Gary. He immediately thinks about all that has been revealed to him. Andrew grew up wealthy because David Taylor adopted him. Now, he's aware that his adoptive father, along with countless others, were part of the Jinn Legion, and the Jinn's God, Lord Moon, made David Taylor adopt Andrew; in order to separate the brothers for a period of time.

Lord Moon is the Vowdun witch that had murdered Andrew and Gary's real parents. Lord Moon, the Vowdun, went by many forms and countless names, but Andrew witnessed its true form, and knows the real name of the alien creature.

Etherea.

He also knows that the staff, and AU and AG, are back in the possession of the eternal one who originally created them.

The memories the creature has given him are enormously complex, and Andrew's mind is still trying to adjust to it. He now knows, the reason for it all, Andrew and Gary, and the other two chosen's purpose.

The Etherea is the source of their gifts of their immortality. Its essence is combined with every atom of their being. But, it will take all four of the chosen, to fulfill the destiny of the *Sonz of Darkness*.

Andrew's telepathic mind instinctively senses his brother approaching behind him, "Yes, Gary?" he says, without turning to face Gary.

Andrew's eyes remain locked on the vast blue sea ahead, staring oddly beyond what can be seen with normal sight. To Gary, his brother seems possessed.

"I just feel like I have to say I'm sorry. I feel like I destroyed your life, and if—"

"It was me, Gary," Andrew interjects, interrupting his brother.

Gary moves in closer to him: "What do you mean?"

"When the Etherea first gave us our powers, I knew what I know now. I knew what it was that we had become. When I was taken away from you, I used my special powers, and embedded the memories in your mind, so that you would never forget what happened to us; so you wouldn't forget me," Andrew reveals

259

before pausing, now feeling the unspoken confusion of his brother's mind.

"It was you?"

"...I'm the one who's sorry, Gary. I gave you that great burden, and when I was taken away, I was too *weak* to face our destiny. I used my powers on myself, and erased my mind of all that I was, but you still found me. I guess you had to, that's the *real* reason you hated me so much. You weren't even aware of it."

Gary doesn't know what to say...

He turns and gazes at Melody.

She's looking out at the sea, off the coast of *Japan.*

Andrew senses the doubt that clouds his brother's heart.

"Melody, do you love her?" Andrew questions, startling Gary.

"Yeah, I do!" his brother answers immediately.

Andrew turns to face Gary: "Then you *must* let her go. The Etherea will...will harm Melody, *just* to make you despise it even more."

"No! I'll *protect* her, no matter *what!*" Gary defends. Even as he says these words, Gary's heart grows faint. *But how can I stop someone who can't be killed?* he asks himself, Gary knowing he would find no answer.

"...With the two others who are like us. I can feel them, and we *must* find the other chosen, before it's too late." Andrew's vision returns back to the sea. "The Etherea grows desperate...if we don't succeed in the destiny it has forged for us, the Etherea will destroy this world, to regain its balance of solitude. We have no other choice."

Suddenly, Gary sees the silver eye open in the middle of his brother's forehead. Andrew turns to him and unleashes a powerful force, causing Gary to stumble.

Andrew catches his brother before he falls.

Gary now tries to move...

But can't.

He struggles...

Tries to control his physical and mental capabilities...

But can't.

Nothing works.

Not even Gary's own supernatural powers.

His nose begins to bleed, as Gary tries hard to fight what's happening. Andrew now enters his mind.

"I once gave you a great burden, now let me take one away, Gary."

"N-O-O-O-O-O-O-O-O-O-O-O-O!" Gary screams out silently, as his brother tears into his conscience.

Andrew begins erasing the memory that Melody Black survived that night at Sharon Puwa's home.

It's will be for the better.

This is his gift to his brother, a decision, Andrew knows Gary can't force himself to make.

Andrew sees Melody rising from her seat, as she notices what's taking place. Instantly, Andrew shuts down Melody's mind. He soon will do the same to her, as he's doing to Gary, knowing it will save Melody's life from the chaos, they're about to encounter.

She will never remember that Gary Romulus or Andrew Taylor, ever existed. From this day forward, they will only be known as "Messiah" and "Exodus"....

GLOSSARY

AG – Symbol for silver
AI –Artificial Intelligence
AU – Symbol for gold
Boughie – Slang for bourgeois/affluent middle-class people
Bro – Brother
Cherubim – Guardian angel representing the glory of GOD
Chump Change – A small amount of money
FBI – Federal Bureau of Investigation
FDA – Food and Drug Administration
Hammer – Gun
Jack – Phone
Knocked – Locked up
LCD – Liquid-crystal display
NSA – National Security Agency
Off-The-Charts – Live/exciting
OPS – The controlling of organized military
Paper – Money/cash
Pen – Penitentiary
Pigs – Derogatory term for police
Shanty – Hut/shack
Simian – Characteristics of monkeys or apes
Slim Jim – A thin metal tool
Snitch – To inform sneakily
Weed – Marijuana

An excerpt from *SONZ OF DARKNESS 2* by
DRU NOBLE
A GHETTOHEAT® PRODUCTION

Deep beneath the busy streets of *New York City,* in its literal bowels, feces, urine, and stench of human waste, pools in rivers from loosened pipes too old to fix. This is the place where rats and other indescribable vermin call home, and in this place, an amorphous, ghost-like shadow, returns to the physical flesh and blood form of Attila.

The abilities the immortal possess are eerily strange, but for the sweet taste of the Attila's own demise, the being would wager and forfeit its soul if Attila was sure, such a thing exists. His body is beginning to sluggishly heal, as Attila journeys through the dark, dank tunnel of the sewer system, feverish, and battling to overcome the foul stench that his heightened senses make even stronger.

He almost doesn't hear the nearly silent footsteps mimicking his own behind him. The assassin pauses...his trembling hands reaches into his leather jacket, fingers tightly gripping his gun.

"Don't move! ...That was a nice trick you played back there, but you're not getting away from me," tells a very deep, commanding voice.

Attila becomes startled by the very notion that he could be followed. His nerves are electrified by the impossibility. As sweat runs down his brow, Attila takes a lungful of air and holds it. Bracing himself for what he knows he has to do, he only has one shot. Attila body spins, gun aiming at the figure's head, and on impulse, he fires.

Twin shots echoes throughout the tunnels, whistling through the stale air. One of the bullets hit its target dead on, the other tears through Attila's chest, busting out of his back. The assassin's heart fatally bursts before he hits the ground in an ungraceful slump.

Attila can't move at all, already he's succumbing to shock. He struggles effortlessly, as his forced breathing becomes shallow. Attila has endured death, many times in his uncanny, violent life, but would never find the final rest. Attila is amazed that he can still hear footsteps approaching his immobile body, as his large black eyes stares blankly at the oval ceiling of the sewer.

A man named, Wolf, stares down upon Attila, while the grotesque bullet hole bleeds from the middle of his forehead. Attila is baffled to witness that this man is still alive, as he takes his last gasping breaths. He glares into the frightening familiar face of his murderer. Attila's vision begins to darken in a haze, as the world grows cold, so unbearably cold.

A name surfaces in the core of his stomach, swimming in agony. It fights it way through his constricted throat, willing its way to be said. It has to be spoken—the name was sealed in the past. His vocal cords tremble, as it escapes the assassin's dry lips.

"Koshat?" he whispers. There is nothing—nothing but darkness.

An excerpt from ***GHETTOHEAT*®** by
HICKSON
A GHETTOHEAT® PRODUCTION

***GHETTOHEAT*®**

S-S-S-S-S-S-S!
Can you feel it? Scaldin' breath of frisky spirits
Surroundin' you in the streets
The intensity
S-S-S-S-S-S-S!
That's GHETTOHEAT®!
The energy – Electric sparks
Better watch ya back after dark!
Dogs bark – Cats hiss
Rank smells of trash and piss
Internalize – Realize
No surprise – Naughty spirits frolic in disguise
S-S-S-S-S-S-S!
INTENSITY: CLIMBIN'! CLIMBIN'! CLIMBIN'! CLIMBIN'!
GHETTOHEAT®: RISIN'! RISIN'! RISIN'! RISIN'!

Streets is watchin'
Hoes talkin' – Thugs stalkin'
POW! POW! POW!
Start speed-walkin'!
Heggies down – Rob that clown
Snatch his stash – Jet downtown
El Barrio – Spanish Harlem:

"MIRA, NO! WE DON'T WANNO PROBLEM!"

Bullets graze – I'm not amazed
GHETTOHEAT®!
Niggas start blazin'
Air's scathin' – Gangs blood-bathin'
Five-O's misbehavin' – Wifey's rantin'-n-ravin'!
My left: The Bloods – My right: The Crips
Niggas start prayin' – Murk-out in ya whip!

Internalize – Realize
No surprise – Naughty spirits frolic in disguise
S-S-S-S-S-S-S!
INTENSITY: CLIMBIN'! CLIMBIN'! CLIMBIN'! CLIMBIN'!
GHETTOHEAT®: RISIN'! RISIN'! RISIN'! RISIN'!

Mean hoodlums – Plottin' schemes
A swoop-down – 'Bout to rob me – Seems like a bad dream
Thugs around – It's goin' down
'BOUT TO BE SOME SHIT!
But I'm ghetto – Know how to spit
Gully mentality – Thinkin' of reality of planned-out casualty
I fake wit' the trickery:
"ASS-ALAMUALAIKUM"
"STICK 'EM UP!"
"YO, DON'T FUCK WIT' HIM – HE'S MUSLIM!"

Flipped script wit' quickness
Changed demeanor – The swiftness
Not dimwitted – Felt the flames of evil spirits!
Hid chain in shirt – I don't catch pain – Don't get hurt
No desire gettin' burnt by the fire
Thermometer soars, yo, higher-and-higher
In the PRO-JECTS – Fightin' to protect ya neck
Gotta earn respect – Defend ya rep
Or BEAT-DOWNS you'll collect
The furor – The fever – My gun – My cleaver
Bitches brewin' – Slits a-stewin'
Sheets roastin' – Champagne toastin' -- Gangstas boastin':

"The ghetto – Nuthin's mellow
The ghetto – Cries in falsetto
The ghetto – A dream bordello
The ghetto – Hotter than Soweto"

Internalize – Realize
No surprise – Naughty spirits frolic in disguise
S-S-S-S-S-S-S!
INTENSITY: CLIMBIN'! CLIMBIN'! CLIMBIN'! CLIMBIN'!
GHETTOHEAT®: RISIN'! RISIN'! RISIN'! RISIN'!

Red-hot hustlers – Broilin' at the spot
Boilin' alcohol – The lucky crackpot
Streets a-scorchin' – Crackheads torchin'
Stems ignited – Junkies delighted
Money's flowin' – Pusherman's excited
The first and fifteenth: BLOCK-HUGGERS' JUNETEENTH!
Comin' ya way – Take ya benefits today
Intoxication – Self-medication – The air's dense
Ghetto-suffocation – Volcanic maniacs attackin'
Cash stackin' – Niggas packin' – Daddy Rock's mackin':

"The ghetto – Nuthin's mellow
The ghetto – Cries in falsetto
The ghetto – A dream bordello
The ghetto – Hotter than Soweto"

BedStuy – Do or die: *BUCK! BUCK! BUCK! BUCK!*

They don't give a FUCK!
In The Bronx – You'll fry – Tossin' lye – WATCH YA EYES!

Walk straight – Tunnel vision – False move – Bad decision
So hot – Starts to drizzle – Steamy sidewalks – Begin to sizzle
HOT-TO-DEF! Intense GHETTOHEAT®

"DO YOU FEEL IT? DO YOU FEEL IT?"
"THE HOTNESS IN THE STREETS!!!™"

So hot – Got ya mase?
Too hot – PEPPER SPRAYIN' IN A NIGGA'S FACE!
The Madness – Sadness: Don't you know the flare of street-glow?
OH! Meltingly – Swelteringly: *S-S-S-S-S-S-S!*
HOOD IN-FER-NO!
Internalize – Realize
No surprise – Naughty spirits frolic in disguise
S-S-S-S-S-S-S!
INTENSITY: CLIMBIN'! CLIMBIN'! CLIMBIN'! CLIMBIN'!
GHETTOHEAT®: RISIN'! RISIN'! RISIN'! RISIN'!
INTENSITY: CLIMBIN'! CLIMBIN'! CLIMBIN'! CLIMBIN'!
GHETTOHEAT®: RISIN'! RISIN'! RISIN'! RISIN'!
S-S-S-S-S-S-S!

An excerpt from *CONVICT'S CANDY* by
DAMON "AMIN" MEADOWS & JASON POOLE
A GHETTOHEAT® PRODUCTION

"Sweets, you're in cell 1325; upper bunk," the Correctional Officer had indicated, as he instructed Candy on which cell to report to. When she heard 'upper bunk', Candy had wondered who would be occupying the cell with her. As Candy had grabbed her bedroll and headed towards the cell, located near the far end of the tier and away from the officer's desk and sight, butterflies had grown deep inside of Candy's stomach, as she'd become overwhelmed with nervousness; Candy tried hard to camouflage her fear.

This was Candy's first time in prison and she'd been frightened, forcefully trapped in terror against her will. Candy had become extremely horrified, especially when her eyes met directly with Trigger's, the young, hostile thug she'd accidentally bumped into as she'd been placed inside the holding cell. Trigger had rudely shoved Candy when she first arrived to the facility.

"THE *FUCK* YOU LOOKIN' AT, HOMO?" Trigger had spat; embarrassed that Candy had looked at him. Trigger immediately wondered if she was able to detect that something was different about him and his masculinity; Trigger had hoped that Candy hadn't gotten any ideas that he might've been attracted to her, since Candy had caught him staring hard at her.

She'd quickly turned her face in the opposite direction, Candy wanted desperately not to provoke Trigger, as the thought of getting beat down by him instantly had come to Candy's mind.

She couldn't exactly figure out the young thug, although Candy thought she might've had a clue as to why he'd displayed so much anger and hatred towards her. Yet, this hadn't been the time to come to any conclusions, as Candy was more concerned with whom she'd be sharing the cell with.

When Candy had reached cell 1325, she glanced twice at the number printed above on the door, and had made sure that she was at the right cell before she'd entered. Candy then peeped inside the window to see if anyone had been there. Seeing that it was empty, she'd stepped inside of the cell that would serve as her new home for the next five-and-a-half years.

Candy was overwhelmed with joy when she found the cell had been perfectly neat and clean; and for a moment, Candy had sensed that it had a woman's touch. The room smelled like sweet perfume, instead of the strong musk oil that was sold on commissary.

Right away, Candy had dropped her bedroll and raced towards the picture board that had hung on the wall and analyzed every photo; she'd become curious to know who occupied the cell and how they'd lived. Candy believed that a photo was like a thousand words; she'd felt that people told a lot about themselves by the way they'd posed in photographs, including how they displayed their own pictures.

Candy then smiled as her eyes perused over photos of gorgeous models, both male and female, and had become happy when she'd found the huge portrait of her new cellmate. Judging by his long, jet-black wavy hair, facial features and large green eyes, Candy had assumed that he was Hispanic.

Now that she'd known the identity of her cellmate, Candy then decided that it would be best to go find him and introduce herself; she'd hoped that he would fully accept her into the room.

As Candy had turned around and headed out the door, she'd abruptly been stopped by a hard, powerful right-handed fist to her chiseled jaw, followed by the tight grip of a person's left hand hooking around her throat; her vocal cords were being crushed so she couldn't scream.

Candy had haphazardly fallen back into a corner and hit the back of her head against the wall, before she'd become unconscious momentarily. Within the first five seconds of gaining back her conscious, Candy had pondered who'd bashed her so hard in her face.

The first person that had come to mind was Trigger. Secondly, Candy also had thought it might've been her new cellmate who obviously hadn't wanted Candy in his cell, she'd assumed by the blow that Candy had taken to her flawless face.

Struggling her way back from darkness, Candy's eyes had widened wide, at that point, being terribly frightened, as she was face-to-face with two unknown convicts who'd worn white pillow cases over their heads; mean eyes had peeked from the two holes that was cut out from the cloth. The two attackers had resembled members of the Ku Klux Klan bandits as they'd hid their faces; both had been armed with sharp, ten-inch knives.

269

Overcome with panic, there was no doubt in Candy's mind that she was about to be brutally raped, as there was no way out. Candy then quickly prayed to herself and had hoped that they wouldn't take her life as well. Yet, being raped no longer was an important factor to Candy, as they could've had their way with her. All Candy had been concerned with at that moment was continuing to live.

An excerpt from *HARDER* by
SHA
A GHETTOHEAT® PRODUCTION

When I finally arrived back home, Tony was heated. I
didn't even realize I was out that long.

"WHERE THE *FUCK* YOU BEEN, KAI?" he yelled as I
walked through the door.

"I went to the range and then shopping. I had a lot on my
mind to clear and I just needed to get away. Damn, is there a law
against that?"

"Nah, ain't no law, shorty! Just watch yaself, cuz if I
finds out different, we gonna have major problems."

Tony was taking on a "Rico" tone with me that I did not
like whatsoever.

"Who the *fuck* is you talking to, Tony? I *know* it ain't me.
Ya better keep that *shit* in ya back pocket before you come at me
with it."

I had never seen Tony like this before, and it made me
very upset. I knew I had to calm down, before I said something
that I would live to regret.

"Oh word? It's like that, Kai? Fuck you forget or
something? This here is *my* house! *I'm* the star, baby girl! You
used to be the co-star, but now you just another *fucking* spectator!
Show over, get the *fuck* out!"

Just when I thought things couldn't get any worse!

"Get the fuck out? You get mad over some *bullshit* and
now it's 'get the fuck out'? Tony, think about that shit for a
minute." I started talking slowly and softly. "I'm ya 'co-star'
alright, but do you *know* what that means? ...It means, everything
you own, *I* own. All the work you put in, I put in, too.

"You forget who sees over the cooks and make sure ya
deliveries are made on time? That's me, *motherfucker*. You *sure*
you wanna have me running the street with all ya info, baby
boy?"

That weird laugh echoed out of me again. This time, it set
Tony off. He grabbed me by my throat, and *threw* me into the
hard brick wall! When I hit the floor, Tony started to strangle me
as he screamed, "BABY BOY? BABY BOY? HUH? YOU

271

FUCK THAT NIGGA? HUH? DON'T YOU *EVA* IN YA LIFE
CALL ME 'BABY BOY' AGAIN, YOU FUCKING SLUT!"

Tony let go, and I hit the floor again. It took all the air I
had in me, but I managed.

"Tony-I-ain't-fuckin'-nobody!"

"Oh word? You come in here acting brand-new, and you
ain't *fucking* nobody? We'll see!"

Tony then picked me up by my waist and ripped my jeans
off. He proceeded to remove my panties. I didn't know what Tony
was up to, until he threw me onto the couch. Tony then spread my
legs wide-open, as he stuck three fingers in me at the same time.

I screamed in pain…

Tony bowed his head in regret.

"I'm sorry, Kai," was all that he said, before Tony left the
house for the night. I laid there until he came back early the next
day. When Tony walked in the house, I'd pretended to be asleep,
as he started to play with my hair.

"Kai, I hope you're listening to me. You know shit's been
kinda hard since *Five Points*. You know it's hard knowing that I
can't make love to you. I be seeing how dudes look at you and
shit. I know your type, ma, you got the sex drive of a 18-year-old
man."

I stifled a giggle.

"I just be thinking when you're gone, you out there
getting the only thing I *can't* give you. I know you've been on my
side since I came back home, but I still be bugging. You're a
trooper, baby and that's why I love you. Please don't leave me—I
need you. All this shit, is 'cause of you. I know that, ma-ma; I
love you."

That became my driving force. The man that ran Queens
needed me. It's true that behind every great man, was a great
woman. I wanted to go down in history as being the greatest.

Tony would be my link to the city. I already had him in
my back pocket, so that meant I had Queens in my back pocket!
All I needed was the other four boroughs to fall in line.

Sure, I would step on some toes, but I would stand to be
retired at twenty-five—with enough money to finance my life, for
the rest of my life. AJ was right, but I had a point to prove, and
money to make! After that was done, I would be game to anything
else.

I started stashing away as much money as I could. I told Tony that I would no longer sleep at his house, since he put his hands on me.

Tony begged for me not to.

Instead, we came to the "agreement" that, I would *only* sleep over two or three nights out of the week, and I *had* to be on his payroll.

Tony agreed.

Every Friday morning, I got five thousand in cash.

I *never* put it in the bank.

I used some of it as pocket money, and had my checks from work directly deposited in my bank account every Thursday. I used my work money to pay my bills and other expenses. I didn't want to give "Uncle Sam" a reason to start sniffing up my ass! Instead, I hid the money that Tony gave me in my bedroom closet at my father's house.

My game plan was clear: I would be the Queen-of-the-NYC drug empire.

I had Tony do all of the dirty work, and I stopped managing the cooks. I became his silent partner, so to speak. With a little coaching from me, and a lot of strong-arming, Tony could definitely have a heavy hand in the other boroughs. In case the Feds were watching, I had a sound-proof alibi:

I was a student...

I worked full-time, and I lived at home with my pops.

Technically.

The only way I would be fucked was if they ever wanted to search my father's crib. Tony *never* came to my house, so I doubt that would ever happen.

An excerpt from *LONDON REIGN* by
A. C. BRITT
A GHETTOHEAT® PRODUCTION

Back in *Detroit,* Mercedes is bragging to her sisters about how great the sex is with London. She's truly falling in love with "him", and wants to do something really special for London.

Tonight, Mercedes goes over to the *Lawrence House,* and convinces the landlord to let her into London's room. Mercedes has all kinds of decorations and gifts for "him", wanting to surprise London when "he" comes home.

"I can't *believe* you're going through all this," Saiel says before she starts blowing up balloons.

"I know. I can't believe I'm *feeling* this *nigga* this hard. I think I'm just whipped!" Mercedes replies.

"From what? You and London *only* did it once."

"But London can eat the *fuck* out of some *pussy* though! That *nigga* stay having me climbing the wall. You know...I have never been in here when London wasn't home. I wonder what he got *going* on around here that he doesn't want me to see," Mercedes says, as she begins to go through London's things.

"Mercedes! Don't go through the man's *shit!* You might *find* something you *don't* want to see—and then what?" Saiel spits.

"...This *nigga,* London keeps talking about how there's *shit* I don't know about him anyway, so I *might* as well play detective. He's taking *too* damn long to tell me." Mercedes then picks up a pile of papers out of a file cabinet and starts flipping through them. "Pay stubs...bills...bills...more bills," Mercedes says to herself.

"Mercedes, you *really* need to stop."

"Perhaps you're right, Saiel," Mercedes answers, as she puts London's papers back and opens the closet door. Saiel then looks in the closet.

"Mercedes, why you leave so many *tampons* over here? That's weird."

"...Yeah, it is...because those *ain't* mine." Mercedes pulls the box of tampons out the closet, and looks in it to see how many are missing. "I don't even *use* this kind, must belong to some other *bitch.*" Mercedes then put the tampons back where she

274

found them, yet, Saiel now picks up a stack of medical papers that had fallen when Mercedes opened the closet.

Saiel reads the contents of the paper, and her mouth practically *drops* to the floor. Mercedes notices her sister's reaction, so she immediately walks over to Saiel.

"What, Saiel? ...What is that? What does it say?"

"U-m-m-m...doctors' papers."

"What? London ain't got no *disease,* do he? Because I don't even know if London used a condom," Mercedes confesses. Saiel looks at Mercedes again and shakes her head.

"Naw...no disease...and whether London used a condom or not, doesn't matter," Saiel answers worriedly, having a traumatized look upon her face. "Mercedes...I think you better sit down."

"Why? What that *shit* say?" Mercedes asks anxiously.

"London ain't...Mercedes, this nigga...damn! Mercedes. W-O-W! London *ain't* no dude!" Saiel says emotionally; completely shocked.

"WHAT?" Mercedes asks with much confusion.

"London...Mercedes, London is a girl!"

Mercedes can tell by the look in her sister's eyes that Saiel isn't kidding. Mercedes immediately snatches the papers out of Saiel's hand, and reads everything from the name of the patient, to the diagnosis of a urinary tract infection.

"A girl? ...But I *fucking*...I *fucked* him! Her...it! We had *sex,* Saiel, how the *fuck* is London a girl?" Mercedes now being hurt, quickly turns into anger: "THAT'S WHY THAT *MUTHAFUCKA* NEVER WANTED ME TO TOUCH DOWN THERE! AND WHY HE...I MEAN SHE, *WHATEVER,* DIDN'T REALLY WANT TO HAVE SEX WITH ME!

"I am so *fucking* stupid! He made me...*FUCK!* She made me wear a blindfold. Said she wanted to try something new.... I don't understand Saiel, I've seen London's chest, and she *ain't* got no breasts. I mean, there are nubs, but I ain't think nothing of it," Mercedes explains as she begins to cry.

"Mercedes...sweetie, she had us *all* fooled! London don't *look* like no girl! She doesn't *sound* like no girl, and London *sure-as-hell,* doesn't *act* like no girl! We had no reason to think otherwise. Sweetie, just leave this *shit* alone and let's go!" Saiel instructs, taking the papers out of her sister's hands while ushering Mercedes to the door.

An excerpt from *AND GOD CREATED WOMAN* by
MIKA MILLER
A GHETTOHEAT® PRODUCTION

Some people call me a *hoe* because I strip for niggas and hustle for cash.

Yeah, I turn tricks.

I tell niggas, "If the price is right, then the deal is real."
My momma used to say, *"As long as you got a pussy, you sittin' on a goldmine. Never give your shit away for free."*

If that means I'm a hoe, so be it!

None of these *bitches* pays my bills or puts food on my mutha...fuckin' table, so fuck 'em!

God didn't give me the type of brains where I can understand all that "technical" book shit. In elementary school, I was never good at math and, to tell the truth, I was never that good at readin' either.

It's not like I didn't try.

It's just that, when it came to school, nothin' really registered. In high school, I tried to learn the secretarial trade. I figured that if I had some sort of technical skill, that I could at least get a halfway decent gig after I graduated. Well, it turns out that typin' and shorthand was just another thing that I failed at.

So bein' somebody's secretary was out of the question.

With no real education or skill, I had to settle for minimum wage jobs. My first job was workin' as a maid at a five-star hotel. After about two weeks, I got tired of cleanin' after rich bitches that shitted all over the toilet seats, and hid bloody tampons all over the *goddamn* place!

And I wasn't 'bout to work in *nobody's* fast-food restaurant. So I had to come up with a new plan. And that's when I met this f-i-n-e-ass, Puerto Rican *muthafucka* by the name of Ricky.

Ricky was a straight-up thug. He had tattoos all across his chest and stomach like *Tupac* and shit. When I met Ricky, I had two kids. I was single, workin' my ass off as a hostess in a restaurant and braidin' hair on the side.

I was finally maintainin', you know, gettin' money. But I was always workin', so I didn't have no time to enjoy my kids or my money.

Ricky came on the scene and promised me all kinds of shit. He was like, *"Baby, you ain't gotta work that hard, why don't you lemme take care o' you and nem kids."*

Ricky had my head gassed up, for real!

Plus he was layin' the pipe on the regular. Fuckin' me *real* good wit' his fine ass. So one night, after Ricky got finished eatin' my cooch, he was like, *"Baby, I'ma take you to Philadelphia wit' me. You an' the kids can come wit' me, and I'll hook ya'll up wit' errythang."*

Me, bein' naive, I followed his fine ass all the way to Philly and shit, and the nigga started trippin'! Beatin' me up, knockin' me all upside my head, accusin' me of cheatin'..., which I wasn't. Ricky started kickin' my ass to the point that I was too ashamed to go to work with black eyes and busted lips, and I eventually got fired.

Long story short, after a while, I finally had enough. I packed me and my kids up and went to a shelter. I didn't know no fuckin' body, I didn't know shit about Philadelphia—all I knew that I was broke and I needed a place to stay for me and my kids.

So I went to the welfare office....

I tried to work within the system. Well, welfare was draggin' they feet, and in the meantime, I needed to make some cash, fast.

That's when Marilyn popped up on the scene. Marilyn was basically a po' white trash version of myself. She was stayin' wit' me at the shelter.

Marilyn told me between puffs of her *Marlboro* cigarette: *"Mekka why don't you strip? You got a beautiful body, and I know you would make plenty of money 'cause you tall, you got them big, perky titties, and you high yellow. You could make some good money and be outta here in no time; you perky-titty bitch!"*

I figured what I lacked in the brains department I'd make up for with the "gifts" that God did give me: my pretty face, this small waist and these big ole titties!

So I took Marilyn's advice. I rolled around wit' her, and she took me to some strip clubs. That's how I got this gig where I'm at now. Strippin' at a hole-in-the-wall called *Dutch Gardens*. *Dutch Gardens* is where "Mekka" was born, but I gotta finish this story another time, I think I hear them callin' my name.

"Hey Mekka, you go on in five," Trish hollers from the entrance of the locker room. Trish is a white bitch who *swears* she's black!

Only fucks Black men....

And she can get away wit' it 'cause, Trish got a ghetto-booty and a body like a sista. And some niggas think that "white is right", but they'll be alright. Trish is kinda cool though, as far as white girls go.

"Hey hoe; Mekka, you hear me?" Trish calls again.

"Bitch wait! I heard your *muthafuckin'* ass!"

I check my face in my magnetic mirror hung on the inside of my locker, spray on a hint of *Bulgari* "Omnia Eau de Toilette" body mist, adjust my g-string and tighten the laces on my thigh-high boots. Other bitches wear them tall shoes, but I'm gettin' old, and my old-ass feet and ankles need a lil' mo' support.

Plus, it's easier to slide them dollar bills in your boots and keep it movin'.

I slam my locker shut and take inventory of my surroundings. There's a room full of beautiful bitches all *hatin'* on me!

They wanna know how I make it-do-what-it-do! How I make all dat dough in the course of three hours, and they been in here all night lettin' niggas suck on they titties and finger their coochies...and still comin' up broke?

FUCK BITCHES!

Like I always say: "Money over niggas; bitches, stick to the script!"

An excerpt from **GHOST TOWN HUSTLERS** by
CARTEL: CASTILLO
A GHETTOHEAT® PRODUCTION

It was early in the morning when I heard someone knock on the door, calling my name. I sat up and reached for my watch that I'd placed on top of the nightstand.

It was seventy-thirty.

"WHO IS IT?"

"Senor! Lo estan esperando pa desallunar! (Sir! They're waiting for you to come have breakfast!) I hear the voice of Maria yell from behind the door.

"Dame unos cuanto minutos!" (Give me a couple of minutes!"

I hear footsteps going away. I get out of bed, walk over to a table on the far left corner of the room, where a vase full of fresh water has been set. Once downstairs, I see the boys sitting down at the table along with Emilio. I sit next to Pedrito.

"Where's Martha?" I ask.

"She didn't want to eat," Pedrito says while shrugging his shoulders.

Minutes later after we'd eaten, Pedrito and I got up and walked out onto the porch, sat down and lit up our cigarettes. Emilio lit up a cigar, like the one Don Avila used to smoke.

Pedrito then said he wanted to show me something, so we stood up and walked away from the house. He explained to me that the two men that were sent to pick Don Avila up from the airport had betrayed them, and that Emilio had all of his men looking throughout Medellin; having his connections search the rest of Colombia for any signs of them. So far, no one was able to find anything.

We notice that the house was barely visible, so we decide to go back. When we reach the house, the boys were inside, and Emilio was waiting for Pedrito with three men by his side.

"Come," Emilio says, gesturing with his hand to Pedrito. "I want to show you something I found." Emilio had a smile on his face, but I noticed that it was very different than any other smiles he'd given before. It was as if Emilio was smiling to himself and not at Pedrito.

"Can Raul come, too?" I heard Pedrito ask. I stop midway up the stairs, proceeding to go into the house. I look back and see Emilio staring at me, almost as if he was thinking about what to answer.

"Sure," Emilio replied shortly. "He can come." Emilio began walking towards the back of the house, where there were three smaller houses that weren't visible from the front of the main house. One of the smaller houses were guarded by two men. One was holding a rifle, the other had a gun tucked inside the waist of his pants.

"Donde estan esos hijo-eh-putas?" (Where are those sons-of-bitches?) Emilio asked once he, Pedrito and I were before the guards.

"Hai dentro patron!" the guardsman with the gun at his waist answered, as he opened the door for us.

We walked into an unfurnished room, yet, it was well lit. In the center of the room, there were two men on the floor on their knees, with their arms raised above their heads; tied up with rope that had been thrown over a beam and secured to a pole. They're shirtless, and it seems as if someone has been beating them badly with a whip—the two men having cuts on their chest and faces. They were bleeding profusely from their wounds.

"These are the ones that sold out your father," Emilio said, pointing to the two men who are still on their knees. "They're responsible for the death of your father. That's Angel, and that's Miguel."

Pedrito walked up to the two badly beaten men: "Who killed my father?" Neither of the two men answered. Pedrito then forcefully kicked Angel in his stomach. "QUIEN?" (WHO?) Pedrito shouts.

"Pedrito—" I say while taking a step forward. I immediately stopped when I felt a hand rest upon my shoulder firmly. I look back to see that it's Emilio.

"Leave him," Emilio commands. I turn to look at Pedrito, who's now violently shaking Miguel's head, grabbing him by his hair as he continues to yell loudly.

"QUIEN FUE? DIME!" (WHO WAS IT? TELL ME) Pedrito asks and shouts. Moments later, Pedrito looks around, still holding Miguel by his hair. He then let's go of Miguel and walks toward Emilio and I.

The guardsman who let us inside is now standing next to Emilio. Pedrito walks up to him, snatches the gun from his waist, cocks it, and runs back to where Angel and Miguel is. I see that Angel and Miguel's eyes are dilated before Pedrito blocks my view of the two men, now standing in front of them.

"Por f-f-f-avor no-no-no-no me maates!" (P-l-e-a-s-e don't kill me!) Angel begs for his life. "Yo no fui quien le mato." (It wasn't me who killed him."

"Entonce fuiste tu, eh?" Pedrito says, turning the gun to Miguel.

"N-O-O-O-O-O-O-O!" Miguel screams.

An excerpt from *GAMES WOMEN PLAY* by
TONY COLLINS
A GHETTOHEAT® PRODUCTION

A woman always sees a man before he sees her. Then, in a blink of an eye, she completely checks out everything him about him from head-to-toe—without him even knowing what the woman is doing. Even faster than her lightening quick assessment of him, she studies very swiftly, all of his surroundings; including any other woman who is interested in him.

Yes, a woman notices every little personal detail about a man. That's right, not one thing about him escapes her laser-like focus. So, as she studies him, at the same time, the woman makes a complete mental list of the number of turn-ons and turn-offs regarding any or all of his personal details. These turn-ons or turn-off may include: details about his personality, his looks, a man's level of personal grooming and cleanliness, body type, clothing, shoes and accessories, financial status, a man's relationship status, and so on.

However, a woman doesn't just stop at this point, the level of merely making a "check list" of superficial observations about a man. She doesn't stop her analysis of a man at the point that most men would end their analysis of a woman. A woman looks beyond the surface of a man's visible details, when she considers whether or not to pursue him. A woman analysis of a man is more complex.

Not only does a woman make a mental check list of all the personal details that a man possess, but also, she notices how well he maintains his personal details. Yet, a woman doesn't stop even at this point in her study of him. She is still not done putting him under her mental microscope. She takes her analysis of him to an even deeper level.

A woman notices if any of his personal details lacking, and she observes which personal details a man should have, but are completely missing. Why does a woman go through all these levels of observation regarding a man's personal details? Well, a woman makes such an in depth study, because she knows that by analyzing the presence, and/or the absence, and/or the condition of a man's personal details, that these three factors raises questions in her mind about him, making the woman go "Hmmm, I wonder why that is?"

Once she begins to ponder, then her naturally-analytical mind, kicks right into high gear. Instantly, a woman starts trying to figure out what's the most probable answer to each of the questions raised in her mind—from studying a man's personal details; putting two-and-two together.

By taking this approach, and backed by a lifetime of observing men, combined with her training from the "Female Mafia", a woman knows that what she can come up with quite a lot of accurate information about a man. Although she may not always be exactly correct with all of her on-the-spot analysis, and "guesstimates" about him, usually a woman is very accurate with most of her breakdown regarding him.

Even more amazing, and usually to a man's complete bewilderment, a woman's reading of him, using his personal details, can be so on point, that she even figures out things about a man that he was purposely trying to conceal.

So, from studying the presence, the absence, or the condition of a man's personal details, and then "guesstimating" the most probable answers to the questions raised by studying them, a woman gets not only a superficial understanding of him, but also, she gets a deeper insight into who this man really is, and what he is really about; at the core of his being, beyond the image that he is presenting to the world.

Therefore, given this scenario, let's follow along as she studies, analyzes, questions, and then figures out, everything about a man without him even knowing what she is doing; all of this taking place in a blink of an eye.

An excerpt from *TANTRUM* by
CHARLES D. ELLISON
A GHETTOHEAT® PRODUCTION

Walking past *Broad Street,* delusions is the anonymous,
homeless and dirty dread-headed dark man of no darkness, but the
blackness of bad happenings consuming him. It's not time that
weathers the man as much as the distance of many endless
avenues, nameless streets and missed beats thrown off by skips
and fits of gambled fate. Owns little beyond an empty wallet and
a ripped backpack that survives the dogged survivalist terrain of
his depressing urban adventure. This is what he does, how he
exists, the day-in and day-out of a vagabond walk that never ends.
And so, on this day, the man tackles a long stretch of *Broad
Street,* tripping over buckled sidewalk when—for no reason
because, his life has no reason; worn sneakers from the local
shelter suddenly spring a right turn into a gas station.

There's nothing unique about this particular gas station
because, it resembles every other gas station in the city that has
pumps, broken car vacuums and dingy mini-marts selling junk
food, expired condoms and cigarettes behind bulletproof
windows. He then attempts to add a little personality to it,
adjusting into street-beggar mode while sticking his hands out:
"Excuse me—do you have a *dollar* for a bite to eat?" He poses a
very strategic question, because it somehow cracks the irritated
faces and gritty *Nicetown* dispositions of people passing him by.
A polite question, but it's also fast and pointed enough, yet
touching in his acclaimed search for food.

Which is bullshit, he's thinks, *because there's a
methadone clinic only blocks away where I might be able to grip
a bottle of Oxycontin to wash the day's sins away.*

Most ignore his requests for random charity; a few are
pretty damn nasty about it. But, a good number offer loose change
and crumpled dollar bills—a rare few out of compassion; the rest
out of guilt or something like that. The man despises the
occasional smart-ass who will test his *"bite to eat"* by offering to
buy the food instead. Those walks to the carryout across the street
waste time, and he gets vicious heartburn from the MSG. But he
has little choice but to play it off.

We will call him "Dread". His identity is unknown because it is filed away in abandoned houses, train yards, warehouses and cardboard boxes under bridges. There are the humiliations, of course: the muggings at night; drunken kids looking for a bum fight; he might score nauseating sex from an infected crack-head who requires his scarce dollar for the next fix. At some point, Dread figured *he* was all worth forgetting. Driver's license; Social Security card; an old photo of a daughter Dread thinks is his—all of that is at the bottom of a brown, polluted *Schuylkill River.* Strangely enough, though, he possesses a library card. The books keep a fraction of sanity maintained and he always brings them back on time. While at the gas station, Dread stops for a moment to case the scene. It's morning, and the stress of stressed out people are moving about their business quickly, moving briskly in an effort to end the day as soon as they humanly can. They all shower him with petty looks and pitiless stares, as a frigid fall wind blows through *Broad Street.*

The ominous, refitted brick and metal frame of an abandoned clothing factory, rises above the corner of *Broad* and *Lehigh* like a haunted Scottish castle on an urban landscape. Within two years, Dread expects a multi-million dollar condominium park to replace the old factory halls across the street from the gas station. If he doesn't get harassed by the impending police presence in the wake of yuppie emergence on his corner, Dread anticipates new revenue streams from wealthier individuals. He argues this point just yesterday with another lost, dingy soul under the *Ben Franklin Bridge,* while on an extended evening drink binge.

"Them yuppies movin' in? That's loot, son. That's guilty modern professionals tryin' to get a conscience, so they throw money at you." Dread was loquacious that night, lit and limed on a killer pint of rum he snatched from the corner liquor store. All Dread could see was a blurred crescendo of *Camden's* skyline lights dimpling the *Jersey* side of *Delaware,* and the distorted, hamburger meat face of his other homeless friend—who was just as hopeless as Dread was.

"Dread—what you talkin' 'bout? That's called gentrification, my friend. And I will bet that it's not as progressive as you make it sound. It's overpriced condos, rising property taxes and poor folks getting pushed out of homes because of unfair property assessments," his friend piped on about

285

the evils of outsiders moving into blighted neighborhoods, as if he had personal knowledge about it. Perhaps it was the reason behind his present misfortune.

Dread snorted. Speech slurred. Back slumped. Genitals burning from some unknown STD: "Seems like people livin' there should've been takin' better care of the hood," laughing and spitting spittle of rum. "Now they want to get vexed because the man then moved in and figured how to make profit and high life off rundown homes." With an unorganized band of raggedy vagrants and addicts crowding around them to listen in, that evening's conversation carried a political talk show quality to it.

And so, in the meantime, Dread watches his progress arrive: the construction crews banging away, nails hammered, wood split, massive cranes slowly moving unidentifiable objects in mid-air. The noise scrambles the concrete serenity of a *Northtown* morning, transforming it into a cluttered neo-ghetto symphony. Contractors and day laborers with scarred fingers and aging faces, bleed the filth of work that flows into puddles of caked drudgery on stubbed chins. They are like a battalion of ants building out a mound of dirt, but it's a louder, stronger, defiant intensity that rocks cold metallic atmosphere, and stirs stained pigeons into wing-flapping fury.

Angry birds looking for breadcrumbs and cigarette buds flutter about the building's noise in aimless drift. Dread sees glimpses of opportunity in this, but his sanity is long consumed by a defeated soul worn rough. Dread's life's file is heavy from the weight of unkempt locks bearing on the skull. Pacing asphalt amid the alcoholic ads, lottery billboards, and scent of price-gouging fuel, Dread pokes his soul for new answers.

"How can I find work with the hard hats banging away up there," he asks while scanning the organized chaos of construction. *My situation*, Dread continues, *is as dry as that salty stretch of burning funk I can't seem to shake. Damn!* he curses. *That funk of no direction. That funk of regression. That odor of no hope, broken promises and exhausted salutations.*

It is here where the *BANG! CLANK! BANG! CLANK!* of a ground excavator is overheard, blasting the bitter silence of the begging man's introspections.

I am in need of a much-needed break from misery, Dread cries. *I am misery. ...A job sure could reverse it*, he screams back at the excavator, and the God he thinks will hear him.

An excerpt from *SKATE ON!* by
HICKSON
A GHETTOHEAT® PRODUCTION

Quickly exiting the 155th Street train station on *Eighth Avenue,* Shani, walking with her head held down low, decided to cross the street and walk parallel to the *Polo Grounds;* not chancing bumping into her parents. As she approached the corner, Shani contemplated crossing over to *Blimpie's* before walking down the block to the skating rink. She craved for a *Blimpie Burger* with cheese hero, but immediately changed her mind; fearing of ruining the outfit Keisha gave her.

Shani then headed towards *The Rooftop*, feeling overly anxious to meet with her two friends. As she walked down the dark and eerie block, Mo-Mo crept up behind Shani and proceeded to put her in a headlock; throwing Shani off-guard.

"GET OFF OF ME!" Shani pleaded as she squirmed, trying to break free. Already holding Shani with a firm grip, Mo-Mo applied more pressure around her neck.

Trying to defend herself the best way she knew how, Shani reached behind for Mo-Mo's eyes and attempted to scratch her face. Mo-Mo pushed her forward and laughed.

"Yeah, *bitch,* whachu gon' do?" Mo-Mo teased. "SIKE!" Startled, Shani turned around with a surprised expression on her face.

"Mo-Mo, why are you always *playing* so much? You almost scared me half-to-death!" Shani said while panting heavily, trying hard to catch her breath.

Mo-Mo continued to laugh, "Yo, I had ya heart! You almost *shitted* on yaself! I could've put ya ass to sleep, Bee!"

"Mo-Mo, please stop swearing so much," Shani replied, as she smiled and reached out to hug Mo-Mo. Mo-Mo then teasingly tugged at the plunging neckline of Shani's leotard, pulling it down to reveal more of Shani's cleavage.

"Since when you started dressin' like a lil' hoe?"

Shani, quickly removing Mo-Mo's hand from her breasts, became self-conscious of what she was wearing.

"I knew I shouldn't have put this on. Keisha made me wear this. Do I *really* look sleazy?"

Mo-Mo frowned. "Whah? Shani, stop *buggin'!* You look aiiight. I'm just not used to seein' you dressin' all *sexy* and shit."

Shani then looked towards *Eighth Avenue* to see if Keisha was nearby.

"Mo-Mo, where's Keisha? I thought you two were coming to *The Rooftop* together."

Mo-Mo then pointed across the street, as she loudly chewed and popped on her apple flavored *Super Bubble* gum.

"Yo, see that black *Toyota Corolla* double-parked by *The Rucker?* She in there talkin' to some Dominican *nigga* named, Diego we met earlier. We made that *fool* take us to *Ling Fung Chinese Restaurant* on Broadway. Keisha jerked him for a plate of Lobster Cantonese—I got chicken wings and pork-fried rice."

Shani shook her head and chuckled, "You two are always scheming on some guy."

"And you *know* it! A *bitch* gotta eat, right?!" Mo-Mo asked, before blowing a huge bubble with her gum, playfully plucking Shani on her forehead.

Mo-Mo was a belligerent, lowly-educated, hardcore ghetto-girl who was extremely violent and wild. Known for her southpaw boxing skill and powerful knockout punches, she'd often amused herself by fighting other peoples' battles on the block for sport. That's how Mo-Mo met Shani.

Last January, Sheneeda and Jaiwockateema tried to rob Shani of her *Bonsoir* "B" bag near Building 1. Mo-Mo observed what has happening and had rescued Shani, feverishly pounding both girls over their heads with her glass *Kabangers.*

She didn't even know Shani at the time, but fought for her as if they were childhood cronies. Since then, the two have become close friends—Mo-Mo admiring Shani's intelligence, innocence and sincerity.

In addition to her volatile temper, ill manners and street-bitch antics, Mo-Mo was rough around the edges—literally and figuratively. Eighteen-years-old and having dark, rich, coffee-colored skin, Mo-Mo's complexion was beautiful, even with suffering from the mild case of eczema on her hands—and with her face, full of blemishes and bumps from the excessive fighting, junk food and sodas she'd habitually drank.

Bearing a small scar on her left cheek from being sliced with a box cutter, Mo-Mo proudly endured her battle mark. *"The Deceptinettes"*, a female gang who jumped Mo-Mo inside of

Park West High School's girls' locker room last year, physically attacked her. Mo-Mo took on the dangerous crew of girls all by herself, winning the brutal brawl, due to her knowing how to fight hard and dirty.

With deep brown eyes, full lips and high cheekbones, she highly resembled an African queen. Mo-Mo wasn't bad looking, she just didn't take care of herself; nor was she ever taught how. Because of this, Mo-Mo was often forsaken for her ignorance by most.

Awkwardly standing knock-kneed and pigeon-toed at five-foot-seven, big boned with an hourglass figure, Mo-Mo was a brick house! Thick and curvaceous with a body that wouldn't quit, she had ample sized forty-two D breasts, shifting wide hips, big legs, with well-toned thighs.

Having the largest ass in Harlem, Mo-Mo's behind was humongous—nicely rounded and firm. It automatically became a sideshow attraction whenever she appeared, as everyone, young and old stared in disbelief; amazed at the shape, fullness and size of Mo-Mo's butt. A man once joked about "spanking" Mo-Mo's rear, claiming that when he'd knocked it...her ass knocked him back!

Her hair length was short, in which Mo-Mo wore individual box braids, braiding it herself; having real, human hair extensions. Often, her braids were sloppy and unkempt, having naps and a fuzzy hairline. Mo-Mo's coarse, natural hair grain never matched the soft and silky texture of her extensions, but she always soaked the ends in a pot of scalding, hot water to achieve a wet-and-wavy look.

Mo-Mo never polished her nails or kept them clean, having dirt underneath them regularly. Rarely shaving the hair from under her armpits or bikini line caused Mo-Mo to have a rank, body odor. Someone even left a package at her apartment door one day, filled with a large can of *Right Guard, Nair* and a bottle of *FDS Feminine Deodorant Spray* with a typewritten note attached. It read: *"Aye, Funkbox, clean ya stank pussy and stop puttin' Buckwheat in a headlock—you nasty bitch!"* Mo-Mo assumed it was either a prank from Sheneeda and Jaiwockateema, or Oscardo—still sulking over Mo-Mo kicking his ass six years ago.

She'd now lived alone in the *Polo Grounds,* due to her mother's untimely death six months ago—dying of sclerosis of the liver from her excessive drinking of hard alcohol. Just days after Mo-Mo's mother's death, she'd received a letter from *Social Services,* stating that they were aware of her mother's passing, her only legal guardian, and that she would receive a visit from a social worker; one who would be instructed to place Mo-Mo in an all-girls group home in East Harlem.

Mo-Mo had begged her other family members to allow her to live with them, but they refused, not wanting to deal with her nasty disposition, constant fighting and barbaric lifestyle. Nor did they wish to support Mo-Mo emotionally or financially, resulting her to rely on public assistance from the welfare office. At that point, Mo-Mo hadn't any relatives whom she can depend upon—she was on her own and had to grow up fast.

Luckily Mo-Mo's eighteenth birthday had arrived a day before she was accosted in the lobby of her building by a male social worker, having the rude investigator from *Social Services* antagonize her with legal documents; indicating that she was to temporarily be in his custody and taken immediately to the group home.

"SUCK A FAT BABY'S ASS!" was what Mo-Mo yelled at the social worker before defiantly slamming the door in his face.

Failing most of her classes, Mo-Mo barely attended school. She was in the tenth grade, but had belonged in the twelfth. Mo-Mo was still a special education student, now having a six-grader's reading and writing level. Her former teachers passed her in school, being totally unconcerned with Mo-Mo's learning disability.

Their goal was to pass as many students as possible, in order to avoid being reprimanded by superiors for failing a large number of students. The school system had quotas to meet and didn't receive the needed funds from the government for the following term—if a large amount of students were held back.

Along with other personal issues, Mo-Mo was hot-in-the-ass, fast and promiscuous, having the temperament of a low-class whore. She was a big-time freak, a sex fiend with an insatiable appetite for men with huge dicks—becoming weak at the knees at the sight of a protruding bulge.

Mo-Mo's self esteem and subsidized income was low, but her sex drive was extremely high, having sex with men for cash while soothing her inner pain. She didn't sell her body for money due to desperation and destitute—Mo-Mo did it for the fun of it.

She *loved* dick and decided to earn money while doing what Mo-Mo enjoyed the most—getting fucked! She was going to have frivolous sex regardless, *"SO WHY NOT GET PAID FOR IT?"* Mo-Mo often reasoned.

Academically, she was slow, but Mo-Mo was nobody's fool; being street-smart with thick skin. A true survivor, who persevered, by hook-or-crook, Mo-Mo was determined to sustain—by all means necessary.

"AYE, YO, KEISHA, HURRY THE *FUCK* UP!" Mo-Mo beckoned.

"Hold up! I'm comin'!" Keisha replied with irritation in her voice; concluding her conversation with Diego, "My friends are callin' me—I gotta go."

"Can I see you again and get ya digits, mommy?" Diego begged, talking extremely fast with his raspy voice.

"Maybe! And *no* you can't get my number—gimme yours," Keisha snapped.

Diego immediately was attracted to Keisha's good looks, snootiness, nonchalant attitude and bold behavior. He smiled as he wrote his beeper number on the flyer he received for an upcoming party at *Broadway International*—while exiting the Chinese restaurant with Keisha and Mo-Mo an hour earlier.

While handing Keisha the flyer, Diego attempted to wish her goodnight, but Keisha interjected: "Can I get three hundred dollars?" she said, looking straight into Diego's eyes.

"Damn, mommy, what's up? I just met you an *hour* ago and you *askin'* me for money already?"

Keisha paused for emphasis.

"...Are you gon' give it to me or *not?*" Keisha coldly asked, still looking into Diego's eyes—not once she ever blinked.

"Whachu need three hundred for, mommy?"

"First and foremost, my name is *Keisha,* not mommy! And I don't *n-e-e-e-e-e-d* three hundred dollars—I want it!"

Diego sat silently, bewildered and turned on by Keisha's brashness.

"Diego, don't you want me to look cute the next time you see me?" Keisha asked innocently while batting her eyelashes; deceiving Diego with her fake, light-hearted disposition.

"So I'm gonna see you again huh, mommy?" Diego nervously asked, smiling as he pulled out a wad of cash from his pocket. His large bankroll, wrapped in jade-green rubber bands caused Keisha's eyes to widen.

"Uh-huh," she effortlessly replied while staring hard at Diego's money while turning up the volume on his *Benzi* box.

Diego was playing his *DJ Love-Bug Starski* mixed tape and Keisha bobbed her head, rocked her shoulders from side-to-side and rubbed her thumb swiftly against her middle and index finger, while singing to *Money: Dollar Bill, Y'all* by Jimmy Spicer; *"Dollar-dollar-dollar-dollar-dollar bill, y'all!"*

Diego looked at her with his right eyebrow raised, peeling off money from his bundle. He handed the bills to Keisha and hopelessly gazed into her eyes.

Keisha, who became annoyed with Diego for showing too much of an interest in her so soon, rolled her eyes and retorted harshly, "Gotta…go," as she attempted to reach for the car handle. Before grabbing it, Keisha pulled out a napkin from her brand-new, blue and white *Gucci* bag with the signature G's, wiped her fingerprints off the console and opened the car door with the napkin in her hand.

"Yo, Keisha, why you wipe down my car like that?

Keisha ignored Diego's question and beckoned to Shani and Mo-Mo, signaling them by waving her five-carat, diamond-adorned right hand in the air, before quickly bringing it down to slap her right thigh.

"Yo, I'm ready, y'all—let's go!"

Keisha then walked around the front of Diego's car and proceeded to cross the street; now eager to enter *The Rooftop*. Shaking his head in disbelief, chuckling, Diego couldn't believe Keisha's sassiness.

"YO, WHEN YOU GON' CALL ME, MOMMY?" Diego yelled out to Keisha from his car window.

Keisha immediately stopped in the middle of the street, causing the flow of traffic to halt. She flung her long hair, looked over her shoulder and tauntingly replied, "As soon as you step-up ya whip, *nigga*. Do I *look* like the type of girl who be *bouncin'* 'round in a dusty-ass 'one-point-eight'?"

Diego froze as Keisha continued to speak.

"You don't even take ya *whip* to the car wash. And stop callin' me 'mommy'!" Keisha concluded, flinging her hair again by sharply turning her head. She then stuck her butt out and switched while crossing the street.

Diego stared long and hard at Keisha's rump as she walked away, noticing how good her behind looked in her skin-tight jeans. He then drove towards Eighth *Avenue,* repeatedly hearing Keisha's last comments over in his head.

Keisha stood at the entrance of the skating rink and observed the huge crowd outside as—Shani and Mo-Mo greeted her.

"It's about time!" Mo-Mo snapped. Keisha ignored her and reached out to hug Shani.

"What's up, college gurrrl?" Keisha asked.

"Hey Keisha! I'm fine. I'm chilling like a villain." Shani replied awkwardly, not use to using slang in her daily dialect.

"Shani, it's *'chillin''* not 'chill-i-n-g'! Why you be always talkin' so *damn* proper anyway? I wonder sometimes, yo, if you *really* from the hood!" Mo-Mo snapped.

As Shani attempted to politely respond back to Mo-Mo, Keisha rudely interjected.

"So, Shani, how's DC?" Keisha asked, cleverly examining her outfit from head-to-toe without Shani realizing she had.

"I like DC so far. I'm very excited about attending *Howard University.* I just need to learn my way around campus," Shani answered. Feeling jealous and left out of the conversation, Mo-Mo interrupted the two.

"Can you two *bitches* learn y'all *muthafuckin'* way inside this skatin' rink?" Mo-Mo snapped before entering *The Rooftop.*

"Mo-Mo be illin'! She *betta* watch her mouth 'cause I'm-not-the-*one!"* Keisha retorted while rocking her neck and waving her right hand in the air.

Shani, experiencing cramps from her period and the stress from sneaking from DC to New York City for the grand opening of *The Rooftop,* shrugged her shoulders to relieve the tension she had felt, as she inhaled a breath of fresh air. Shani then slowly exhaled, and quickly adjusted the plunging neckline of her scoop-neck leotard to conceal her cleavage—as she and Keisha followed inside.

An excerpt from *SOME SEXY, ORGASM 1* by
DRU NOBLE
A GHETTOHEAT® PRODUCTION

BIG BONED

"I need you, Melissa; oh I *love* your body! Let me taste you, mmmph, let me *love* you—just give me some sexy!" Jezebel begged while still squeezing the woman's luscious crescents. Melissa had no hope of resisting this sudden passionate impulse that flooded her.

She felt Jezebel's grip tighten on her, then a finger slowly traced between her curvaceous legs. The unexpected jolt of excitable pleasure caused Melissa to rise on her side, throwing Jezebel off of her. She palmed between her own thighs, trying to silence the rest of the roaring waves threatening to overcome her preciousness.

Jezebel couldn't take her eyes off of Melissa, as she breathed erratically, while Melissa couldn't help but to stare back with conflicting desperation. Melissa's hand reached out and grasped the back of the Native-American woman's neck, as she pulled Jezebel towards her forcefully.

Their lips touch, melded, then opened. Jezebel's tongue dove into Melissa's mouth, finding the versatile muscle was eager to wrestle her own. A groan vibrated down Melissa's throat. Her hand came up, and two fingers strung like guitar strings on Jezebel's upturned beady nipple—first playing with it, then catching Jezebel's hardened nipple between her index and middle fingers; closing it within tight confines.

Jezebel then straddled Melissa, the two women's hands meeting, immediately intertwining before their kissing ended.

"I wanted you since I *first* saw you; I've been wet ever since that moment. You're so *fucking* sexy, Melissa. I *need* you, can I have some sexy? Give it to me," Jezebel said in a low, hushed voice.

The twinkle in her beautiful brown eyes affected Melissa like an intoxicating elixir. Melissa watched on, as Jezebel took her captured hand and began to suck on two fingers with her hot, steamy mouth. Jezebel's checked hollowed, as she continued to close in on Melissa's dainty fingers.

Melissa, voluptuous and womanly, petals became slick, and damp—natural juices now running down towards her rounded rear end. "I want you, too Jezebel, come get some sexy!" she pledged. Jezebel smiled as Melissa's fingers slid from her mouth, leading them down her body. With her lead, Melissa allowed her hand to enter into Jezebel's bikini. A glimpse of her fine, black pubic hair came into view, as Melissa then felt the lovely grace of Jezebel's vagina.

A soothing hiss breathed out of Jezebel. The moistness of her internal lake coated the fingers that ventures to its intimate space. Melissa then bent her hand so the bikini could come down, and she was grand the delightful vision of where her fingers ventured.

Jezebel's outer labia had opened, as Melissa's fingers split between her middle, like tickling a blooming rose. She tipped her hand up, and used her thumb to peel back the protective skin over Jezebel's engorged clitoris. The pink button revealed itself exclusively, and Melissa used her thumb to caress it; stirring up Jezebel's burning desire.

Melissa had never seen or touched another woman's pearl, but found that she'd loved it completely. Two of her fingers then slipped within Jezebel's hot, oily insides, and the Native-American woman had thrust her hips forward to take all Melissa had to offer.

"You're so *hot* inside; burning up my fingers, baby."

"Just don't stop; *please* don't stop what you're doing," Jezebel instructed. Her hips began to undulate, rocking herself to a sweet bliss. Jezebel rode Melissa's fingers like she would her fiancé's long, pleasure-inducing dick.

Melissa then curled her wet fingers back slightly, as she would if she were touching herself, searching inside for that magical area most women long to discover—the G-spot.

Melissa felt Jezebel's tunnel pulsate, and a shock ran through the humping woman, giving Melissa total satisfaction that she'd found Jezebel's spot; now also realizing that, by her being a woman, she had full advantage to knowing another woman's body, better than any man could.

An excerpt from *TATTOOED TEARS* by
BLUE
A GHETTOHEAT® PRODUCTION

INTRO

When I began brainstorming for what I consider, will be the perfect novel to reach the desired audience (everybody), I didn't know that *TATTOOED TEARS* would come pouring out of my state-issued pen, and onto state-issued writing paper. I didn't know if I would have the motivation and drive needed to put it together. Now that it's done, I can honestly say that, I didn't know I had the stomach to do something like this.

The reason: being that our youth, children, younger generation, or whatever else you choose to call our leaders of tomorrow, mean so much to me. So much in fact, I didn't want to do them an injustice by not telling it like it is, for our kids.

Our children go through so much at such a young age, I myself sometimes wonder, how it is that some are capable of making a future for themselves; a future without gangs, a future without violence, a future without hate and ignorance, a future that doesn't involve dealing directly with the hypocrisies, of this system of so-called justice we live under in America.

Despite what our news broadcasts, newspapers, politicians, jails and institutional statistics may lead you to believe, along with our juvenile detention centers, we as a society must realize that not all of our youth are going to crumble under the pressure.

TATTOOED TEARS, however, is about those who suffer through more trials and tribulations than your average convict on Death Row. And they're not even old enough to drive, yet they find the strength and willpower in themselves, to overcome those obstacles and trying times that are laid before them, in order to succeed in their own little worlds.

My father used to tell me, *"Boy, listen to me and listen good. I done already been down the road you on…"* I'm sure that 90% of our up-and-coming generation has heard this at least once in their lives. But did my father *really* understand what I was going through?

Had he really gone down the same roads that I've been on? I mean, my father didn't go to school with me, didn't get locked up with me, nor did he didn't drink alcohol with me, or smoke or sell marijuana with me. My father also didn't get into the fights I got into, or get shot at with me. Do you understand the point I'm trying to get across to you?

Now, we as adults can do what we can, to detour our children from doing the things we did, or from getting into certain types of situations we got into, but the fact remains that, they will make their own decisions, with or without our guidance. In a way it's scary—frightening even, but what can we do?

All we can do is hope and pray that they make the best choices possible with the hands they're dealt. All the advice in the world—given to any random child, means nothing if the child it's directed to, doesn't grasp the true meaning of what he or she has been told. And if that kid *does* understand the concept of what's been taught to them, it now becomes a new weight on their shoulders; a new "pressure" to deal with—a new rebuttal to what they were probably originally thinking, contemplating or anticipating.

We want our youth to be responsible, and become right-minded enough to act on the positive voices in their heads, opposed to the negative ones. With peer pressure coming in all forms from sex, drugs, gangs, and guns, battling the anxiety of getting good grades, going to college, carrying a team to the state championship, and holding a job all at the same time, a kid can really become a victim in his or her own world, which can result in becoming, his or her own worst enemy.

That, in itself, is what I feel is the biggest problem facing our children today, and has been in years past. It's the stress they feel, the depression they suffer, and the grueling temptations they need to avoid, yet seem to fall prey to it every time.

I guess what I am trying to ask in writing *TATTOOED TEARS* is…why? *Why* must they go through it? If we as adults claim to have been down that road of suffering, and of every problem in the book that these kids can endure for the benefit of them, so they wouldn't have to undergo it themselves, *why* does it still happen? *Why* are more kids carrying guns? *Why* are more children having sex? *Why* are more-and-more kids joining gangs, or even associating or affiliating themselves with these groups?

WHY? WHY? WHY?

If these *same* children are our future—truly 'our' future—*why* aren't their lives being molded today, for the betterment of that future?

There are a million answers to these questions, along with some potentially powerful debates that can be brought forth for a much needed discussion on this topic. However, to make sure our youth are going to be the productive citizens in society, we should be hoping them to be, we have to do more than just *talk* about it. We, as the leaders of today, must take the initiative to *do something* about it.

NOW!!!

Granted, there are issues that are a part of a young person's life that we cannot understand because the fact remains: this is a new generation coming up—a new breed. That means new problems, new barriers to get around, new hindrances, that are affecting their everyday living.

With that said, maybe we—the role models, heroes and saviors in our children's lives, should just fathom that, we can't save the world. We can't do it all! We can't be there for our kids twenty-four hours a day, seven days a week, because it's just not physically possible. We can't be at school in class with them, and we can't be at their jobs.

We just can't do it all!

Yes, as I said before, it's scary. But *they* are *our* children—*our* future—so what can we do? We can love them, share with our youth, and listen to our kids. We can occupy their lives with an unconditional amount of appreciation, showing we value their existence, showing that they're wanted, and needed.

In *TATTOOED TEARS*, Amir struggles with his own issues and demons—the types of things that most kids experience at one time or another in their young lives. But will Amir make it pass the temptations, struggles, and everyday battles that all kids encounter as part of just doing the one thing nature asks of him, growing up?

As a writer, I am *desperately* asking you, the reader, to pay attention to this story carefully. Even though it's a complete work of fiction, I need you to understand that these things really do happen to our children on an everyday basis. Not to *all* kids, but to our youth in general. The problem is that, they constantly feel as if they're alone in the process, and that no one is expecting them to succeed in the first place.

What is also disturbing to me is that, a lot of children are labeled as having certain disorders, after they've made a 'cry for help'. Labels that many, in my opinion—and I stress my opinion, are wrong in various cases—'misdiagnosed' for lack of a better term.

Ritalin is *not* always the answer!

I know from having more than eighteen years of experience, living with a kid that was 'diagnosed' with Attention Deficit Disorder (ADD), Attention Deficit Hyperactive Disorder (ADHD), and admitted to classes designed to meet the 'special needs' of the Behavior-Emotionally Handicapped (BEH).

He took Ritalin for many of those years. I'm not in any way trying to talk down the prescription drug, as it has worked for some, yet Ritalin just didn't always prove to very effective in our household.

Once again, I say that *all* of our children are in danger of failing in life, or taking the wrong path. I say that all of our children are potentially at risk of doing so, because 'growing up', simply isn't the same as it once was.

We can, however, help our youth get through it, be there for them, do what we can for the kids, without robbing them of a childhood.

This is *TATTOOED TEARS...*

Shed some if you'd like.

An excerpt from ***DIRTY WINDOWS*** by
JOI MOORE
A GHETTOHEAT® PRODUCTION

Forty-three beautiful angelic souls drift above the "Triple Platinum Night Club", on a cold wintry night in the city of Chicago. What happened? A brawl jumped off, triggering panic, and forty-three children, mothers, fathers and friends lives are lost. Sadly, they were all trapped and left suffocating, leaving a city gripped with pain.

When Dr. Brighton Miller, Senior Medical Examiner for the city, comes face-to-face with the lifeless corpse of one of the victims, his loyalty is questioned, and his world becomes smaller when a scandal erupts, and the doctor learns that it's someone from his past.

Brighton, once labeled a "white tee boy", back on the street corners of the city, pitching pennies and sleeping three-deep on piss-stained mattresses, is no longer a part of the doctor's world. Brighton has come up! These days, the only part of his old hood he sees, is through the rearview mirror of his black-on-black *Maybach Mercedes Benz*. A man educated with street wisdom, and blessed with genius in the books, he struggled hard, earned himself a scholarship, and took off on a one-way ticket out of the ghetto.

Sixteen years ago though, a hot kindling affair with his "ride-or-die" girlfriend produced a love child, a precious baby girl. However, when the allure of his newly found, wealthy world begins to clash with the precious moments spent with her, Daddy's little girl is left to roam the big dark city alone.

When Brighton's little "Ms. Riding Hood" is murdered, is it too late for daddy to go after the big bad wolf, or has he totally lost touch? Does Brighton even have a clue about who this mysterious character is? Is he even someone from the dilapidated bowels of the ghetto, or a cold-blooded and sinister monster, dwelling amongst the secret world of the elite?

Brighton's baby's mama, now a well-known attorney, will beg to differ. *Law and Order* will meet *CSI* when the blood of the two love child, stains the concrete jungles of the hood! Surrounded by people who hide behind the scenes, and you, not knowing who they are, watch as their shadows lurk behind *DIRTY WINDOWS*.

ghettoheat®

TOUGH by JAA'MALL
CLUB AVENUE by JAY BEY
UGLY/BEAUTIFUL: ME by GOD MATH

Coming soon…

GHETTOHEAT®: THE HOTNESS IN THE STREETS!!!™

ghettoheat®

THE GHETTOHEAT® MOVEMENT

THE GHETTOHEAT® MOVEMENT is a college scholarship fund geared towards young adults within the inner city, pursuing education and careers in Journalism and Literary Arts.

At GHETTOHEAT®, our mission is to promote literacy worldwide. To learn more about THE GHETTOHEAT® MOVEMENT, or to see how you can get involved, send all inquires to: MOVEMENT@GHETTOHEAT.COM, or log on to GHETTOHEAT.COM

To send comments to DRU NOBLE, send all mail to:

GHETTOHEAT®, LLC
P.O. BOX 2746
NEW YORK, NY 10027

Attention: DRU NOBLE

Or e-mail him at: DRU@GHETTOHEAT.COM

Artists interested in having their works reviewed for possible consideration at GHETTOHEAT®, send all materials to:

ghettoheat®

P.O. BOX 2746
NEW YORK, NY 10027

Attention: HICKSON

GHETTOHEAT®: THE HOTNESS IN THE STREETS!!!™

ghettoheat®

ORDER FORM

Name_____

Registration #_____(If incarcerated)

Address_____

City_____ State_____ Zip code_____

Phone_____ E-mail_____

Friends/Family E-mail_____

Books are $15.00 each. Send me the following number of copies of:

__ CONVICT'S CANDY __ LONDON REIGN

__ AND GOD CREATED WOMAN __ TANTRUM

__ AND GOD CREATED WOMAN 2 __ GHETTOHEAT®

__ GHOST TOWN HUSTLERS __ HARDER

__ GAMES WOMEN PLAY __ HARDER 2

__ SONZ OF DARKNESS __ TATTOOED TEARS

__ SONZ OF DARKNESS 2 __ SKATE ON!

__ SOME SEXY, ORGASM 1 __ DIRTY WINDOWS

Please send $4.00 to cover shipping and handling. Add a dollar for each additional book ordered. *Free shipping for convicts.*

Total Enclosed = _____

Please make check or money order payable to GHETTOHEAT®. Send all payments to:

GHETTOHEAT®, P.O. BOX 2746, NEW YORK, NY 10027

GHETTOHEAT®: THE HOTNESS IN THE STREETS!!!™